TWIST

Book Two of the Faceless

RIKKAINE THOMPSON

For Robert

ACKNOWLEDGMENTS

There are so many people I'd like to thank.

Robert, my husband, for his love, patience and late-night cups of tea. My parents and my wonderful sister, Felicia, for their ongoing love and support. My brother, who would've loved the puns. My children, for the noise when they're happy and the quiet times which always have me wondering if they're up to no good. The ever-growing Frakking mob, purely because reasons.

Katie Luisier and Elle Tharp for their love, advice, and help in bringing this book to life. This would still be just an idea if it weren't for you.

Cheyenne Phakousonh, Haideé T. H, Sabrina Sheldon, Zhanna Postupalyo, Mélanie Bourgelas, Eden Ellis, Elizabeth Burns, and Emily Combs for their comments and support.

And you, my reader, for giving this series a chance.

In loving memory of Mae.

CHAPTER 1

The computer beeped.

Belinda Bell dragged her attention from yet another boring report to peer over the top of her glasses at the computer across the other side of the room and ponder whether it was worth getting up to check. That particular search had been picking up false-positives all week, thanks to some new movie release.

Sighing, she reached over to her bedside table and picked up her motel-grade coffee to gulp, before she returned her attention to the report. It was due by morning and she hoped this final report would close the whole Alyson Gale debacle and allow Belinda to continue doing her job without being under constant surveillance.

The computer beeped again. Belinda frowned at it. Two tags, in a short space of time, was at least worth a check. She sighed and heaved herself from the lumpy motel bed to carry her coffee mug over to the computer.

She almost dropped her mug when she saw what her search had found.

A blurry set of pictures depicting a partially decomposed and misshapen carcass. The strange circumstances surrounding it and its incredibly odd appearance meant the images were fast going viral. The hiker who took the pictures posted the caption that the remains were somewhere near the woodlands below Three Chimney's Peak in Tuolumne County, California, but he commented he was deep in the woodlands and not sure where the body was located to be recovered.

Belinda quickly collated all comments surrounding the picture. The majority of theorists had decided the remains to be some type of bear suffering from mange or some other skin disease to explain the gray and almost scaly appearance of its skin. Some hoped it was a grizzly, thought extinct in California, but most thought a black bear was more likely the case. Almost all of them believed the hiker should've gotten better shots of the creature, as well as the surroundings so it could be located again. Almost all of them were certain it couldn't be human. Some of the more outrageous claims were that it was alien in origin, asking if the hiker saw lights in the area or strange markings.

No matter what the general public believed, Belinda had seen corpses like this before, all in varying stages of decomposition. What's more, the location of the supposed creature was within the vicinity of the location Alyson Gale was discovered, confused and disoriented and suffering a concussion.

Typing out a quick email, Belinda attached the image she'd pulled from the internet and sent it, then reached for her cell.

"Identification," came the soft voice of Tegan, her contact and head of communications within the Mimic Identification and Prevention Unit.

MIPU was the only thing which stood between the mimic abominations and the general public. *They can replace anyone. A loved one. A friend. The President. Imagine.'* had been the tagline which had ultimately recruited Belinda. Imagine an assassin who could literally change their appearance and get away with murder. Imagine a mimic impersonated the President and the havoc that could cause. Would anyone really want the country in the unscrupulous hands of a mimic?

There were no known numbers of mimics and only vague theories about their abilities. At least, none of which the higher-ups were willing to share with a hunter like Belinda. Only certain trusted people within MIPU were given a mimic detection device, the only sure way to tell a mimic from a civilian, and Belinda wasn't one of those. Still, she was good at what she did and the more mimics she captured and processed, the safer the world would be.

A few years ago the 'Faceless' had emerged and had completely shaken up the Unit. Hideous, misshapen, mindless beasts built only to charge and destroy. Guns had little effect on them. Capturing them alive was impossible and they decayed so fast after death, assuming they could even get their hands on a corpse, dissection yielded no results. Rumors surfaced regarding other Faceless with the ability to blend in with the general population.

No one knew where the Faceless were coming from, but one thing was clear. Someone was building an army and that had the higher-ups worried.

"BB dash seven-six-zero."

"Hello, Belinda," Tegan said, her voice brightening. "How's life treating you? How's Glenn?"

Glancing at her motel room and not wanting to let her superiors know she hadn't gone home like they'd instructed her too, Belinda lied, "Pretty good, he's enjoying having me home, but I really hate sitting on my ass all day long."

Tegan laughed. "I would *love* to be able to sit on my ass all day. What can I do for you today?"

"I sent an email of a Faceless corpse," she said. "The location where it was found leads me to believe Alyson Gale knows more than she was letting on. Seeking permission to follow-up."

"Hmm, one sec," Tegan said, drawing out her words and Belinda had the impression she was accessing the image. "Huh. Wow. Hold on."

Belinda waited while she listened to Tegan type.

"Okay," Tegan said, elongating the word before she picked up her speed, "I see what you mean about the corpse. However, the directors have instructed you to stay clear of Alyson Gale."

Belinda made an irritated noise. "She's a person of interest and I've already built a rapport with the girl—"

"I'm only repeating what they told me. Everyone's being instructed not to pursue the 'Braddock daughter' angle. You pissed off someone high in the command chain."

Well, wasn't that interesting. Going after Alyson Gale stepped on someone's toes. Now, Belinda had to find out who. And why. "It wasn't my fault—"

Tegan's voice held a hint of bite as she interrupted, "The whole situation was an absolute mess. You went in because Gomez said his mimic detection device was giving confusing results. You were provided with a team of men to help you locate and tag shifters, yet you decided the best option was to kidnap some girl because she *might* be some non-existent daughter of Braddock—"

"I had information and—"

"—off the street, just weeks after you murdered the mimic who was her friend instead of tagging them."

Belinda raised her voice in the hopes of cutting Tegan off. "Tegan—"

"Did you think that wouldn't be noticed by the local authorities? They're watching her now. This…" A moment's hesitation suggested Tegan was looking up the records. "Deputy Locklear seems convinced something else is going on. The whole operation was a fuck-up."

Belinda ground her teeth together. "I've heard all this before, Tegan—"

"The word is they're calling in the twins."

Dread settled in Belinda's belly. "Shit."

"Mmm-hmm." Tegan hummed, then sighed. "I've

passed on your message. Feel free to investigate the corpse, but I'm advising you to stay away from Alyson Gale."

Sighing, Belinda hung up from the call and reached for her laptop to organize travel plans. The corpse was her first priority because it degraded so fast, but after that, she'd head to Bellhollow. Alyson knew more than she was letting on and Belinda would discover what that was, regardless of her orders. Preserving mankind meant sacrifices and Alyson Gale was another in the long line to keep everyone safe. She would reveal her secrets.

He came at her and Aly went cold.

Figures loomed, shrouded in shadow. Grasping hands in an alleyway. A nameless Faceless crashed through trees as it chased her through a forest. Snatches of sound and flashes of memory laced with terror.

Her heart pounded so hard it felt like it could burst free at any moment. She could hear the blood rushing through her head. Her mouth was dry and her clenched fists were slippery with sweat. An unfamiliar anxiousness swept through her. She took a half-step back, braced her knees and raised her forearms to shield.

His chest hit her arms and it didn't stop him moving toward her. Hands seeking, he invaded her personal space and made a grab for her upper arm.

Panic overwhelmed and fled with her remaining bravado. Aly squeaked and, with flailing arms, she managed to clout the man in the jaw. In her hasty backward skitter, her foot collided with her opposite ankle and caused her legs to tangle. She went down, landing on her backside with a hard thump.

"Aly!" Grace cried, scampering across the mat on all fours. "Are you okay?"

Aly blinked as Grace wrapped her arms around Aly and things swam into focus. Grace. A training room. A mat cushioned her as she struggled to sit up.

They were at the self-defense class. Del was here, looking shocked and ready to protect her, but unsure how. Kayla, the instructor, positioned between her and her attacker, who stood a small distance away, rubbing his chin.

She didn't know him, she didn't know him and... except she did. She didn't know the body; hair too light, too tall, freckles... but the eyes were that deep chocolate she'd known most of her life so the person inside... her heart and feelings fought a vicious battle with her eyes, and reason won as she realized who she'd smacked. With a gasp, her hands flew to her mouth. "Oh my gosh, I'm so sorry."

Kayla patted the air ahead of her in a placating manner. "It happens when you're learning," she told Aly. "That's why he has so much padding." She turned, smiling at her teaching partner. "All good?"

"Did I hurt you?" Aly fumbled, scrambling to kneel. "I really didn't mean to—"

Fletcher, or Noah as he'd asked to be called, her best friend returned from the dead and hiding in a different form, smiled. "Don't worry, this thing is designed to take a hit." He patted the protective suit he wore and nodded to her. "You've got a good swing there."

"How about you?" Kayla asked Aly. "Are you okay?"

"I... er..." She still felt nervous and anxious, even if the feeling was fading rapidly. She hadn't expected she'd react like that at all, but when Kayla had talked about how to protect herself, and mentioned assault, both sexual and physical, this pressure began to build inside Aly. Glancing around the room at the other participants, men and women ranging in age from late teens to early forties, she wasn't the only one who felt anxious.

Kayla nodded. "These sessions can be quite confronting," she said, sweeping a coil of black hair over her ear as she looked at all the participants of the session.

"For some, the first session dredges up memories and brings anxieties to the forefront, so it's not uncommon to feel overwhelmed. Noah has to invade your personal space so that I can teach you moves which, over time and practice, we'd like to become intrinsic. But for that to happen, you have to allow him to put himself in an attacker's place, and you in the place of the victim, and *that* can be both challenging and disturbing." She glanced at the clock on the wall. "We'll take a ten-minute break, and then I'll show you all what I'd like you to work on between now and the next lesson next week."

Smiling, Grace offered Aly her hand. With an apologetic look at Noah, Aly allowed her friend to pull her to her feet. Wrapping Aly up in a hug, Grace asked, "Are you okay?"

Aly clutched at her friend and suppressed a shiver of fear. "Nope."

Looping an arm around Aly's shoulders, Grace led her toward the wall.

Del, awkward and unsure of what to do to help, ran a hand over his tight, black cornrows, tugging at a handful at his neck. "I'll get snacks," he announced. "There's a vending machine outside."

Grace nodded and suggested, "Something with sugar."

With her back against the wall, Aly hugged her legs to her chest and tried to slow her heartbeat by taking calming breaths. Sitting next to Aly, Grace stretched out her legs ahead of her and crossed her ankles. Placing her hand on Aly's shoulder to offer support, Grace asked, "How're you doing?"

"I've been better," Aly said and leaned over so her head rested on Grace's shoulder.

"I didn't realize how anxious this would make me," Grace said. "I did martial arts when I was eight and this… it's like a gut reaction." She shrugged. "Perspective, I guess."

Not really wanting to talk, Aly fixed her eyes on Noah

as he listened to Kayla and one of the other women attending the self-defense class. "Possibly."

"Dad said he's gonna show me how to use a taser again before college," Grace continued, referencing her deputy sheriff father, Jonathan. "He's extending the offer to you as well."

Aly raised an eyebrow. "He's fussing."

"Yup," Grace said, clicking her tongue. She tugged her long, raven hair from its ponytail and swept it over her shoulder so she could braid it while they sat there. "They're all gonna fuss, long after we've left. Mom's even threatening to close the restaurant and move there, just so we won't be by ourselves."

Aly nodded. "Mom said her agent in LA sent her through some apartments. She's doing her 'mom' check before she shows them to me. I get the feeling our moms are in cahoots."

Lijuan 'Grace' Locklear was one of Aly's best friends and had been since Grace's family moved to town when Aly was fifteen. Their creative personalities made for interesting conversations. Grace was a musician and composer while Aly strived to be an animation artist, a combination of talent which allowed the pair to collaborate and produce short cartoons as they tested out techniques. While that practice had fallen by the wayside during their final year of high school, Aly hoped they'd be able to start again, especially when they lived together in LA. Aly had been accepted into Otis, while Grace had secured a place at LA College of Music and both of them hoped to secure transfers into CalArts in a few years.

A real estate agent with a large property portfolio of her own, Aly's mother, Penelope Gale, had decided that since Aly had her own trust fund from her deceased biological father which could support her through college, Penelope would use some savings to buy an apartment in Los Angeles for the girls to use. Aly knew why her mother insisted they stay in an apartment rather than their college dorms. An apartment lifted some of Grace's financial burden for college, but it also would have its own security. Penelope and Roger, Aly's adopted father, were still overprotective.

"Undoubtedly. Did she veto the sex dungeon?" Grace asked with mock seriousness.

Aly giggled. "Yup. And the Jacuzzi."

Grace snapped her fingers and pretended to be upset. "Dang it."

"Mom's still trying to suggest that we convince Del to come with us," Aly said, her eyes drifting across to Noah again. "The amount of three bedroom apartments she's had on her list is staggering."

"Yeah," Grace sighed. "My mom too. I wish he would."

"Me too, but he says he'll be too loud when he records videos," Aly said.

Delwin 'Del' Cook was the third side of their triangle. Del and his mother, Cassidy, had moved to Bellhollow following her divorce. The last to leave the nest, Del had an older brother who followed in his mother's footsteps and was in the last year of Law. By contrast, Del was a gamer and wanted to explore a career revolving around that. Del always had a smile on his face and while recent loss had dimmed the smile, it hadn't diminished Del's sense of ridiculousness. Although he was accepted into LA Film School under a Recording Arts degree, he was tossing around the idea of deferring for a year so he could spend time on his YouTube gaming channel, something which he hadn't told his mother about.

Tying her braid up with a band, Grace flicked her hair over her shoulder. "Liiiiies. There's this thing called 'soundproofing'."

"Yup."

"I'm happy he's taking this risk, but I'll miss him. Here," Grace continued, widening her legs and patting the floor between them. "I'll braid your hair."

Aly scooted across so she sat ahead of Grace, accepting the hairband to hold while Grace combed her finger through Aly's hair. Stuck with light brown hair with enough curl to frizz if she didn't care for it, Aly's hair was shorter than Grace's long locks and almost always a mess. So much so that Grace often amused herself by playing with Aly's hair and Aly found it relaxing.

As Grace played, Aly contemplated Noah. He'd kept Fletcher's dark brown eyes, a feature she was very glad to see. While Fletcher's hair had been dark, this version of Noah had light hair, almost a dusty brown. Freckles dotted his cheeks and nose, matching Aly's. Given his appearance, Aly believed he could almost be a cousin of Fletcher's. There had been a flare of recognition from Del and Grace when they'd seen him.

A few months ago, Aly might've laughed if anyone had told her shapeshifters were real. Not the fanciful animal-to-human kind of shifters popular in fiction, but people who could change their appearances on a whim. Her best friend Fletcher had been one of them, and he'd been killed because of it. Barely two weeks after that, as Aly's shift at Dirk's Diner finished, men in dark clothes had lunged from a van and stolen her. She'd been interrogated by Belinda Bell, a Purist who later claimed she was an FBI agent, about a man called Rex Braddock, who Belinda mistakenly believed was Aly's father.

In the chaos of the kidnapping and subsequent escape, Aly learned about the existence of shifters. Fletcher wasn't dead because 'Fletcher' had never existed. Instead, he'd been Noah, a genetically engineered shapeshifter. Called Faceless and shunned by natural shifters, he and his siblings were created in a lab by a company they knew as the Institute, run by someone known only as 'Darcy'. Their abilities had been modified and experimented on, allowing them to do things with their bodies natural shifters couldn't. After escaping, he'd happened upon Bellhollow and fallen into friendship with Aly. While they'd met at the physical age of eight, Noah's age reflected a complicated shift, one that aged in tune with her.

Noah, under the guise of 'Will', had rescued her and with the help of his sister, Elaine, they'd escaped the Purists, only to be set upon by a group of people who destroyed Elaine's car. After fleeing from them, and accidentally separating from Elaine, Noah and Aly were chased through a forest by a misshapen Faceless. Genetically engineered, like Noah, except these were wrong somehow. Distorted and trained to follow orders without thought, their mutations were why all Faceless were a horror story to the naturals. Ghastly beasts capable of monstrosities. Mindless murderers.

After escaping and returning home, Aly pretended not to remember a thing about her ordeal to protect Noah. It was better in the long run, especially since she hadn't really been sure she remembered some of it correctly. She'd thought she'd caught flashes of Penelope in the forest, but some of the details had become fuzzy, so she chalked a lot of what she'd seen up to a concussion.

One fact still troubled her; Rex Braddock and Madeline Spenser. Although Aly's birth certificate listed Penelope Spenser and Leon Braddock, the two names Belinda had supplied her with rattled around in Aly's mind since. According to Noah, Rex was the leader of a group of renegade shifters. What that meant, Aly wasn't sure. What Aly did know was that Belinda Bell, and various factions of shifters, believed she could possibly be the daughter of this Rex Braddock. The factions were at war and if she was Rex's daughter it could be used against Rex.

She had so many questions for Noah.

Like what was the misshapen Faceless who hunted them in the forest? Who were the factions and what did they stand for? What happened to Elaine? Although Noah had said he hadn't seen anyone, was it still possible that she was being watched? Who were Madeline Spencer and Rex Braddock? Had Aly really seen her mother in the forest?

Seeing she was watching, Noah's lopsided smile bloomed, lighting up his whole face and Aly felt her heart crash against her chest. All she wanted to do was dart across the room and hug him so she could feel safe.

Which would be completely misinterpreted by Grace, Del, and practically everyone in the room. So she sat, twisted up inside, and hugged her legs tighter to her chest.

Noah's smile slipped into worry and he excused himself from Kayla and the woman she spoke to. He went to the bags beside the wall and removed the protective gear. Squatting down near a black backpack, he rummaged through, then wandered over toward them, trying to look nonchalant.

Nervous, Aly tried not to tense. They'd decided to play an introduction by ear if the opportunity arose. They knew that if Noah was serious about staying in her life any way he could, Grace and Del came with that promise and there was no telling how they would react. First impressions were everything and Aly's reaction in this session already painted him in a bad light. But now, the moment seemed to be here and Aly desperately wanted it to go well.

Reaching them, he crouched down to appear less intimidating and held out his hand. "Peace offering. I hope you don't mind Snickers, the machine was all out of everything else earlier."

Grace's hands stilled in Aly's hair and she made a soft intake of breath. Snickers had been Aly and Fletcher's chocolate of choice and still carried a portion of pain and remembrance for their friends.

Aly was quick to accept so Grace would know she was okay. "They're actually my favorite. I'm sorry for hitting you."

"No big," he replied with a one-shoulder shrug. "Happens all the time."

"I bet," Grace said.

"Yup." Noah smiled. "Everyone has a limit and,

generally, we don't know what that is until it's pushed. Now we know yours, and I'll make sure I won't push you beyond it until you're comfortable. But next time, tell me to back off before you belt me, okay?"

Aly's embarrassed giggle sounded strange to her ears. "I'm really sorry."

"Doing better now?" Noah asked and she watched a shadow cross his face as he tried to appear less emotionally invested in her answer than he was.

Aly smiled to put him at ease and tore open the Snickers. "Yeah."

Returning to the training room, Del stated, "The dumb machine was out of—oh," he said as he reached them, spotting the Snickers in Aly's hand. "You got one. Gonna share?"

Staring at him, Aly took a deliberate bite. "Do I ever?"

Making a huffy and somewhat playful noise, Del flopped down on the floor beside them. "Never get between you and a Snickers. Learned that early." He flicked his eyes to Noah. "Hey, bro. Noah, right?"

"That's me," Noah replied. He pointed with a single finger and lifted his eyebrow. "Delwin?"

Del nodded and glared at Grace. "Just 'Del'. *Someone* had it in their head to be funny."

Grace shrugged and smiled. "Don't know who that could've been."

"Great to see guys in a self-defense class," Noah mentioned. "It's a good idea for everyone."

Del nodded. "Literally needed in this day and age. A black kid like me can barely walk down the street without getting side-eyed. But, I'll refrain from learning the 'knee to the boys' from you. Literally can't think of a worst thing."

Noah snorted. "I hear that. You do you, man. It's just my job to let you beat on me."

Del studied Noah. "You look really familiar."

Noah tried to look nonchalant while Aly held her

breath. "Don't think we've met."

"I'm sure I've seen you before," Del said as he tapped his fingers against his knees.

Aly chewed slowly, trying not to shoot Noah a panicked look. The form Noah had chosen was similar to Fletcher but now she worried it was too similar. He'd mentioned it would be Clark Kent syndrome. Not seeing the obvious because there was no possible way it could be true. Noah would feel familiar and maybe that would be enough to connect with Del and Grace.

"I've only been in Bellhollow for a week," Noah replied. "Came in to help Kayla with a few things before college."

"Oh?" Grace asked, intrigued. "Have some schools already had exams?"

"No idea. I deferred for a year." Noah shrugged. "Couldn't really decide what I wanted to do, so I decided not to make my life miserable by accumulating debt until I knew for sure. I gotta be in LA by fall."

Noah's lies flowed like silk. It wasn't easy for Aly to lie and hearing Noah do it with such ease was disturbing for her. Necessary, if she wanted him back in her life, but still unsettling.

"Going to college in LA?" Grace asked, curious. "Us too."

"Yeah?" Noah asked. "Where at?"

"College of Music for me," Grace said. She held her hand over Aly's shoulder and tapped her fingers against her thumb in a demanding gesture. "Share."

"I got accepted into Otis," Aly said, offering the chocolate bar over her shoulder but refusing to let it go. Grace had to take a bite of what Aly offered.

"How come she gets some?" Del complained.

"She loves me more," Grace teased and took the hair band from Aly.

Noah flicked Aly a mischievous look. "Oh, I have seen *you* before. Last weekend, you were at the lake, sitting under a tree and drawing."

Aly laughed and hoped it didn't sound fake. "Oh yeah. I remember."

"Ooh, right," Del said, bemused. He tugged at his cornrows sheepishly. "Maybe that's where. So, deferring for a year worked for you? Don't wish you went straight on?"

Adjusting from the crouch to sit more comfortably, Noah replied, "I got to see a lot of the States. Worked in a lot of jobs and got a variety of experience. It was liberating and I enjoyed it. It worked for me but others I know who did the same thing aren't going to college now. Why?" he asked Del. "Thinking of taking a year off?"

Del lifted a shoulder, in a half-shrug. "I got accepted into a film school in LA, but I also run a YouTube channel and I'm thinking of taking a year off to see if I can make it work."

Noah grinned, pleased by that. "Oh, that sounds cool! What sort of channel do you run?"

Taking another bite of the Snickers, Aly pondered on their little friendships traditions which could be carried over. Fletcher and Aly had met in a tree and she'd stolen his Snickers, and now she and Noah could claim almost the same thing. As they tended to do when she thought about Fletcher, her fingers found the bee pendant hanging from her neck to toy with.

Grace leaned forward and wrapped her arms around Aly's shoulders. "Doing okay?"

Aly dropped her necklace to hold onto Grace's wrist. "Snickers helped." An unexpected shiver ran down Aly's spine and goose bumps rose along her arms. Noah stiffened in response and Aly felt his tingles chase the goose bumps along her skin as he scanned the room, and probably beyond, without breaking conversation with Del. Trying to be subtle about it, Noah glanced around behind him turned away, running his hand through his hair to help hide his expression.

Aly rubbed her hands along her arms. Was it a shifter or was she just having a moment? She couldn't be sure but the speed of Noah's response worried her. The shiver vanished, almost as fast as it had appeared, but Noah's tingles lingered.

He glanced back at her with a frown and lifted one shoulder a minute amount to shrug in silent communication. Aly shook her head a fraction since she didn't understand either.

"Alright, gang," Kayla said, calling the attention of the class. "Let's get started on that homework!"

CHAPTER 2

There were several diners around Bellhollow the trio liked to go, and while Dirk's Diner had the best burgers, Aly found she couldn't go near the place anymore. Even though she was pretending she didn't remember a thing about the attack and kidnapping, her friends accepted it when she said the place made her anxious. Barry, her boss at Dirk's, hadn't been surprised when she'd regrettably quit her job as a waitress.

Today they'd decided to go to Deedee's because Grace had a craving for pancakes and Del had one for burgers and Deedee's made both.

Aly sat facing the main entrance so she could glance up each time the bell tinkled to see who entered. She found if she had her back to the door she would turn obsessively and fret, so this was easier and her friends were happy to accommodate her on it.

Cupping her chin in her hand, Aly rested her elbow on the table and doodled in her sketchbook, only half listening to Del and Grace discuss music. It wasn't really a conversation she could contribute to, since she couldn't create music or manipulate sound like they could. Grace and Del seemed to be aware that she didn't want to talk and worked to fill the silence with friendship.

All her recent character creations looked like a lizard version of Voldemort, which would've only caused questions from Del and Grace, so Aly fell back on her tried and true method of drawing a cartoon bee in various poses. Right now, her little bee wore a Southern Belle inspired outfit and pranced through flowers bigger than she was. It was cute and easy and anyone who saw the image wouldn't be concerned about her state of mind. She might even color and animate it later.

Aly glanced up as Del and Grace dropped to uncanny silence. Del, with Grace's headphone buds in his ears, had closed his eyes to listen to something Grace played via her cell.

Grace noticed Aly's attention and smiled. "Needed a second pair of ears." While Del wasn't musically trained like Grace, he was an excellent sound technician and could be counted on to give an honest opinion. Both Aly and Grace often asked him about their creations, especially when they did cartoons together.

"Latest piece?" Aly asked. "Is that for prom?"

"Nah, that one's done." Grace pointed at Del's ears. "This one I've been working on for a while, but I benched it so I could see if I could figure out what it was missing."

Aly nodded. "Ahh."

"You can have a listen after," Grace offered.

Aly tucked a strand of stray hair fallen from her braid over her ear. "You know I think anything you make is beautiful. I'm not much good at telling flaws."

Grace waved her hand to dismiss that. "Doesn't matter. First impressions count too."

Aly watched Del's face as he listened to the music and waited for him to pull the buds out of his ears. When he did, he set a scowl on Grace. "That was absolutely horrible. You fail music. Change your career to professional nose picker."

Grace laughed. "Professional nose picker? Well, that

blows."

Del grinned at her and winked. "I was swinging between nose and toe. Either or."

"Take her pick?" Aly asked, giggling.

Del held his stomach as he laughed. "Oh, that's awful, Aly-cat."

"You started it," Aly protested.

"What'd you really think?" Grace asked when they'd stopped laughing among themselves.

Del stroked the wisps on his chin in thought. "Literally beautiful. It's more melancholy than sorrowful. I dunno if that's what you were going for, but you're right about something missing."

"Yeah?" Grace asked and waited for him to elaborate.

"Mmm." He shrugged.

Grace chewed her lip and offered a partial solution. "There's space for a second violin, I suppose."

"What about vocals?" Del suggested.

Grace laughed. "You just like me singing."

He winked at her. "True dat."

"Not this one. I can't find words to fit the tune."

"I didn't mean words," Del said, picking up his cell from the table as it buzzed at him. "I mean… what about humming? Or '*oooooooh*'," he said, singing out a long note. "Just something floating over the top. Enya that shit up."

"You're dead to me," Grace dismissed, laying on the sarcasm even as she struggled not to laugh. "Enya that *shit*? Honestly, I don't know why we put up with you. Bums rides all the time. Wears his corn rows too tight. Thinks Enya is shit."

Del gave her a flat stare. "Dude, like, Enya is *the* shit. Her track stacks are on point. You know that. Stop taking it the wrong way. Just, add some siren-type croons over the top and see what happens."

Grace tilted her head as though she could hear a melody. "Mmm… That's an interesting idea."

"Of course it is," Del preened, pretending to shine his

nails against his chest. "I thought it. And I'm amazing."

Aly snorted.

Grace, seeing a chance to distract, asked, "How's the bee?"

Dragging her eyes to the sketchpad, Aly smiled at the drawing. "Buzz-tastic. But then she always is."

"You really should name her," Del suggested.

Aly lifted her other hand to her bee necklace and ran the pendant along the chain. "Nah. For the moment, she just is. If I name her, I'll get attached."

"You're *already* attached," Grace said. She sat back, lifted her hand and, with an air of great grandeur, announced, "I hereby name her Phoe-bee."

Aly snorted. "Bee-trice."

"Honey," Grace countered.

"Oh," Del crowed and thumped the table. "I know! Bay-bee."

The face Grace pulled caused Aly to burst into laughter. As Grace went to retort, her cell chimed, and she lifted it to check. "Ick," she said, wrinkling her nose at the screen.

Focusing on her doodle, Aly offered a, "Hmm?" to invite Grace to talk.

"Oh, Madison-Lee's having a panic attack about prom again."

Aly rolled her eyes. Madison-Lee Campbell was Bellhollow High's resident party girl. Most of the teenage shenanigans happened at her place, including the prom after party. "She is?"

Grace arched an eyebrow at her. "Haven't you seen the Snapchats?"

Aly shook her head. "I try to steer clear of her mess."

"We all do," Del muttered, concentrating on his own cell and Aly guessed by his thumb use he was either typing or playing games.

Grace nodded. "Lucky you." She heaved a sigh as she swiped her cell. "The color of her dress is the wrong shade of carnation pink and she's demanding that Kate fixes it. Somehow."

Aly gave a short burst of laughter. There wasn't much Kate could do about a wrong shade, even if she was inclined to help. Kate was a fledgling fashion designer and a marvelous seamstress but she was only making hers and her best friend, Tamara, dresses for prom. "Why would she even *want* to help Madison-Lee out?"

"Kate's ignored her all day. Madison-Lee's now wavering between being irate and bitchy, and downright begging. Tamara's trying to tell Madison-Lee that re-dyeing it will take days and probably ruin the fabrics."

"But Madison-Lee's not listening."

"Nope." Grace shrugged. "Not much that can be done at this stage. Her loss."

The bell to the diner dinged as the door opened and Aly glanced up, then sat up straight as Noah met her gaze. By his unsurprised and slightly smug expression, he'd known or at least suspected she was going to be here, even though they hadn't planned meeting tonight.

At Aly's reaction, Grace twisted so she could peer behind them. "Well, well. It's our punching bag."

Del swiveled around, then lifted his arm to wave at Noah, who waved back. Aly hesitated, wondering what she should do. Should she invite him over? Was it too soon for that?

She was saved from making a decision as Noah approached the front counter and a frazzled waitress appeared at their table laden with plates.

Grace beamed. "Food! Awesome! Mine were the pancakes with extra honey."

Aly pushed her sketchbook to the side to accept her meal. "Chicken salad for me." Taking a moment to smile at the waitress as she slid the plate in front of her, Aly said, "Thank you so much. It looks great."

The waitress gave her a relieved smile as she slid the third meal in front of Del. "Anytime. Enjoy your meal."

"Regretting not getting a burger?" Grace asked as Aly helped herself to some of Del's fries.

"I was feeling queasy. Now I'm not. Besides," Aly said, picking up her fork, "their dressing is *amazing*. No regrets."

Del turned around, mock-glaring at Aly. "Dude, how come I have to share my fries, but you didn't have to share your Snickers."

"Because, *Snickers*," Aly replied, rolling her eyes at him.

Over Del's shoulder, Noah nodded at the waitress behind the counter and made his way across the diner to them. "Hey, guys."

Grace, straw in her mouth as she took a drink, opted to wave while Del grinned. "Hey, man!"

Noah adjusted his stance and looked awkward. "Look, would you mind if I sat with you? It'll be just while the order gets done. I'm on fetch duty tonight, but the tables are all full."

Aly scooted over so she wasn't taking up as much of the booth. "Sure. Take a seat."

Noah flopped down beside her and smiled gratefully. "Thanks. I don't know many people in town yet and… well… I've awkwardly loitered a bunch."

"No probs, dude," Del said as he picked up his burger. "We know what it's like."

"You're still working?" Aly asked and then flushed with how familiar that sounded.

"Yeah," Noah said, nodding. "Kayla has a few other classes I help with tonight."

"Do you like getting punched on a regular basis?" Grace teased.

Noah laughed. "As long as it helps people learn, I'm happy with it. I'm glad I caught you," he continued, looking at Del. "You mentioned a gaming channel, but I didn't have time to get the name or what sort of games. I'm a gamer too and I'm always looking for new content to watch—"

Del grinned at Noah, sensing a kindred spirit and

launched into an explanation of his channel and the type of games he played and soon they were both talking about a first-person shooter game, the name of which escaped Aly.

Aly munched on her salad and surreptitiously stole Del's fries, smiling to herself. It felt like old times when the four of them would get together after school and talk about whatever popped into their minds.

It made her heart twang. She knew her and Noah's friendship would appear easy to outsiders. All she had to do was pretend they bumped into each other later and got to talking, but she didn't begrudge Noah this chance to reconnect with Del. They were never going to get back that shared history or the comfort and ease they had with each other, not while Grace and Del didn't know about shifters. They didn't know the boy sitting opposite them was Fletcher in a different form. It didn't feel fair that only she could know.

But Noah had been right. His sort of life was dangerous. It could hurt them.

Couldn't it hurt more if Del and Grace became friends with Noah, only to have him vanish too? Or die like Fletcher had. That would be even worse.

Aly wanted Noah back in her life. She truly did. But now she knew what kind of life he might have to lead, now she knew what else was out there, was it really the best thing? For her? For Grace and Del? Could they have a normal life?

Did she even want normal?

Something nudged her knee, breaking through Aly's musings. She blinked, moving her leg away and sat up straighter, glancing at Grace across the table. Grace was typing on her cell, not waggling her eyebrows at Aly like the bump suggested she would be.

Her knee was nudged again and Aly turned to look at Noah, who flicked her a glance and raised his eyebrows at her in a silent question.

Aly lifted her shoulder a fraction and looked away so she could shove a forkful of salad in her mouth. She really didn't know what to say. It was nice having him here and if Del continued to respond the way he was, then Noah had a way into the group. She felt more relaxed than she had been in a while and she wasn't compulsively watching the door. She felt safe, but she didn't know how to tell him that without it sounding too strange.

"Are we boring you?" Noah asked.

"Huh?" Aly asked. Noah nodded toward the sketchpad. A blush pinked her cheeks as she realized she'd been doodling hearts around her bee while she was eating. "Um. No. Not bored."

"May I have a look?"

It was for show, for Grace and Del, Aly knew that, but she still balked before she slid the sketch pad over to him. "This one's just for doodles," she said. "I'm more into animation and character design."

"Digital or traditional?" Noah asked.

"Digital, but carting a laptop or tablet around is a pain." She waved her hand at her small sketchpad. "This fits in my purse."

"Especially when she's forgetful and accidentally leaves them places," Del added, winking at her.

"Once," Aly complained and pulled a face at him. "It happened once!"

"That we know of," Del teased.

"Sometimes she just has to draw," Grace said. "Plus, this way she can rip pages out and give them to people."

"That would be handy. You really like bees," Noah said, staring at the page. "These are really good."

Aly shrugged and touched her fingers to the bee pendant around her neck. "She's my bay-bee," she punned, winking at Grace.

"Oh, hell no!" Grace declared, outraged, while Del snickered. "We're *not* calling her that!"

Noah lifted the page to see the next image, then stared.

"Wow," he breathed in a tone of voice which said he wasn't kidding about the awe.

Realizing who he was looking at, Aly flushed. A full-faced sketch of Fletcher. Something she'd been working on when she missed him the most. Something she hadn't let anyone else see, not even Del and Grace.

Noah's lips quirked up as he teased, "Who's this? Boyfriend?"

It was for show but she couldn't resist. Returning Noah's smirk, Aly said, "You could say that."

Del stopped chewing and Grace's eyes blew wide at Aly's white lie. Noah's jaw dropped before he caught himself and schooled his expression to something more appropriate than a gape.

Aly held out her hand. "Can I have it back please?"

"Oh. Um. Sure." Noah passed it over, still staring at her. "Thanks for letting me look."

Aly closed the sketchbook and hugged it to her chest. She left it on her lap and picked up her fork to pick at her meal.

The awkward silence was broken by Grace. "So, you said LA in the fall? What are you going to be studying?"

"Should be," Noah said. "California State in Computer Science, if all goes well."

Aly raised her eyebrows and Del perked up. "What are you going to do with that?"

"Not sure," Noah said with a shrug. "But probably—"

The waitress paused at their table. "Excuse me," she said, speaking to Noah. "You're picking up meals for Sports and Rec, right?"

"That's me," Noah said and pushed away from the table. "Thanks for letting me sit with you guys. See you on Wednesday."

Waving, Del said, "Seeya then, dude."

Aly watched Noah pay the waitress and pick up several bags of food from the counter.

"He seemed nice," Grace commented.

"Hope he likes the channel," Del said, focusing on his food. "Maybe we can hook up and game."

Leaning back in her seat, Aly spotted Noah's cell on the seat beside her. Restraining her eye roll, she went with it. "Oh, he's left his cell," she blurted and scooted to the edge of the booth. "I'll be right back."

Del wiped his mouth on a napkin, giving off signals that he'd deliver it. "I'll—"

She waved her hand at him and flounced toward the door. "Stay. Eat." She flexed at him. "I'm tough. I got this."

Noah was storing the paper bags into the saddlebags of his new motorbike by the time Aly caught up with him. He'd parked around the corner, out of view of the windows of the diner. "That was *so* subtle, bumble-butt."

He chuckled, glancing over his shoulder at her. "That's me, embodiment of subtleties."

Curious, she asked, "How'd you know we'd be here?"

"Didn't," Noah said, lifting his shoulders in a shrug. "It was Kayla's turn to order, so I got really lucky." He turned around and held out his hand for the cell. "Thanks for bringing it." As Aly placed it in his palm, he curled his fingers around her hand to keep it. "How are you?"

Startled by the sudden seriousness in his voice, Aly blinked. "Fine."

"Uh-huh," he said in a tone which suggested he didn't believe her.

She huffed out a sigh. "Okay, so I overreacted. No big—"

"I scared you."

Something in his voice caught her attention and Aly dropped the blasé attitude in favor of consoling him. "No. No, it wasn't *you*, Fletch."

Looking like he didn't believe her, Noah scrunched his eyes closed and dropped his head. "Aly, I know—"

"You don't scare me," she promised. "It was the situation. I wasn't prepared and I will be next time."

He peeked at her. "You said you were okay."

"I am," she insisted. She squeezed his fingers and pulled a face to offer him the truth. "Alright, so I'm okay *most* of the time. That was… the whole thing made me anxious, all the talk of assault… but it made Grace anxious, too," she added. She hadn't wanted to admit how much the self-defense class had unsettled her, but knowing it unsettled Grace as well made her feel like her reaction was within the scope of normal. "I didn't know I was going to react like that. Honest to Snickers."

He considered her. "Have you been anxious a lot?"

Turning her eyes aside, she evaded, "I was already booked into that course. I would've gone even if you weren't here and probably had the same reaction to someone else. Me being anxious because of it doesn't mean anything."

He frowned. "Aly, if you need to talk to someone, you can talk to me—"

She withdrew her hand. Hugging her arms to her chest, she nodded. "Yeah. I know."

"I know what PTSD is like. And I know it's hard to talk about since you're pretending not to remember anything."

She raised her eyes to his, knowing that it was better to face that head-on than hide. "It's not PTSD. At least, my therapist says not yet anyway. And I *am* coping. I might be nervous and overly alert, but I haven't lost interest in what I love and I'm not pushing my friends away."

"Do you blame yourself for what happened?" he asked carefully, his voice soft.

Aly blinked and gave him the truth. "No. Not really. I mean, I was stupid for going down that alleyway at night… but, I mean"—she shrugged—"they would've come for me anyway, right?"

He nodded.

Deciding to switch subjects, she forced herself to relax her stance. Shaking a finger at him, she planted a hand on her hip. "You know, you're cheating with Del."

If he was surprised at the topic change, he didn't show it. "How so?" he asked, tucking his cell into his pocket.

"You already know all of Del's interests. You just have to play to them. Plus, your appearance is very similar to Fletcher's. They both thought you looked familiar, but can't place why."

Noah leaned against his bike and crossed his arms over his chest, his stance stiff and defensive. "I was trained to use everything to my advantage."

"I didn't say it was a bad thing," she reassured. "It's... well, it's interesting to watch, that's all."

He ran his hand through his hair. "Do you think I came on too strong?"

"No, I don't think so. Judging by the Del-o-meter, he seems to like you, so that's good." She smiled at Noah's snort from her joke. "Are you really going to college?" she asked, curious. He'd never said anything about it to her, and she wanted to know if he was serious.

He winked at her. "Better than pest control, don't you think?" He sighed and lost his playfulness. "It's part of the cover. I mean, I could go to college, but then when you move to CalArts..." he shrugged. "I want to be a part of your life, but there will be places I can't follow you. If I'm going to college... if that's part of the cover, I can't drop it and move with you."

She nodded. It made sense. "Assuming I'll get in."

"You'll get in."

"I suppose forging college stuff is more difficult than high school," Aly replied.

"Yup. We'll revise our plans closer to August. It..." he waved a hand, "depends if all this works. If we screw up, we can try again, right?"

"Okay." Pointing over her shoulder with her thumb, she gestured the diner. "I should get back before they come and get me." She hesitated and decided she needed to ask for her own peace of mind. "That... that thing before. The shivers."

Eyes widening, he blurted, "I couldn't see anything. I'll do an in-depth sweep tonight." He made a frustrated noise. "Could you tell anything?"

"I don't really know how this works, you know."

He raised his eyebrow at her. "Sure you do. You feel a shifter close, you get goose bumps."

The strange tingling feeling Aly got around him was her sensing the shifts he made. And since he only made them intermittently, she only felt them intermittently. But the man at the diner before she'd been taken by the Purists had set off a sustained shiver, indicating he was a natural shapeshifter who had shifted. "How close?" she asked. "I have no idea on the range. Or… you know, tell if it's someone walking over my grave or not. And what about the differences in it?"

He frowned at her. "What differences?"

"You don't give me tingles," she continued, "unless you're shifting. And Elaine only prickled when she shifted. I couldn't tell her just by looking the first time and I don't know that I can tell her in the future. What if I can only tell you because I know you so well? Jonah's out there and… I mightn't be able to tell her… him?"

Noah's sibling's all had gender non-conforming, biblical names. She knew there was a possibility they could switch gender since Noah could. Since she hadn't asked about the others, she couldn't be sure. Jonah, Elijah or Elaine as she'd preferred, Seth, Solomon, and Adam were the siblings she knew of, but there could be others.

"Her," Noah said and rubbed his chin. "It could be that you need to see a Faceless first before you can tell if you see them again." He looked up at her with a furrowed brow. "Tingles? Prickles? Strange distinction."

She shrugged, not sure how to explain what she felt.

"You'd know, Aly," he assured her with a confidence she didn't feel. "I… you're the strongest sensor I've ever encountered, including me and I was built for this. Jonah and Elaine haven't... I mean, despite what she said they haven't been here and I don't know why that is. I spotted a few other people, but I don't know why they were here or which faction they're from. They sort of... passed through, and then nothing. I'm torn between worrying that I'm just not good at this anymore and being happy that you're not an interest to them."

She frowned at him. "Isn't that what we wanted?"

He sighed. "Yeah. I guess."

She tapped her fingers together and shuffled. "Honestly, I'm not even sure it wasn't just a delayed reaction to the... um..." She raised her fists up to protect her face in an awkward boxing pose to illustrate. "Situation."

"Ahh."

Feeling silly, she dropped her hands. "Maybe we should do some tests on range?"

Scratching his cheek, he nodded. "I think that would be a good idea. Why don't we meet at the gorge tomorrow? Say four?"

She smiled. "Sounds good."

"Maybe, once we've checked your range, we should work out some sort of code so you know if I'm around." At Aly's nod, Noah continued, "How opposed are you to learning Morse code?"

An odd request, but Aly pondered it anyway. "Do you think it will be needed?"

"I have no idea. Better safe than sorry. It's... practical. Things like 'yes' and 'no', would be helpful. Or if I had a way to warn you if something wasn't right."

"Okay. I'll learn it." She smiled at him. "Things I do to keep you around."

He laughed, then sobered. "If it happens again, you need to—"

"I'll call you. Straight away. Promise."

"Good." He reached for his helmet and straddled his bike. He clenched his fist and offered her his forearm. "Be careful, okay? Best judgment. I'll always try to be close, but—"

Bopping her forearm against his, she smiled. "You're but one man. Plus you have a job. I did alright without you, you know."

"I know. I just worry my presence will bring them all back."

"If that happens, we'll deal with it," Aly said and turned away. "Night."

"Hey, Als?"

She turned around, eyebrows raised. "Yeah?"

"That… that boyfriend comment?" he said, looking bewildered, nervous and a little hopeful.

She shrugged and continued to walk backward away from him. "Seems easier to explain without having to go into it." She winked at him. "Have to give you some sort of hurdle to get over, don't I?"

"But… we… um… we didn't talk about that—"

"Don't forget," she called over her shoulder as she flounced back the diner. "You still owe me the world's biggest Snickers for being a dumbass. That little peace-offering was just the beginning."

CHAPTER 3

A large stretch of woodlands nestled between Bellhollow and the gorge. The ancient river carved a divot in the rocks, producing crumbling cliff edges. Woodlands trimmed the edge and ran to the freeway. There were several cliff paths to the pebbled river below the bridge for fly fishing and there were a few overused bonfire sites teenagers hung out at. Walking tracks wove through the woodlands for those who liked to wander and there were many sights to behold along the paths.

On Tuesdays, Aly used to play paintball in a portion of woodlands not far from the gorge, but Thursday afternoon meant the space felt deserted. She pulled into the almost-empty parking lot and chose a spot close to one of the hiking paths, beneath the shade of a tree. Pushing open the front door of the car, she kicked off her flats and reached for socks and hiking boots.

After she'd put her boots on, Aly went to the trunk for the small hiking backpack which contained her water bottle and a few frozen Snickers. She slipped her cell into the back pocket of her shorts and dropped her hat on her head, turning at the sound of a motorbike pulling into the parking lot.

Taking the bay beside her, Noah pulled off his helmet and ran a hand through his hair to loosen it. "Hey."

Hand on the open hatch of her trunk, she smiled at him. "Hey. Do you wanna store your stuff in here?"

"Nah," he replied, kicking down the stand. "Saddlebags lock on this one."

She shut the trunk and locked her car. "Nice addition."

"Was about time."

"How did you afford it?" she asked, curious, and tucked her keys into her pocket.

He paused, then continued to store his gear. "This one's a rental. I have a few investments in various names and... um... well... Life insurance."

She gaped at him. "You didn't."

Noah couldn't meet her eyes as he shrugged. "It's... easier. It's never... I mean, I know it's fraud, but I never go for the expensive ones."

"You hack," she teased.

After a tense look, he saw she was teasing and grinned in response. "Shall we?"

"Where are we going?"

"Up near the falls. All the fishermen are congregating near the split, so the falls should be empty. I want to have a bit of warning of anyone approaching while we practice." He smiled as they fell into step along the dusty path. "I'll be able to see the walk and the parking lot from there."

A mile, through dense trees. "Wow," she breathed, amazed. "Really?"

"Yup." He shrugged. "Heat signatures and such."

She blinked at him. "*Really?*"

"You know I can do X-ray," he said. "Heat signatures isn't much of a stretch. It's just a matter of changing the wavelength my eyes and ears can see and hear. Animals do it all the time."

"If you tell me you can see through clothes too, I will smack you."

Noah lifted an eyebrow at her. "X-rays don't work that

way."

"Uh-huh, sure they don't, Superman." Happy, she bounced beside him, swinging her arms as she walked. "Shapeshifter; super strength and stamina, age manipulation, eyes and hearing, speaking ultrasonically. Wait, I suppose you're more like... oh, what's-his-name... the green alien?"

"Martian Manhunter?"

Aly clicked her fingers. "Yup! What *can't* you do?"

Noah laughed. "Well, I can't fly."

"Why not?" she asked, only partly serious about the question. Waving her arms around, she blurted, "Can't you, I dunno, sprout wings?"

"Wings aren't a natural extension of the human body," he said, shaking his head at her. "I can't make feathers. I have no idea where to put muscles or bones or tendons to make them work." Scratching his cheek, he continued, "Best I could do was stretch out my skin and glide. Maybe."

She stared at him. "If... if you did know... could you build them?"

He shrugged. "Probably. I've added extra limbs before, as an experiment. It never works very well. I tried wings, it was a very painful mess... What?" he asked, bewildered. "Why are you looking at me like that?"

"Who's your best friend?" she prompted with a sing-song tone. She turned to walk sideways while grinning at him.

"You are?"

Using the same tone, she tugged on his shirt, "And what is it I do?"

Now it was his turn to stare. "Huh?"

"I've got pages and pages of character design," she said, practically skipping with excitement. "Anatomically correct mermaids and angels, or as close as I can get without a medical degree. Not to mention I *know* there are wing designs out there people have drawn for a human body, bones and muscle structure included. We could do bat wings."

He snorted. "Sure."

"I'm dead serious. I bet I could even render 3-D ones and animate movement so you can study that."

Noah stopped walking, his face a picture of comical surprise. "Shit. You could?"

"Yes." She turned her nose up at him and kept walking. "You'd have to commission me, though. After exams."

He pounced on her, his arms roping around her stomach so he could squash her back to his chest. "Aly, you're the best."

She squeaked in surprise when he picked her up to spin her around, then burst into laughter. "Yeah, I know."

He nuzzled the back of her head with his face. "Does this mean I get downgraded from Superman to Batman?"

"Absolutely. Can you let go now? You're squashing my Snickers." He released her and she shoved him on the shoulder as they resumed walking. "You are *such* a dork."

He laughed exuberantly and nudged her with his shoulder, then draped his arm across her shoulders. "But you love me anyway."

Smiling, all she did was shake her head at him.

The falls were quaint and peaceful. A ten-foot drop into a pond of water that rushed away into the small river which eventually met up with the gorge. A semi-popular spot for adventurous teens looking to jump from the rocks at the top to the pool below, despite the copious warning signs around the area not to. A graffiti-covered concrete picnic table sat in the shade of a tree beside the pool of water at the bottom of the falls.

Aly sat on the table, propping her feet up on the seat. "So, how do we do this?"

"Well, first I want to make sure you can tell when I stop and start shifting. If I do it rapidly, do your tingles match the shift?"

She rested her wrists on her knees and clasped her

hands. "No clue."

Standing before her, Noah smiled. "So, we test that first." He rolled up the sleeve of his red flannel shirt to reveal his forearm. "Short bursts, I'll do it so you can see. Let me know if the tingles match the stop-start rhythm I'll do, or if there's a delay."

Aly nodded. "Sure."

A patch of skin on his forearm changed from pale to dark, spreading in an oval circle until it was about the size of a quarter. The tingles which tickled through Aly matched the growth of the mark almost exactly, stopping and starting when it did. Giggling, she wriggled.

Noah frowned. "What?"

"It *tickled.*"

His lopsided smile burst onto his face. "*Ooh.*"

Aly's eyes widened as she realized the ammunition she'd inadvertently given him. "Oh no."

He drawled, "That sounds promising."

She waggled a finger. "Don't you dare."

"When you least expect it," he told her.

"I will smack you!"

"Not"—he planted his hands on either side of her and leaned forward—"if you're laughing too hard."

Tickles ghosted down her spine and spread out at her hips. They danced up and down her arms and delighted her ribs. Aly tensed and gave Noah a deadpan look as she struggled not to give in to the temptation of laughter. "That's not going to work. It doesn't tickle *that* much."

"Uh-huh. Just like you really, really hate having your feet tickled." He drew closer, a silly smirk spreading across his stupid face. "Can you feel it, niggling its way under that steel armor of yours and—"

Aly scowled, then snorted. Slapping a hand over her mouth to contain any more giggles of betrayal that might sneak by, she stuck her hand on his chest and pushed. "Stop. Or I'll never share another Snickers. Ever."

"Okay, okay," he said and stopped his shift.

She breathed out in relief, then crossed her arms over her chest and huffed at him. "Meanie."

"You're the one threatening to deprive me of Snickers." Still grinning, he said, "So the basic skin shifts tickle. Interesting." He adjusted his stance. "Pretty cool that you can tell the difference."

"It's probably just you," Aly pointed out.

"Maybe. Let's try again." Holding out his arm to her, Aly watched as the mark faded from his arm. "Well?"

Aly lifted her head to look at him. "Did you stop in the middle?"

Noah didn't reply but she interpreted his pleased expression as confirmation. "Close your eyes this time. Tell me when I start and when I stop."

Aly wriggled to get comfortable and closed her eyes. "Okay." She concentrated hard on the sensations tickling through her. "You started… stop."

"Good," Noah crooned. "Okay. I'm going to take about ten paces away from you. Same deal."

"Alright." Keeping her eyes closed, she listened to the crunch of his boots as he walked away from her, then focused on the tickles. "Started… and stop." She frowned as they restarted. "Start… stop."

"Good," Noah repeated. "Could you tell which part of my body I was shifting?"

She scrunched up her face. "No… not really. It… always starts, like, between my shoulder blades first, then sort of travels."

"Could you tell my direction?"

"Um… I don't know. I didn't concentrate on that." She shrugged and waved her hand at him. "I mean, I already know where you are."

Noah laughed. "Okay. Keep your eyes closed. I'll move away and I want you to really concentrate on those three things. Direction, stop-start and body part, okay?"

"You don't ask for much," she muttered.

"I know."

Her hands clenched involuntarily at the thought of being left alone. "Please don't go far."

"Sight and hearing distance the whole time," he assured her.

"Yeah, but *whose* sight and hearing?" she retorted.

"Touché. Just call out what you feel."

She did. She told him when she thought he stopped and started. She pointed the direction she thought she felt him, although she wasn't at all confident in that respect. Once she thought she felt the tickles leading down to her leg, so she pointed there. It felt like he moved around all over the place. Keeping her eyes closed, she strained her ears as she searched for any clue she might be getting any of the directions right.

The change from tickle to tingle caught her off guard. It was still him, she could tell, but stronger. Like someone had been blowing on her skin and changed to stroking it with a gentle finger. Feeling confident in the distinction, she said, "That's an augment."

He didn't answer, so she pointed in the direction which the tingles felt like they were coming from.

Then came a strange sort of fading. One moment she felt the tingles, the next they dissipated, but it felt different than his normal stopping. Like it petered out. "Stop? It's… it's different?"

They faded in, then back out, then in again, before they stopped and she reported every feeling. She waited but no more tingles returned.

After a minute, Noah called, "You can open your eyes now."

She blinked them open and squinted from the sudden brightness. Turning her head to watch him approach, she asked, "Well?"

"Enlightening. Your range seems to be about two hundred feet, which…" He tilted her head at her inquiringly. "That feels bigger than it was before."

Aly nodded, turning her face into the breeze and

breathing in the soft scent of leaves it carried with it. "The guy in the diner, I didn't feel him until he entered."

He scratched the back of his neck. "Yeah, but you probably weren't taking much notice. We'll do another test again in a couple of weeks. See if it's growing."

Trying to get a judge on range, she asked, "How far can you see?"

He jumped up on the chair so he could sit on the table beside her. "X-ray and heat signatures only go so far before it gets too noisy and I can't tell anymore, but I can also do something like an eagle can, and see great distances pretty clearly. Depends on cover and such." He smiled at her. "I can look at a person and tell they're a shifter, but you— you can *feel* them coming, even if you can't see them. *That's* an amazing skill."

As impressed as he seemed to be, she wasn't sure. "Think so?"

He nodded.

Reaching for her bag, she pulled out two Snickers and handed one to him. "What about the rest?"

"You were *perfect* on the stop and starts," he said, tearing into the packet. "Even the quick ones. So Morse code will be definitely useful." His tone turned from eager to reflective. "Decent on the directions. It wasn't exact, but it was close. Body parts," he cringed and sucked in a breath through his teeth. "We can work on that, I guess."

"It'd only be useful for you anyway, wouldn't it?" Aly asked. "You said the most others could do was a skin shift."

Nodding, Noah took a bite of his Snickers. "My siblings can augment too. It might give you an idea if one of them is around."

"And what if it's just you I can sense like this? A natural shifter felt different... I think." She frowned and struggled to explain. "I... that guy at the diner did, and those others... felt very weird but they were all at a distance, I guess, and—"

Noah nodded. "I thought about that. There are a few places we can go where I know natural shifters live. After you graduate, we can test it if you want. We'd just have to sit in a public place for a while and see what happens."

Aly took a bite of her chocolate bar. "Do you think, maybe, I could be a shifter? I mean, you said shifter ancestor—"

Noah breathed out through his nose. "You know, I considered that when I figured out those shivers you got corresponded to my shifts. But no. You would've had an incident by now. I'm told shifting manifest naturally around the time toddler's temper-tantrum. Something about the emotion triggers it involuntarily and then they get taught to control it."

"Ahh. Yeah. Mom said I was a rather 'explosive' tantrum-er. So I guess no shifting for me."

"Are you disappointed?" he asked, lifting an eyebrow at her.

"Well… maybe." She shrugged and tossed her head. "I mean, it would've been cool to have a superpower that I didn't know about."

Noah laughed. "I guess."

Taking another bite, she considered as she chewed. "Do you think things will ever go back to normal?"

He rested his elbows on his knees, staring out into the woodlands. "Normal is relative."

"Okay, do you think there will ever be a time where there's no threat from shifters or Purists or anyone like that?"

He swallowed. "Not for me."

She pressed her lips together at the unspoken meaning in his words. As long as she wanted him in her life, she'd be under threat from shifters too.

"Once upon a time, I thought there could be. But Elaine *knows* you're a sensor. That alone…" He pinched the bridge of his nose. "I made a mistake telling her."

She leaned sideways and rested her head on his

shoulder to offer him comfort. "You had no reason not to trust your sister."

"Yeah, but it still might come back and bite me in the ass."

"Is she working for Darcy?" Aly asked, referencing the leader of the Institute and the person behind the creation of the Faceless. She didn't know much about them, but she suspected neither did Noah. "Or is it a ruse?"

He shrugged and looked up at the sky. "I have no idea. See, if I'd seen Elaine watching you, I'd know for sure, but as far as I can tell, she hasn't been here. And I don't know if that means she's playing me or she's playing Darcy and I don't..." He sighed and rubbed his face. "There's nothing stopping you from living your life, Als. But, if you want me in it, there's always going to be a risk."

"Uh-huh. Except that I'm a sensor gold mine, right? I'm safer with you. And we shouldn't let the possibility that we might be discovered stop us from living, right?" She wasn't going to let him try to push her away or feel guilty about being here.

He nodded. "Right. It's no way to live. Tried it. Yeah, I might have to leave at a moment's notice, but you're right. We shouldn't let it stop us."

Her heart gave a thump at the thought of being left behind again. Would she go with him if he asked? "There were no answers on that flash drive Elaine slipped you?"

He straightened his spine in surprise and the action rocked his shoulder, bumping Aly. "Oh, I didn't tell you, did I?"

"Nope."

"It was a bunch of photos. Selfies mostly but there were some pictures of the ocean or trees. A few landmarks that I recognized, but yeah, it felt like... it felt like it was her blog or something. I honestly don't know why she wanted me to get them." He tilted his head until his cheek rested on her head. "Maybe this artist I know will look at them and tell me what she thinks."

"Sure."

"After exams."

"Yeah. My weeks are pretty full up." She took another bite of her chocolate bar, thinking while she chewed. "Fletch, I wanted to—"

His expression was morose as he nudged her. "You probably should get used to calling me Noah, Als."

She lifted away from his shoulder. "Oh—"

He wrapped his arm around her waist to keep her close. "It's okay when we're alone, but if you slip, especially around Grace and Del…" She scrunched up her face and he gave her a squeeze. "I know. I don't like it like this either."

She sighed. "No. You're right. I should be more careful."

He grinned and bumped her with his shoulder. "How about a game of hide-and-seek?"

Aly lifted her eyebrows at him. "Are you twelve?"

He laughed. "No. We're seeing if we can refine your direction. I hide and keep shifting until you find me. Best way I can think of. After that, I can run you through some more self-defense moves."

Aly hid her smile. "Fine. I'll give you to the count of twenty."

CHAPTER 4

Pulling into the school parking lot on prom night, Aly could see Del and Grace, both dressed elegantly and chatting as they waited for her at the top of the stairs. Getting out of the car, she fixed her dress and picked up her clutch. Touching her bee pendant, she glanced around, wondering if Noah was out there somewhere. While she was sad he couldn't attend prom, she still wanted to get his reaction to her dress. A small tickle down her spine told her that he was close, so she flashed a bright smile in the direction she felt and twirled so he could see.

Her dress was bright yellow, her favorite color. A layered A-line skirt, a jeweled bodice, something she could wear again if she chose. A tiny bundle of flowers from Roger curled around her wrist and a black band twisted around her arm. Although her parents had ignored the black band on her arm, Aly caught Penelope looking at Fletcher's portrait in the hallway as Roger, her adopted father, took photos. Aly knew they both wished he was here. She wished she could tell them the truth but she knew they wouldn't believe her.

Another tickle, longer this time as Aly flounced off to join her friends. "Sorry!" she called to Del and Grace as

43

she climbed the stairs. "Roger wanted photos."

"S'all good," Grace said. "We know about 'because parents'."

"You look sexy as hell," Aly told her friend. "It's gorgeous."

Grace beamed and brushed her hands over the skirt. "It's the red silk."

"Striking. That little bit of lace, it just screams 'look at my cleavage'."

Grace laughed. "It's a *bodice*."

"A change of word doesn't make it any better," Aly teased. "Bodice, cleavage." Feeling silly, she combined them. "Cleavice? Bodage?"

Del perked. "Bondage?"

"Oh, you *would* hear that." Grace gripped the lapel of Del's suit and dragged him forward so he stood beside her instead of lounging on the brickwork beside the stairs. "Cassidy dropped Del off; she even took photos of him walking up the stairs."

Aly grinned at Del. "Wow, Del, you look smokin'."

He preened, touched his fingers to the brim of his top hat and gave a small bow. "Thanks, Aly-cat. You look gorgeous too."

"That top hat," Grace said and reached up to adjust it while Del was still bent. "It's so," she growled out the word, "*manly*."

Del pulled a face at her. "Be nice and I'll let you wear it later."

"I'll hold you to that."

Del turned toward the entrance and offered both girls his elbows. "Shall we go, miladies? Or do we literally want to linger on the stairs all night? I really want to get my photo taken with the two best looking ladies around."

Aly wove her arm through Del's and grinned at Grace as she took his other elbow. "Time to sparkle."

Joining the line for the photographer outside the gym, they greeted the other members of the senior year as they came across them. They took two photos, one for their parents, and one for them. The parental one was filled with decorum, grace, and seriousness, while the one for them had Grace wearing Del's hat and posing like she was a 1940s pinup girl, while Aly got a piggy-back ride from Del.

The design of the gym decorations was simplistic yet effective. A ribboned podium set on the stage, a DJ hired for the night set up in the corner, a buffet, and tables and chairs set at one end of the hall leaving room for a large dance floor. Long streamers of red and gold roped between support beams around the outside of the gym while the tables and chairs were also swathed in the same colors. Most of the tables were already full of chatting and laughing seniors taking selfies for their various social media accounts. Aly's eyes drifted across the gym, looking at the various balloon arrangements on the tables and then to the stage where the podium was. The white drop-down screen, used for large-scale presentations, had been pulled down but nothing was playing on it at the moment.

Upon scoping the room, Del heaved a mock sigh and overacted slumping his shoulders.

"Well, I like it," Grace told him.

"Elegant," Aly agreed. "Nice use of color."

"Nah, it's the music," Del said, nodding to the DJ in the corner, who currently played a waltz. "Hope he's not gonna keep that drivel going."

"He's setting the mood," Grace informed him.

"Yeah, but ain't nobody going to dance to that shit."

"You have absolutely no elegance," Grace said with a small scowl. "That's Lehár."

"And that name means absolute jack to me," Del teased.

Grace whacked his chest with the back of her hand. "Uncultured."

"Come, darling," Aly drawled, lifting her nose to Del. She held up her hand to Grace, palm down and pretended to be snobbish. "Let us leave this riff raff behind."

"Pish posh," Grace responded, placing her hand over Aly's. "We must away."

"Save me a seat," Del laughed after them.

Grace stuck her tongue out at him over her shoulder. "You can sit on the floor."

Spotting their friends, Aly tugged on Grace's hand. "There's Tamara and Kate."

Grace lifted her hand to wave. "Darlings!"

Tamara, Kate, and Lloyd turned from where they were chatting. "Darlings!" Tamara responded in an over-the-top haughty voice as she sashayed over to them. "Oh, you look divine! Kiss kiss," she said as she reached them, leaning in to give both Aly and Grace an air kiss.

"*Please* tell me you're not doing that all night," Lloyd muttered.

"Excuse me?" Tamara asked, turning to her long-term boyfriend. "We are Victorian princesses for the night. I have the tiara to prove it."

"You're totally my princess," Lloyd said. "But can the fake accents and posh-ness."

"No," Tamara said, dusting her peach dress with the back of her hand. Peach looked striking against her olive skin and her hair had been curled into ringlets.

"Essential part of tonight," Grace included.

Aly said, "Authenticity and all that."

"Deal with it," Kate said, trailing her fingers along her pale blue skirt.

Lloyd scoffed and kissed Tamara. "I'll be back. I need to find some testosterone."

"Return with punch," Tamara called after Lloyd.

"Yeah. Sure," Lloyd responded with a wave over his shoulder.

"Toodles, my love! Hurry back!" Tamara called in a loud, pompous voice. "For every second we are apart feels like an eternity!"

Aly descended into giggles. "He's right. That was really

over the top."

"It's not my fault they picked an English era," Tamara said, dropping her hand. "We could've done Southern Belle, but nooo, someone had to be tricky."

They chatted and laughed and teased the boys when they returned laden with drinks before standing in their own chat semicircle. Claiming a table, the group sat to continue their conversation while they waited for the hall to fill and the 'real music' to start. They intermingled, members of their group going to talk to others and being replaced.

Finding her drink empty, Aly abandoned her shoes and picked up her cup. "Do you want another, Grace?"

Grace, deep in conversation with Kate, nodded and smiled.

Aly padded across to the punch bowl where the school nurse stood guard to prevent intentional spiking. She smiled as she filled Aly's cups. "Enjoying yourself, dear?"

After some polite conversation and receiving her drinks, Aly's attention was drawn to rambunctious laughter by the podium. A large group of seniors had gathered, all of them watching the screen which Aly saw was now turned on.

Pictures. Photographs taken throughout the year. Short movies set to piano music with an upbeat tempo. A mash of happy faces, football games, class trips, lessons, teachers, and important moments throughout the year. In the few seconds Aly watched, Tamara flashed on the screen at one of her empanadas sales smiling brightly at the camera. The image swiped and showed a football game, causing a rousing cheer from the seniors watching.

Aly smiled and made her way to their table. As she arrived, she interrupted Del's conversation with a touch to the shoulder. "Senior's tribute playing."

He laughed and twisted toward the screen. "Lloyd! It's you!"

"Huh?" Lloyd asked and turned toward the screen to

laugh. "Oh, wow, remember that?"

While the group around the table repositioned their chairs to see the screen better, Aly passed Grace her drink and sat down. The conversation turned to memory and laughter as they watched the pictures unfold.

Aly had been expecting one. By the way Grace squeezed her arm, Aly knew Grace was waiting too. It was a tribute after all. Winnie, the school photographer, had been out and about at every event for the year, so Aly knew it was inevitable that Fletcher would appear in a photo. While it was agony to wait, she'd been prepared to see him when he appeared. It seemed others weren't. Conversation died off even from those not at their table and awkward glances commenced.

Aly fixed her eyes on the screen and ignored it.

Fletcher was in a few photos. Sometimes in the background, sometimes with a group of friends. One which caused laughter involved him and Del standing in a canoe out in the middle of the lake, giving salutes to the camera while the canoe sunk. Another was him leaning on his bike, chatting to Grace after school. Fletcher in his track and field uniform holding up a medal. Fletcher in his usual flannel, grinning madly at Del. Fletcher carrying Aly's art bag as they walked through the hallway together. Fletcher and Lloyd helping out with lighting for the drama club.

The piano music changed, slowing down to single, lingering notes and sounded reminiscent of a music box winding down.

The next picture Fletcher featured in was one Aly hadn't been aware of. She and Fletcher sat together in the quad at one of the concrete tables. Back to back, Aly had been animating on a peg board and leaning on Fletcher while he played Del's PSP. They were laughing, Aly's head thrown back onto Fletcher's shoulder and he was hunched forward with a mischievous expression.

Smiling, Aly leaned forward and cupped her cheeks

with her hands as she watched the screen.

His face caught her attention the most. Longing and love, it wasn't the face of someone who wanted to remain a best friend but someone who wanted more.

He was asexual, someone who lacked sexual desire, not gay like he'd told her he was. That had been a lie so he could maintain his distance and she understood that better now. She had to rethink all she knew of him. All the moments they'd shared. All the conversations and laughter. So many moments where they'd screamed their affection at each other. He'd been her measuring stick, the man she assessed all others against.

He was back in her life and she no longer knew where they stood. He couldn't *be* Fletcher anymore, but he also wasn't hampered by the fact people knew Fletcher was gay. If he wanted, then he could. They could. If she wanted to and she still didn't know.

She loved him, more than anything, of that she was sure. And there had been a point where she'd considered herself to be in love with him. It had taken her such a long time to get over that and still, sometimes she'd looked at Fletcher and wondered.

The animation Aly had been working on as tribute appeared. Fletcher straddled his bike staring into the sunset with his hair flowing in the breeze. Words scrolled across the image, Fletcher's name followed by his birth and death dates. The screen faded to black and the piano finished it's winding down tune to turn into silence. As the last note sounded, the senior group photo appeared.

Up near the screen, Ethan leaped up on the stage and lifted a glass toward Aly and their table. "To Fletcher." The sentiment was quickly echoed by the rest of the seniors.

Grace made a noise that sounded like a mixture of a whimper and a sigh. Del leaned sideways to put his arm around Grace's shoulder. A knife twisted in Aly's chest but it wasn't one for Fletcher, it was for those he left behind.

Those who didn't know. She looked around at her group of friends, watching the emotions flit across their faces.

"Guys," Lloyd began. "Um…"

"Did you like it?" Del said, giving Grace a squeeze. "Grace wrote the music. She did a fantastic job."

Grace smiled. "Del made the slideshow."

Del nodded. "And Aly worked her ass off to get her animation tribute finished. We couldn't stand the thought of someone else making it. We didn't want it sappy, but we didn't want him ignored either."

"It was beautiful," Aly sighed.

Del nodded. "It's going up on the school website. Feel free to download a copy. We can get you stills too if you want." He thumped his palms on the table. "Alright then. Enough sappiness. Who wants to do the chicken dance?"

Smiling, Aly shook herself free of melancholy and bounced to her feet.

CHAPTER 5

Stars hung in the sky, winking down at the waters of the lake outside Bellhollow. A waxing moon provided little ambient light, but enough so Aly could see. Shoes in hand, Aly wiggled her toes, feeling the grass beneath her sore feet. Lifting the skirt of her yellow dress so it wouldn't get dirty, she picked her way down to the water's edge. Summer made the night air warm with moisture, but not overly hot.

No one else was around and the silence was a rare treat. Overprotective parents and friends made it difficult to be alone and although she felt safer with them around, tonight was different. Tonight, the solitude felt alluring and sweet.

Aly picked a concrete picnic table at random and dumped her shoes and clutch on the seat. Lifting her cell, she checked on her social media pages. Grace was an avid Instagram and Snapchat user and had spent the night documenting prom. One post caught Aly's attention. It was of Aly and Del, mucking around and dancing together ridiculously. Del looked especially silly in his off-center hat. Grace had captioned it with 'Good to see her smile again.'

Smiling to herself, Aly chuckled and dropped her cell into her clutch. Hugging her arms to her chest, she stepped away from the table and stared out at the glittering water, wondering if she should hike up her skirt and dip her tired feet in.

Such a wonderful night, she'd enjoyed the time with her friends more than she thought she would. Dancing, laughing and having fun, then skipping Madison-Lee's post-prom party to head to Tamara's house for a horror movie night. With Kate falling asleep on Grace, and Tamara and Lloyd starting to make eyes at each other, they'd decided to call it a night. Aly knew her parents weren't waiting up for her, and while she would wake them when she got home, she knew she wouldn't be missed. Grace had been half asleep when Aly dropped her home, and Del said he was going to wind-down with a game or two before bed.

She waited on the water's edge for the one person missing from her amazing night.

"You look beautiful." His voice was soft and warm and sent a delighted shiver through her.

Aly looked over her shoulder, dragging the curl of hair caught in the wind over her ear. Noah walked toward her, wearing what seemed like dark pants, a white shirt and a jacket. Smiling, she said, "Thank you."

"Yellow is really your color."

She grinned at him and ran her teeth along her bottom lip. "I like it."

Noah shuffled. "Did you have fun?"

"I did. It was nice. No strings attached nice time." The smile drooped. "I missed you. I'm glad you were around."

"I wish I could've been there, but it was... I left coming back too late."

Aly nodded. "Couldn't be helped."

"But, hey, um..." Dragging one hand out of his pocket, he gripped the back of his neck. Aly tilted her head as she regarded him, unused to seeing him unsure. "I'm here now."

Trying to figure out why he seemed nervous, Aly spoke slowly, "Yes? I know?"

"We could…" he cleared his throat. "Dance."

Her eyes flared wider. "Oh."

"If you wanted." He fumbled in his pocket and pulled out his cell. "I mean, I have music. We could… um…"

"What kind of dance?" Aly asked. "Because all Del wanted to do was the chicken dance. And the nae-nae. And dab. My feet are kind of sore and—"

"Slow."

She blinked. When he asked her to meet him after prom, she hadn't expected this. Considering everything, maybe she should have.

"It's an integral part of prom," Noah said, clasping his neck again as he looked away from her. "Del and Tish danced, and Grace danced with everyone."

Aly smiled. "Grace had a lot of fun tonight."

"You didn't… you wall-flowered for the slow dances."

"I don't need the complete prom experience," Aly said, then teased with tongue-in-cheek humor. "Because I asked for a limo and I didn't get that. I had a fun night, even without slow dances."

He met her gaze for a fraction of a second before it dropped in embarrassment. "It was the one thing I was looking forward to."

She didn't know what to say to that beyond, "I'd love to dance."

He puffed out a breath. "Really?"

"Of course."

A flash of a smile, before he fumbled with his cell. The light from it illuminated his face while he selected a song and then set the cell on the concrete table behind them. Stepping closer to her, Noah hesitated.

One of Grace's self-composed piano pieces trickled through the speaker of the cell to fill the night air with romance and Aly smiled. "Oh, you sap."

A burst of nervous laughter. "It's one of my faves."

"Mine too." Aly stepped in closer and looked up at him. "What made you decide to be so tall?"

He smiled. "What made you decide to be so short?"

"I'm not the one who can pick my height."

"This is my real height," Noah replied, teasing. "Fletcher was shorter because *someone* complained."

She slid her arms around his waist and rested her ear on his chest. "I can't reach your neck without my heels on."

"Lies," Noah scoffed as he wrapped his arms around her, clasping his hands together at the small of her back. "I'm not *that* tall. You can reach my neck."

She giggled. "With a step-ladder."

With a snort, he asked. "Do you want me to shrink? Or…"

"Or?"

He teased, "I could pick you up."

She laughed. "No. This is a good cuddle height."

"You can stand on my toes."

"Stop being a bumble-butt and dance."

Her body fit along with his perfectly as they gently swayed together and she wondered if that was by design or a natural melding. It felt amazing to be pressed against him and wrapped up in his arms. Safe and warm and loved.

Tiny circular steps, rocking in time with the slow beat of the music, they enjoyed each other's company. Smiling to herself, Aly rested her ear on Noah's chest and listened to the steady beat of his heart. His fingers flexed on her back, then he unclasped his hands to slowly drift the tips of his fingers up and down her spine.

He pressed his face into her carefully styled hair. "Did I mention you looked lovely tonight?"

"You did."

His hand followed the path of her spine until it reached her neck. "Aly?"

She was drawn to his voice, lifting her head from his chest to look at him. "Yeah?"

"I… I'm… we never talked about… the stuff that was said at the gas station."

The night air gained a heaviness Aly couldn't explain. The gas station where he said he'd been lying about his sexuality, and was actually in love with her. "Do we need to?"

"We should… Don't you think?" he asked, uncertain.

She gave him honesty. "I don't know."

He sighed. "I'm no good at this."

"You being you has always been enough for me."

He hesitated. "Is it really enough?"

She nodded, disliking the sudden awkwardness between them. "You're my best friend. I don't want that to change."

"You don't?" he blurted, his eyes flaring wide.

Aly chewed on her lip as she considered. "You saw the senior's tribute."

Somber, he nodded. "It was nice that they included me and didn't make it too sappy."

"Del made it."

"Ahh. Yeah, he would've—"

Sensing he was going to go off on a tangent, Aly said, "There was a picture."

He lost a bit of the tension in his shoulders. "The one of me and Del in a sinking canoe? I remember that; it was such a fun day."

She snorted. "No. Not that one, although I will admit that was a favorite of mine. The one of you and me sitting back-to-back, laughing."

He grinned. "If I recall, you fell off the bench after that. Then proceeded to chase me around saying it was my fault."

Aly laughed. "It *was* your fault."

"Was not. What about the picture?"

Her smile faded. "It sort of sums up our entire friendship."

He picked up on her expression. "What's wrong?"

She swallowed. There were things she needed to know, but if they talked about them, would things be the same between them? Would they change? Did she want them to? "When you told me you were gay, did you have feelings for me?"

Noah's hands tightened on her. Not painfully but enough for her to know he reacted to her question.

"There's two ways to look at the picture," she said. "Two different meanings."

"What do you see?"

"Your expression, it's… it's not… I saw what I wouldn't let myself see before because you were… you were unattainable. I couldn't—*we* couldn't be more because we were hampered by that barrier you put in place very early on. But that didn't stop me from treating you like we were more, did it?"

He said nothing.

She pointedly looked at the way they were standing, at where their hands were, at how they pressed together. "This is… us. The way we are together and… the way we shouldn't be together if we're just friends. Cuddles and holding hands. We fell into that old routine so quickly and… Dancing like this; this isn't the sort of things platonic friends do."

"Yes, it is."

She tried to be succinct. "I hug Grace. I don't cuddle her. I hug Del. I don't cuddle him. Not like this."

Confused, he said, "This is us, though. You're tactile and I…"

Smiling, she teased, "Like it."

Their swaying had drifted to a standstill but they didn't release each other. "Well, yeah. Is that a bad thing?"

She pursed her lips. "I've been trying to think how it started and I can't. I can't remember if this is what we were like before you told me you were gay, or if it evolved afterward because you were safe and I could practice on you. Like, if I hadn't had the barrier of you being gay and

I'd treated you like I do, there would have come a point where I questioned why you didn't kiss me. I can't remember if that's the reason I did kiss you."

Noah remained silent, letting her talk.

"The reverse is also true. What if these feelings you have for me developed because of how I treated you? What if…" Trailing off, she shrugged helplessly.

Frowning, he prompted, "What if what?"

She steeled herself. "What if you're caught with the idea of being in love and *I* was safe? I wouldn't push you into any sort of commitment because I thought you were gay."

Noah stiffened. "You've been thinking about this a lot."

"I've had a lot of time to research. I don't even… I mean, you said you were asexual but what does that mean? For you personally? There's such a spectrum for it. What are your boundaries? Shouldn't we talk about that first? Is sex like a hard-no thing? Or a maybe one day if you're really comfortable? Or, like, is it on par with folding laundry, you could do it, but you don't really get anything from it. Do you kiss or is how we are right now all we'll ever be?"

A grave silence hung between them, thick and burdensome, a fog which wasn't ready to be lifted. Hunching her shoulders, she stepped away from him and he let her go. Questions needed to be asked before any step taken or any decision made and the heaviness of the questions had broken the fragile ground they stood on. Aly hugged herself and waited for his response.

Noah cleared his throat. "It wasn't until after you kissed me that I saw you as anything other than a friend. I don't think that way about people. I remember…" He gave a deep sigh. "The month before the kiss was incredibly awkward."

She didn't remember it like that. "It was?"

He put his hands in his pockets and stared out at the

water. "Something was going on, I just didn't know what. You were... different. Girly."

She raised her head at his choice of words. "Girly?" she asked, incredulously.

"Over the top giggling. Playful flirting or doing the arm stroke thing. Battering of eyelashes. Wearing skirts and putting on too much lip gloss. Like those movies you made me watch." He snorted. "You weren't proficient at flirting back then."

She bared her teeth at him. "*Grr.*"

With a laugh, he continued, "I remember wishing you'd go back to normal. Then you kissed me, and things made sense. Afterward... I knew that was going to be hard. I waited for you to pull away. To not want to be my friend anymore. I'd seen movies." He coughed to cover embarrassment. "Not that that's a reliable source, but... you know. I expected things between us would change."

She turned so she stood beside him to stare at the water. "They did."

"Not as much as you might think," he said. "It took a while. But things did return to normal. *My* normal. Punches and elbows and wrestling. Leaning on me while you drew. Using me as a footrest. Hugs when I needed it and Snickers galore. All that stuff that you don't seem to think is platonic. We did that before the kiss."

Relief swept over her. "We did?"

He nodded. "Which, as you said, is probably why you kissed me."

"Oh."

"Then we had the week of Josh."

Aly screwed up her face and grunted in disgust.

His expression grew tender at her reaction. "I spent the week hating him and hoping you wouldn't change and I'd lose you. You didn't."

"He wanted me to stop spending time with you. I wasn't going to give you up for anyone."

"I know and... that astounded me. The simple fact that

someone, that you, wanted me to be a part of your life. That you were willing to fight for me…" There was a sense of wonder and awe in his voice. "No one's ever… It made me rethink everything. I didn't want to watch you live your life. I wanted to be that person who made you happy."

"You do make me happy."

His lips quirked up. "When… we kissed, I didn't have feelings for you beyond friendship. They developed over time."

She waited for the 'but'.

He didn't disappoint. "But I… I… I can't…" he huffed and resorted to blurting, "I can't sexualize you, Aly." He pressed his fingers to his temple. "In my head. I can't do it. You're wonderful and amazing and any straight guy would be picturing you naked and thinking about…"

"Boobs and butt," Aly supplied.

"Yeah. I… don't." He looked crestfallen at that. "I can't. I tried and… I can't."

She wasn't sure how that made her feel. "Oh."

"There are other ways to be intimate that don't involve sex. Cuddles and snuggles, and yeah, we might have gone beyond what platonic friends are supposed to, but keep in mind… I'd never had a friend before."

She hadn't thought about it like that. "Oh."

His expression was earnest and determined and he kept his gaze on her as he spoke. "You and me, we shaped each other. I took my cues from what you thought was acceptable. You treated me as family. You've been in my life for nine years." He paused. "It's ten now, isn't it?"

"Yeah."

"Ten *years*," he said, astounded. "That's more than half our lives."

"It's a bit incredible."

Ducking his head, he said, "You taught me what it was like to be normal, all the things I never got to experience. You *are* safe." His lopsided smile grew. "But you're also incredibly dangerous."

Her head reared back in surprise. "I am?"

"I came back to be near you, in whatever way I can. That's very dangerous. I've already been 'killed' once here."

A bolt of panic surged through her and she grabbed his arm. "Fletch—"

He cupped her elbow and pulled her closer. "Best friend or something more, I don't care, I need to be a part of your life. Just because I can't desire you, doesn't mean I don't want to be with you. You're my favorite person, Aly, and to me, you're *home*."

A lump clung to her throat and tickled the back. She looked up at him with tear-bright eyes. "Fletch…"

Noah took a deep breath and exhaled slowly. "Sex… I don't know. I really don't. For everyone else it would be something I wouldn't even consider but, for you?" He shuffled and his expression tightened. "I could try—"

Forcing herself to speak around the lump, she said, "If sex is a no for you, then it is. If we start something, I'll go in knowing that. I would *never* push you for more than you're willing to give, don't force yourself to do something because you think it's what I want."

He swallowed. "If?"

She blinked several times. "I… um…"

"Do you want to try?" His fingers brushed her cheek. "Cause if you do, I'm going to make heaps of mistakes, and I have boundaries others don't have and sometimes I don't even know what they are. Kissing," he said, his voice turned husky and his gaze dropped to her lips before they locked on her eyes. "I could do that. I want to do that."

His other hand followed his first until he cupped her face before he let his hands slide down to her neck. She anticipated his touch, concentrating on the feel of his hands and tried not to shiver as he brushed over the bare skin of her shoulder. Every movement was so careful, almost choreographed as he checked himself and her reactions and for a fleeting moment, she wondered if he was copying a move he'd seen in a movie.

Then his hands tangled in her hair, stroked her neck and things felt *different*.

Good different. Wonderful different. Scary different. A tickle settled in her belly as an old fire was stoked and Aly felt thirteen again, standing on the docks by the lake, pouring out her heart and embarking on a journey she wasn't ready for. Nervous and scared, yet curious and hopeful too.

"Aly?"

He was close. So close their noses brushed and the contact sent a thrill coursing through her. So close and waiting for her permission before their lips could graze together.

She could rise up on her toes and press her lips to his and...

Start something she wasn't ready for. Things were still too new, too up in the air, too exposed right now. What if none of this worked? What if his presence here brought the Purists or the shifters back and refocused their attention on her? He only just got back, who was to say this peace would last? What if he had to leave, had to run, what then? Would he take her with him? Would she go?

Could she let him go if she'd had a taste and then had it ripped from her?

A pain rippled through her heart at the thought of losing him again.

Her fingers curled, gripping his shirt to keep him in place as she drifted her head away. "Things are... confusing and kind of scary right now. I..." She moistened her lips. "I don't feel safe. I question everyone I meet and wonder. I'm... there's still so many things I don't know. And I... I don't know about this."

Leaning forward, he pressed his forehead against hers to murmur, "I never wanted you involved with any of this."

"So many things are changing, Fletch," she said and slid her hand up to cover his heart, feeling its thump beneath her palm. "Shifters and factions and Faceless. College and exams and leaving home. I feel... I'm so scared and unprepared for it all and I'm struggling so much with normal now I know what's really out there. I have no way to defend myself and I was so lost without you and trying to be brave and... You *just* got back, but I still feel so wound. Twisted and coiled and ready to snap and ... I... I need something in my life to stay the same as it always has. I need that anchor."

He swallowed. "Best friends."

She touched her fingers to his wrist of the hand on her face. "Best friends with exclusive snuggle benefits."

His lopsided smile bloomed slow, and hurt, but accepting. "That sounds nice."

"I love you," she said, shuffling closer and desperate for him to understand. "More than platonic. I always have. I just... can't right now. I need time. We need to talk more about expectations when we're not in this overly romantic situation and you're making doe eyes at me."

He snorted. "Am not."

"You are," she insisted. "You're cheating. I'm trying really, really hard not to be affected by them."

Ducking his head down, Noah pressed his lips to her cheek, grazing the corner of her mouth and Aly's heart rattled in her chest. "I love you too."

"See?" she said, letting out a shaky breath as he moved back. "Cheating."

Noah chuckled and eased them back into a slow dance.

CHAPTER 6

A week before exams, a heat wave latched onto Bellhollow and refused to leave. Studying for exams had taken up all of Aly's spare time and the heat made it extra difficult. While Aly's home had central air, Grace wasn't as lucky.

So when Tamara's group text regarding Lloyd's swimming pool, plus non-alcoholic sangria, and an invitation to lounge arrived, Aly immediately called Grace.

"Pick you up in ten," she chirped as she rummaged through her cupboards for her swimsuit.

"Girl, you know it!" Grace replied, happily.

The only child of absentee parents, Lloyd lived in one of the larger houses in Bellhollow. His longtime girlfriend, Tamara, was outgoing and enthusiastic while Lloyd was her polar opposite, quiet and reclusive, so an invitation to his home was a rare treat, even if Tamara was the one making it. And because it was Lloyd's home, not Tamara's, Aly knew there would only be their group of friends and not Tamara's large family packed in as well.

They'd have the whole pool to themselves.

Kate beeped behind them as they pulled into Lloyd's driveway and Grace turned around to wave at her.

"Couldn't study in this heat either?" Kate called as she

left her car, locking it with a click of a button.

"We're melting," Grace answered, pressing the back of her hand to her forehead dramatically. "What a world, what a world."

"Never pegged you for the Wicked Witch of the West," Kate teased as the three of them wandered through the side gate. "Tammy! We're here!"

"Darlings!" Tamara called. "Back here, come on through!" When they got to her, she looked up from where she and another girl loitered at Lloyd's outside bar. While Tamara wore a crimson bikini, the new girl was still in casual clothes. "Nice of you to join us."

"Swimming pool," Grace said. "Sangria. You know exactly how to coax us out of our study caves."

"Not that it was hard," Aly said.

"This is Ilana," Tamara said, waving her hand at the girl who sipped at a glass of sangria. "She's Zek's girl from Redding."

"That would explain the extra suit you asked for," Kate said, rummaging around in her bag. "Hi, I'm Kate."

Tamara grinned. "Zek did the"—she deepened her voice—" 'I'll just be a minute'."

"Over an hour ago," Ilana included with a solemn nod.

"They're talking livestream, right?" Aly asked, glancing up at Lloyd's bedroom window.

Once a month, Del ran a gaming livestream, something which he planned to increase to weekly once school finished. Aly and Grace's roles on Del's live-chat was to help provide conversation while he waited for game match-ups, as well as act as chat moderators. On occasion, Aly would run her own drawing livestream of Del's YouTube thumbnails simultaneously, so that those fans of his who were interested could watch. She had plans to do one tonight, which meant she needed to rest her wrist and was a big part of why she didn't mind having an afternoon of fun in the sun.

"Del takes that very seriously," Grace said.

"Even more seriously than exams," Aly added.

"Especially since he wants to do it as a career," Grace continued.

"Yeah," Tamara said, waving her hand. "I get that. But Zek's not usually part of the stream. He just wants to gossip."

Aly and Grace nodded. "True."

"So, we're gonna swim and drink sangrias and the second he's ready to go, we're not going to be. The terrible twosome are Aly and Grace," Tamara told Ilana, pointing at each of them, while Aly and Grace waved at the sound of their names.

Kate gestured, holding open her bag to show off several swimsuits. "Take your pick, Ilana."

Tamara hopped off her stool. "I'll get the sangrias while you get changed."

Because Aly had a tendency to burn rather than tan, she'd opted to wear a long-sleeved swim shirt with her bikini boy-shorts, as well as applying sunblock. The last thing she wanted through her exams was to be nursing a nasty burn. Kate, and her similar skin tone, had the same idea, but Grace, with her browner skin, opted for a one-piece.

The water was wonderfully cool against the bite of heat in the sun and Tamara's sangrias were divine. As was custom with a new person, they chatted and stayed on neutral topics while they learned about her.

"How do you know Zek?" Kate asked Ilana as they lazed in the water.

"Through our synagogue," Ilana said and lifted her hand from the water to watch the drops slide from her fingers.

"Are you a senior?" Grace asked, rolling onto her stomach and clutching a water polo ball to her chest to use as a floatation device.

Ilana nodded. "Yup. I'll be going to Sac to study teaching."

"Oh awesome," Kate said brightly. "This here's my new girl, since y'all are abandoning me in the fall," she said, flaring dramatically, then told Ilana in a more serious tone, "I'm going into fashion design in Sac. We should totally hang out."

Ilana looked pleased. "Sounds good."

"We'll be back for Thanksgiving, Kate," Tamara deadpanned, looking over her sunglasses at Kate.

"Nope," Kate said, splashing water at Tamara. "Abandonment. All of you."

Trying to be polite, Ilana asked the rest of them, "What are you studying?"

"Public Relations," Tamara said with a playful scowl at Kate. "In SF, so it's not too far away."

Kate rested the back of her hand against her forehead. "Abandonment!"

"Drama queen."

"Music Composition for me," Grace added with a wink at Kate. "In LA."

"I'm going into animation," Aly said. "In LA too, Grace and I are—"

Ilana's eyes blew wide. "Oh. Oh, *you're* Alyson Gale, the one who was—" she paused, noticing the instant, stony silence from the group.

Aly felt her stomach lurch, and Grace accepted Aly's sudden need for comfort with a soft smile and moved closer so Aly could lean on her friend.

With a cringe, Ilana corrected herself, "Oh. You... um... probably get that a lot."

"All the time," Grace said.

"I'm sorry."

Aly nodded.

"Um..." Ilana's eyes darted around the group as she fumbled. "You said music? Do you sing or play?"

Grace, seizing an opportunity to change the subject, launched into a discussion about music that gradually turned into a more enthusiastic discussion about their favorite bands.

The patio door slid open. "Oh, I see," Lloyd called, wandering out into the backyard. "Having a party without me?"

"I was bored," Tamara called.

"You were supposed to be over to study, not swim," Lloyd replied. "Gratuitous use of my AC, right?"

"Hard with you hyenas laughing upstairs," Tamara replied, tart. "Plus, it would've been rude to Ilana. Zek left her all alone."

Ezekiel, having joined Lloyd, looked abashed as he rubbed the back of his neck with his hand. "Sorry. I didn't mean to spend that long."

Del came out, grinning broadly. Coming to stand at the edge of the water, he puffed out his chest and put his hands on his hips. "Ladies! Looking mighty fine!"

Aly said to Grace, "Think he's got his cell in his pocket?"

"I don't care," Grace said, lifting out of the water to toss her ball at him. "He's getting wet." Strong strokes across the pool brought her to Del's side quickly, but he danced out of the way.

"Nuh-ah!"

Aly hauled herself out of the water, cutting off his escape. Spreading her arms, she dripped, "Give us a hug, Del!"

Eyes blown wide, Del held up his hands to ward her off. "Wait!" he blurted and fumbled for his pockets. Knowing he stalled to save his electronics, Grace and Aly stalked him slowly. His cell, keys, and wallet went up on the bar and he kicked off his shoes before Grace grabbed him and, laughing madly, pulled him toward the water.

He put up token resistance against Grace, enough so that Aly could clamber onto his back to weigh him down and give Grace a hand. As the three of them reached the edge of the pool, Del leaped in, hauling both girls in after him. Aly surfaced, laughing, and Del pounced on a spluttering Grace to dunk her under the water before she could complain.

"Now, that does look like fun," Noah said.

Aly's head snapped around and she gaped at him. He stood next to Lloyd, looking like he belonged there. While she knew Noah had been spending a lot of time with Del outside the classes, she hadn't expected him here and it completely derailed her. "What are you doing here?" she asked as she swam over to the side.

"Well, hello to you too, Als," he said, with a wink as he crouched down to talk to her. "Nice to see you."

Holding onto the edge of the pool, she wiped water from her face to complain, "I never know when to expect you."

"I'm like the Spanish Inquisition in that way."

She giggled and it came out too high-pitched for her normal giggle. "No, seriously, what are you doing here?"

He poked her nose. "It's stream night, ergo, I'm helping Del. Shouldn't you be getting ready?"

Del was normally picky about who joined him and Noah had only been around a few weeks, but Aly wasn't surprised at the invite at all. Noah had mentioned he'd spent a lot of time with Del outside the self-defense class as well as online, even joining the trio for dinner after their last class. "I *am* getting ready. I'm stopping myself from melting." Smiling, she placed both her hands side-by-side on the edge of the pool and peeked up at Noah in an attempt to appear cute. "You look hot," she said in a sing-song tone.

Noah laughed. "Well, thank you."

"I could totally pull you in."

"You could try."

"Get off me, Gracie!" Del called, thrashing water behind Aly and Noah danced away to avoid getting splashed. A wave caused by Del and Grace knocked into Aly.

"Get dunked on!" Grace replied, her laughter echoing

across the pool.

Tamara spoke as she hauled out of the water, "Well, there goes our quiet time. Babe, you coming swimming?"

"Abso-fucking-lutely. Hey, Del," Lloyd called in a teasing voice. "You know I've got spare trunks. You should've asked!"

"Man, I'm gonna need a complete change of clothes," Del called. He stripped off his shirt and threw it onto the paving beside the pool with a wet slop.

Laughing, Lloyd said, "You want a pair of trunks, Noah?"

Caught off-guard by the casual invite, Noah balked. "Ahh—"

"You're welcome to join us," Lloyd said.

"Please?" Aly said and fluttered her eyelashes at him. She drifted away from the edge, lifting up her torso to float. "Tamara made sangrias."

Taken aback, Noah blinked at her, then narrowed his eyes in consideration.

"Oh, she did?" Ezekiel blurted, overhearing. "Score! Tammy, you are the best."

"I know," Tamara crooned.

Ezekiel turned toward the pool. "Ilana, have you tried—"

Floating in an inflatable pool chair, Ilana replied, "Someone left me alone for over an hour, I absolutely have."

"Dude, I'm so in."

Gesturing Ezekiel to follow him, Lloyd asked, "Noah? You in?"

Hands lazily treading water beneath her to keep her floating, Aly waggled her eyebrows at Noah.

"Sure," Noah said after a moment's consideration. "Me too."

Pleased, she rolled over, then swam toward Del to join in the wrestling.

It wasn't long before Lloyd and Ezekiel dive-bombed

into the pool, swimming straight for their respective girlfriends. Aly turned from her three-way wrestle to greet Noah. Catching sight of him, her eyes widened and she swallowed hard.

It was like he'd picked every single body trait he knew she found attractive and merged it into one form. Toned arms, defined torso, but not exaggerated or overly buff. Lean and flexible. She hadn't felt him shift, which meant he'd been walking around with that under his clothes since the beginning.

Noah tilted his head at Aly and cocked an eyebrow in confusion. Aly felt her face heat as she looked away.

She was allowed to look. She was. He might be asexual but she wasn't and, *damn it all*, he was attractive and he'd *chosen* to be attractive and that wasn't fair.

Side-glancing Noah as he slipped into the pool, Aly bit her lip, then slipped under the water to float just beneath the surface and hide.

It was only a body. One he could change at will. He could, quite literally, tailor-make his body for her if he wanted to. There would be no way he would, however, because he didn't see attraction the same way she did. He worked in a gym, so the more obvious reason was his job being behind his chosen physique, no matter how hot it was.

She wondered if that was similar to how he felt. Feeling little but aesthetic appreciation for her non-fluid body and everything else for her personality. It kind of made sense, the more she thought about it. To him, bodies were fluid, personality was not.

It was *him* she was interested in, even if she was taking her time to sort through her feelings. It was hard reconciling that with an ever-changing body. She was still keyed into including a visual aspect into attraction.

She watched him wade through the water toward her and surfaced when he got close.

"That's a pensive face," Noah said.

"I'm a very pensive person," she replied and splashed him.

A water fight followed. Alternating between squealing and giggling, Aly splashed whoever was closest with water. She warded off waves and caught tossed balls, returning them at random. She pounced on Del and Lloyd, pushing them under. She teased and tickled Grace. She dove around legs and splashed unsuspecting victims. Del caught her around the waist, hoisted and tossed her back into the water. Ezekiel swam around while slowly singing the theme from Jaws, dragging people under the water if they didn't get out of the way. Noah and Del pounced on Grace, lifting her up and sending her crashing down into the water again.

After a time, Aly sat on one of the pool lounges beneath a patio umbrella, drying her face so she could apply more sunblock and watching as Noah, Del and Grace wrestled in the water.

Tamara flopped down beside her and stretched out. "He's cute," she said, indicating Noah.

Aly smiled to herself as Del tried to get Noah in a headlock and was foiled. "He is."

"Your self-defense teacher, right? Lloyd told me about him. Kick ass moves, plus he's got some sort of…" She snorted. "I dunno… high kill ratio in… gah, I can't remember what their latest game is! I'm a bad girlfriend."

Aly laughed. "I can never remember their shooting games either. Give me an RPG any day. Which Battlefield are they up to?"

The laughter in Tamara died and she watched as Grace surged out of the water and clambered onto Del's back to dunk him under. "He fits in well. Del really likes him. Non-stop chatting whenever I poked my head in to listen."

Aly nodded and rubbed sunblock on her legs. Screwing the lid on, she waited for whatever Tamara wanted to say. Tamara always had a way of getting to the heart of matters. If something bothered her, she talked about it.

"Are you okay with that?" Tamara asked, her voice soft and gentle.

"Yup," Aly replied with a smile.

Relieved, Tamara nodded. "Good."

"No one's going to replace Fletcher," Aly said, smiling at her wrestling friends. As Del went to dunk Grace, Noah body-slammed him into the water, then was tackled by Grace.

"No," Tamara said quietly.

"Noah's not asking to replace him," Aly said. "He's just… asking for friends and… we can make room for one more, can't we?" Noah turned his head and smiled at her, lifting his hand to wave and Aly waved back, smiling.

Beaming, Tamara said, "Absolutely."

Lloyd called for Tamara's attention from the water's edge. "Tam! Chicken fight! C'mon babe!"

Laughing, Tamara dragged Aly into the water. Lloyd hoisted Tamara onto his shoulders, declaring that they were unbeatable in a chicken fight, Grace accepted that challenge by diving between Kate's legs and hoisting her up, pushing through the water to attack Tamara and Lloyd. Ezekiel and Ilana were such a mismatched pair, neither could decide who was going on whose shoulder.

Aly turned toward Del, only to find Noah diving down beneath her to lift her up on his shoulders. Surfacing, he snorted and wiped his face free of water while Aly clutched at his head to regain her balance. She wriggled, settling on his shoulders.

"Aww, what?" Del complained, pouting.

"You snooze, you lose," Noah teased, curling his hands around Aly's thighs, just above her knees.

Del wagged a finger at Noah. "That's *my* girl you're stealing."

"Do you wanna be stolen, Als?" Noah asked.

"Yup," she chirped, poking her tongue at Del. "Steal away."

"The woman has spoken, Del," Noah teased. "Mine

now."

Well, didn't that do odd things to the butterflies nestled in her stomach.

Sulking, Del flicked water at them. "I don't wanna be the odd man out."

"You can referee," Aly suggested as Noah waded through the water, heading for Kate and Grace.

"Or lob balls at people and try to unseat them," Grace called. "Get a workout."

"There's enough balls around for you to make a great distraction," Kate agreed. "Really, Aly? You're gonna take us on?" She dropped her eyes to Noah and smiled. "Who's this? I didn't get your name yet. I'm Kate."

"That's Noah," Grace said, adjusting her grip on Kate. "Told you about him, didn't I? He's our punching bag for the self-defense class we're taking."

"Sign me up for the next one," Kate chirped and locked hands with Aly. "So, you know how to take a hit then?"

"Take one, dish one out," Noah replied and although Aly couldn't see his face, she guessed he was smirking at Kate.

Aly had to admit, the training Noah'd been giving her, both in the self-defense class and one-on-one when they had time, made battling Kate a lot easier. It helped that Noah was a rock beneath her, able to read Kate and Grace's movements and compensate so Aly never lost her seat.

After Kate was successfully dethroned and sent tumbling to the water with a splash, Aly and Noah moved onto Tamara and Lloyd, who were busy lording their victory over Ilana and Ezekiel. The smack talk between Lloyd and Noah started, while Aly giggled at Tamara as they locked hands. Tamara, always competitive, kept issuing Lloyd instructions on how to stand and how to move, and while he did his best, he wasn't quick enough to follow all her instructions.

Aly lifted her arms into the air in triumph as Tamara hit the water. "We are the champions!" she sang.

"Nice work, Als." Noah lifted his arm from around her leg and held it up and she bopped her wrist against his.

"Yo!" Del bellowed loudly and tossed a volleyball at them. "Fletcher, heads up!"

An icy hand gripped Aly's spine and froze her through.

Noah lifted an arm to block the volleyball from hitting Aly in the shoulder and twisted around so they could see Del. "What?" he asked and Aly wondered how his voice didn't crack. If she'd spoken, hers would have.

Del's face was awash with horror as he recoiled.

Grace's hands covered her mouth as she muffled out Del's name. Aly's eyes filled with tears at the pain on Del's face. Water lapped against the edge of the pool, loud compared to the people standing frozen in its girth.

"I… I…" Del's Adam's apple bobbed hard and he rushed, "I gotta go."

He made it to the water's edge before Aly could think to move. Squirming free from Noah's shoulders, she belly-flopped into the water. Surfacing, she swam after Del. "Del, wait—"

"I'm sorry, Aly-cat," he said, picking up his cell, keys, and wallet and shoving wet feet into his shoes. "I gotta jet."

Dripping, she hurried after him and caught him at the gate. As he wrestled with the latch, she flung herself at him and hugged him hard from behind. "Del, please, just wait—"

"I'm sorry," Del said again, his voice cracking. "I dunno why I said that. I… it… I mean… it looked…"

Aly understood what he was going through but she couldn't find the words to reassure him. Del had seen Aly laughing and having fun on someone's shoulders, whose face was, most likely, obscured by her legs, and was thrown into a memory of a similar situation. She'd been feeling it too. It was like old times.

Del cleared his throat. He twisted his torso so he could get one arm around her to return her hug.

Tears pricked her eyes and burned her throat. She hated seeing her friends hurt like this. All she wanted to do was tell him the truth, about everything. About Noah and Fletcher. About herself. About what happened. About shifters and what she'd learned. Lies burned her tongue and she couldn't speak. Instead, she buried her face in his chest.

"I feel like such an idiot," Del said. "Gonna go before I embarrass myself more and it literally wouldn't take much right now."

She lifted her head. "Del—"

He cupped her face and brushed away a stray dribble of water that dripped from her hair. "I'm okay. Just need some alone time. Talk tonight? Stream's still on, if you're right to go."

Not knowing what else to say, Aly nodded and released him.

She stood at the gate, wringing her fingers as she watched Del walk briskly down the street, throwing his shirt over his shoulder while he dried in the sun.

"Aly?" Noah asked from behind her.

"It's our fault," Aly murmured. "We weren't being careful."

"We knew it was going to be hard." His hand clasped her shoulder briefly as he moved past her. "I'll talk to him. Call you later."

She nodded, watching as Noah broke into a jog to catch up with Del. Shoulders slumping, she hugged herself and went to find Grace. "I hate this."

CHAPTER 7

Eyes skimming the pages of the biology textbook, Grace caressed the edge with a thumb and index finger. Pausing her reading, she reached across to her laptop to check a definition, then returned to her page caressing. Turning the page, she frowned at the next one.

Across the table, Aly let out another deep sigh and tapped her pencil against her notepad. It would've been fine, had it been the first time Aly sighed, but the girl had been a constant nuisance of noise in the quiet of the library. Tap and sigh and tap some more.

Grace couldn't even remember the last time she saw Aly turn a page in the textbook she was supposed to be studying. "You're being really, *really* annoying."

Cringing, Aly stopped tapping her pencil. "Sorry."

"It's not that," Grace said. She clasped her hands together and rested them on her notepad to give her friend her complete attention. "I mean, it doesn't help, that's for sure, but it's the constant sighs and noises you're doing."

Aly chewed on her lip, looking everywhere but at Grace. "I've got a lot on my mind, that's all."

"Do you want to talk about it?" Grace offered, ready to be distracted from studying.

Skittish and clearly avoiding the question, Aly reached for her water bottle. "Nah. I'm good."

Grace squinted at her, not ready to let this lie. "This wouldn't happen to be why you were doodling all those hearts at Del's livestream yesterday."

Aly choked on her water. Her eyes widened and she wiped her mouth on the back of her hand. "I was not," she protested.

With a sly grin, Grace couldn't resist the opportunity to tease. "You were too! There's video evidence."

Last night, when Grace checked on Aly's doodles, she'd seen little 'Bay-bee' with big flirtatious eyes and hearts everywhere. And it just so happened to coincide with Noah's first time in the stream. Plus, Aly had been flirty with him at Lloyd's place yesterday. Not hard to put two-and-two together.

Covering her face to hide the growing pink, Aly groaned. "I shouldn't have streamed."

"Who were the hearts for, Aly?" Grace asked, her smile spreading across her face. "They wouldn't be for a certain self-defense punching bag, would they?"

The pink of Aly's cheeks turned red which confirmed that it was.

Aly with a crush. Now, that was a rare thing indeed. Grace had had multiple crushes on various people, from Mitchell and Lloyd, to most recently Kate. Grace had even had a crush on Aly when they'd first become friends. But her kind-natured friend really only had one or two noticeable ones in the time they'd been friends. Carter had been one, and that had died as fast as it had begun.

The other had been, as much as she tried to hide it, on Fletcher.

Noah was cute. He seemed nice and kind and genuine when he spoke to them. He reminded Grace of Fletcher in the ways which really mattered. Recalling Del's slip yesterday, she wasn't the only one who thought that. But it was Aly's reaction to him that had Grace excited. Aly was smiling more and seemed happier and Grace thought that could only be a good thing.

Eyes shining with delight, Grace cupped her face with one hand. "Wow. It's been a long time since you had a crush on anyone. I mean, I suspected, especially with the whole 'Fletcher's my boyfriend' lie but now… Were you trying to shut him down or yourself?"

Frazzled, Aly went into protest mode. "I'm not. I don't. Can we get back to biology, please?"

"What an artist doodles is a window into their soul," Grace replied with a knowing smile. "And you were doodling hearts *every* time he talked. I wonder what I'd find if I looked at your doodles from today."

Aly groaned and wouldn't meet Grace's keen eyes. "Shuddup. Noah's… he's… just a friend."

"A friend who makes you light up so much when he walks in the room."

Aly flopped back on her chair and rolled her eyes skyward dramatically. "Maybe."

"Maybe? Girl, you went *scarlet* when he was teaching us that technique to get the 'attacker on top' off. I like him; he's got a nice ass and a good smile. Del has a big old man-crush on him. He seems to like you. It's obvious you *like*-like him. Ask him out."

Fumbling for words, Aly touched her fingers to her bee pendant. "I can't, Grace. It's… it's—he's nice and I—but—"

Grace knew what the touch to Aly's pendant meant. Fletcher had given her that for her birthday. Being reminded caused Grace's mood to swing to somber. "Fletcher would've wanted you to be happy."

Head down, Aly nodded. "Yeah. I know he would've."

She tried to be reassuring. "I bet he would've liked Noah. They have a similar sense of humor. That's probably why you like him."

Aly made a non-committal noise.

Trying to keep things light, Grace snorted. "Fletcher

might've even been competition for all we know."

Aly's laughter was more boisterous than Grace expected. "Maybe!"

"It can't hurt to ask him out, you know. Or get his number and talk to him—"

"I already have his number," Aly said and flushed.

Grace was entirely too pleased with that development. "Oh-ho!"

"He gave it to Del too!" Aly responded.

"Yeah, but *I* don't have it yet," Grace crooned. "Del and I can make ourselves scarce on Wednesday if you want. That way you two could get your own"—Grace waggled her eyebrows—"biological studies done."

Aly groaned. "Grace!"

"Kisses, Aly. Kisses are *amazing*. You deserve to have some. When was the last time you got kissed?"

Aly chewed her lip. "Um… I…"

"*Aaaages*," Grace sang.

"Well, when was the last time you got kissed?" Aly retorted.

"Prom night," Grace replied, smiling in remembrance. Dancing forms and hands clasped. Soft lips hidden in shadows. A giggling face. Kate's smile swum into Grace's mind and made herself at home. She'd hoped for more kisses yesterday at Lloyd's, but the party had broken up after Del and Noah left.

Aly's eyes widened. "Why am I only just hearing about this? For shame, juicy gossip like this should not be kept to yourself."

Grace waved her hand dismissively. "I may or may not have gotten a little handsy with a certain someone who's not ready to come out to the greater population of Bellhollow yet."

Aly seemed pleased. "Go Kate."

"You didn't hear it from me," Grace said with a sassy finger waggle before she turned wistful. "Aly, you need someone to make you breathless, to kiss until your lips are numb and you're all gooey, just so you can experience that. If you don't want to have a summer fling before college…" Grace shrugged. "Well, hey, he's going to be in LA. You could always… keep flirting and see where it takes you."

Aly squirmed. "You're not supposed to be enabling me."

"Girl, I am enabling *me*. I can't wait. A time of experimentation and finding one's self. There's so many things I want to try or do. Courses and clubs and music and paint! I plan to do a *lot* of experimenting." Grace let out a blissful sigh and flopped back in her seat. "I want deep and meaningful friendships and frivolous romances. I want to do everything I couldn't do here."

Aly raised her eyebrows. "While I'm concerned you don't think we have a deep and meaningful friendship, I'm suddenly envisioning we're going to need a 'Do Not Disturb' sign on your door and a secret code so I know when you're otherwise engaged."

"Absolutely," Grace said with a light laugh. "But you know I'll be sensible. Try things out at my own pace. See what fits."

"Of course you will."

"Life's too short," Grace said, serious. "It… it can… disappear and then it's gone and you never get to say the things which were important or do the things and—" So many things she wished she'd said to Fletcher and never had the chance to. Things she made sure to tell Del and Aly. Fletcher was a big part of why she'd approached Kate, rather than waiting until college.

Tears welled in Grace's eyes for a brief, heartbreaking moment before she shoved them away. If she cried, that might set Aly off and Aly deserved a chance at happiness. Clearing her throat, she said, "No regrets, Aly. Fortify and no regrets."

"You're right." Face sympathetic, Aly stretched her hand across the table and clasped Grace's to offer comfort.

It felt odd that Aly seemed more concerned about offering Grace support than grieving for Fletcher, but it had been the norm since Aly had been kidnapped. Concerned with everyone else over herself and harboring a secret. Grace could practically see it lurking around Aly at times.

If Grace had been kidnapped off the street and subjected to God-knows-what, Grace might be loathed to burden her friends too. Or maybe she was reading too much into it.

They held hands, lost in thought and memory. Shaking her head, Grace roused herself. With a wink, she forced a playful tone. "We should get a 'Do Not Disturb' sign for you too."

Aly pulled a face. "So subtle. Wow. Queen of subtleties right there."

Laughing more naturally, Grace waggled her eyebrows.

"Grace?"

Grace twisted around, then leaned back on her chair to peer down one of the library aisles. A warm feeling spread through her as she saw who lurked in the aisle. "Hey, good looking! What's happening?"

Beaming, Kate bounced over with a satchel over her shoulder and several textbooks clutched to her chest. "Hey! I thought that was your cackle! Hi Aly!" Eyeing their textbooks, Kate continued, "Tammy and I are on the way to grab a pick-me-up snack. Tammy's complaining about a distinct lack of sugar required for studying. Do you guys wanna come? Or we could bring you back something?"

"Absolutely not," Grace said with a straight face as she shoved the lid back on her pen and shut her textbook. "What a ridiculous idea."

"We're neck deep in study here," Aly echoed, similarly packing up. "How dare you interrupt us with the promise of sugar."

"I shall have my father arrest you," Grace said, piling up her textbooks. She slung her purse over her shoulder and picked up the books so she could return them to the bay.

"You've done it now," Aly told a giggling Kate as they fell into step. "She's gone Malfoy on you."

"I'm quivering in my boots," Kate replied.

As the four of them returned to the library after sundaes, elbows linked and full of sugar as they told each other funny stories, Grace heard someone call Aly's full name.

"Alyson Gale?"

Without looking, Grace knew by the tone that it was probably a reporter. So many of them had been after Aly for a story.

With a sigh, Aly replied, "Yes?" Then her hand on Grace's arm clenched, causing Grace to turn.

In a professional gray pantsuit, with a sky-blue silk shirt beneath the jacket, a woman stood a small distance away, staring at Aly. Her dark hair tied up in a tight bun, her dark eyes felt somehow foreboding, and she held a manila folder in her hands.

Aly, for some strange reason, was frozen, her fingers digging into Grace's elbow.

"I don't know if you remember me," the woman said, "but my name is Belinda Bell and I'm with the—"

Responding to Aly's sudden fear, Grace tried to usher Aly toward the safety of the library. "She's not doing interviews."

"Ahh, no," Belinda said. "I'm with the FBI."

Aly snatched an incomplete breath, then took another one. "We've met?" she asked in a voice which wavered only slightly, but enough for Grace to understand something was wrong. "I don't remember you."

"Understandable," Belinda said, smiling. "I suppose you met a lot of people after the incident."

"Yeah."

"I was wondering if I could have a word." Belinda's eyes slid over Aly's friends. "In private."

Aly stalled. "Um… I'd rather not."

For whatever reason, this woman scared Aly, and Grace wasn't going to allow that. "Can I see your badge?"

Belinda's eyebrows rose, but she reached into her jacket pocket to retrieve her identification, and there was no mistaking the weapon she had holstered against her side. "And you are?" Belinda asked as she opened the small wallet that held her identification and held it up to be viewed.

"Grace Locklear," Grace said, peering at the identification.

"Ahh, the deputy's daughter," Belinda said with a nod and a smile.

Well, at least Belinda had done her research. "That's me." Grace looked at Aly and pressed her lips together. Behind her, Tamara and Kate hovered uncertainly.

Belinda said, "I have some photos I would like you to look at, Alyson. It shouldn't take more than a few minutes of your time."

Aly blinked. Then blinked again and Grace wondered what was going through her head. "Did you find out who took me?"

"Please, it'll only take a moment."

Aly shuffled and pried her fingers away from Grace's arm. "Uh… alright."

There was no way Grace was going to leave her alone. "We'll be close."

"Thanks," Aly said and allowed Belinda to draw her away. "Do you have suspects?"

They didn't go far; to the shade of a tree at the entrance to the library but it was out of earshot for Grace.

"Don't like this," Tamara muttered as Grace whipped out her cell.

"Aly seems really uncomfortable," Kate mentioned.

As discreetly as she could, Grace took a photo of the woman with Aly and sent it to her father as a precaution. "She does."

"They really have *nothing* on the scum who took her?" Tamara asked.

Grace shrugged. "Daddy says that's not uncommon. They have heaps of evidence, but nothing that can match up in the system and... well, Aly doesn't remember. There's only so much they can do."

"Small blessings, I suppose," Kate said. "I can't imagine what she went through."

"Should we really be allowing Aly to talk to an FBI agent alone?" Tamara asked, shifting her weight from side to side. "It doesn't seem right."

"I hear that," Kate said, throwing her blonde locks over her shoulder. "Grace?"

"She knows we're here," Grace said, watching Aly closely.

Belinda handed Aly pieces of paper and Aly pondered each one then shook her head. The more pieces of paper Belinda handed over, the more relaxed Aly seemed to become with her, so Grace wondered if Aly's unease was anxiety related to being startled.

Still speaking to Belinda, Aly took a step back. As she looked toward Grace, Aly made all the signs she was ready to leave.

Something shifted in Belinda's body language as she handed over one last piece of paper.

Aly went stark white. She recoiled with a cry, dropping the paper as she lifted her hands to her mouth.

Grace moved in without thought.

"You *have* seen one!" Belinda said, triumphant. "Was it in the forest? Tell me where you saw it."

Aly doubled over and gagged. "Oh, God."

Belinda crooned, "I can protect you—"

Grace shoved herself between Aly and Belinda. "What did you show her?!" she demanded and snatched the picture from the ground to look for herself. It was... what was it? Some sort of animal? That looked to be gray scaly skin. A mouth that was nothing more than a gap filled with misshapen teeth. It was dead, decomposing. A bear, maybe?

"You need to return that," Belinda chided. "It's classi—"

"Oh my God," Grace blurted, outraged as she waved the paper around. "What the hell is this? Are you showing Aly pictures of decomposing bodies? That—that doesn't look human! Is it a bear? Gross!"

"That's disgusting," Aly said and gagged again. "Is it dead? What is it? Why did you show me that?"

"Kids see worse things on TV," Belinda said, unimpressed, snatching the photo from Grace.

Grace turned, gathering Aly into her arms and glared at Belinda. "Yeah, sure, when they *consent* to see it. When they're ready to be confronted by that sort of stuff."

Huddling, Aly said, "You said photographs of people. Suspects. Is that… is that a person? You can't just shove that at me and not expect me to react."

"It's entirely possible you encountered this creature in the forest. It's of vital importance that I find it—"

"That?" Aly blurted and pointed her shaking finger at the picture. "I encountered a bear?"

Grace pressed, "A creature? And you want to find it? What is this, X-files? What kind of agent are you? Aly was kidnapped off the street by crazy men and you're showing her pictures of *dead bears*."

"What's going on?" Tamara asked, coming to lend support. "Aly, are you okay?"

Aly shook her head and whimpered.

"I'm calling my father," Grace snarled. Placing her hands on Aly's shoulders, she marched Aly toward the library. "That was so unprofessional."

"Ms. Gale, I can protect you!" Belinda called.

"From what?" Grace retorted. "Dead bears and creepy FBI agents? We can get rid of one of those threats right now!"

As they strode away, Kate wrapped an arm around

Aly's shoulders and Tamara wove her arm through Aly's so the three girls formed a shield around her. Grace snorted like a bull getting ready to charge. "What an absolute bitch. I'm sure there are laws against that sort of thing. Charges we can press."

"Aly, are you okay?" Tamara asked.

Pale and hands shaking, Aly nodded.

"You sure?" Grace asked as Tamara and Kate looked at each other in concern. "It's okay if you're not. We can study another day—"

Aly's smile seemed forced. "No, it's okay. She took me by surprise, but I'll be okay." Straightening, she squared her shoulders. "C'mon girls," she said with obviously feigned bravado. "Finals are next week. Let's put the sugar rush to good use."

Lips pressed into a line, Grace made a mental note to call her father as soon as she was able.

Sitting cross-legged in the middle of the bed, Belinda kept half her attention on her laptop as she spoke to her husband on speaker. "I'm in Bellhollow, California," she said and glanced around the room. "In the tackiest motel room you've ever seen."

Glenn laughed. "Really?"

"They have soap in the shape of ducks," Belinda told him in conspiring tones. "The walls are pastel pink. There was a ceramic greyhound in the reception area. And it's called 'Apex Inn' because it sits on a triangular piece of land. And I know that because they told me. They're proud of it. I feel like I've time traveled back to the eighties."

"So tacky."

"All the tackiness," she replied, carrying on the teasing. "It's *horrid*. At least the AC works."

"Oh, excellent. Better than traipsing around the wilderness and camping in a tent," Glenn joked before he became serious. "You'll be careful."

"It's not a dangerous one, but I'll be careful. I always am."

Glenn sighed and sounded regretful. "I'm in meetings all day tomorrow. The Henderson account is due."

Belinda cringed. She'd forgotten about that and part of her knew she should be home supporting Glenn. "Oh, that's tomorrow? Good luck! You've worked so hard, I'm sure it'll be a success."

"I'm just sad you're not going to be around for the celebrations should it all go well."

Smiling to herself, Belinda imagined the pouty look on his face. "I am sad too. I'm sure you'll be fantastic."

"Thanks. Love you."

"Love you too. I'll call tomorrow night."

Glenn's tone turned lofty. "Hurry back to me, my little chime, for the days apart will surely break me."

She played along, being sour and grumpy. "Ugh. Somehow you are tackier than this motel."

She could hear the pout in his voice. "I was going for cheese, not tack."

"You got tack," Belinda said, smiling. "But I gotta go. It's not a holiday and I have some work to do."

"Okay. Talk to you tomorrow. Enjoy the ducks."

Hanging up, Belinda shook her head at her cell and tossed it on the bed. She lifted the remote for the television, unmuting the news so she could listen while she was working on her research submission. She was halfway through when her cell rang.

Glancing at the number, she put it on speaker. "Hey, Tegan."

"What the hell are you doing in Bellhollow?" Tegan snapped.

Belinda raised her eyebrows at the ire in Tegan's voice. "Following a lead."

"I told you to stay away from Alyson Gale. Deputy Locklear lodged a complaint which you are *so* lucky I intercepted! The directors want answers."

"She knows about the—"

"I don't *care* what she knows. You disobeyed an order! We were all instructed to stay clear of—"

"She's *seen* one," Belinda insisted. "A *live* one. I could see it on her face. Do you know what a unique opportunity that is? Someone who saw a live one and *lived*."

A heavy pause, then Tegan blurted, "Jesus Christ, did you show her the picture?"

Belinda made a noise of confirmation. "I had to know."

"I'm going to say this once, Belinda. Get out of there. Alyson Gale is off limits."

"With all due respect—"

"The twins are on this."

"I am better suited to—"

"Regardless, the twins are on this. This is way over our heads, Belinda, but if you want to continue to do good works, I suggest you let this one go."

CHAPTER 8

Fleshy, gaping mouths and scaled faces. Guttural cries from beasts that chased her. Crashing through the foliage, relentless pursuers snapped at her heels and clawed at her back. She dashed through a tunnel of darkness which closed behind her. The light ahead, so far away, dimmed the closer she drew. A figure haloed against the black, holding the circle of light open.

Held it open? No. The figure drew it closed. She scrambled and ran, screaming for him, but he closed the light and left her in the dark.

Nightmares tore at her. Claws sunk into the tender flesh of her belly and pulled. Teeth tore at her neck. A face which only held a laughing mouth filled with sharpened teeth rose above her and grinned.

Aly fell out of bed, dragging half the bedding with her. She cowered in the corner while the shadows on the walls echoed the remnants of her dream. Certain the shadows were preparing to attack, Aly kept her eyes on them as she bolted for the light switch. Light flooded the room, chasing away the dark and Aly gulped in a sob.

These infrequent dreams had haunted her since the kidnapping, and robbed her of a full night sleep when they appeared. Although she remembered them as nothing more than a collection of jumbled up images tangled with fear, the sweat drenching her body indicated this one had been the worst yet.

It hadn't helped that Belinda had all but confirmed her worst fear. Aly had remembered the Faceless correctly.

Scrambling for her cell, she dialed Noah's number. While waiting for him to answer, she curled up at the head of her bed and wrapped herself in blankets.

Voice thick with sleep, he answered after the third ring. "Als?"

Aly whimpered and gulped in a breath. The panic wasn't ebbing. "Fl—I—" It was silly and stupid. She never used to call him when she had a nightmare, but he was the only one who could understand.

He woke up. "What's wrong?" he blurted, half-panicked. "What's happened?"

She shuddered so strong her shoulders shook. "Nightmare."

"Oh," he puffed a breath out. "Are you okay?"

She wanted to be. She really did. But Belinda's photograph was still so fresh in her mind. With a stifled sob, she mumbled, "Nope."

"Okay," he said. "I'll… give me ten minutes. Open the window. If the lights are on, dim them."

"Okay."

By the time Noah scaled the wall to appear at her window, Aly was in a strange, numb void. Calmer, but poised to return to the panic at any given moment. Nightmares still lurked and her mind churned. She knew she wasn't going to be going back to sleep tonight. Studying was out of the question, and drawing would only result in the Faceless making an appearance again.

Remaining hidden in the shadows, Noah gestured for her to come. She knew there were listening devices in her room. They'd made the decision together to leave them alone so they wouldn't appear suspicious, but it meant they couldn't talk candidly here.

Crawling through the window, Aly wrapped her arms around Noah's neck and her legs around his hips. Placing one hand under her thigh for support, he scurried upward toward the roof. This late at night, Aly doubted there would be anyone around to see them, and with several large trees around the Gale garden, they were hidden by foliage from casual gaze.

Once he put her on the tiles, she didn't hesitate in huddling into him for comfort. Holding onto her, he hunkered down so he was sitting on the roof and arranged her on his lap. "Do you want to talk?"

Sitting sideways on his lap, she rested her forehead against his neck and sighed. "It's just stupid dreams."

"Been getting them a lot?"

"On and off."

He stroked his fingers through her messy, bedraggled hair. "What about?"

"I'm sorry," she mumbled. "It's ridiculous and needy and I don't know why I reacted like this."

"Hey, *shh*," he crooned. "I don't care. Was it Belinda?"

"No... no..." she swallowed heavily. "I mean, yeah, sometimes it's her, and sometimes it's men in shadows coming out of the darkness for me but tonight... it was the Faceless from the forest. It... chases me sometimes." She swallowed. "And sometimes it catches me."

He tensed. "And tonight he caught you?"

"Yeah." She shuddered and Noah hugged her closer. "I know it's because of that image Belinda showed to me and I don't want to be afraid of it—him—but I can't—I don't know... I half expected him to have been a delusion. So many things from the forest are hazy, I was hoping he was too, but then Belinda... and the picture and..."

"I should've been there," he lamented, sounding guilty.

Aly felt pained. It wasn't his fault and she didn't want to imply that it was. "You were at work and—"

"Doesn't make it okay."

"I'm not helpless," Aly said. "You came back to be a part of my life, not to babysit. Stop being Atlas and taking the weight of my world along with yours."

With a forced laugh, he lifted an arm to flex. "Are you sure?"

Smiling, she shook her head at him. "Bumble-butt. Yeah, she took me by surprise, but I'm pleased with how I handled it."

With a less forced laugh, he dropped his hand to her knee, then sighed. "I have nightmares," he admitted. "Lots of them. Had them for years after we escaped from the Institute, and they came back after seeing that Faceless with Solomon's face. It… it wasn't easy seeing that and I don't expect you to be okay with this. I'd be more worried if you weren't showing signs it affected you."

Fingers slid along the small of her back, a gentle stroking designed to soothe. "How do you cope?"

"Time. Training." He sighed. "I dunno that I do, really." He shrugged. "Bottle approach. That's me, though. You don't bottle well, you never have."

"There wasn't anyone I could talk to."

"There is now, lovely. You've been so chill about everything."

Aly blinked at the endearment. He pronounced it differently than the word, including an 'a' sound in the middle of the word. 'Love-a-lee.' The emphasis of her name included in the word sounded pretty and did wonderful things to her.

"It's okay to be scared," Noah continued. "Or angry at me. Or furious. Or frustrated."

"Why would I be angry at you?"

"I left you," he said as though it was that simple.

"You didn't have a choice."

"I could've given you a way to contact me. I could've let you know I was watching." He lifted her hand to her neck, touching the bee pendant with the tips of his fingers. "I could've been back for your birthday."

"Things never work out the way we want them to," Aly said. "Do you want me to be angry with you?"

"I didn't come back expecting acceptance," Noah admitted.

"You're a dick," Aly responded. "Leaving me to fend for myself. How dare you." Smiling, she softened to a playful tone. "Is that better?"

He snorted. "Thanks."

"You did what you felt you had to do. You sent random bees to show you were thinking of me and... well, push comes to shove, I could've called you on one of those numbers." She sighed. "I didn't like being left. But I understand. It was necessary. We can't second-guess decisions made in the spur of the moment. We both did the best we could with what little information—and *time*—we had."

"Well... thank you."

"You came back and that's what matters."

He kissed the top of her head.

"I didn't expect Belinda to still be around," Aly muttered. "Is she FBI? She had ID, but I mean, I can't tell for sure."

Noah shrugged. "Maybe. If she's real, then shifters in general are in trouble. But it's also entirely possible she *thinks* she is, and isn't." He snorted. "Purists get us in trouble for impersonating, but they do it too, all in the name of humanity. She appears to be alone, though. I'll keep an eye on her."

"Should we worry?"

"No," Noah soothed. "Let's not overreact. There's no point jumping the gun and reacting if she's passing through or... I dunno, trying to catch you in a lie or something."

Aly sighed. "What if she's here to make another attempt?"

Noah breathed out slowly. "If we start running, then we'll never stop. I don't want you to give up the life you want to build, Als. It was an unfortunate coincidence last time, and it's sort of feeling the same this time. We're aware, we're both being vigilant. As long as we keep our heads down… I think we'll be fine."

She turned her face away and looked up at the moon. Shuffling sideways, she sat beside him on the tiled roof instead of in his lap. "Can you grab my laptop? I want to show you something."

"Yeah? Sure." He heaved up from the roof and disappeared over the edge, scurrying back a moment later with her laptop. Handing it to her, he plopped down beside her.

Balancing the laptop on her knees, she opened it. Typing in her password, she said, "You know how I said I was in therapy."

Noah nodded. "Roger being Roger."

"My therapist was excited when she found out I was an artist. The whole 'draw what you feel' concept."

Noah's shoulder brushed hers as he extended a hand out behind her to lean on. "Ahh."

"I couldn't show her a real one. I had to make up a few… like angsty-confused pictures to satisfy her. Swirling darkness and scribbles just out of reach."

"But you did a drawing of what you feel anyway, didn't you?"

She looked away. Shuddering from a sudden cool breeze, she hugged her arms to her chest. "The thing is… I don't…" She glanced at Noah's alarmed look. "No. Sorry, that was a chill."

He relaxed. "Okay. Do you want your blanket?"

She shook her head and continued, "A lot of what happened in the forest is… fuzzy. Some things feel clear, but others I'm not sure if I remember or my mind embellished."

"Like?"

"Like… I think I saw my mother among the people in the cars."

Noah drew back in surprise. "Really?"

Aly nodded, her eyes fixed on her screen. "But... I'm guessing it had to be a shifter. And then Belinda showed me that picture and... I hoped I'd remembered him wrong, I really did. But that picture..."

"Ahh."

Aly clicked on the file once and stopped. "Maybe... I mean... it might be hard for you to see this too—"

Lifting from his slouch, Noah pressed his chest to her shoulder as he leaned around to open the file. The low light from the screen flickered across his face as he blanched.

Staying silent, Aly waited and watched Noah rather than the screen.

So many expressions seemed to flit across his face. Pain and torment before he carefully schooled his expression and let out a long breath. "Well..."

Ash gray, reptilian-like skin, glassy gray eyes, a misshapen mouth and a flap for a nose, the leer chased Aly through shadows and into the light of the waking hour. All her nightmares and horrors in that one image which she'd never show anyone else. Despite what her therapist had said, drawing it hadn't helped.

Noah said these Faceless were corrupted. Elaine had said they were something like what Solomon, Noah's brother, had done. He'd shifted wrong or too fast and couldn't come back from that. It was hard to think that this Faceless could be the similar to Noah's true form.

Noah closed the laptop and rested a hand on the top as he stared out into the night. "Solomon."

Aly cringed and hunched her shoulders. "I'm sorry. I shouldn't have said anything."

"No." Bumping her shoulder with his chest, he tapped a finger on her laptop. "I said you should talk to me about this." Leaning back on his hands, he extended his legs out in front of him and crossed his ankles. "That was... an accurate rendition."

"I... don't... I mean, not much made sense. I don't really understand what... why he's like that."

Noah nodded. "That one had dysplasia."

"He shifted wrong."

"Elaine implied he was *made* shifted wrong, that Darcy somehow was able to...I don't know anymore. I've been away too long." He sighed, then scrunched up his nose. "How to explain this..."

"You don't—"

"I want you to understand," Noah said and squinted at the dark sky. "Just... okay... Solomon was never... he wasn't good at augmenting. Shifting he could do, like, as long as the image was close to his own, and he had time and peace to do it in, which was kind of difficult with Smith always breathing down our necks. Taking that step to augment—when I shift wrong, too fast or too much, I get headaches which sometimes knock me flat. For Solomon, building enough cartilage to create a proper nose was agony for him. It took him hours to slowly modify his muscles so he could run longer and faster, something that can take me a second. But he had all the same theory we did. He knew how, even if he couldn't do it himself."

Leaving the laptop balancing on the tiles beside her, Aly wrapped her arms around her legs and rested her cheek on her knee as she listened to Noah.

"When M—" He cleared his throat. "When Seth died, when we found out why... Solomon took all that theory and forced his body to become the strongest thing it possibly could to avenge her. I knew just by looking his heart couldn't take it but I also know..." He flinched and twitched and changed what he was going to say. "Rex helped us escape but he was there for another reason too, one I didn't find out until much later. Remember how I said after us, clones didn't live for long?"

Aly lifted her head. "He did that?"

Noah nodded. "Foxtrot was the last group which Darcy considered unflawed and useful but I don't know what happened to them. Golf… four of them made it out, including mine, but they… died *so* quick. Rex told us he changed something and after that I…well… Rex wouldn't let us tell them what was happening and I couldn't watch Hotel go the same, so I left."

"Oh."

"I don't know if Darcy found out about the augments, or about Solomon's shift, but I guess… she must've somehow gotten her hands on his DNA after his last shift."

She hugged her legs tighter. "Is that what you look like?"

Noah lifted his shoulders. Sitting forward, he draped his arms over his knees. "Yes and no. Take away all that bulk and… skin tears and… that was—the color's right— scales too, but I'm… refined, I guess. I don't know. Human shaped, with scales. Sort of."

"Can I see?"

He tensed and turned his face away from her. "You… don't really want to see that."

"It's you. Whatever you look like, it's still you and I love you, scales and all."

He breathed out through his nose and glanced at her. "It's… different, Als, and maybe off the back of a nightmare isn't a good idea."

She had to concede that. "Yeah, okay. Maybe."

"I figured you would want to, one day." He nudged her with his shoulder. "And I will show you, but not today, okay?"

Aly nodded. Cupping her face with her hands, she rested her elbows on her knee and stared out into the night. "How do you do it?"

"Do what?"

"Lie. All the time. To everyone."

Noah turned his head and stared at her. "I… is that what you think I do?"

"What happened… it's like… always on the tip of my

tongue. I feel like I'm always a breath away from telling Grace everything. Telling her what happened. Letting slip about you. I want to, so bad. They're hurting, Fletch, and they miss you so much"—Aly blinked back tears and tried to swallow the lump in her throat—"and I know if I just *told* them, all that pain they're feeling would go away, like it did for me."

He looked agonized. "You can't."

"I know. I… I just… I don't like lying. I never have and this… sometimes it's all too much."

"Would you prefer not to?" he asked, every word carefully spoken. "Do you want everything back the way it was before?"

She shook her head. "No. If this is what it takes for you to be able to stay here, I'll do it. I just… I want to know how it's all so simple to you."

He turned away. Reaching down, he dug a pebble out from between the roof tiles and held its weight in his hand. "You really think it's simple?"

She shrugged. "You make it seem like it is."

"Not even remotely." He tossed the pebble off the roof. "I don't like lying to Grace or Del any more than you do, Als."

"You lied to me for years," she said, keeping her tone mild and non-accusatory.

"Out of necessity," he said, turning his face away from her. "And… I never… I've never tried to come *back* to a life before… I never stayed in one place long enough to form attachments to anyone other than my siblings. This is… it's weird. And new to me too. I don't know what I'm doing…"

Aly didn't know what to say.

Noah sighed. "Okay. Fine. We tell them. Then what?"

Aly frowned. "I…"

"They can't tell a shifter. Even if I *show* them—and you know I'd have to before Del would believe me—I'm Faceless. I'm… Purists and shifters alike, none of them would really let me be. The first Purist I came in contact with in ten years tried to off me on contact. What's worse is that she *knew* about Faceless, which means… I don't know. But it can't be good. There might…" he ran a hand through his hair.

"But… we don't know," Aly said. "Not for sure. I mean, you lived here for ten years without incident."

"Ten years in secrecy, lying to you, thinking every day might be my last." He shrugged. "And maybe I shouldn't have. Maybe had I told you, you would've been able to react differently in that alleyway. I don't know. But you… you can sense them. You *know*. Grace and Del don't have anything like that. How… how would…" he sighed. "So we tell Del and Grace. They know. What next? Do we tell Penelope? Roger? *Tim*?" He gave a half-hearted laugh. "And have it blasted all over the schoolyard? The more people who know who don't have something to hide, the likelier it is that knowledge of shifters will get out."

"We don't know that," Aly said. "Shifters have been around forever and people still don't—"

Noah shook his head. "Most shifters can't shift like I can, it's hard to catch them in a shift. And we'd have to catch them or expose myself before the general population would believe it. Plus, with video editing and movies… it'll be explained away." He laughed, low and somewhat mocking. "I would *love* to blow their precious secret and tell everyone. But, with the state of the world right now, can you imagine if we added common knowledge of shapeshifters to the mix? Reptilian skinned ones at that? I'm persecuted enough." He sighed. "Where do we draw the line on who knows and who doesn't? Adding in that you're a very strong sensor… we'd be endangering them all. One wrong word… They have nothing to protect them. They couldn't even see a shifter coming. You can."

Aly said nothing. There wasn't anything else to say about that. He was right.

"I want to tell them," he assured her. "I wanted to tell

you. But I felt your safety was more important than my feelings."

"Mmmm..."

He regarded her. "What happened today? This... this seems to be more than just Belinda's scare. Or... this has been building for a while?"

"Both." Aly sighed. "Girl talk. Grace... well... she was trying to tease me about Noah-you and how Fletcher-you would've liked Noah-you and..." she paused, then giggled. "That's a lot of yous."

"Yup." He chuckled and teased, "Cause of the hearts on stream, right?"

Aly cringed. "Oh... You saw that?"

He bumped his shoulder into hers. "May-*bee*."

Her face felt so hot. Not ready to talk about this at all, she tried to hide by covering her head with her arms and buried her face in her knees.

Arm roping across her back to her opposite hip, Noah pressed his side to her shoulder. "What else did Love Doctor Locklear say?"

"Nope. Uh-ah. Not telling." Aly raised her head and turned it to scowl at Noah.

His face was closer than she thought and she froze.

Startled by the sudden swell of butterflies in her stomach, Aly said the first thing on her mind. "She suggested that Fletcher-you might've been competition."

He chuckled and his breath tickled her face. "Well. I don't think that would've been a problem."

He didn't seem to realize how he was affecting her, he was being his normal, playful self. Sitting close, teasing her and being affectionate. If they became a couple, that wouldn't even have to change, they were already there.

All they really had to do was start kissing and...

Aly's belly cartwheeled. Desperate to stop thinking about his lips and how much she wanted to taste them, she bit her lip, hard.

"Your expression is weird," he said, frowning. Aly

caught the quick dart of his eyes as he registered the position they were in. "I'm making you uncomfortable?" He rocked away to give her space. "I didn't mean to but I don't understand why this is making you uncomfortable—"

"No," she assured him quickly and grabbed his shirt to keep him close. "I just…"

"I thought you wanted best friends," he said, baffled. "This is what we always did."

"I know and I don't want you to stop."

His eyes narrowed. "You don't?"

"It… feels different. That's all." She flushed again, releasing his shirt and smoothing the fabric back against his chest. "Now that I'm aware it's possible for us to… um… be a couple… it feels strange."

"Oh," he said, subdued.

She tilted her head at him. "Things don't feel different to you?"

He shook his head.

She echoed his '*oh*' with a faint one of her own.

He studied her for a moment, then turned away. Downtrodden, he bent his knees, draped his arms over them and clasped his wrist with his opposite hand. "I wish I could be normal for you."

"I don't," she said, looping her arm through his. "What's normal anyway? Everyone is different. I like who you are." She squeezed his arm. "This one's on me, Fletch. I keep… I'm overthinking things and my emotions are a mess right now and—don't you see? It's a good thing."

"How?" he asked. "How is me making you uncomfortable a good thing?"

"You're not making me uncomfortable. You're making me nervous and excited."

His eyes widened. "Oh!"

She flushed. "Yeah."

He seemed confused as he sought clarification. "And that's a good thing?"

"Yes."

He considered that. "What happens when it goes away?" he asked. "What happens if *this*"—he gestured the two of them—"is all there ever is between us? I'm not ever going to be that raging fire of passion you see in movies, Aly." He sounded sullen, like he was warning her away. It felt like an odd thing for him to say, considering they hadn't really been talking about that aspect of things.

"Fletch—"

"I'm not blind," he said in a resigned sort of way. "I saw the way you were looking at me at Lloyd's."

She felt obliged to defend herself and that made her tone tart. "Oh, and you're taking that to mean, what exactly? One, I've *always* been attracted to you, so this isn't a new thing. Visually, you're appealing and I'm allowed to appreciate it. Two, I spent years dealing with that and was still capable of being your best friend. Don't you dare think I can't do that again." She made herself lose the standoffish tone. "Are you having second thoughts?"

Noah swallowed. "I... I'm afraid of what will happen if it doesn't work."

She rubbed his arm. "That's the risk, Fletch. That's why I want us both to be sure. To talk and take our time. You're my best friend. I'm not going to give that up." She laughed, soft and gentle. "Grace said I should just keep flirting with you and see how that goes."

"Keep?" Noah asked, surprised at that and turned his head to focus on her again. "Have you already been flirting with me?"

She poked him on the nose. "I promise, when I start flirting with you, you'll know."

He twitched his nose beneath her finger. Dropping her hand, her fingertips brushed against his lips. He caught it before she could move too far away, lifting it back up so he could kiss her palm. Stifling a gasp, she murmured, "What did I say about doe eyes?"

"To not to," he said, using Tim, her six-year-old half-brother's, favorite phrase.

She giggled and dragged her gaze away. "Bumble-butt." Leaning into him, she lifted her gaze to the stars.

After a while of companionable silence and stargazing, he plucked at the shirt at the small of her back. "I know you're having a real hard time with all this, but…"

"But what?"

He shrugged, jostling her head against his shoulder. "It's nice to have someone to talk to about it all."

Aly's jaw dropped. "Fletch," she breathed. "I… I didn't—I'm so sorr—"

Disregarding her stammering, he interrupted with, "Are you going to be able to get back to sleep?"

Taken aback, Aly stared at him.

He tapped her back and rose, extending a hand to help her up. "C'mon. Let's go for a ride. We haven't done that in ages."

Rousing enough to smile at him, Aly said, "Yeah. That sounds like fun."

CHAPTER 9

The air filled with graduation caps and Aly found herself wrapped up in an unexpected hug from Casey Giles. Turning in a haze of excitement, she ducked falling hats to give Sevasti Fotopoulos a hug. A sea of black robes rolled around her as Grace forced her way through the rows of seats and celebrating seniors. "We did it!" she yelled and threw herself at Aly.

Aly laughed and hugged Grace. "We did!"

Arms still around Aly, Grace blew black bangs from her face. "God, that ceremony took forever. I mean, Laura's speech was banging, but the rest of it was *boring*."

"I know, right? Get to the good bits already!"

Grace bounced up and down with her hands gripping Aly's upper arms. "No more speeches!"

"No more homework!" Del announced, lurching out of the black robes to sweep them both into a hug. Squashed up against Grace, Aly struggled to get in a position she could return his hug. "Literally!"

"For you, maybe," Grace said, laughing. "Some of us want to further our education!"

Grinning, Del scooped Grace up and spun her around, an action which was promptly returned with a battery of playful smacks around his shoulders and a demand of, "Put me down!"

He did, right on top of a chair instead of on the ground. Twisting, and with his arms still around Grace, Del waggled his eyebrows at Aly.

She stepped backward, bumping into a celebrating senior. "Don't you dare." She brandished her diploma like it was a sword.

"Aly-no-fun," Del complained, releasing Grace to yell: "Lloyd! Get off her face, bro, and give me a hug."

Aly stretched out her hand to Grace to give her some extra balance as she hopped off the chair. "He's an idiot."

"Yeah, but he's our idiot," she said and sighed. "Gonna miss him."

Aly laughed. "You know he's gonna be calling us every night. We'll have to set up a computer just for permanent video chat."

"Not the same as having him there."

"Lijuan!"

Grace turned at the sound of her name and grinned. Standing on tiptoe to wave, she said, "Gotta go, family duties. See you at the Dragon."

Aly waved as Grace hurried off to her family. Lan, Grace's mother, had decided to host a banquet for their group of friends and their families at her Chinese restaurant, the Happy Dragon, and Aly looked forward to the meal. Lan was an incredible chef, as were the people who worked with her, and tonight was bound to be a delight.

Weaving her way through the crowd of slowly dispersing seniors, taking group selfies and receiving hugs along the way from friends, Aly made it to her family.

"Oh honey, we're so proud of you," Penelope gushed, wrapping her arms around Aly.

"Thanks, Mom," Aly replied, extracting herself to turn toward Roger.

"Congratulations, Aly," Roger said, sweeping her up

for a hug. "You've earned this."

A bright smile burst across her face. "It's a high school diploma," she said into his shoulder. "No big."

"Aly, Aly, did you see me?" Tim said, bouncing around her feet. "I waved when you were on stage, did you see me?"

"The first of many qualifications," Roger said as he released her. "Still important in the grand scheme."

"Aly! Aly!"

"Yes, I saw you," Aly said, bending over to hug her little brother. "You were hard to miss."

"It was so *boring*," Tim told Aly. "But Mom said I had to sit still then I could have fried ice-cream for dessert."

"Aren't you lucky?!" Aly exclaimed with a smile for him.

Tim twisted to Penelope to grab her skirt. "Mom, Mom, can I have dessert first?"

Roger laughed. "And if you promise to eat *all* your dessert you can have the main course."

Tim looked delighted. "Yeah!"

Roger leaned down and scooped up Tim, arranging him on his hip. "We'll see."

"Oh, I need photos," Penelope blustered and reached into her purse for her cell. "Let's go by the stage."

"Poppy, didn't you take enough when she walked up?" Roger asked.

"Yes, but now I can get one with family. And I want to get some of her teachers too!"

Seniors slowly spilled from the gym as they met up with family and friends to celebrate their success. With fewer people packed in, it was easier to walk to the stage. Tamara pounced on Aly before she reached the stage, hugging her long enough to spin Aly around before she sailed away. "Have you seen Kate?"

"Yup. Up the end," Aly said, walking backward away from Tamara.

"Awesome. Thanks!" Tamara called over her shoulder.

"See ya at the Dragon!"

"Can't wait!"

A hand touched her shoulder. "Hey, Als."

Ecstatic, Aly swung around and jumped on Noah before he could protest. "You came!" Arms around his neck, she squeezed him tightly.

He picked her up so her toes dangled above the ground as he hugged her close. "Of course I did." Remembering himself, Noah cleared his throat and placed her back on the ground. She gripped the fabric of his long-sleeved shirt to make sure he didn't go too far. "It's your big day," he said with an easy smile. "Congratulations."

She bounced on the spot. "Thank you!" She puffed out a breath. "So much hard work, but good too."

He grinned at her, his brown hair flopping on his forehead. "You earned it, lovely."

"Noah!" Del exclaimed, wriggling by Ethan and Carter to stride up to them. "Dude! What are you doing here?"

"Wanted to say congratulations," Noah said and held out his hand for Del to shake. "I wasn't doing anything else and you guys are really the only friends I have in town, so I came."

Del's eyes dropped to Aly's hand on Noah's arm and he arched an eyebrow as he looked between them. Blush blooming on her cheeks, Aly removed her hand and stepped back.

Ignoring Noah's offered hand, Del embraced him. "Dude, you should totally come to the Happy Dragon with us. Grace's mom owns the place and we're having a celebratory banquet tonight. There's more than enough food," Del said, stepping back. "Good company. It's open invitation, plus, I need a favor."

Exchanging a glance with Noah, Aly shrugged.

"What sort of favor?" Noah asked.

"Aly!" Penelope called, standing on her tiptoes to see over the crowd of people.

Aly twisted her head to peer at her mother, then back

at Noah and Del. Pulling a regretful face, Aly said, "I gotta go—"

"Yeah, okay," Del said and gripped Noah's arm. "See you at Grace's." To Noah, Del said, "I have a problem that you might be able to help me with—"

Aly twisted away, pushing herself through the crowd of families and their newly graduated children, and managed to slam straight into someone. "Oh!" She tilted, off-balance, and dropped her diploma.

"Careful," the man she'd bumped into said, backing away from her.

"I'm so sorry," Aly blurted, flustered, and bent down to retrieve her diploma. "I wasn't looking where I was going."

"No harm," he said and shoved his hands into the pockets of his jacket. "Congratulations on your graduation."

Aly beamed. "Thank you." The smile faded as she looked at the man. Although he didn't produce prickles, his presence made her uneasy. Nervous. Like she was juggling mismatched déjà vu. Blue eyes etched with worry lines, he sported a light brown beard with wisps of white, set on an oval face. She tilted her head at him, trying to determine why he felt familiar. Perhaps he was the parent of one of the seniors or maybe he was an old substitute teacher. There were so many semi-familiar faces drifting around as families of graduating seniors attended.

But there was something there. Like he was waiting for some sort of reaction from her and was confused when he didn't get it.

Aly frowned. "Do I—"

"Aly, c'mon!" Roger called across the room. "Your mother's getting anxious."

Aly turned and the smile returned. "Coming!"

Walking away, Aly lifted up the sleeve of her robe to check that she wasn't subjected to goose bumps. Her arm was free of blemishes and she didn't know what to make of the encounter or whether she should mention it to

Noah. Then Tim grabbed her hand, dragging her over to her family and she pushed the man from her mind.

Penelope delved deep into a hidden passion for photography. By the time she was satisfied, Aly's face hurt from smiling and there were several blind spots in her eyes when she blinked. All of Aly's teachers had been accosted for a photograph by Penelope and they were well on their way to being late to Lan's celebration dinner.

On their way to the car, Aly spotted Del leaning on his mother's car looking disgruntled while he waited for Cassidy to finish on her cell. As a single mother, Cassidy worked hard as a lawyer to support her boys, but often found it difficult to juggle work and home life. Del spent all his time on the computer at home so it didn't trouble him, but school events were often interrupted by calls from clients. While he graciously accepted that, Aly could tell this particular instance hurt.

"Be right there," she told her parents and bounced away before they could say anything.

Del glanced up as she skipped up to him, then grinned, relaxing out of his gloomy stance. "Hey, you're still here."

"Mom wanted so many photos I'm blind in one eye," she said and flopped against the car beside him.

"I hear you. Mom did the same."

Aly nudged Del with her shoulder to tease him. "You're the baby. Last one to leave the nest."

The smiled died. "Yeah."

Tilting her head, Aly regarded the sudden sullenness in him and tried to piece together why he was sad. It felt more substantial than his mother being on the phone. "What's wrong?"

Del heaved in a breath and let it out slowly. "She found out about the YouTube stuff."

Aly winced, knowing Del had been waiting for the right time to tell Cassidy. "Ahh, frick. Who blabbed?"

"Oh, I did," Del told her in a bland tone. "She started talking about taking leave so she could 'escort' me to school in August, and wanted to know when you two were going and whether or not I'd given any thought to moving in with you guys, rather than staying in a dorm. So, I told her about my plans for a gap year."

"She didn't take it well?"

Del glanced over his shoulder at his mother. "She's on the phone to Dax right now planning an intervention."

Aly nodded. "Dax knew, though, right?"

"Yeah." Dejected, Del's head went down. "He'll defuse as much as he can but you know how Mom loves her compelling arguments. She's convinced I'll flop. She can't even give me gap year to try."

Aly nudged into Del's side to comfort him. "What do you need?"

"Nothing. Nah, it's literally why I asked Noah to join us." With a small smile, he jostled her with his elbow. "I'm hoping if she sees the fact *he's* still going to college even after a gap year, she'll give me a chance."

"Ahh. Very sly. I did wonder." Fiddling with her sleeve, she tried to be nonchalant as she asked, "Is he coming?"

Del snickered and returned to her happy-go-lucky friend so he could tease. "Yup. That way you can keep flirting."

She blushed and tried to hide it behind a scowl. "I was not flirting."

Del laughed. "Uh-huh."

"I wasn't!" she huffed.

Losing his smile, Del asked, "You like him, don't you?"

Aly narrowed her eyes at him. "Yeah. So do you. So what?"

Scuffing the toe of his shoe on the ground, Del said, "Can I be cliché friend for a sec and say I don't wanna see you get hurt?"

Aly tilted her head until it rested on Del's shoulder. "I know."

"Fletcher... he's—"

Aly knew what Del was thinking. It was the same thing

Grace had been worried about. "Always going to be a part of me, Del. Forever and always. I'm *never* going to forget him. Noah's... not replacing that. But, I also know that Fletch wouldn't want me to throw my life away. He'd want me to be happy."

"And you think Noah can make you happy?"

"I have no idea," Aly said with a smile. "That's half the fun, isn't it?"

Del snorted.

"I'll be careful. I promise."

Del nudged her again. "Fine. Talk over. Go on, shoo, Aly-cat. Grace'll be wearing out the floor waiting for us. Mom 'n I will be along soon. Just be prepared for her to be all pouty and making snide comments."

Aly lifted away from the car with a laugh. "Okay. See you soon."

Clambering into the back seat of Roger's car, Aly reached across the gap between her and Tim to tickle his belly. "Sorry," she told her parents.

"It's fine," Roger said, sliding the car into gear. "It's your day. We can wait on you."

Reaching for her cell, she flicked it off silent to check her messages. Nan and Pa, Roger's parents in England, had sent her messages of congratulations. Her adopted cousins from Roger's brother had bombarded her with messages as well. She smiled as she read through them. "Did you send out a general announcement?" she asked Roger.

"Gale family tradition," Roger told her, and exaggerated his clipped English accent. "When I graduated, we didn't have these fan-dangled cell phones."

Penelope laughed. "Good, old-fashioned snail mail."

Roger laughed with her. "My grandfather sent me a telegram with Morse code that I had to decipher. That's how ancient I am."

Aly giggled and continued to check her messages. "Good thing I had this on silent," she muttered.

"Would've been embarrassing."

"Especially since I changed your ringtone to 'We are the champions'," Roger said.

Aly laughed at his joke, knowing that he couldn't get through her password. "Sure you did."

The Happy Dragon was decorated in the traditional sense; Chinese paper screens, paper lanterns covered in gold and green dragons, tables laid with chopsticks and fine china, and incense burning in the corner. As Aly had expected, Lan, and the mouthwatering smell of her banquet, greeted them at the door, sweeping Aly into a bear hug. "Oh, we're so proud of you!"

Aly returned the hug, grinning madly. "Thank you, Lan!"

Lan peppered her face with kisses, then bopped her on the head with her knuckle. "Go, Lijuan is waiting for you to start the celebrations. Oh, Poppy," Lan gushed, making overly dramatic come-here gestures to Penelope. "Our girls are growing up so fast!"

Penelope leaned down to embrace Lan. "I know! I wish they'd just slow down for a moment!"

"So where's the party tonight?" Jonathan asked as he stood beside Lan. "Grace won't tell me."

Innocent, Aly gave him a wide-eyed stare. "What party?" She raised her voice. "Grace, is there a party tonight?"

"This here's the only party we're having," Grace yelled from across the room.

Being as charming as she could, Aly smiled at Jonathan. "See? No party."

"Uh-huh. Sure."

Rolling her eyes playfully, Aly swished regally away and went to pounce on Grace.

Lloyd, Ezekiel and Ezekiel's younger brother, Tobias, chatted together, Ezekiel waving his arms around animatedly as he described in detail the incredible kill he got in the game he'd been playing. Aly congratulated them both on graduating as she walked by. Still in their graduation robes, Grace, Tamara and Kate took selfies and posed for group shots. Extracting herself, Grace swept Aly up in a hug. "You're late!"

Aly laughed. "Nuh-ah!"

Stretching her arm straight out, Grace lifted her cell then pressed her cheek to Aly's. Smiling, Aly flashed a peace sign while Grace pursed her lips.

"I'm right on time to make a grand entrance."

"And you're earlier than Del," Grace said, looking toward the door. "Did you see him on the way in?"

Aly's smile drooped. "Cassidy found out. He's being lectured."

Eyes wide, Grace's head swung back to Aly. "Oh shit. Battle stations then."

"Absolutely. Del invited Noah tonight. I think he plans to use Noah as an example for Cassidy."

Grace nodded. "Good plan. There's more than enough. In the meantime, fun, food and friends!"

Tamara, overhearing that last part, raised her hands above her head and trilled, "*¡Fiesta!*"

True to their words, it was an awesome night; food and friends especially. While Lan's staff rolled out the banquet, Aly sat beside Grace and the pair tried hard to look like they weren't were eavesdropping on the conversation occurring at the next table as Noah and Del talked to Cassidy about college. They could only hear snatches of conversation, especially with other people talking around them, but both Aly and Grace were optimistic it helped. Cassidy looked like she was listening and Aly knew that would be half the battle.

Toward the end of the night, with graduation robes discarded and people beginning to filter away to other events, Kate dragged Grace over to the makeshift dance floor in the corner. Cranking up the music, they giggle-waltzed around Tamara and Lloyd's slow dance.

With Del and Noah deep in conversation, Aly headed

for where Tim played on his PSP in the corner. Scooping him up so she could dance with him while she still had the chance, Aly passed by the parent's table.

"We're going to take him home soon," Penelope called, taking a sip of her wine. "Don't rile him up."

Lifting Tim onto her hip, Aly called, "Just one dance!" as she joined Kate and Grace's playful waltz, laughing and spinning her brother around.

One of the things she loved the best about her brother, beyond his silly sense of humor and cuddles, was his laugh. A high pitched, chortling belly-laugh which shuddered through him every time he found something hilarious. Tim found many things hilarious, especially being waltzed around by Aly, with Grace making faces at him over Kate's shoulder.

It didn't take Aly long to tire from carrying Tim and move from waltzing to an exuberant bounce-dance and twirl Tim beneath her arm. Laughing as she tried to keep Tim from getting dizzy with his spins, Aly backed into Noah's chest. "Oh!" she blurted, whirling. "Hi."

He graced her with his lopsided smile. "Hey. May I have this dance?"

"Nope," Aly said, grinning. "Taken."

"Who're you?" Tim asked, glaring as he clutched Aly's hands tighter.

"This is Noah," Aly said, aware that Tim hadn't met this persona. "I told you about him."

Tim's expression cleared. "Oh yeah! He's teaching you to kick butt! Can you teach me?"

Noah laughed and got down on one knee so he could look Tim in the eye. "Absolutely. But you know, your mom's looking lonely over there. Why don't you ask her to dance and allow me to dance with your sister?"

Tim released Aly's hand to rush toward his mother. "Okay! Hey Mom!"

"That's cheating," Aly accused.

Clasping one of her hands, Noah put his other one on

her hip and tugged her in closer. Heat swelled in the small gap between them. "I'm apparently good at that. You look gorgeous tonight."

Pleased, she rested her hand on his shoulder. "Thank you." As he spun them, she caught a glimpse of Roger watching. "Uh-oh. Parental alert. Please stand the regulated distance apart or we'll have questions."

He chuckled. "I've already been warned."

Aly tilted her head up at him. "Huh? By who?"

"Roger *and* Del. They're conspiring."

That surprised her. "Really?"

Noah laughed. "Yup." With a wink, he teased, "Roger caught you looking."

"Me looking?" she scoffed. "Was not. What'd they say?"

He released her hip and raised his arm to spin her underneath, making the skirt of her blue sundress flare. Settling back into a sway, he curled the hand they clasped to his chest and splayed the other one on the small of her back. "You'll be pleased to know Roger's 'talks' have evolved since we were fifteen."

Aly giggled. "That's such a relief."

Tucking her against him, he said, "In addition to the 'I'm watching you, don't hurt my baby', I was also given a crash course on Fletcher and not once was it mentioned he was gay."

Heat rose to her cheeks from how intimate the dance was. "Oh."

"Del didn't mention it either. I'm not sure if I should be offended or not. Being gay was an integral part of that persona and I don't like that—"

Squeezing his shoulder, she said, "Hey, Noah?"

"Yeah?"

"Fletcher was gay."

He stared at her, then chortled. "Thanks for that. Good to know."

She caught her bottom lip between her teeth and tried

to ignore the delicious tickle in her belly. "Is this why you're being so coy?"

"Well, I figure we're busted, why not roll with it?" He lifted the shoulder her hand was on to shrug as he smiled at her. "No use hiding how I feel about you. I know where we stand."

The butterflies in her stomach took flight. "Better not be on my toes."

He ducked his head down closer. "Me? Never."

His expression set her aflame. Aware that eyes were on her, she wanted to bury her face in his chest to hide but she couldn't take her eyes from his. "You're doing the doe eyes again."

His smirk said he knew. "I think I finally got this flirting thing figured out."

"No kidding. How many movies did you have to watch to nail it?" she teased.

"Are you picking on my smolder?"

"Is that what you're calling that look?" she replied, being mischievous so she could ignore the steady increase of her heartbeat. "I thought maybe it was a stomach ache."

His laugh was light and free and she felt herself tumbling harder. "Should I stop?"

"No."

Noah flicked his gaze away from hers moments before Grace's announcement of, "Smile!" and Aly was blinded by a flash.

"Grace!" Aly scolded, blinking rapidly to clear her sight.

"Not sorry!" Grace chirped as she twirled away with Kate. "That was too cute not to record. You can get a copy off Instagram later!"

A woman sat in her car opposite the Happy Dragon, giving off the appearance of reading her cell, when in reality she was carefully noting details. A notepad filled with garbled letters and nonsensical sentences rested on her knee.

A man opened the passenger door and slid in. "What do you think?"

Carefully, the woman placed her pen on the paper, then lifted her hands to reply. She signed, "She is a nothing. A no one. I do not understand why everyone is so interested."

He rubbed his chin, then removed his hand to speak. "We have our orders."

Bonnie glanced at her notepad, then at the restaurant. "We should not linger much longer, Ross," she replied and then grunted, scratching at the scar on her forehead before she continued to sign, "We have already been here long enough and no sign of who we are supposed to be watching for."

"And someone who no one thought to look for."

"Yes. It troubles me. Whoever this girl is, she knows."

Together they watched the girl in question walk out of the Happy Dragon with a young boy sleeping on her shoulder. "We can use that."

CHAPTER 10

During winter and fall, there was a shady spot in the garden where Aly liked to sit during the day. She rarely used it during the summer months but as her room was bugged and she didn't want to spend more time there than she had to, she decided to use her spot to draw.

With school over, Aly had lots of free time and she didn't need to start packing until mid-August. While she and Grace needed to make a trip to Los Angeles soon to look at the shortlisted apartments, she didn't have any other solid plans for a few days. It was nice to have nothing pressing to do, and Aly was contemplating opening up her commissions to get a bit of extra money for the trip.

Her chat pinged at her, interrupting her drawing, so she rearranged the windows on her laptop so she could see the chat and her picture, allowing her to multitask.

I-Noah-guy: [So what are your plans for this afternoon, Ms. No-more-school lay about]

Smiling at his silly username, she replied,

Bee-casso: [I have the arduous chore of doing absolutely nothing.]

I-Noah-guy: [Wow. So lucky. You and Del seem to

be doing the exact same thing. So jealous.]

Bee-casso: [IKR? You poor people who have to work.]

I-Noah-guy: [Rub it in more. I think you missed a spot.]

Bee-casso: [I have salt to help with that burn.]

I-Noah-guy: [Since you're gonna be bored, would you take a look at something for me?]

Bee-casso: [Sure.]

I-Noah-guy: [I'll email. It's some of what was on the drive Elaine left me. It's not everything (because reasons), but these are the pictures confusing me the most.]

Bee-casso: [What do you want me to do?]

I-Noah-guy: [That's the thing. I don't know. I don't know why she gave them to me. They're selfies. Lots of them, but I can't see a reason for them.]

Bee-casso: [K. I'll look.]

I-Noah-guy: [Most of the other images were like pictures of street signs, or landscapes, things like that, which have been from all over. It's like a map of where she's been and I've plotted it out. But if there's a hidden message in these selfies, I'm not seeing it.]

Bee-casso: [Couple of ways to hide hidden messages in photos. Do any of them have layers?]

I-Noah-guy: [How would I tell?]

Bee-casso: [File extensions. Any PSD files? Anything other than jpeg?]

I-Noah-guy: [They're all jpeg.]

Aly sighed.

Bee-casso: [k I'll work mah magic.]

Bee-casso has sent sparkles.

I-Noah-guy: [Haha. I appreciate it.]

When Noah had to leave for work, Aly stayed in the shade looking through the photos he'd sent. The zip file had about twenty of them and he'd been right about the fact they were selfies. The woman was different in each shot, and although Aly had thought that maybe knowing it was Elaine in different forms would help her identify shifters, it seemed the sense didn't transpose to images. Other than the fact these had come from Elaine's drive, there was no proof the pictures *were* Elaine.

Opening a document, Aly jotted down notes, the first one being '*how do we know this is Elaine?*' Maybe he could tell from pictures, but she couldn't.

The first photo was a woman at a beach, her arm extended to take the photo. Behind her, the ocean crashed onto white sand. The next was a different woman in a vibrant rainforest, a straw hat perched on her head as she grinned. By her clothes, she appeared to be hiking through leafy green ferns, Aly could see a rocky path behind her. The pose wasn't the same as the one on the beach, but it was similar.

Another touristy type photo was next; a woman on wooden decking, the sky darkening to twilight. Instead of looking at the camera, she looked into the distance and behind her was a myriad of market stalls on either side of a pier.

They were the kind of photos Aly and Grace took of themselves when they went away on holidays. Or in the schoolyard when they were being silly. Selfies and memories. Reminders of good times. Aly filled an entire hard drive with pictures from her life without even thinking about it. Grace's Instagram was full of candid shots like this. At first glance, it appeared Elaine documented her life in the same way.

Aly hit the next image button. More images. The analytical side of Aly's brain switched on as she regarded the image with a more of a creative view. "Hmm."

A smudge. Evidence of background cloning. A blur where there shouldn't have been. Disguised editing. Something removed or something added, Aly couldn't be sure. It wasn't in every image she flicked through but there was evidence on enough for it to be a clue.

She made notes of which images had the smudges as well as the vague shapes the smudges appeared to be. Most of the smudges seemed pretty close to the woman, and none of them were in the images with a lot of people in the background. It seemed only scenic pictures were affected.

On a whim, she checked the metadata of the images. As an artist, she often put her signatures in metadata, as well as signing and watermarking, if she put her pictures online. It didn't prevent art theft, but it did make proving she was the original artist easier. Nothing much of anything in the metadata, but she did find one which confused her.

"Isidora?"

A google search brought up the fact it was a name of Greek origin as well as a brand of clothing. Enlarging the picture she found the metadata in, she traced around the smudge.

Conceivably, the smudge could've been a person removed from the picture but Aly didn't know what to make of it. The remaining shadows weren't enough to rebuild the image but she made a note to tell Noah. She pulled up several of the images with many people in them to see if she could see a common person in the background.

As the sunshine started to shift from pleasant to biting and her shady spot was close to vanishing, Roger brought her a drink. "Hey Aly," he called as he ambled down the grass toward her.

She looked up from the screen and blinked at him. "Hey!"

"Getting some sun?" he asked, holding out the glass.

"Getting some shade," she replied with a smile. "Nice day for it. Thanks."

"Not really a nice day," Roger replied, grimacing. "I'm sweltering already."

"I'm not the one wearing a doctor's coat." After taking

a sip, she placed the glass on the grass beside her. "Are you going on or coming off?"

Pulling a disgruntled face, Roger tugged on his cuff. "Saturday night at the ER. Not my ideal way to spend it."

"I hope you won't be needed," she said.

"Me too."

Tim bounded out of the house, full of energy. "Dad! I'm ready!"

Roger turned. "Yeah, yeah, off we go."

Aly raised an eyebrow. "Where's he going?"

"Sleepover at Ryan's," Roger explained and started to walk toward the house. "It's just you and Mom tonight. Can you do me a favor? There's a shopping list on the kitchen bench that I didn't have a chance to pick it up. Just sundries. I left you some cash; grab them before Mom gets home?"

Since she didn't have any other plans, Aly nodded. "Sure."

"Thanks, hon," Roger called.

Tim poked his head out the door. "Bye Aly!"

She straightened enough so she could wave. "Bye! Bye Tim! Have fun!"

With a soft sigh, she made several notes regarding the file she'd been working on, then closed the laptop. Wandering inside, she left her laptop on the kitchen table and fetched an apple to chew while she checked the list Roger wanted.

Bread, milk and a few other items. Easy enough to pick up at their local corner store. Taking another bite of her apple, she went upstairs to fetch her shoes and purse before she headed out.

While small, the corner store had basic necessities. There were several of them scattered around Bellhollow and a larger grocery store in the center of town. The store itself had several other stores attached to it; a florist, an electronics store, and a hairdresser.

Collecting a carry basket, she wandered through the

store grabbing the items on the list. Bread and milk. Some batteries. Ketchup. Stopping at the candy section, she picked up a couple of Snickers.

Maybe she'd invite Noah over for a movie after he'd finished work. They hadn't had a movie night in such a long time and she missed it. It'd be a good way of getting her parents used to him again and—

Shivers slid down her spine and goosebumps covered her skin. She froze in the middle of the aisle, clutching her carry basket. Her eyes flashed around as she tried to determine which direction the shivers came from. She was alone in the aisle, but she could see people at both ends. A tall woman and a short man spoke in sign language over by the milk, and an old man by the cashier waited behind a mother and child.

Slipping her hand into her pocket, she pulled out her cell. The shivers dispersed as fast as they appeared, leaving Aly panicked. Was someone stepping in and out of her range? Noah said about two hundred feet and that was a big circle around her. The shifter could be anywhere and they weren't necessarily close. Still, she lifted her cell and left a brief voice mail for Noah.

Breathing out, she hurried through the shop to pick up the remaining items on the list. Standing in line at the cashier, she pondered her options. What should she do? People and population. They couldn't take her if she was around others. If they were after her. What if they weren't here for her? What if—

The pinpricks returned, edging to a constant prickle along her skin. Cemented to the spot, Aly considered. Seconds ticked by and the sensation remained constant. She concentrated, trying to get a location, but could only tell it was somewhere ahead of her. The parking lot, perhaps. Maybe beyond in the street, but she wasn't sure.

Nothing happened and she breathed out a trembling sigh and glanced around again as some of the panic ebbed. The woman by the milk used a flurry of sign language as she spoke to the crooked-nosed man beside her. The old man in the line ahead of Aly paid for his shopping and the cashier prompted Aly to pass up her basket.

As the last item was scanned and bagged, a man passed by the front window and, as Aly focused on him, the pinpricks intensified.

Clipped beard with wispy white strands among the brown, he seemed in his mid-fifties. Casually dressed, he had an unremarkable appearance but Aly was certain of one thing. He was the same man she'd seen at graduation last night. Only now he was out of his natural form.

She needed to leave without drawing attention to herself. Picking up her shopping, Aly headed for the door and kept her face turned away from the man. He didn't appear to see her as he opened the door to the florist and she hastened to her car.

Aly arrived home a bundle of nerves. She'd been constantly on edge in the car, watching her rear-view mirror more than she should have. Her mind played tricks on her, leaving her holding her breath until the car which seemed to be following her for the last few streets turned away.

Shutting the front door behind her, she peered through the peephole to see if she could see anyone following her. Nothing. No slowing cars. No parked ones with people in it. No pedestrians.

Heaving out a sigh of relief, she hurried to the kitchen to put away the groceries. She needed to call Noah again and let him know what was going on.

"Aly," Penelope called from upstairs. "Is that you?"

"Yeah!" Shoving the last of the groceries into the fridge, she grabbed her laptop from the kitchen table and hurried up the stairs. She couldn't hide in her room because of the bugs, but she could sit in Tim's room to call Noah.

Pausing at the top of the stairs, Aly was surprised to find Penelope standing at Aly's bedroom door, staring into the room. "Mom? What are you doing?"

Without turning, Penelope said, "The first time I ever held you in my arms, I thought you were the most perfect being ever created."

Aly shuffled and hunched her shoulders. She didn't have time for this. Not now. "I'm not leaving until August," she mumbled, staring at a small smudge on the carpet by her door. "You really don't need to—"

"Ten fingers, ten toes, beautiful blue eyes, your birthmark. All the best parts. Everything about you was wonderful. I got to watch you grow, take your first steps, hear you call me Mom, meet Fletcher, fall in love, have your heart broken. All the best things in life. I wouldn't give up the last eighteen years for anything."

Aly, not knowing what to say or do to get out of an awkward situation, let her mother talk. She rested her shoulder against the door frame and peered into her room.

"And your father…"

"Yeah, I know," Aly mumbled, trying to avoid a tearful conversation. "He missed it all. Look, Mom, I need to—"

Penelope sighed. "No, honey, you really don't. Things are about to change for you and not in the way we expected."

With a frown, Aly looked at her mother. "Mom?"

"I can't stop it anymore. I'd hoped—I wanted you to have a normal life. Go to college. Get married. Make animations or games; whatever made you happy. I never thought…" She sighed again and rubbed her face. "Things haven't been the same since those… people took you."

Aly pressed her lips together. "I know."

"You don't sleep, you don't eat right. The other night you weren't even in your room at four in the morning. I feel like we don't even talk like we used to."

Shrugging, Aly said, "I'm trying, Mom. I am. I just… it's hard."

Penelope sighed. "Honey, I need you to pack a bag."

Aly fought against herself to step away. Warning flared

down her spine as paranoia woke. "Why?"

"We're going on a road trip," Penelope announced with false cheer.

Aly studied her mother. Twins, Noah had said. Her brain could be tricked if the images were close enough. Everything about Penelope felt real. No shivers so she wasn't a normal shifter, but she could still be Jonah or Elaine. Penelope had made a point of detailing things only someone who knew Aly well would know about, but Aly was still skeptical. "A road trip."

"Yes."

"That doesn't sound like you," Aly noted, gripping her laptop while her mind whirled. She should run. Her keys were on the counter by the front door. She could make it to her car and go hide at Grace's place. What would she tell Grace if Penelope showed up and Aly wouldn't go with her?

The house was empty. There was no one close who could help. They weren't going to get to Noah through her.

Penelope said, "We should do something impulsive before you go to college, just us girls."

Her purse. Beside her keys on the downstairs vanity by the front door. She'd need money. "That really doesn't sound like you."

"It's been years since we did something spontaneous," Penelope continued. "A road trip. We can head up to Seattle, see the sights along the way. Chat and have some fun. Oh! Manicures and pedicures! There's a great little place up in—"

"Sounds like you have a place in mind already."

"Could you be a little excited about it?" Penelope asked, the false cheer over-the-top.

"You gave yourself away," Aly said, turning her attention to her room. If she could manipulate Penelope, confirm her as either her mother or a Faceless. Risky with the bugs in her room, but... maybe they wouldn't be able to pick up much *outside* her room. Struck with sudden inspiration, she faced away from her door to muffle her voice and said, "Considering you didn't tell Rex about the trip, he doesn't expect us to pack up and leave. So, what's really going on?"

Her bluff and wrong name drop didn't have the intended effect. Penelope paled and took a step away. "What did you say?"

Aly tensed.

An ugly look filled Penelope's face. Her hand dove into the pocket of her skirt and withdrew a small gun. "Who are you?"

Aly leaped backward. "Whoa! What are you doing?"

"Don't move!" Penelope snapped and clicked off the safety. "Who are you and where is my daughter?"

Aly cowered and shielded her head with her laptop. Trying to keep from panicking, her eyes darted for an escape route. Down the stairs, through the door, she could be out of here.

"I *knew* something was off."

Heartbeat increasing in fear, she inched backward. "Mom—"

"Don't call me that!" Penelope snapped.

"Why do you even have a gun?" Aly blurted as her back hit the cupboard at the top of the stairs. "Roger hates guns!"

"Don't you dare," Penelope snarled. "You're not getting to Rex through us. I won't let you use her! She has nothing to do with any of this. She's an innocent!"

Strength drained from Aly as the horrible reality crashed over her and her worst fear confirmed. Penelope knew about shifters. Penelope knew about Rex. Penelope *knew* and she'd kept it secret.

Penelope yelled and shook her gun at Aly. "You *replaced* her! I was warned you would try again! Where is she?"

Everything Aly had learned came surging back. Rex and Madeline. The forest where she'd thought she'd seen

Penelope. The certainty Belinda had that Aly was the right one. Noah's evasiveness when discussing Rex. Something pinched in his face when he'd thought about her being Rex's daughter. Betrayed, her head shook of its own accord, her feet moving her away. "You *were* there. In the forest. You knew, all this time and you never told me."

Confusion from Penelope and the gun quivered in her hand. "What?"

"Who's Madeline?" Aly asked, her voice rising.

Penelope stared at her. "*What?*"

"Rex Braddock and Madeline Spenser," Aly wailed. "That's *why* they took me. Is she my real mom?"

Penelope's expression melted from ferocious into horror. "Oh God, Aly—" The gun wavered and dropped. Appalled, she covered her mouth with her free hand and shook her head. The pain on Penelope's face was all Aly needed to know the truth.

Panic doubled as pinpricks spread across her skin and Aly flipped into flight mode. They were not going to get her again. She bolted, racing down the stairs to snatch her keys and purse and made for the door.

"Wait!"

Aly didn't. Out the door. Glass rattled as the door slammed against the wall. She'd barely made it down the stairs of the front porch when her gaze fell on the man getting out of a parked car a few doors down.

The same one who'd been going to the florist.

Rex. It had to be.

Her car. She had to get to her car. After that, she didn't care.

Penelope cried, "Aly! Please!"

Upon hearing her name the man's expression went confused and he hurried in her direction.

Aly dashed for her car and yanked the door open, then locked herself in. Throwing her laptop and purse on the passenger seat, she jabbed her key into the ignition.

Penelope ran down the path toward the car and Aly

knew if she got behind the car, Aly would have to face what truths Penelope had to offer. Who the man was. What relationship she had to him. To Penelope. Why they'd lied.

She didn't want to. Not right now.

The man ran onto the lawn, heading for Aly's car and Penelope almost collided with him. "Rex! What are you doing here?"

Caught in indecision, Aly stared at the man. Her father. If she were to believe that truth, then everything, including the woman who said she was her mother, had been a lie. This was the man who'd vanished from her life. Who'd crashed Elaine's car. Who was the leader of the renegade shifters. Who, by the flowers and the fact he was at her graduation, might want back *in* her life.

Nope. No. She wanted none of this. Not a single bit.

Aly jammed the car in reverse and floored it.

She shouldn't be driving. It was stupid and reckless. Brushing away the tears on her face, she sped down her street. Not thinking about where she was going, she checked behind her.

In the distance, Penelope and that man got into a car the man had arrived in.

What should she do? Grace's place? No. Grace would think she was crazy. Noah? No, he was at work and she *couldn't* lead Rex to Noah. Go hide at the lake? No. Too close and Penelope would find her. She didn't want to face this right now. Or ever. Her whole world was upside down and she couldn't find the way out.

Fumbling for her cell, she called Noah. Putting it on speaker, she left the cell on her thigh while she drove. With every ring, her heart sank more, until message bank answered. "Call me. Right now."

She hung up and dialed it back in case he hadn't been able to get to his cell in time. Message bank again. "It's all true," she blurted, unable to contain the information. "Madeline. Rex. All of it. My mother just pulled a gun on me. My mother. Had a gun. A gun! She could've shot me! Only she's not actually my mother, is she? Not if Madeline and Rex and—she was there in the forest and... there was a shifter *at* my house. At my house! I sensed him before at the store and then—Fletcher, I don't know what I'm doing. What do I do?" She glanced behind her and swore again. "They're coming after—"

The message bank pinged and hung up on her.

Frustrated, Aly hit the steering wheel with the palm of her hand then redialed. When the message bank came through, she blurted, "Did you know? Did you know she wasn't my mom? Tell me you didn't know. Tell me you weren't in on this too. I asked you and you said I looked like my mom! I *asked* and—you lied to me, didn't you? I thought we were done with lies, Noah!" Her heart sunk and she felt sick. "Were you *assigned* to me? If Rex is my dad and you worked for him and—and... and I can't do this," she blurted and hung up.

Switching her cell onto silent, Aly tossed it onto the passenger seat. "I don't know how much more I can take."

CHAPTER 11

Hands delved into the pockets of her shorts, Aly hunched her shoulders as she walked. She'd found one of Fletcher's old flannel shirts tucked away in her trunk and wore that over her top to help hide. Her hands ached from clenching the steering wheel and her back felt stiff from sitting rigidly. Her mind whirled with so many thoughts and theories and depressive resolutions. Questions churned and spawned more questions. Aly knew she'd get no answers until she found courage.

Penelope hadn't caught up with her. She hadn't found Aly at the gas station or followed her along the freeway. While she'd thought she'd lost her mother and that man in Redding, she'd *never* expected to make it to Sacramento. Doubling back with as much unpredictable driving as she could, she'd still been sure Penelope would have caught up with her by now.

She'd hidden her car on one of the suburban streets not far. A distance from the freeway, she'd driven around for a while to make sure she wasn't being followed before she parked.

Aly's cell buzzed again. She checked it before setting Do Not Disturb mode, then slipped it into the breast pocket of Fletcher's shirt. Penelope had left a stream of messages and texts which Aly hadn't listened to or read. Grace had left a message inviting her over. Del had sent her a text asking about a senior's party and wanting to know if he could score a ride, so it seemed both her best friends didn't know. Roger had called and since Aly couldn't be sure it wasn't Penelope on the other end, she'd ignored it. Noah's number hadn't appeared yet and she knew he had to be close to finishing his shift and would probably be incredibly angry that she'd run to Sacramento.

Turning the corner, she paused to scope her surroundings.

Sprawling grass, manicured flower beds and tall trees for shade, Aly had come to this cemetery for one reason only. Leon Braddock was here, the man cited on her birth certificate as her father. Aly visited his mausoleum annually in December to mark the day he passed. The visits were purely for her mother's sake to honor a man Aly didn't remember but she was never allowed to miss the date. With everything that happened, Aly questioned why those visits were so important. If Leon wasn't her father then whose grave did she visit? Or was it an empty one? Or someone else's grave who matched?

Or, perhaps, was there someone who watched her change from year to year, never coming close?

The outdoor mausoleum had several parallel corridors. Leon's was furthest away from the road, around the middle but as Aly reached the place where the slot was, she couldn't find his plaque. Frowning, Aly ran her hand over the surface, looking for screw holes. Perhaps it had fallen off and was being replaced. As she checked the names beside it, she discovered none of the others had screws.

She had to face it. Leon Braddock's memorial didn't exist.

Stunned, Aly sat in the grass and stared at the spot the plaque was supposed to be. Dragging her legs toward her chest, she hugged them tight as her world tumbled around her. With tears threatening, Aly turned her concentration to her breathing, determined not to cry.

She failed.

Large tears rolled down her cheeks and dripped onto Fletcher's shirt. A sob ripped through her chest, causing pain as she tried to stifle it. Not really knowing why she tried to stop it, she buried her face in her knees and let go.

Crying only ever left her feeling drained, but it did relieve her of some of the pent-up tension she'd stored. Left exhausted, all she wanted to do was curl up in her bed and sleep. An impossibility at the present moment.

Her cell shrilled at her and there was only one person she'd allowed through the Do Not Disturb function. Sniffling and trying to control herself, she answered. "Hey."

"Aly!" Noah blurted, sounding panicked. "Where are you? Are you okay? What happened?"

She hiccupped and looked at the mausoleum. "I'm in Sac."

A sharp intake of breath and the expected anger came tumbling out. "What, the absolute fuck, are you doing in Sac?"

Aly snorted. "Funny story," she said, her tone as sarcastic as she could make it. "Turns out the man I thought was my father doesn't have a grave here at all. It's gone."

She could hear him breathing noisily as he either tried to control himself or walked quickly somewhere. "What happened?"

"He was *at* my house," Aly rushed. "At my house and the store *and* my graduation yesterday."

"Who was?"

"Rex!"

Noah sucked in a breath. "Aly—"

"Don't tell me I don't know for sure. I know! I know it's him and I know yesterday at graduation he was in his natural form and I know today, when he came to my house, he *wasn't*. Mom *called* him Rex. She thought I was a shifter and pulled a gun on me and said she wasn't going to let anyone use me to get at him!"

"I—"

The words steamrolled out of her, her voice rising pitch with panic. "And she *was* in the forest and, Fletch, I saw her and I saw him and she was there. She let them shoot at me. I thought I was imagining it! Fletch, what do I do? I was really stupid and I ran and I should've come to you, but I didn't want to lead Rex to you and by the time I shook him, I was in Redding so I just kept going and now I feel so exposed but I had to know! I had to know if Leon's grave was here or if—"

"Lovely, calm down. Breathe. It's okay."

"It's not okay!" she scolded. "It's definitely *not okay*!"

"Shh, shh," he soothed, being as patient as he could. "I'm coming. I just need you to breathe before you pass out."

Realizing he was right, she gulped in a shaky breath. Following his reassuring instructions, she took another, and another to relax as much as she could. "Okay."

Seeking clarification, Noah said, "You're in Sac. At the cemetery you visit in December."

"Yeah. Only his grave's not *here*. It's always here and it's not and what does that mean and—" she could feel herself panicking again and couldn't stop it.

"Let's not worry about that right now," Noah soothed. "Where's your car?"

It was a struggle to calm herself enough to answer. "In a side street not far. It stands out, so I hid it as best I could."

"Yeah. Yellow. Ick. Okay. Do you have money? Credit cards?"

She concentrated on her breathing and his voice. "Yes."

"Walk to the closest safe motel and get a room. Cash over card, it's harder to track. If you don't have enough, look for an ATM not close to the hotel and get some. Don't use your name, use 'Rose Ward'."

Aly raised her eyebrows at the name. Rose was her middle name, and 'Ward' was the surname Noah had used when he was in his 'Will' persona. "Really? You're serious."

He sounded slightly amused at her disbelief. "I have a credit card for Will and ID for both of us under those names."

She was astounded at how prepared he was. "You... you..."

"If you can't get cash, call me and I'll pay over the phone. Don't attempt to on your own, it can be tracked."

She swallowed. "Okay."

"Lock yourself in and *don't* open the door for anyone. I'll... I'll be there as fast as I can, okay? I'm picking up my stuff and then I'm coming. We'll figure this out."

She swallowed. "Okay."

"Don't go back to the car, Als."

"My laptop's there."

"It's encrypted, remember? We did all that work securing it and backing up your images. There's nothing there that we can't afford to lose."

"Those files you sent me."

She could practically hear him cringe. "Ahh. Shit." He made a noise and she didn't know what that meant. "Okay. Okay. Go get it, and anything else you want in the car, then leave. Consider it abandoned until further notice. It's dangerous to go back. If you see anything out of place, or feel a hint of a shifter, you gotta consider whatever's in that car lost. Promise me."

"I promise."

"Walk with purpose. Don't run. Keep an eye on your surroundings and trust your gut."

"Okay."

He made a frustrated grunt. "God, I wish you hadn't run that far."

She sniffled. "I'm sorry. I didn't mean to—"

"No, don't," he soothed quickly.

"We're gonna have to run, aren't we? I made a mistake and now we have to—"

"Don't. Don't second guess; we don't know anything yet. Maybe you overreacted, but maybe you didn't. We can't make any decisions until we're together. Get somewhere safe. I'm coming."

She didn't feel any better. "Thank you."

"I love you."

"Love you, too. Please hurry."

Hanging up, she shoved her cell into her pocket and began the brisk walk to her car. She passed a few people walking dogs or running on her way back and listened to the ever-changing noises occurring in the suburban houses. People listening to music or chatting with a neighbor over the fence. Children playing in their gardens. Normal, everyday occurrences that she was now hyper-aware of.

As she approached a t-intersection, she saw a gap in the hedges with a clear view of a white sedan parked directly behind her yellow car. Aly froze, peering through the gap. A man looked into her car. Someone who didn't seem to be setting off her shifter sense, but… someone she also felt deep in her gut she'd seen before.

A woman sat on the brick wall of the house on the corner and looked the opposite direction of Aly. A white cat rubbed along her arm and the woman stroked it with her free hand.

Aly's breath lodged in her throat. She *had* seen them before. Platinum blonde pixie cut. Man with a crooked nose. The couple from the grocery store who had been using sign language to communicate with each other. They weren't shifters… were they like Belinda then? Purists?

She crossed the road and headed down a side street, hurrying away as fast as she could. Her laptop sat hidden under the driver's seat and she knew she couldn't retrieve it. All her drawings, all her photos of friends, her whole life was in that car. While it was a heavily secured laptop and all her animations and illustrations were backed up on the internet, she still mourned its physical loss.

Knowing she was going to jump at shadows until she was safely inside somewhere, Aly kept walking. Hands clenched into fists so tight her nails dug into her palms and she had to hide them in her pockets, Aly waited for the inevitable call of 'stop'.

She didn't dare look behind her.

Belinda idly scratched a mosquito bite as she listened to Tegan. "I see. So. Is this the part where I dance and say 'I told you so'?"

Tegan's sigh echoed through the phone. "Yes. You earned it."

"But the twins are there," Belinda said, keeping her tone mild. "And I thought I was supposed to stay away."

Tegan sighed again. "Every tagged mimic along the North Coast who has known ties to Rex Braddock are showing signs of erratic behavior. It's troubling."

"Six low-level mimics doesn't warrant attention."

Sounding irritated, Tegan said, "Look, I'm passing along information, that's all. We know there was an altercation outside Alyson Gale's bedroom. We know the name Rex was used. We know she ran and her car's been seen in Sacramento. And we know CCTV cameras in Bellhollow logged a man who matches the description we have on file for Rex."

"An old, unconfirmed file."

"Which is why the directors want you."

Belinda pressed her lips into a thin line. "They're doubting the loyalty of the twins?"

"No. It's because you're the *best*, Belinda, and you saw this coming and they didn't believe you. Now you have to see this through. Make them remember why they enlisted you in the first place."

She'd already made the decision to go, but she wanted to milk this as much as she could. "I want a mimic detection device."

Tegan hesitated. "I am unable to authorize that. However, Gomez is in the area. I'll arrange for him to meet you with his."

With a sigh and a roll of her eyes, Belinda said, "Fine. I'm on my way."

"You're angry."

"Very astute of you."

A soft sigh. "Poppy—"

Penelope ground her teeth. "I had to lie to my husband. I've had to lie to my family for years. I had to lie to *Aly*. Then you turn up and want back in her life. So yes. I'm angry. Did you really think I wouldn't be?"

"I didn't ask you to lie."

Stiff back and arms crossed, Penelope stared straight out the car window and watched as a motorbike zoomed by them fast enough that the highway police would take notice. For one brief and painful moment, Fletcher popped into Penelope's head, but that might have been because of the blue flannel shirt the cyclist was wearing. Scowling, she said, "The minute you came to my door, you've asked me to lie. That's what you do."

Anger filled the car. "I gave you everything I could. I purchased a house to help you provide for her, I secured Alyson's trust fund, I—"

"A trust fund that won't do anything for her if she's got to go into hiding! It's not about the money, Rex," Penelope snapped. "It's *never* been about the money. She doesn't belong in your world. She's not like you."

"You made sure of that."

Penelope scowled. "Damn right I did. She has plans. A future. You have no right to take that away from her."

"Things are in motion I can't stop. I can't protect her from the shadows anymore. And maybe I shouldn't have waited until after she graduated—"

Penelope grabbed the seat belt and yanked it down so she could twist in her chair to face him. "She doesn't know anything about your war. She thinks you're dead!"

Blue eyes met blue. "Two months ago you *begged* me to find her. You were prepared to let me back in then, what would running now have achieved?"

Penelope glared. "It would've given me a chance to explain things."

"Except you botched it. She ran. On her own. Into danger."

Her face twisted into a scowl. "It's your fault. Calling me like that and giving me so little notice, I thought something had happened! Then Aly referenced you. What was I supposed to think? I can't tell who is and who isn't! I have done everything you asked. I kept her safe. I gave her a normal childhood. I loved her to pieces, I *raised* my daughter. I sent you photos and videos and made sure she visited that fake grave once a year so you could see her. What more do you want?"

Rex thumped the steering wheel hard enough to make Penelope jump. "Do you think I *wanted* this for Alyson? She's allergic to shifters. She's allergic to me! Don't you think I *regretted* leaving her with you? Every time I touched her I risked killing her and with Maddie gone… how was I supposed to care for her? The longer she's exposed to shifters, the more detrimental it will be for her!"

Penelope wasn't going to allow him make her feel guilty. "Then *stay* away."

"This is bigger than me. The wrong people have taken notice. If she hadn't run, then I could have quietly secreted her away. But the twins were in Bellhollow and now they're following her, and that means the Welchers know, and they're very dangerous people. *We* have to get to her first."

The names didn't mean anything to Penelope. Only Aly mattered. "She ran because she remembered."

"And we need to know how much."

Lips pressed together, she returned to her stare out the window. "She knew Maddie's name. How did she know Maddie's name?"

Rex didn't have anything to say about that.

CHAPTER 12

Curled up in the corner of the room, Aly stared at the furniture she'd dragged in front of the door to use as a barrier. She'd made sure to get a second-floor room so that the window wasn't easily accessible. While that wouldn't be an issue for Noah, she hoped no one else could scale a wall like he could.

Redding was over two hours away from Sacramento and she had no idea how long it would be before Noah could get to her. It had taken a while for her to find a motel she felt comfortable enough using. Somewhere out of the way and not even close to the cemetery. Somewhere her mother wouldn't think she'd go. Somewhere away from those people by her car. She'd jumped on the first bus she'd seen and gotten off at a large shopping district and searched for motels around that.

She thought, if needed, she could flee where there'd be people and make a scene and hope someone would be willing to help her. And she hoped it was far enough from her car to confuse people who might be looking for her.

Tapping her foot on the floor, Aly gnawed at her thumbnail. Sitting alone, in the dim light and silence, only served to make her more paranoid. Jumping at every noise and clutching her cell tight, waiting with bated breath every time someone walked by her door. Though time felt like it was racing away, whenever she glanced at the clock, only scant minutes had passed.

She didn't know what this all meant. Was she going to have to leave her life? Or was there still a chance to salvage everything? She had to hope this was just a setback and it would all be over soon. Noah would know.

To distract herself, she began sketching the people she'd seen following her. The room had complimentary pen and paper and, while she hated sketching with pen, sketching on her the small screen of her cell was an even worse prospect.

As she watched the clock on her cell, she knew it would be soon. She sank her hand into her hair and clutched at her skull, trying to alleviate some of the tension. She chewed the end of her pen to pieces but the sketches took shape.

A spiky pixie cut for the woman, a shock of almost white-blonde hair that she couldn't duplicate because she only had a blue pen, so she made it as light as she could and she drew an arrow to indicate it was blonde. Blue eyes. She wrote sign language in the corner.

The man had close-cropped brown hair and a strange bumpy nose, as though it had been broken several times and never healed correctly. She'd only caught him in profile and the nose had been the one thing that stuck with her.

Rex, in both his forms, was harder to draw. She couldn't detach herself like she normally did when she drew. This man… the probability he was her father was astronomical now and a part of her wanted to know everything. To find herself in his features. Another part of her screamed at her and called her names. If he was her father, he'd allowed her to believe a lie her entire life. Penelope had allowed her to believe a lie.

Wiping a tear away from her face, she tried to

concentrate. Noah would need to see this. He'd need to know. Tears stained the paper, making splotches of her pain visible and she tried not to let it smudge the ink. If she had her laptop she could've done this properly, with full color and shading, but the pen would have to do.

She scrambled between the four images, refining features as she remembered them. A jagged scar on the woman's forehead. Attached earlobes on Rex's natural form and unattached on his shifted one… or was it the other way around? What else? Wrinkles lining blue eyes. A mark on the man's neck.

Taking a picture of all of her sketches with her cell, she backed them up online to her secure account which housed all her pictures, then emailed them to herself as well.

Having set her cell on Do Not Disturb for everyone other than Noah, her ringtone startled her so much she let out a shriek and dropped the cell, then had to scramble for it. Breathless, she answered, "Hey."

"Hey. I'm here."

"Here *here*?" she rushed. "Or in Sac here?"

"I'm downstairs." Noah's tingles shivered down her spine and Aly let out a puff of relief. "I'm coming up."

She sagged, then surged up so she could dismantle the barricade she'd secured against the door. When Noah's knock came, she hadn't freed the door up enough for it to open. "One sec!"

A sudden sharper tingle told Aly Noah had augmented, before she heard a chuckle. Cheeks flaming, she unlocked the door and twisted the handle. Noah was through the door, scooping her up before she could even open the door completely. One arm around her, he lifted her off the ground to hug her. Aly squeezed her eyes shut as she wrapped her arms around his neck and let her body dangle.

Noah re-secured the door and replaced most of Aly's barricade one-handed. She could feel him moving around, thumps and bumps and jostles as he did so, before he bent and scooped up Aly's legs behind the knees. A couple of steps and he sat on the bed, pulling her into his lap.

Burying her face in his neck, she lost the battle against tears.

"Shh, it's okay. We're okay," he murmured and stroked her hair. "Talk to me."

She leaned into his touch and couldn't find her voice.

He didn't press. Instead, he held onto her, crooning comfort while her tears dried on his shirt. As time passed, she felt her heartbeat settle and the fear she'd held seep away. A minor tingle told her Noah changed something, especially since he rubbed her back as the tingle appeared.

Cradled in the strength and security of his arms, she asked, "Are we safe?"

He sighed. "Safe is relative."

Aly tensed.

"No," he hastened with a tight hug. "I didn't mean… We're safe. I searched around the motel, I did several passes around before I even came close and I didn't see anyone at all. I just don't know how safe or for how long. We're safe and I'll work to keep us that way." He raised his hand until it cupped her neck and pulled her up so he could see her face. Pressing his forehead against hers, he murmured, "I need you to tell me what happened."

She wriggled free of his grip and dashed for her sketches, grabbing the two she'd made of Rex. "This is him," she said, handing one to Noah. "This one was him at graduation, and I bumped into him and somehow I knew him—I *knew* him—but he didn't—he wasn't shifted then. There were no prickles."

Noah frowned at the first image.

Aly handed over the next one. "And then today, I was at the corner store and they flared up and this guy walks by and I knew, I *knew* it was the same guy from graduation but I don't know how I knew. But all the prickles came from him, so I got out of there. And when I got home,

144

Mom's lamenting over my life and wanting to make a trip and… you said twins, right? Sometimes a shifter gets things wrong, a tiny detail and… it was out of character for her, so I wanted to test her, to make sure she wasn't Elaine or Jonah, because I still don't know if I could tell and so I said Rex instead of Roger and she pulled a gun on me. I ran, and that guy"—she tapped the paper—"is out the front of my house and Mom called him Rex."

Noah swallowed. "And that's the one you felt was out of form."

Aly nodded furiously, her hair bouncing up and down from the force.

"Because this one," Noah said, indicating the shifted Rex. "This is the one I thought *was* his natural form. This is how I know him, and I never got *any* sense he was shifted."

That riled her. "You don't believe me?" she shrilled.

"Of course I do," he said and cringed. "My ears are augmented, lovely. Try not to yell."

She shrunk. "Oh. Sorry."

"I'll probably be shifting periodically," he warned. "So that I can check—"

"You don't need permission. Do what you need to do. I'll deal."

"Thanks. I believe you about Rex. Your ability to sense is extraordinary. I'm… I've never had a shifter that could hide a shift from me, that's all."

She bent down to scoop the other two pictures up. "These two were in the grocery store near home. And then they were at my car here. They don't feel shifted, but… I mean… they feel different, though, but not like 'shifted' different. I can't explain it."

Noah frowned as he studied the images. "They're not anyone I recognize," he said. "But… if one was Jonah, I couldn't tell from a picture. That being said, the fact that they didn't change forms from Bellhollow to here, tells me they're probably not Faceless."

Aly puffed out a breath. "Okay. So maybe they're like Belinda?"

"Maybe," Noah said and picked up Rex's sketch again.

Aly swallowed. "Did you know?"

He eyed her. "About?"

"About *any* of it?" she asked, suspicious. "Rex being my father. Or Mom not being my mom. Because I asked you and you evaded and—"

Noah scrunched up his face.

"You did know!" she accused.

He held up his hands. "Not... not for sure. This is not an exact science. And to be fair, you asked me about Rex, not your Mom."

Aly balled her hands into fists. "Noah!"

He exhaled. "She *is* family."

"Noah, tell—"

Noah's voice was gentle as he said, "She's your aunt."

Aly wobbled. "My aunt."

He steadied her with a hand on the shoulder. "Aly—"

"And you never told me! Why wouldn't you tell me that?!" She didn't mean to get angry at him, but her jumble of emotions was hard to navigate.

"Your anger is misplaced," he pointed out.

She knew and being told only served to make her more upset. "You should have told me!"

He kept his tone infuriatingly even. "Families have secrets. Families *need* secrets and I am not delving into that. I thought there could be a perfectly innocent reason why she never told you and I wasn't going to betray her like that."

"But you're perfectly willing to betray *me*!"

Hurt splashed across his face. "That's not fair!"

She retorted, "My *aunt* has been lying to me for years and you knew and—"

"So have I," he said simply.

She faltered. "That's different."

"It really isn't."

His pity only made her angrier. "You never pulled a gun on me."

"She was scared. She probably thought—"

"So am I!" She ground her teeth together, then snarled. "You lied about your past. She lied about *mine*. That's the difference."

Noah was silent as he considered her. Then he pulled a face and tingles ran down Aly's spine.

She cocked her head at him.

"The… erm… revelry occurring three doors down is"—he cringed—"getting to the point it's uncomfortable to listen to."

Aly stared at him, then burst into nervous laughter. She flopped down on the bed and shook her head. "Wow. Poor you."

"Yeah," he drawled, elongating the word. "You wouldn't believe the shit people say when they think no one's listening. There's only so much I can take. To be fair, they're in their own room. They're not expecting to be overheard." Shuffling, he thrust his hands into his pockets and refocused the conversation. "It's not easy being able to look at a person and tell stuff like that, Aly. Yes, I knew Penelope wasn't your birth mother. It wasn't my secret to blab. I mean… take Carter for example. The man he thinks is his father is really his uncle and I think his mother is still playing both of them."

That surprised her. "Really?"

With an exaggerated shrug, he continued, "Maybe they all know about it and are fine. Maybe so many things. Do you really think I should break up a family like that? Do you really think I like knowing that Tim…" He broke off.

Knowing what he had been going to say, Aly put her head in her hands. Her precious baby brother was actually her cousin. It hurt even to think that. "No."

"Me either. What do you want to do?"

She wiped away a traitorous tear. "I dunno, Fletch," she mumbled. "I didn't expect this."

147

"If you're Rex's daughter, there's not going to be many places you'll be safe," he pointed out.

"I'm probably safer if he doesn't know where I am," she muttered. "From what you've told me, I don't know that I want to meet him."

"Rex… always was very secretive," Noah said, and ran his hand through his hair at the back of his head and down until he could clasp his neck. "The idea of him having a daughter is jarring. And the fact he's come out of hiding for you… something's happening and I don't know what it is. Maybe we should talk to him."

"I don't want to. The man has been absent my entire life, I don't—"

"I don't think you understand how serious this is."

"He *caused* Elaine to crash!" she spat, infuriated by his calm tone. "I *saw* him and Mom in the forest. I was *in* that car and he *let* his men crash it and—"

"I'm sure there's an explanation."

"I don't owe him anything. Not even a conversation."

"We need information and—"

Her head snapped up. "Do you work for him?"

Noah closed his eyes and braced. "I understand why you'd ask that—"

"It's all very convenient, isn't it?" she ranted. "You happened to decide to stay in the same town his daughter lives. Do you even hear yourself defending him?"

"I swear by the Snickers, I didn't know."

Aly snorted a laugh at that.

Noah rushed, "I did work for him. I don't deny that, but I haven't seen him in years. I haven't seen anyone in years."

Even though she believed him, she muttered, "So you say."

"Look,"—he swallowed heavily—"when my siblings and I escaped, Rex helped us. We were somewhere in the desert in Utah. He took us across Nevada and into California. When Solomon… when he…" he shook his

148

head and shrugged.

Feeling guilty, she said, "Fletch, I believe you, you don't have to—"

Not looking at her, Noah continued, "Rex took us to San Francisco and south along the coastline… The ocean scared the shit out of me." He spread his arms wide and turned in a circle. "It's so big, Aly, all that space!" He shook his head again. "Suffice it to say, I'm not comfortable with it. But the rest… California is gorgeous. Almost all of Rex's bases have been here. I grew to like the place. But… we were green. We didn't know how the world worked. We had no experience, so we didn't know any better. Friendships and free will and all that… When I broke from Rex, I left. I wandered through all the States, trying to find something. And I couldn't, cause I didn't know what that something was. I missed my family. I missed being part of something. So… I came home. I went aimlessly up and down looking for them but I couldn't… I thought maybe if I stayed in the State, I could…" He shrugged. "I don't know."

Aly had relaxed as she listened to Noah talk, now she smiled. "Then you met a girl reading a book up a tree."

"Yeah. I gave up looking for an old life and started looking for a new one."

"I thought you had ways of contacting them?"

Noah swallowed. "I… well… Adam… he found me after about two years in Bellhollow. I decided to stay hidden. He accepted that and gave me a way to keep in contact if I chose, which, I assume, all of us had access to. All that he found anyway. I didn't use it other than to let him know periodically that I was okay. I figured… he knew where I was if he ever needed me."

She looked at her shoes. "So, this is another massive coincidence?"

Noah glanced toward the door. "I've always felt drawn to you," he admitted. "From the first moment I saw you, I was drawn. You were… interesting and different and vibrant. I don't know if the reason I was drawn was because of your shifter sense responding to my abilities, or if I subconsciously knew you were connected with Rex. So I can't answer that." He shuffled and shoved his hands into the pockets of his jeans. "I can say that I never knew he had a daughter."

She pulled a sour face. "Guess we know what caused Rex's infatuation with the State."

"Guess so." He looked back at her. "But Aly? Even if I was drawn to you, that's not the reason I stayed. Not the only reason. Penelope—she was so accepting. Here I was, this dirty kid, and she welcomed me into her home and..." He snorted. "You remember me then. Little lost boy who confused his slang and didn't know how basic things worked."

Aly smiled at the memory of teaching him how to use the microwave and dishwasher. "Yeah, I remember."

"I'd never experienced... what you had before."

Nodding, she appreciated his clarification. In a small voice, she said, "I'm sorry. I didn't mean to get angry and yell at you. I'm just... I—"

His voice stayed gentle. "You're scared and frustrated and your world is upside down. You're blurting out thoughts as you have them. I get it. I do."

"Yeah. But I shouldn't have accused you of working for him."

"I'd much rather know what you were thinking than have you bottle it. That way it doesn't fester."

He watched her, waiting but Aly didn't know what to say.

After a time, he ventured, "I think we should call your mom. She needs to know you're okay."

Aly dropped her head into her hands. "I'm scared."

"Why?"

She flopped on the bed on her stomach and buried her face in a pillow.

"Running won't make it go away. Believe me, I've

tried."

Sighing, she angled her head so her voice wasn't muffled. "Right now, it's all conjecture. If I talk to them, I'm going to know for sure. I'm scared of what that means."

Noah's hand pressed between her shoulder blades as he sat on the bed beside her. Leaving his hand there, he shuffled up the bed and Aly turned her head so she could watch as he arranged himself at the head of the bed, fluffing pillows behind his back. Once settled, he patted his chest in invitation.

Discarding the pillow, Aly crawled over to drape an arm across his belly and rest her head on his chest. A gentle, comforting warmth bubbled up inside her as he slung one arm across her back and she felt a lot of the tension she carried drift away.

"Penelope loves you," Noah said, running his fingers through her hair. "She opened her home to you, she put your well-being first and foremost. She's an amazing woman. Is it really the end of the world if she's not your biological mother?"

She sighed and snuggled closer to his warmth, letting it seep into her. "Yeah. I know. And no. It's not. It's… a shock that's all. I don't doubt she loves me. I've never doubted that. It's more… I don't remember a Madeline in the family tree."

"Families have secrets," Noah reminded her.

"And Nanna had Alzheimer's," Aly said. "So, it's not like there's anyone from that side who'd be able to tell me."

"That too. I don't remember any Madeline's among Rex's group."

Curious, Aly rolled her head so her chin rested on his chest instead of her ear. "How long ago were you a part of that group?"

He made a noise of consideration. "Um… I joined about fourteen years ago. We think we were at the Institute for about two years. Well, Rex said it was two and we didn't have any reason not to believe him. Tracking time was hard because they kept knocking us out. Lasted three years in his group."

"So, I would've been four-ish when you joined."

"Yeah. At a guess."

She screwed up her nose. "Okay, that's weird."

With a throaty chuckle, he agreed. "Yeah, a bit."

"So Madeline was before your time."

"Or," Noah pondered, "she wasn't a shifter at all. Penelope isn't one. In all the years in Bellhollow, I've never sensed any other shifters."

"Not even him?"

"No."

"I don't think I've seen him around," Aly said. "But he did give me the weirdest feeling of déjà vu. So I dunno."

Swallowing, he said, "I don't think it's a good idea to tell Penelope and Rex about me being Fletcher."

"Why?"

"I can't imagine Penelope would take it very well."

"She loves you."

"She loved Fletcher," Noah pointed out.

She propped herself up on her elbow. "You *are* Fletcher."

He curled a strand of hair behind her ear. "Lovely, it is very difficult for people to make that distinction when they're not expecting it. She can't sense us. If she knew about shifters, how is she going to react when she finds out one of them has been eating from her table for years and she *didn't* know?"

"If we don't mention it, won't Rex question why the great Noah has a sudden interest in someone like me? He's going to think you knew something."

Noah's mouth twisted into his lopsided smile. "The great Noah?"

"You can do *amazing* things," Aly said, beaming at him, then let her smile die to be serious. "Besides, what else could we say? If I have to talk to him, I don't want to do it alone. I need you there and they're going to ask… won't he know by looking at you that you're… um… you?"

"He has to see me first. All I'm saying is we should *call,* not necessarily meet. I don't think we should tell him anything about me." His voice dropped to mutter, "See how he likes people keeping secrets."

Aly studied Noah. "You don't like him."

Noah tucked his free hand behind his head. "He's a good leader. Sound tactician. The man himself… I hate being lied to."

Her ear sought out his comforting heartbeat again. "I know."

"He lied a lot." He grew remorseful. "I don't mean to sour memories before you have a chance to make them."

Aly resisted the urge to pout. "He never gave me a chance."

"Since you're not a shifter, maybe he thought you'd be safer in Penelope's world."

She traced the lines on his flannel shirt, looking at them rather than Noah. "Do you think he even knows I can sense you?"

He scrunched up his face. "Maybe that's another reason he stayed away. It can't feel good to be unable to get close to someone without them shivering. Or, for someone like Rex, staying in his natural form when so many people are looking for him… Except no one knew his natural form so… something just doesn't add up at all." He squeezed her. "It's hard considering your needs before a shift and trying to get so much done at once so it doesn't cause you too much discomfort. I can't imagine what it would be like if you felt me shifted all the time."

She shrugged. "Yours feel nice. But yeah. I… maybe. It was… pretty constant with his. Fletch?"

"Yeah?"

"Are… are we going to have to run?"

He toyed with her hair, lifting it up and letting it spill

from his fingers. "I don't know yet. Let's not jump to conclusions without all the info, okay? But we should at least call Penelope and let her know you're okay."

With a groan, she bopped her head onto his chest. "Nag."

"Yup."

"Fiiine," she complained and rolled away from him to fetch her cell. "I'm not really sure what I should say to her."

"Keep it simple. You're fine. You know who he is and you want to know what he wants. On speaker, if you don't mind. I can check background noise then."

Aly took a deep breath and let it out slowly. "This is going to be bad." Hitting the speaker like Noah had requested, she let it ring. When it answered, no one spoke. Cradling the cell in her hand, Aly lifted it up and said, "Hello?"

Penelope rushed, "Aly? Aly! Oh god, honey, are you okay? Where—"

Surprised that Penelope's voice was cut off by a hissing noise, Aly blurted, "Mom?"

A deep male voice muttered, "Proof."

Noah's hands clenched and his tingles ran through her. Aly glanced at him and addressed the cell, "Who's this? Mom? Who's got your phone?"

The man said, "I need proof you are who you say you are."

Feeling annoyed, Aly said, "Well, since I haven't actually said I'm anyone at all, and you've got my mother's phone, I really should be demanding proof from you."

"Full name and date of birth," the man said, ignoring her tirade.

"No," Aly said.

"Do you really think I don't know her voice?" Penelope's shrilled in the background, then grew louder. "Honey, where are you? I'll come get you."

"I'm fine."

"You're not," Penelope insisted. "You're in danger."

"Yes. I know."

"Sweetie, I'm sorry if I scared you. I thought you were a… there are things you don't know and we need to talk to you about."

"No kidding."

"Where are you?" Penelope asked again. "I want you safe and home."

"Both those things are relative," Aly responded. "Especially since *him* being here means I can't go home, can I?"

Penelope's voice rose in pitch. "Of course you can—"

"I *know*," Aly stressed. "I know about shifters and I know he won't let me go home, will he? Not anymore."

A gasp from Penelope, then the man said, "You know about shifters."

"Yes." Aly made her tone mild, "You're Rex."

Rex replied, "Who told you about me?"

"That would be Belinda Bell. The woman who kidnapped me. She took me because I matched information she had about your daughter." She sighed. "I guess she was right. I know you're the leader of a faction of shifters and I know people are looking for you," she continued. "I know you were outside my house. I know you were at my graduation."

"You were?" Penelope asked and Aly guessed she was speaking to Rex.

Restrained surprise from the man. "I see—"

Without waiting for him, Aly continued, "I also know you were in that forest and you caused the car crash."

"That was an accident. You were with two very dangerous people and members of my group were overzealous. It's not my fault whoever drove panicked and crashed."

She clicked her tongue and wished he sounded at least remorseful. "You *shot* at us. That's what caused the crash. You shot and then you stayed in your car right up until ours exploded."

Rex hummed at her. "So you faked your amnesia. Clever. No one would have believed you so—"

"You don't get to accuse me of anything," Aly snapped. "Not since you faked being dead for eighteen years. And she faked being my mother and—" her throat clogged. "Are you my father? Is that part true?"

Penelope's voice broke. "Oh, honey, we never meant to—"

"Is it true?" Aly insisted.

A heartbeat before Rex admitted, "Yes."

Aly swallowed and tilted her head to stare at the ceiling. "And my mother?"

"Is gone," he said and now he sounded regretful.

Her throat burned. Noah reached over and put his hand on her knee and left it there. Not knowing why she grieved for a woman she'd never met, Aly tried to contain her emotions.

"You're not safe. Tell me where you are," Rex insisted. "We'll come and get you."

"And I'll be safe with you?" she asked, her voice meeker than she meant it to be. More than anything she wanted to believe that. She couldn't look at Noah to judge his reaction to that.

"Yes."

She let that sink in and a heaviness filled the room. Shaking her head, she asked, "And then what? Hide me away so this secret war of yours doesn't find me? That won't work."

"We'll make it work—"

She forged on, "People have been yelling at me and telling me things and I was kidnapped because of you! I don't even know if I *want* to know your side of the story because they're going to keep coming for me, aren't they? Because of you."

"I can keep you safe—"

"Can you? Can you really?"

"I promise."

She didn't want empty promises. "You're not doing a very good job so far. Don't you think I would have been safer if I'd known about all this right from the beginning? No, instead you kept me in the dark *knowing* that it could affect my life at any given moment."

Noah made a soft noise of dismay.

"It's not that simple, Alyson," Rex said, stern. "You're not a shifter. Growing up in shifter society would have been detrimental. Also, there's some concern over your—"

"You *abandoned* me! How would you—"

"Aly, that's enough," Penelope scolded.

"Don't stick up for him," Aly snapped, then sighed. "You need to worry about Tim and Dad"—she used the word deliberately to spite Rex—"cause people have been watching us for *months*. They need to get out of town."

"What?" Penelope squeaked.

Aly said, "Ask *him*."

"Are you sure?" Rex asked.

"Why are people watching my house?" Penelope shrilled. "You said there was no one."

"Am I sure?" Aly asked, her voice rising over the top of Penelope's. "There have been so many names thrown at me lately. Belinda Bell. Wesler or Welcher or Wechsler, or something. The Faceless. Someone called Darcy. Am I sure? Absolutely, because Belinda Bell is the one who killed—"

"Faceless," Rex said, his voice flat. "You've heard of the Faceless."

Aly cringed. She hadn't meant to mention them. Pressing her lips together, she met Noah's gaze for the first time since the call began.

Expression guarded, Noah nodded.

"Yes. Belinda asked me about them. They're a faction of shifters, right?"

"This is not a discussion to be had over the phone."

Aly chewed her lip.

"Alyson, listen to me. I can protect you. Educate you. Please, you need to tell me where you are."

Out of things to say, Aly cast Noah a beseeching look. She had no clue what to do next and Noah's bleak stare at a spot on the bed offered no solutions.

"Please, honey, I want our family back together," Penelope pleaded. "I'm so scared for you and—"

"I'm safe," Aly assured her and then words failed her. "I… um…"

"She's gotta go," Noah said, taking control of the conversation. "Penelope, get your family out of Bellhollow for a little while, they're at risk."

"Who are you?" Rex demanded as Penelope said, "Aly, who's that?"

Aly felt dreadful. She never even considered Tim when she'd run. "Would people really try for them to get at me?"

With a nod at Aly, Noah said, "Not to you. Through you, to Rex. Some of them might, I honestly don't know anymore."

"Who are you?" Rex snapped and Aly got the impression he didn't like to be ignored.

Addressing the cell, Noah said, "Someone who cares about your daughter. Been hearing some disturbing and conflicting reports about you. Serves me right for being away for so long."

"Who are you?" Rex demanded, his voice rising.

Noah said, "I've got many names. Fletcher's one of them."

Aly tilted her head at him and he shrugged in response.

"Fletcher?" Penelope asked incredulously before she rushed, "Aly, it's a trick, it's not possible—"

Noah chuckled. "I'm a shifter, Aunt P. Anything's possible."

"It's really him, Mom," Aly said, earnest. "Promise. Not a trick at all, it's really him."

"You can't be sure—"

"I tested him," Aly said. "I'm not dumb. He knows

things only Fletcher could've known. Plus, I can—" Noah shook his head sharply and the words died in Aly's throat.

Penelope choked on a sob. "Oh, God. Fletcher. You're really alive?" She sounded bewildered and Aly knew exactly how that felt.

Noah smiled. "I am."

"And you're a shifter?"

"Yup."

"Not possible," Rex snapped. "You're lying. Alyson can't be around—" he broke off.

Noah crowed in triumph and clapped his hands. "I *knew* you knew."

Aly frowned at the phone. Noah had effectively trapped Rex into admitting he knew she was a sensor.

Leaning forward, Noah snarled, "How the hell could you leave such an asset unguarded?"

Aly's stomach churned unpleasantly. "Asset?" she squeaked. What was he playing at?

Noah pressed his lips into a thin line and looked away.

"How dare you!" Rex snarled. "My daughter is *not* an asset."

Noah met anger with sarcasm designed to torment. "Uh-huh. Just like the Faceless weren't an asset."

The noise of disgust Rex made closely resembled a growl. "Who are you?"

"You probably know me as Noah."

Sounding awed, Penelope said, "Aly's self-defense instructor, oh baby boy, that makes so much sense—"

"Stay the hell away from my daughter!" Rex blurted, his voice harsh and angry and the cell crackled in Aly's hand as it tried to compensate for the sound.

Aly cringed at the noise. "Whoa."

"Bit late for that," Noah said, off-handedly. "I've spent the last *ten years* with her."

Rex's voice turned frantic. "Alyson, he's a master of manipulation, don't believe a single word he says."

"Oh, you're one to talk," Noah scoffed.

"Rex, what's going on?" Penelope asked and her words melted with Rex's.

"He's a dangerous thing; a liar and a—"

"Fletcher's the kindest, sweetest—"

"It's a farce. He's trying to get to me, he's an—"

"—boy I've ever known and he's been so good to Aly."

Rex snapped, "—abomination of the worst kind—"

Noah stiffened and his hands clenched.

"—this is just another one of his underhanded tactics to—"

Feeling protective, Aly scowled at the cell. "I'll believe him over you any day."

"You fucking monster, you brain-washed her—"

Noah snapped, "Why did my sisters go back to Darcy?"

"I should've left you to rot in that place," Rex snarled, ignoring him. "This is despicable."

"We would have escaped without your so-called help," Noah retorted. "Answer the question."

Silence on the other end of the phone.

Noah's lips thinned into a line. "We can vanish," he threatened. "You'll *never* find us. So you have one sentence to tell me why you sent them back in."

Silence.

Noah nodded as though he expected that. "Right."

A jolt of panic rippled through Aly at the thought she might never see Penelope again. Whatever she felt right now, whatever she was going through, she loved her mother. She loved her adopted father and her brother and the thought of never seeing them again was too much to bear. Her mouth felt dry and she croaked as her eyes flicked between Noah and the cell. "No, but…"

Cold anger was all she felt from Noah, and although it wasn't directed at her, it caused her words to die.

"No, *please*," Penelope implored. "Please don't disappear."

Hesitating, Noah held still. "We'll be in touch." He

stretched out his hand and hung up, then sighed.

Aly slowly placed the cell on the bed and stared at it. In a meek voice, she asked, "We're not really going to disappear, are we?"

"No," Noah muttered. He groaned. "I shouldn't have done that. That was so *stupid*." He smacked himself in the forehead several times. "Idiot."

"You have a lot of pent-up rage against him."

Noah flopped back on the bed. "Yeah. I guess you could say that."

She twisted her fingers and turned her attention to the cell. "What do you think he's going to do?"

Covering his face with his hands, Noah said, "Given that he's trying to keep you a secret, I'm hoping he won't send people after us. Can't say for sure. We'll let him stew then call back."

"Do you think he knows where I am?"

"I think… well, the background noise… I don't think they're in Bellhollow. I wouldn't be surprised if they're here, somewhere. Maybe Penelope guessed you'd come here."

"Maybe."

He sighed again and dropped his hands to his chest. "I'm hungry. There's an In-N-Out not far. Fancy a burger?"

She pounced on the chance to do something normal. "Sounds delicious. Are we staying here tonight?"

Noah nodded.

Sheepish, she smiled. "All I have with me are the clothes on my back."

With a snort, Noah heaved himself to his feet and held out his hand for her. "Walmart here we come."

"You make a crack about me and shopping and I will hit you," Aly said, tart.

"Wouldn't dream of it."

CHAPTER 13

The ex-senior football players had the bonfire ablaze when Del and Grace arrived at the lake. Just on sunset, the dusk still had the bite of daytime heat. Numerous cars were scattered around the parking lot and some of the seniors still waited by them for absent friends.

"Sure you can't make it?" Del asked, speaking into his cell. "Nah. It's cool, bro… late notice and all. How's tomorrow then? I challenge you to… okay! Seeya then."

"Noah couldn't come?" Grace asked as Del hung up.

Del shrugged, staring at his cell. "He's in Redding at the moment."

"Ahh," Grace said, disappointed. Gravel crunched beneath her shoes as she exited the car. "Shame."

"It's not like tonight was planned." Del climbed out the passenger side. "I still don't understand why you brought s'mores," he said as Grace opened the trunk of the car.

Grace raised her eyebrows and removed her guitar from the trunk without a word.

"And so many," Del complained, grabbing two bags.

Grace shook her head at him. "You realize it's so you'll get to eat as many as you like."

"Yeah," he whined playfully, "but I still have to *share*."

"You, sir, are a walking stomach. Mom *fed* you. That one too," she said pointing to one last bag.

Del reached down and grabbed the bag she indicated. "I'm a growing boy."

She closed the trunk and locked her car, sliding the keys into her pocket. "Oh, don't give me that," she scoffed. "I'm a growing girl and I don't eat half as much junk as you do."

"Operative word, 'junk'," Lloyd said, strolling toward them. "Wasn't Del most likely to have a heart attack by age twenty-one?"

Del scoffed and rolled his eyes. "Oh, hardy-ha." Offering Lloyd one of the bags, he said, "Make yourself useful."

Lloyd tossed his brown hair away from his face with a flick of his head as he took the bag. "No Aly?"

"Aly's mom surprised her with a trip apparently," Del said with a shrug.

"Graduation present," Grace added, tugging down her green shirt. "Whisked her off to Seattle. We tried, but she wasn't answering her cell."

"Oh, nice!" Lloyd said. "Some have all the luck. Oh, Grace, could you not mention Tamara's hair? She's a bit self-conscious."

Grace winced in sympathy. "The dye job go bad?"

Lloyd shrugged. "Well, I think it looks amazing, but it's too pink for her liking."

"Pink?" Del asked with a laugh. "Really?"

Lloyd fell into step beside them as they headed for the bonfire. "Tammy says she asked for rubine and it came out cerise." With a cringe, he continued, "So if you could find out what she meant, I'd be eternally grateful."

"It'll fade," Grace assured him. "And cerise is lighter than rubine, so she'll be able to re-dye without bleaching first."

Del and Lloyd exchanged glances. "And that's a good thing?"

Grace smiled. "Yes, that's a good thing."

With a waggle of his eyebrows, Del asked, "You gonna get your hair done too, Grace?"

"Oh, absolutely," Grace lied and stroked her fingers through her locks. "Purple streaks all the way."

"Singing, Grace?" Lloyd asked, nodding to the case.

"It's a possibility. Depends if people get drunk or not."

"Public space, underage, plus Sheriff's daughter equals best behavior. At least while you're around."

Grace laughed. "Good, he's on duty tonight. I'd hate to have to tattle." Smiling to herself and leaving the food to the boys, Grace made her way to Tamara and Kate.

The night was young, spirits were high and s'mores were abundant. The brightly burning bonfire dimmed as it turned the logs to charcoal and embers, then was re-fed. A Bluetooth speaker, which had been playing while dancing occurred, was replaced by Grace's gentle strumming, songs and ghost stories. Friends talked, laughed and shared their hopes for college. Grace knew some of them would be leaving soon either to relocate closer to their college, or go on one last family vacation as Aly had.

Del seemed in a good mood and Grace was grateful about that, especially with all that had been going on with him lately. She sat on a rock so she could play, while Del made himself a home at her feet, chatting to Ezekiel about games. Humming to herself, she improvised an easy five-chord tune and allowed her eyes to wander over the group.

Bellhollow had its niche groups, but the town was small enough they didn't segregate much. So close to college, they clung to their old way of life. Madison-Lee and Ethan snuggled together on the other side of the fire, other couples following their example to express some public affection and Grace idly wondered how long any of them would last.

College was a time for new beginnings and the majority of them were leaving home. Grace caught Kate's eye and they shared a smile. Perhaps that was why Kate'd been so open on prom night, it was a chance to experiment with no strings. Nothing had come from their interaction, but given the flirty eyes and inviting smile Grace was getting now, Kate might be open to another rendezvous. Grace wasn't ready to be tied down, but at least with Kate, they could explore without judgment.

Glancing down at Del, Grace couldn't help but feel worried for him. She and Aly were leaving him behind. Aly had always been worried about leaving Fletcher behind when she went to college and now Grace echoed that worry with Del. Grace was proud he was making the choice for his channel but it didn't make her feel better. Although he hadn't said anything, Grace knew convincing his mother was going to be an ongoing battle.

Grace pushed the negative thoughts from her mind and switched key to bring some Green Day into everyone's life. Del sat up straight and twisted to grin at her. Allowing her to sing the first stanza on her own, he soon joined in and gradually the whole group sang along.

She took requests after that. Popular choices were Weird Al's songs and even House of the Rising Sun. When it degraded to SpongeBob's Campfire Song, they all sang as fast as they could until the group ended up laughing too hard to sing.

To vex her friends, Grace returned to her gentle background strumming and refused to be coaxed into another song.

"That was lovely."

Grace turned her head. A man and woman in their mid to late twenties stood at the edge of their group, dressed too well to be camping or relaxing. With blond, spiky hair, the man was dressed in a black suit, sans tie. His jacket hung open and the white shirt beneath had several buttons undone, while the woman wore her dark hair up in a bun, with long pressed pants and a silk shirt, its color lost to firelight.

"I'm sorry," Tamara said, by far the most polite of

them. "Are we being too noisy?"

"Not at all," the woman assured. "Are you the recent Bellhollow seniors?"

"Just graduated," Ezekiel said and lifted his cup to clink it with Lloyd's. "Free and clear."

"For the next month at least," Grace mentioned.

The woman gestured herself and her companion. "My name is Elaine and this is Joseph, and we're looking for people who knew Fletcher Norman."

Conversation ceased and silence spread across the group around the bonfire. Those who didn't know him well looked at each other to see who would answer first, while Fletcher's friends ducked their heads to hide.

Grace huffed. So many journalists had been around when Fletcher died, vying for a story. She had hoped people would have lost interest by now.

Mitchell broke the silence. "What for?"

Elaine looked at him. "We're journalists with Sacramento Bee. We're currently researching the long-term effects death has on friends and family and I'm looking for people who knew him."

"Do you really think this is appropriate?" Mitchell asked and gestured the group. "We're celebrating."

"Oh, of course," Elaine soothed. "I was simply seeing if there was an opportunity available—"

"Is this going to be on TV?" Carter asked, excited by the prospect.

With a bowed head, Del grunted, "Trust Carter."

"It's a *newspaper*, Carter," Lloyd muttered and was ignored.

Elaine's smile invited them to talk to her. "There is that possibility."

Several seniors perked up and Carter bounced to his feet. "I'll talk to you."

"Of course he will," Grace muttered to Del.

Del nodded and draped his hands over his knees. "Never any doubt."

Elaine beckoned Carter away from the group. "Would you come over here? Joe is also available to talk to, if any of you are interested."

"Sure," Joseph said and sidled into the group to sit down. "So, did you all know Fletcher?"

Madison-Lee's gaggle of friends were the first to answer. "Oh, yes!" Tiana replied, earnest as she leaned toward Joseph. "We're a close-knit community here. Everyone knows everyone."

"No secrets of any kind," Wanita crooned and waved her hand to gesture the entire group of people.

"I find that hard to believe," Joseph mentioned with a small smile. "What was he like?"

"Sweet to everyone," Madison-Lee said as she sat forward to answer. "It's a real shame."

Ethan slung his arm over Madison-Lee's shoulder, drawing her back to him. "Nice guy, but a bit of a loner."

Tiana wiggled sideways, closer to Joseph. "His uncle died when he was thirteen or something, so he had to look after himself."

"No foster parents?" Joseph asked, raising an eyebrow. "Unusual the state didn't step in."

"He might've been, like, fifteen, or something," Lola said, looking at Del for clarification.

Del refused the bait, saying nothing as he stared into the fire.

Grace wrinkled her nose at the sudden interest in Joseph from Madison-Lee and her group of close friends. Unsurprising really. There had been a bunch of people who had over-dramatized everything, not only in Madison-Lee's group, but all over the school. It was so frustrating. They didn't know Fletcher, but they grieved like his death had been the end of the world. Tears in the hallway, running sobbing from a room, staring into space and blaming contemplating mortality as the reason for their inattention.

Grace had been so glad Aly had been absent during

those first two weeks after Fletcher had passed. The majority of the school had wanted to tell how Fletcher's death affected them, personally, when they hadn't known him. They hadn't been concerned at all about how it affected those closest to Fletcher. "Ugg."

Del patted her knee. "I hear you."

"Strange to have a reporter now," Tamara said, her voice clouded with confusion, as she snuggled deeper into Lloyd's arms.

"There were some sniffing around when… at the beginning," Lloyd said. "But the school redirected them. I would've thought they'd lost interest by now."

"Long-term effects, she said," Kate commented and licked her fingers to clean them of the s'mores she'd been eating. "Maybe that's why they're here now."

"It's not really been long," Ezekiel mumbled. "Wouldn't long-term be…" he cast a wary glance at Grace and Del. "Sorry."

"Years," Del finished, staring at the fire. "It's okay to say. Long-term is 'years'."

"I know it doesn't help, but… it gets easier," Tamara said. "You won't ever forget. But someday it mightn't hurt so much to think about him."

Grace stopped plucking the guitar so she could rest her hand on Del's shoulder. He lifted his hand and placed it on the top of hers.

Searching for something comforting to say, she was distracted by Lloyd's sudden, "Oh, he's good."

"Hmm?" Grace asked, as the others regarded Lloyd with curiosity.

"Watch him," Lloyd said, nodding at Joseph. He kept his voice low and conspiring. "Dude knows he's a looker and he's using that. Not over the top or anything, but yeah. Teenage girls, handsome dude, he'll let them daydream. He's searching for something specific. Something that will break this into a full story." He moved his gaze to where Elaine and Carter talked. "She's attentive, but she's not taking notes."

"So?"

"So," Lloyd shrugged. "I wonder what they're really after."

"What makes you think they're after anything?" Tamara asked, tilting her head back onto Lloyd's shoulder so she could talk to him.

"Babe, they're journalists. They're always after something. Looking at the world from a different angle. Everyone has secrets which need to be exposed or stories to be told."

"Fletcher didn't," Grace murmured.

"He had a story," Lloyd said.

"It just wasn't one which should be over-sensationalized by today's media," Ezekiel said.

Lloyd nodded sagely. "Truth."

Sighing, Del looked up at Grace. "You okay, Gracie?"

She nodded and squeezed his shoulder. "It's frustrating. They didn't know him at all. They're attention seeking." She sighed. "I'm glad Aly's not here."

Across the other side of the firelight, basking in the attention of the girls, Joseph turned his head and met Grace's disgruntled gaze. His sudden attention unnerved her and she didn't know why. It wasn't like he could've heard them, he was too far away for that.

"She'd hate it," Del agreed. "She'd go all snarly-rawr and kick 'em to the curb."

Dragging her eyes from Joseph, Grace smiled. "She would and maybe that's what we should be doing."

Del huffed a breath out. "Can't listen to this." He stood and stretched. "Gonna take a walk. Grace?"

"Yeah," Grace said and twisted so she could grab her guitar case. "I'll take this to the car first."

"'Kay. I'll go find us some stones."

"Do you guys want company?" Lloyd asked.

"Nah, bro. Just come get us when this lot's done. Or," Del grinned and shooed his hands at them. "Y'all can take your own walks."

Lloyd snorted. "I think our quote unquote *'walks'* are a lot different than yours."

"Yeah, they involve a different sort of stones," Del leered and danced away from Lloyd's kick to the shins.

After returning her guitar to the trunk of her car, Grace wandered down to the water's edge. The moon was not quite full and with their backs to the fire, there was plenty of light to see by. Del didn't seem to want to speak and she didn't blame him. Instead, he handed her a palm's worth of flat stones to skip.

Skipping stones wasn't her forte, but it was fun to watch them plink across the moonlight-dappled water and count how many she could get before the stone sunk. Del doubled her number easily, but he didn't gloat. Not tonight.

Tossing a stone from hand to hand, Del said, "Taking bets that I can hit twenty skips."

"Doubt it," Grace said and smiled. "What's the bet?"

"Dunno. Next to shout pizza?"

Grace shook her head. "It's Aly's turn. Why waste that?"

"Cause she puts pineapple on them."

"Good point, but I have a better idea." With a sly grin, Grace drawled, "If you don't get it, you have to go back and sing 'I'm a little teapot' in front of everyone. *Including* the actions."

Del laughed. "And if I do, you have to."

"Deal," she said and spat in her hand to seal it.

Del spat in his own hand and took hers. "You are so going down."

Releasing his hand, she wiped it on her jeans and waved him to the water. "Quit stalling."

Not done with the smack talk, Del grinned. "Ain't stalling. Stirring."

"I can stir right back. Gonna record your dance for your many eager YouTube fans."

"Like hell you are." He tossed his stone into the air and caught it. Drawing back his arm, he said, "Watch this—"

"So, you two are the close friends then."

Grace turned her head toward Elaine as she emerged from the shadows. She hadn't heard the woman approaching and her sudden appearance made her jumpy. "What makes you think that?"

Elaine grinned and sauntered toward them. "It's an old trick. Most teenagers haven't seen death yet. They have no experience so they over-dramatize it all. The ones who knew the deceased hide. You two are the only ones who walked away. Dare I say you are Grace and Del?"

It was unnerving to be named with such confidence. "We don't want to be interviewed."

"Not even about Fletcher's apparent suicide?"

Del dropped his stone. Twisting around, he snarled at Elaine. "Fletcher didn't commit suicide. It was an accident."

Elaine tilted her head and a slow, catlike smile spread across her face. "No, it wasn't. He was murdered."

Grace jerked in shock. Stepping backward, she bumped into Del's shoulder and his hand found her arm to steady her. "Murdered?"

"That's not right," Del said, shaking his head. "There wasn't any evidence of—"

"Do motorcycles usually explode into flames when slammed into a barrier?"

Elaine was so blasé, she could have been discussing the weather. Grace's stomach churned thinking about it. An image popped into her mind unbidden and bile rose. Covering her mouth with her hand, she turned away. "Oh, God."

Del, angry on Grace's behalf, rounded on Elaine. "You can't waltz up here and say shit like that. There's no truth to it."

Elaine pressed. "You don't know anyone who would want to hurt Fletcher?"

171

"No!"

Elaine continued, unfazed. "And Aly, his best friend, wasn't kidnapped just weeks after Fletcher was killed?"

"There's no conspiracy here," Del snapped. "Shitty things happen to good people. Get your stupid story someplace else."

"What about Fletcher's family?" Elaine asked, unfazed. "It's odd none of them came to the funeral."

"His *family* was there," Del sneered. "The people who mattered were *there*. Let's go, Grace."

Swallowing hard, Grace nodded. "Absolutely."

Elaine side-stepped so she barred their way. "There's truth to what I'm saying if you'll listen."

Stalking around Elaine, Del shielded Grace, directing her walk with his hands on her shoulders. "Nope."

Something about Elaine's expression made Grace think of a shark circling prey. "Does the name 'Noah' ring any bells?"

Grace tensed and Del's fingers dug into Grace's shoulders as they stopped walking.

Elaine's expression turned sly from their reaction. "So, is this a Noah you've recently become acquainted with? Who somehow feels familiar but you don't know why? Someone who Aly seems to know, even if she's pretending she doesn't?"

Grace, ever mindful and hating the way Elaine's words sank their claws into her mind, said, "You know, I didn't see any identification. How do we know you're reporters?"

Elaine shrugged. "Since neither of you is law enforcement and this isn't private property, I'm not obligated to provide it."

"Nor are we obligated to talk to you," Grace retorted.

Elaine's smirk was infuriating. "Ask Aly about Noah. See what she says."

"We *know* what she'll say," Del snarled and nudged Grace moving again. "She'll literally say you're full of it."

Elaine chortled. "Doubt it. She doesn't have amnesia.

She remembers everything. When you see her, tell her Elaine's looking for her. See what she does. See what *he* does."

Del growled under his breath and Grace felt like she was falling.

Elaine called after them, "There's going to be others looking for her. A lot of other people. We're at the Apex for the next few days, if you feel like chatting."

"Like hell we will," Del muttered to himself. He shoved his hands into his pockets and hunched his shoulder.

Grace matched his pace as they headed for her car. "Aly wouldn't lie to us." She said it because she wanted affirmation from Del but her words seemed somehow hollow. Noah had been familiar. Aly fitted with him so well and so quickly. Why?

"That woman has a way of nipping at the edges of doubt," Del muttered. His face was pinched and his words were strained. "Hasn't Fletcher's death always seemed... odd to you? Especially when you add in Aly being taken. What if... What if Fletcher had something which belonged to someone and they came looking for it. We never learned much about his family or anything like that."

Grace gave him a sympathetic look. "Fletcher wasn't some lost prince or a hero in one of your games, Del. He was a normal guy who died in a shitty way."

Del pursed his lips, reluctant to agree. "Yeah, I know."

Grace felt tears prick. "Life doesn't have to make sense. And it doesn't always give you answers."

He wagged his finger at the air as he walked, deep in thought. "That woman wasn't wrong about Noah, though. He... feels so familiar. Like I've known him a while, and I don't know why."

Grace chewed on her bottom lip. Aly was going through something right now which could lead to acting out and tangled feelings and Grace had felt it more important to be whatever Aly needed. But Noah was nice.

And kind. And he made Aly happy and that's what mattered. Still, there was something about Noah she hadn't been able to put her finger on, something intangible that Elaine's words had brought to the forefront of her mind. "I feel the same."

"He... I had him on my stream," Del continued, sounding bewildered. "He felt... it felt..." He let out a growl of frustration. "It doesn't make sense!"

Not knowing what to do or say, Grace nodded.

"Do you think... maybe it's not about Fletcher at all, but about Noah?"

Del's words buried themselves in her brain and begun to fester.

He sighed. "Reckon Lan'd mind if I crashed in your den tonight?"

Fishing her keys from her pocket, Grace answered with, "Nope."

Del thrust his hands into his pockets and hunched his shoulders. "Good, because I think we need to talk to your dad."

CHAPTER 14

Aly disliked Walmart even on her best days. The closest Walmart had been in Redding and she still keenly remembered getting lost there when she was six. While she preferred to buy boutique clothing, she knew she couldn't quibble. A focused shop, grab what she needed, get out as fast as she could. The possibility they were being followed filled her with anxious energy.

"You'll need jeans," Noah mentioned as they moved through the store. "For the bike."

Aly had a single-minded focus as she mentally ran through her list so they could be in and out fast. A change of clothes, something to wear to bed and toiletries. She didn't know what tomorrow would bring or if she was going to go home and that uncertainty weighed heavily on her. "I figured."

"And a jacket. I'll look for one."

She knew she couldn't buy much because they'd have to carry it. She eyed his large hiking backpack. Black, it looked like it could separate into two bags, a large rucksack, and a smaller backpack. It had everything he needed if he was going to run, including his laptop and she worried her purchases wouldn't fit. "Is there space?"

"Yeah," he said with a smile. "There's space. It's a proper travel bag."

"Why didn't you store that on the bike?"

He shrugged. "Bike might need to be abandoned in a rush. That's why the backpack stays with me. If needed, we can walk out of here and vanish."

"Ah."

He winked at her. "On-the-run, one-oh-one, Als."

"So I'm learning."

"Also, go for guy's jeans."

She considered that. "Pockets?"

Noah nodded. "You'll need to carry all your important things on your person. That's why the bag is split. Laptops and irreplaceables in the smaller one, and things which can be abandoned in the larger."

So many things to remember. Even if it was just precautionary.

Going through the clothing, she found a couple of printed t-shirts, one which was long enough to wear to bed, and a pair of jeans which she liked. Noah returned with a dark jacket similar to the one he wore and she wrinkled her nose at it.

"I know," he said with a fond smile. "It's not very fashionable, but it's reversible."

She ran her fingers down the sleeve. "So?"

"So, in a pinch, you can change what you're wearing. Better to hide in a crowd. If we're hiding from someone, you can take the jacket off, turn it inside-out, and then you're harder to spot because they're expecting you dressed in something else. I do this sort of thing all the time when losing a tail."

She giggled, spotting the cream inlay. "It's a shapeshifting jacket."

Noah grinned, pleased she understood. "Absolutely. You'd be surprised about how little people memorize a face and focus on the clothes, because they're easier to see from a distance. Switch it up and they've lost you."

"Good to know," she said and draped the jacket in her basket.

Underwear was a little embarrassing with Noah there, but fortunately, he spotted something he wanted to look at so Aly ducked away. She was in the toiletries aisle, picking out a toothbrush when Noah bounced back and dumped an assortment of candy in her basket. Lifting an eyebrow at him, she said, "Really?"

"Movie night," he said, rising up and down on his toes in giddy happiness at his idea. "Need provisions."

"I'm looking at toothbrushes and you're buying candy."

He nudged her with his shoulder. "It's been ages. Can't we have a movie night?" Lifting up a Snickers, he waggled his eyebrows at her. "Please?"

Playfully rolling her eyes, she grabbed the bar and shoved it into her basket. "You can't possibly be a teenager. You're a child."

"Excuse you," he said, affronted. Splaying his fingers on his puffed out chest, he said, "This form is nineteen. Respect your elders."

"Uh-huh," she teased and tapped his nose. "You have sixteen years of memories. That makes *me* older, bumble-butt."

"Bah, it would take years to grow a full-sized human. I'm clearly older."

"Keep telling yourself that."

He grinned at her. "So, nearly done?"

"Yup," she said, selecting a toothbrush and slid it into her basket. "Need some lip balm and that's it."

"Okay."

She wandered through the aisle looking for the balm with Noah meandering behind her. Just this morning she'd thought about inviting him over for a movie night so they could spend some time together without sneaking around. It seemed he felt the same way.

Movie night. Popcorn and fun and silliness and maybe some platonic snuggling and… A sly thought crossed her mind and she followed it without really thinking about it. "Any preferences on taste?"

His attention elsewhere, he said, "Huh?"

Angling her head at him, she cocked her hip and smiled. "Cherry or strawberry?"

"I'm not going to wear it," he said. "Get whatever you like."

Aly raised an eyebrow and stared at him as she waited for him to figure it out.

His blank look gradually morphed into a frown and a squint. "I just missed a cue, didn't I?"

"Big time," Aly said and dropped the cherry balm into her basket.

The frown deepened as he mulled. "Ooh. *Wait.* Was that... were you flirting?"

She almost heard the click in his head. "There we go."

"But—" he scratched his head, confused.

"I did say 'when', Fletch."

A brief flash of a grin before it faded. "Can you say it again?"

"Nope," Aly said and turned away. "Moment lost."

"Aww, Aly," he complained, elongating her name.

Turning her nose up, she walked to the cashier. "It's not the same if I have to repeat it."

He skipped sideways playfully to whine at her. "But I wasn't ready. I wasn't even making doe eyes."

"Do better next time."

"I'm not very good at all this."

"And you think I am? *Practice.* Seriously, does anyone become good without hard work first and—"

Her words died in her throat when Noah's hand touched the small of her back as he moved to walk beside her, closer than he would normally walk. Startled, she became hyper-aware of his hand as he drifted fingertips down her spine. The sudden dive into her back pocket of her shorts caused her to twitch and she twisted her head to stare at him in surprise. Something new and different and completely welcome but she couldn't help wondering if he was doing that because he wanted to, or he thought she wanted him to.

Noah stared back, as though daring her to comment or move away. Transferring her basket to her other hand, she leaned into him and copied his action and watched Noah's face light up like a Christmas tree.

They paid for their purchases, packed them in his backpack then wandered across the parking lot toward the In-N-Out. Neither of them were in any hurry to reach it, casting shy glances at each other as they walked in companionable silence.

Halfway across, Noah's cell rang and he lifted his eyebrows in surprise as Del's name flashed across the screen. Untangling from his arms, Aly shot him an inquiring look and Noah shrugged in response.

"Hey," Noah said, answering the call. "What's up?" He listened for a minute and Aly could hear Del's muffled tones. "Oh! Dude, thanks for the invite, but I'm kind of in Redding right now." Noah laughed. "Oh, do you now? It's on. You're going down... yup. Talk then. Have fun!"

When Noah hung up, Aly said, "I'm sorry you're missing out on whatever Del wanted."

Noah slipped his cell into his jeans pocket and shrugged. "Some sort of party at the lake. It's fine."

"But we were working so hard to get you back in the circle and—"

"We're not jumping to conclusions, remember? There's still a chance we'll be able to go back." Looping an arm around her waist again, Noah asked, "Aly?"

"Yeah?"

"This is... nice."

Aly nodded, then grew concerned. "Is it okay?"

His smile was gentle and made her belly cartwheel. "More than okay."

"I can't help wondering..."

"What?"

"Are you doing this because you want to, or because you think I want you to?"

He raised an eyebrow at her. "Doing what? This?" he asked and tucked his hand back into her pocket.

Again with the warm fuzzy feeling. "Hmm."

He hummed. "I'll make you a deal. I'm not going to do anything that makes me uncomfortable if you promise the same. I'm not even going to initiate anything if it makes me uncomfortable. And if anything I do makes *you* uncomfortable, you tell me, okay?"

Smiling, she rested her head on his shoulder. "You said 'uncomfortable' so many times then."

"Aly," he whined.

"As long as you promise to tell me if I make you uncomfortable too, then deal."

He considered her. "Can I ask…?"

Knowing what he wanted to know, she chewed her bottom lip. "Change happens and you can't stop it, but the one thing I've always been certain about was you. I… I don't want regrets. Life's too short for that." She lifted a hand and dramatically clenched it into a fist. "Fortify and no regrets!"

Giving her a squeeze, his smile widened. "That sounds like something Grace would say."

She giggled. "I was quoting her." She sighed. "I mean, this is a really, really *bad* time to start something."

He shrugged. "We have never had very good timing."

"We only get to—wait." She paused and smirked at him as she splayed her fingers on her chest. "*I* only get to be this age once," she drawled and waited for him to laugh. "Let's make a stupid mistake that isn't going to kill us and see where it goes."

"I don't think it's a mistake," Noah said. "And totally not stupid."

She conceded that with a nod. "Impulsive, then."

"It's hardly impulsive either, not with all the talking we've been doing."

"If you're going to be frustrating, I'm going to reconsider." She curled a finger through his belt loop at his hip and tugged him moving. "C'mon. I'm hungry."

Noah laughed as he followed her.

They ordered their food and sat in a booth facing each other to eat. Sitting in silence, Noah alternated between watching people as they entered and exited and looking at his cell while Aly focused on her food.

Dipping her fry into her shake, Aly decided she wanted to talk. She lifted a foot and nudged his thigh. "What are you doing?"

He smiled at her sheepishly. "Memorizing escape routes."

Blood drained away from Aly's face.

"Habit," Noah said, tilting his cell and then enlarged the screen. "Don't read too much into it."

Dread tickled down her spine and flared into anxiety. "Do... do we *need* escape routes?"

"I doubt it." He flicked his eyes up from the cell to her, then back down. "I like to be aware of the best ways out of cities. I mean, we're just off a freeway, which is awesome, but if I have to lose a tail, I need to know routes and I can't do that on the fly on a bike."

"Is... this something I should be doing too?" she asked, reaching for her cell.

Realizing something was going on, Noah looked up, then reached across the table for her hand. "No. No," he soothed and squeezed her hand while he put his cell away. "Als, this is me. This is the way I work. I do this all the time. You don't need to worry."

She thought back to all the times he played on his cell as Fletcher while they were in a group and wondered. "That doesn't make me feel better. I can't... I can't just sit here and do nothing and expect you to do all the work to keep us safe. I need to—"

"You're not doing nothing," he protested. "You have that sensing ability of yours always on. You can give me *so* much more warning than I've ever had."

She shook her head. "That's not—"

"You drew me sketches of the people following you. You sketched Rex. You got out of there on your own, all the way down here. You kept yourself safe. You were clever about everything you did today, even the cemetery you were at is across the other side of the city. Don't doubt yourself, lovely, and don't sell yourself short. You have amazing instincts. Trust them."

She nodded slowly and splayed her fingers so he could thread his with hers. "I guess. I just… I don't want to be a burden. You dropped everything to come and I—"

"I'm the one who dragged you in to begin with." Noah puffed out a sigh. "I'm worried," he admitted. "I'm missing things. I didn't see Belinda. I didn't see Rex arrive. I didn't see those two people following you. I missed it and I… I'm worried about what else I missed and I'm out of practice and… if I do this, then I've got a better chance at keeping us safe."

"It's not all on you." She squeezed his hand. "We're in this together."

He shook his head and changed the subject. "We should finish eating and then go call Rex again."

"And say what?" Aly asked, picking up a fry to dip.

"Ball's in his court," Noah said. "He needs to start giving us information. Offer a solution. Something. I need to know what I'm dealing with before making plans. Vanishing…" He paused and ran his free hand through his hair. "It would be very easy to do that right now, Als, but we'd have to leave Grace and Del and your family behind. I want a solution which means we don't have to abandon your life. He might be able to give us one."

"And he might not," she said. "By the way Mom was acting… I think he might've been coming to take me away." Somehow saying it made it feel real to Aly and she wilted.

Noah nodded like he'd figured that out. "It's possible

and if it is, we'll let him know how unacceptable that is."

"I don't know that I want to know him."

"You don't have to if you don't want to."

She concentrated on her food and muttered sourly, "But he's a resource we need to tap."

He clutched her hand. "Aly… *no*," he whined. "Don't—"

"It's okay," she said, pulling away. "I understand."

"If you want me to work with him, I will. Yes, he's the best resource we have right now, but he's not the only one. If you don't want his help, we won't. We'll do whatever you decide we do."

"*We* decide," Aly clarified.

His expression said he understood. "I feel… if we disappear, you mightn't get the opportunity to talk to him again. We disappear and I think he will too."

Downtrodden, she muttered, "I don't owe him anything."

"No. You don't. But you owe yourself answers."

Aly sighed and picked up another fry. "Yeah. I know." Sighing, she twirled the fry and studied the pattern it made as it spun. "Alright. I'll talk to him."

Night had fallen by the time they finished eating and drove back to the motel. Only a few stars were twinkling above them in the sky, the rest were obscured by the city lights and cloud cover. As Noah navigated through nighttime traffic, Aly hugged his stomach and pondered what she wanted to say to Rex. Maybe it would be better to let Rex take the lead. Would he want to meet? Would she agree to that if he asked? She didn't know. Maybe it was better not to go in with expectations of what she wanted.

Her mind whirled in never-ending circles of questions and she couldn't find a resolution. Noah was right, she needed something from Rex. Some form of closure.

Noah's augments tingled Aly's spine and, because he'd been shifting intermittently to check surroundings, Aly didn't think anything of it until he drove into the little cul-de-sac of shops beside the motel and parked by the gas station instead of driving into the motel. A row of trees and hedges separated the motel and the cul-de-sac and the spot Noah chose was mostly hidden in the shadow of a tree.

Frowning, Aly waited as Noah propped the bike up on one leg and stared ahead intently. Aly's shifter sense increased into a rapid pulse down her spine. She curled in on herself and drew closer to Noah. Because she knew he could be shifting his ears, she stayed quiet.

Noah cleared his throat. "I think someone's in our room."

Her mouth went dry. Keeping her voice low, she asked, "Could it be a staff member?"

"There's two of them," he said. "And I can't see any cleaning gear." He leaned forward on the bike and the tingles increased again. "The angle's wrong, I can't…"

Guilt engulfed her and she licked her lips. "I'm so sorry. I must've—"

The tingles stopped. Noah wriggled, then kicked down the stand. "Off, please. I need to scan you. You did everything right," he said as she got off the bike. "So either they're incredibly good or they have a tracker on you."

Taking off her helmet, she placed it on the seat and adjusted Noah's backpack on her back. "Okay."

"Hold still."

She did, shivering at the sudden flurry of tingles which engulfed her.

"I'll be quick," he said, his eyes roaming up and down her body. Frowning, he said. "Can I have your cell?"

The tingles vanished as she handed over her cell, unlocking it for him first.

Tingles were intermittent as Noah alternated between the cell and their room. He sighed and stopped shifting. "They're not tracking you," he said and returned her cell. "Well, I mean, they *are* tracking you, but they don't have devices that I can see on you. Which means, they might be tracking Penelope's received calls." He glanced at the streetlights. "Or have access to the CCTV. Or... anything really. Depends on the resources."

They hadn't left anything in the room, so Aly said, "So, let's just go. We can... set a trap. Or something."

Noah nodded. "I need to get a good look at the faces. I can't see them from here."

Dread made her stiff. "Oh."

Still staring at the motel, he switched off the bike, then held out the keys to her. "Wait here. I'll be right back."

She didn't want him to go anywhere near that room. "I have a bad feeling."

Taking off his helmet, he left it beside hers and turned his attention to her. "Me too. I won't get close, but if I can get a look at their faces, I'll be able to copy them. Since you're not feeling that they're shifters, they're probably Purists. We'll be able to watch for them."

She tucked her hands under the straps of Noah's backpack. "They might be the same two from before."

He nodded. "That's possible."

Swallowing, Aly asked, "Couldn't we just wait for them to come out?"

"They might see you then," Noah said. He stroked his fingers down her cheek. "I'm just doing a walk by. I'll be quick. Promise."

He bounced off toward the motel, slipping through a jagged hole in the hedge. Aly lingered in the shadows, scanning the parking lot for anyone out of place before she turned her eyes to the motel. It wasn't late and there were a few people scattered around, walking dogs or running along the footpath.

She jiggled nervously, hopping from foot to foot as she willed Noah to hurry with his investigation. She knew she had to be patient and she was fairly certain if she called him, he'd come back. She also knew he'd been doing this sort of thing a long time and he knew what he was doing.

A car drove into the parking lot. A man got out and walked in the opposite direction, toward the gas station. Another car drove in and pulled up at a bowser. A bunch of rowdy boys poured out of the gas station, laughing loudly with each other and being silly as they piled into a car. Turning her attention away, Aly breathed in, then breathed out slowly, trying to force herself to calm down. She was jumping at shadows and that wasn't going to do her any good.

Chewing on her lip, she tried to be practical. If they were going to run and possibly have a long trip ahead of them, being in shorts wasn't a good idea. Not on a motorbike. And there was no way she was going to change in the open. Telling the night air, "I'm going to get jeans on," she walked purposely toward the gas station so she could use their bathroom.

Noah gave her a two-tap acknowledgment tingle in reply and Aly smiled to herself. This way of communicating was beneficial for both of them.

The public bathrooms were hidden down a small alleyway between shops and smelled of disinfectant. Aly hoped that meant it had been cleaned recently. Locking herself in a stall, she changed out of her shorts and into jeans while paying close attention to Noah's shifts. They rippled across her skin in reassuring bursts as he made whatever changes he needed to get information.

Threading her arms through Noah's backpack, Aly stepped from the bathroom and into the night.

A sense of wrongness filled her.

Between her and the exit of the alleyway to the bathroom, a man in a hoodie leaned his back against the wall. Spotting her, he pushed away from the wall and his face beneath the hood caught the light. Gray scales. Pale eyes. A barely-there nose. A Solomon-type face in proportion and undistorted by fleshy skin tears.

A Faceless in natural form.

Aly froze.

Her brief glimpse of Noah's scales had been fascinating. A delicate diamond pattern. Silky and smooth and enticing. The hooded man felt deadly and foreboding. His scales were sharp, cutting slices out of his face. Images of the Faceless bursting through the undergrowth pushed itself to the forefront of her mind. Could he do that at any moment? If she moved, would he explode?

Her lips parted and she breathed, "*Faceless.*"

The man's round eyes widened, then he smirked. "Well, that makes this a whole lot easier."

Noah's flurry of augmentation tingles spurred her into action. She had to get by the hooded man and back toward Noah and the bike.

Her mind raced as she tried to remember the lessons. Make noise. Create a scene. Scream. Do what she'd practiced in the self-defense class. Her voice had deserted her, but her body…

As he reached for her, she reacted, snapping up her arms like a shield. Her forearms hit his chest, and because he didn't stop moving toward her, she jerked her arm up so her forearm was on his neck and pushed.

Gagging, he rocked his head away and made a grab for her. She slapped both hands down on his upper arm, yanked him toward her and kneed him in the groin as hard as she could.

Fast and quick and clearly effective as the hooded man folded in on himself. Still holding onto his arm, Aly heaved, reversing their positions in the hallway, then shoved him as hard as she could.

Close to panicking, Aly twisted and bolted.

The man let out a strangled moan, which turned into a string of swear words. Accelerating, Aly pelted across the parking lot toward the bike. She streamlined as much as she could, concentrating on keeping her speed and hoping that people would notice her predicament.

Noah was the sprinter, Aly was more into distance running and burdened with the backpack, she doubted she'd be able to get clear of an augmented chaser. Throwing a glance over her shoulder Aly saw a flash of movement as the man chased after her.

No time to think. She scanned the parking lot and searched for something, anything, to help her.

Thunder cracked and something zinged against the asphalt ahead of her. Thunder cracked again and tinged on a light pole. Horror flooded her as Aly realized the hooded man had fired on her. A third crack and Aly planted her feet to change direction, skidding along the ground so hard she fell into a slide. Gravel cut at her hands as she braced herself.

Someone yelled and Aly panicked. She pushed to her feet and ran, heading away from the gas station and toward the bike, yet angled toward the highway on-ramp. The more noise she could create, the more notice authorities would give. Especially with the gunshots. She zigzagged as much as she could, trying to create a moving target.

There was a grove of trees ahead of her, sitting on the island of ground between the on-ramp and the highway. If she could make it to that, she might make it to the shops beyond. Or be able to flag down a car. Or hide in the trees.

She tossed her head, wildly looking behind her. She couldn't see Noah but she could feel him.

The hooded man gained.

Don't look, don't look, she chanted in her head. One foot in front of the other. Lengthen stride. Gasp and pant and push so running could continue. Maintain for as long as possible.

The heavy backpack thumped on her back and slowed her down. Noah's tingles grew stronger. As her feet thudded onto the dirt, a car on the on-ramp illuminated the fence line surrounding the ramp. She hadn't seen it in the darkness and there was no way she could get by.

She changed direction again, her shoulder hitting the fence with a clang. Aly sucked in a breath and ran along the fence line, heading for the motel.

"Get back here!"

Fear pushed her faster.

The moment she heard his footsteps behind her and the sharp pants of his breathing, she changed direction, shoving herself away from the fence to bolt out across the dusty garden bed toward the parking lot.

So did he. Instead of grabbing her, he struck a sharp blow. Aly fell forward, tumbling down in a flurry of dust and stone. Sliding to a stop face first, she coughed out dust.

The hooded man snarled, "Did you really think you could escape?"

She hurt. Face and hands the most, but her forearms felt grazed too. Wincing, she propped herself up on her elbows and knees and spat dust.

"You can't outrun me."

He wasn't augmented. She would never have gotten as far as she did if he was, she learned that from Noah. One month of self-defense classes vs military training. She had no chance of coming out on top.

She rolled onto her back, propped up by the backpack with her legs pointed toward the hooded man, ready to kick. One month of training, but she still could make it difficult. Buy enough time for Noah to arrive.

Where was he? Tingles were still strong and felt like they were getting closer, so he was coming. She was sure of that, but she couldn't tear her eyes away to look for Noah.

The hooded man loomed over her, shadows over his scaly gray face and Aly flinched. Blood rushed in her ears and the world gave a sickening lurch. Her mind played tricks on her, throwing her back to the forest and the looming grin as the Faceless extended his misshapen hands toward her. Curling into a protective ball, Aly squeezed her eyes shut and clutched at her head so hard her fingers clawed at her skull. Heart pounding and barely breathing, she waited for the inevitable.

"Get away from her!"

She snapped open her eyes in time to see a form collide with the hooded man. A yell and a flurry of blows and crunching thuds and the hooded man was sent hurtling away.

Noah twisted to Aly, bending down to grab her upper arms to hoist her to her feet. Without saying a word, he scooped her into his arms and broke into a run, heading for his bike. Jolting with every step he made and trying not to burst into tears, she fumbled for the keys in her pocket. A car screeched through the cul-de-sac, skidding to a stop between them and the bike, its headlights blinding. As she turned her face away, Aly heard a splattering of gunfire.

Noah stumbled.

CHAPTER 15

Grunting, Noah planted Aly on her feet and shoved her away from him. Shocked, she yelped, stumbled and hit the ground. Recognizing gunfire, she hunkered down to make herself as small as possible. She didn't know what was going on, but gunfire wasn't a good sign.

Noah twisted back to the hooded man and a gun flashed in his hand as it fired. Aly stifled a shriek, and her ears rang from the crack. A strangled cry of his own and the hooded man went down, clutching at a leg.

Gesturing for Aly, Noah kept himself between the car and her. His augments intensified so much Aly shuddered as a result. Scrambling up, she grabbed a fistful of his jacket to keep them tethered together but stayed behind him.

The driver and passenger side doors both cracked open, with two people ducking behind them to use as shields. Noah's gun swung in their direction as he backed into Aly to keep her covered.

Peeking around Noah, Aly saw people were milling around outside the gas station, looking in their direction. She wasn't sure what she should do, run or stay, and looked to Noah for guidance.

"Put the gun down!" a male voice from the car yelled.

Noah made a gagging sound and Aly yelped as he lurched forward, then staggered, hunching over. "Fletcher?" she asked, concerned.

"Noah! Put the gun down!"

Still hunched, Noah's gun lifted to the man from the car.

Aly's gaze locked on Noah. Something was wrong. Something about the intensity of the shift she felt. Something in Noah's body language. The way his hand shook.

The headlights of the car dimmed as the man turned the lights off. "Hands up and we won't hurt you."

Noah scoffed, then choked on the noise.

The back of his jacket looked damp. Noah's face was stark white and yet he seemed to be sweating. Heart galloping, Aly paled. "Fletcher?"

Noah shook his head and his body shook with it. She couldn't hear him breathing. She was panting heavily, from the run and out of fear but Noah didn't seem to make even a noise.

"Shoot him!" the hooded man bellowed from the ground.

The man at the car yelled, "Tango, stand down!"

Aly pressed her hand to the dark patch on Noah's jacket. It was wet and sticky. Blood. That was blood. "Oh God, he shot you!"

Aly's action must have knocked him as Noah wobbled and teetered. Aly caught him as best she could, looping her arms beneath his to help him stand. He was heavy, his back leaving damp patches on her shirt. She braced, weighed down by both him and the backpack.

The woman bolted out from behind the door and rushed toward them.

"Bonnie! Wait!"

Noah's gun came up, then slipped from his fingers and thumped to the ground. "Boaz?"

Aly lost the battle to keep them on their feet as Noah became dead weight. They collapsed on the ground, with her legs beneath him. She wriggled, trying to scramble out from beneath him so she could get the gun to protect them. The backpack tangled with Noah and made her reach awkward. Stretching out as far as she could go, she inched forward and touched the hilt of the gun with her finger.

The tall woman reached them, kicking the gun away and Aly recognized her as the same woman who'd been sitting on the wall.

"Leave us alone!" Aly shrieked, lashing out at the woman. She couldn't quite reach, not around Noah, but that didn't stop her from trying. She swiped, her fingers curled like claws, and forced the woman to tilt away from them. "Get back!"

"But you're dead," Noah gasped, his breath coming in ragged pants. "I saw you die."

Aly hesitated, not sure what to do. Did Noah know her?

The woman, Bonnie, shook her head and smiled, touching her fingers to the scar on her forehead. She lowered down to her knees beside Noah and reached for him.

Aly snarled. "Leave him alone!" Tingles rippled down her arms now, leaving great waves of diamond impressions on her skin. The hair on her arms, all the way to the back of her neck, stood on end as the tingles swelled.

Noah's head tilted, looking over toward the man approaching them. "Ruth?"

"Ross," the man corrected. His gun, while ready to be used, was held with the muzzle pointed toward the ground. "And we've been looking for you a long time, brother."

"Brother?" Aly blurted, looking between both of the newcomers, then back at Noah. "They're siblings?"

Noah nodded.

Bonnie looked at Aly, then gestured at Noah, smiling in

a kind way that confused Aly. Aly blinked as the woman seemed to sign something and Aly shook her head, not understanding.

"Bonnie, that's not what we're here for."

Bonnie signed again. More insistent this time, twisting to glare at Ross.

Ross sighed and holstered his gun. "She wants to know if she can touch Noah."

"No," Aly responded, curling around Noah protectively.

"She's a medic. She can help."

"You *shot* him," Aly scolded, glaring at the hooded man. "He doesn't need help." Clutching at Noah, she shuddered so hard her shoulder shook.

Noah touched her arm, running his fingers over the goose bumps. "Aly—"

"Doesn't matter," Aly said, glaring at Bonnie.

Noah gasped, his eyes rolling. "Cops!"

Bonnie and Ross shared an alarmed look. Ross snapped, "Did you call them?"

Aly shrugged and nodded toward the gathering crowd outside the gas station. They kept their distance, watching from behind cars and dumpsters. "They might've."

Ross growled. "You're coming with us. Bonnie," he said, running toward the hooded man. "I'll get Tango. You get Noah and the girl in the car."

"We are not going with you!" Aly snarled.

Bonnie's hands fluttered.

Shaking her head, Aly snapped, "I don't care who you are, I'm not—"

The tingles died.

Shocked and panicked, she jerked her attention to Noah. "No. *No*," she blurted, shaking him. His head lolled from the force and hung limp. "Fletcher, wake up. *Please*."

Bonnie scampered forward, her body low and unthreatening and without a gun in hand. She sought Noah's wrist for a pulse and Aly, panicked and unsure, didn't stop her. After a moment, Bonnie nodded at Aly, an action which Aly took to mean Bonnie found one. Bonnie rolled Noah onto his side and yanked up his shirt.

Aly gave a wordless cry at the weeping blood on Noah's back. Her hands covered her mouth in horror and she couldn't tear her eyes away.

Bonnie's grip was rough and unapologetic as she tore Aly's hands away from her face and jerked her forward. Cloth was shoved in Aly's hands, then they were forced on Noah's back.

Blinking, Aly applied pressure. "Oh."

Now jacketless, Bonnie patted the air then stood and sprinted toward the car.

Holding the jacket against Noah's back as hard as she could, she watched as Bonnie went for the trunk of the car. Ross had his arm slung around Tango's shoulders, helping him limp toward the car.

Aly didn't know what she should do. Going to a hospital would be a bad idea. She knew Noah had healed bullet wounds before, but he had to be *awake* to shift. The last time he'd healed himself, it hadn't been as intense as what she'd just felt, but the last time hadn't been as bad as it was right now. One bullet vs… well, she didn't know how many times he'd been shot. Three? More?

A tear trickled down her cheek and dripped from her chin. "Please don't leave me."

The headlights of the car came on and Aly flinched, squinting at the brightness. There'd been enough light to see, but now it was overwhelming.

Noah's blood on her hands and on his shirt shimmered at her, tiny pinpricks of light glistening in the blood. Aly blinked, thinking she was seeing stars, but the light remained. It wasn't the first time his blood had shimmered at her, but every other time she'd been hurt as well and assumed it was a trick of the light. She wasn't sure what to make of it.

Bonnie rushed over and the moment was broken.

Bonnie jostled Aly aside, then busied herself around Noah. Duct tape stretched and tore under Bonnie's teeth as she taped the jacket in place. Aly fell back and stared at the blood on her hands.

"We need to leave," Ross said from somewhere close. "We can help him, but we have to go right now."

An impossible choice.

"Get in the fucking car."

Or no choice at all.

Aly lifted her head to glare at Ross in defiance. With a roll of his eyes, he reached down and hauled her to her feet, manhandling her across to the car. Wrestling the backpack from her, he plopped her in the backseat. "Stay," he snarled. "Or Tango will shoot you too."

Aly threw a startled look at the front seat of the car, seeing Tango clutching his leg with one hand while pointing a gun at her with the other. "With pleasure," he seethed.

Ross drove fast, weaving through the traffic and more than one time Aly found herself squashed against the door from the rough pace Ross took corners. Noah's head and upper chest rested on Aly's lap while Bonnie his held lower half and tended to his wounds. It had taken a bit of work to get him in the car, both Bonnie and Ross laboring to lift him.

Aly wondered why they didn't augment. She hadn't felt anything from them and she'd felt something from Elaine almost straight away. She had more questions than answers and nothing explained Tango's appearance either. While she recalled something about newer clones being unable to access the shift, she wasn't confident in her knowledge.

Aly kept her eyes on Noah, watching for each laboring breath he took. Part of her was aware she should be trying to figure out where they were taking her, but she couldn't bring herself to tear her eyes away. Her fingers stroked his face as she willed him to wake. If he woke, he could fix himself.

Bonnie stretched out her hand and tapped the front seat.

"Yeah, yeah, we're nearly there," Ross said. "Maybe, to pass the time, you'll answer a few questions."

Aly looked up to see him staring at her through the rear-view mirror. "I don't have anything to say to you."

"You've been kidnapped before," Ross remarked. "You should be used to it."

Aly lowered her head, brushed Noah's face with her fingers and refused to speak.

"She's an enigma, eh Bonnie?" Ross said, sounding conversational. "Kidnapped by Purists, rescued, feigns amnesia, gets contacted by Rex, runs away and is found in the company of our brother." He addressed Aly again. "You really can't expect us to believe that's all a coincidence."

"Why do you care?" Aly snapped.

"You're the first loose end he's ever left. There's more to you."

"Good to know," Aly muttered. "Keep thinking that."

"You might want to be more polite to someone who's going to keep him alive."

Ross' tone was mild and that scared Aly more than his words and she bit her tongue to keep from retorting.

Ross shrugged and turned his gaze away with a mild, "Suit yourself."

Unable to keep quiet, Aly blurted, "Who do you work for?"

"What makes you think we work for anyone?" Ross asked mildly.

"Everyone works for someone."

Ross smirked. "Then who do you work for?"

Aly curled up as much as she could. Hatred for Ross filled her, as well as a deep sense of terror. She couldn't predict him, she couldn't fight him. She didn't know what to do.

Bonnie tapped on Ross' chair again, urgent this time. "I

know," Ross replied. "I'm going as fast as I can."

"What's wrong?" Aly asked.

Ross didn't answer and Bonnie returned to monitoring Noah's pulse.

The fear in Aly felt like a ravenous beast, threatening to burst free of her and every time it reached brimming point, her eyes would find Tango's gun. She wanted to run. Escape. Flee. Hide. Hunching over, she focused on Noah. She had to hold it together until he woke up. Until he was able to heal himself. Until he opened his big brown eyes and looked at her again. She had to endure.

She concentrated on her breathing to keep herself going. Curling up, trying not to be noticed, trying not to provoke.

Ross slowed, pulling into what seemed to be a decrepit warehouse. The walls appeared rusted and several of the upper windows were broken. Aly gulped as a feeling of foreboding settled over her as they drove through the doors and into the darkness inside. The headlights illumined dilapidated boxes, rusted shipping contaners and empty space before Ross switched them off. He parked next to another car similar to the one they were in.

Ross snapped off his seatbelt and shoved the driver door open. Striding to the warehouse entrance, he yanked on the chain to shut the warehouse door.

Aly curled up tighter around Noah's head, alternating between watching Tango, who smirked at her, Bonnie, who ignored her, and Ross, who strode back toward the car.

Opening Aly's door, Ross grabbed her arm and dragged her from the car. Aly fought him, kicking and yelling as she tried to free herself and stay by Noah. Turning, Ross used both hands to attempt to subdue her. As he did so, she jabbed him in the throat with the side of her hand, then gripped his arm with both hands, pulling the same defensive strike on Ross as she had on Tango.

He was ready for it, his hips jutted backward while

simultaneously shoving her. She slammed into the side of the car, putting her hands out to brace herself.

Ross grabbed Aly by the hair and yanked her head back. "I don't have to play nice."

Aly shrieked in pain as he dragged her across the floor. She reached back, grabbing his wrist to take some of the pressure off her hair. "Let me go!"

Ross released her at the base of one of the rusted support columns around the place. Aly fell to the ground and tried to scramble away. He grabbed her wrist and pulled her closer to the column. Twisting, Aly sunk her teeth into his arm.

With a wordless cry of pain, Ross smashed his fist into her face. Stars exploded in front of her eyes as her head collided with the concrete floor. By the time she came back to herself, he had her hands wrapped around the column and tied with plastic tags, with the column pressed to her chest.

Scowling, Ross wiped his bleeding arm on Aly's shoulder. "I will have Tango shoot *him* if you don't behave."

Aly groaned in pain and pressed her forehead against the metal column.

Ross left her line of sight. "C'mon, Bonnie."

Her head hurt. Her face hurt. Her scalp prickled and itched. She felt sick to her stomach. She wanted it all to stop. She wanted everything to stop. Her hands hugged the column, seeking comfort. Tears dribbled down her cheeks.

Someone behind her grunted and Aly glanced over her shoulder. She couldn't see what they were doing, so she wriggled around the column until it was between her and the car and watched as Ross and Bonnie hauled Noah and left him on a patch of concrete about ten feet from her. Tango sat on the floor with his back to the wheel of the car, his hands clasped over his wound.

Bonnie rolled Noah onto his stomach and stood, holding out her hand to Ross.

He peered at her, then plucked up one of the objects in her palm. "They're out already?"

Bonnie nodded.

Ross held a bullet up to the small overhanging light by his thumb and forefinger and let out a low whistle. "Tango, how many times did you fire at him?"

Tango's voice sounded pained. "Three or four. What do you mean 'they are out'?"

Ross snorted. "We did tell you what we thought he could do."

Aly frowned as she added that nugget of information to the growing list of clues about the trio.

Ross reached into his pocket and pulled out a mangled gun to show Bonnie. She snatched it, studying it intently, turning it over and over in her hands.

"Statistically impossible," Tango muttered. "Shooting like that."

"You don't know Noah," Ross said.

"And inherently stupid," Tango said. "I am still alive."

"Don't be ungrateful," Ross said. "If he wanted you dead, you would be. Instead, you have a bruised hand and—"

"A gunshot wound to the leg."

"I was getting to that."

Aly twisted her wrists, trying to see how tight Ross had made the ties. She tried to remember the technique Noah had mentioned to break them. Something about shoelaces or making them tighter, then a sudden jerk. If she had a plan, or access to a weapon, she might stand a chance.

After they helped Noah. Aly scolded, "You said you were going to help him."

Ross glanced over at her. "Right after you tell us who you work for."

Her eyes darted between them. "I don't work for anyone."

Ross strode across to loom over her. "Do you want to try that again?"

Cowering, she tried to keep the conviction in her voice. "I don't work for anyone."

"You really expect me to believe that?"

"I really don't care what you believe."

Ross snorted. "Welcher is interested in you. Rex has been spotted in your presence. Darcy sent men after you. Noah's *with* you. And you expect me to believe you don't work for anyone."

Aly twisted her wrists as she stared at Noah. Was he breathing? "Can you *please* help him?"

"Why is *everyone* so interested in you?"

"I don't know," she muttered, sullen.

Ross reached down and gripped the front of her shirt to focus her attention on him. "I will break every finger if you don't start giving me answers."

A sudden influx of saliva caused Aly to swallow hard and try to quell the churning in her stomach. "What?" she squeaked.

"Starting with your pinkie."

As Ross reached for her hand, Aly panicked and struggled, curling her hands up so Ross couldn't get at her fingers. "Wait! *Wait!*"

"Talk!"

"I don't know anything," she wailed, cringing away from him. "Until a few months ago, I hadn't even heard of shifters or the Faceless or all these factions and wars and now everyone's coming and I don't know why!"

Ross squinted at Aly. "What's Noah to you?"

"He's *everything* to me," she answered. "He's my best friend. I've known him since I was eight. That's all this is. They came after me because of him, and then they came after him because of me and he made the stupid decision to come back instead of running like he should've and now they won't leave us alone! Please," she implored as tears trickled down her cheeks. "Please, you have to help him."

Ross looked taken aback. "How old are you?"

She blinked and sniffled and wondered why that even

mattered. "Eighteen."

"Can you believe this shit?" Ross asked, peering back at Bonnie. "She expects us to believe she knew him since she was eight."

Bonnie shook her head.

"We *saw* you working with Darcy."

Aly's brow creased. "Darcy?" She blinked. "Elaine. You saw us with Elaine." Noting Ross' confusion, she shook her head and corrected, "Elijah."

"Yes."

"We didn't know she was working with Darcy," Aly protested. "We were fleeing from the Purists who kidnapped me and ran into her. She helped us escape! We didn't know she was with Darcy until she sent one of those Solomon things after us!"

Bonnie jerked forward, her face aghast, her hands fluttering as she signed while Ross went pale. "Solomon?"

Aly swallowed. "I'm not sure what… Elaine said they were shifted out of control and that's what Solomon did and I…"

Ross and Bonnie shared a look. "You're not making any sense."

She struggled for another way to explain them. Looking at Tango, she lowered her voice, "Shifter clones with dysplasia. That's all I know."

"Why 'Solomon' though?" Ross asked. "Why *that* name?"

"Because that's how Elaine described it. She said… they were Solomon and Noah told me that's what Solomon did when… when Seth died," Aly replied.

Bonnie gasped, her hands covering her mouth and she turned away.

Looking unnerved, Ross checked on Bonnie as he asked Aly, "How much do you know about our siblings?"

Aly shook her head and shrugged. "Elaine's the only one I met. I know about Jonah. Noah told me about Seth and Solomon. And Adam. But that's it. I swear."

Bonnie darted forward, her hands flying as she addressed Ross. He lifted his hand and patted the air at her. "Okay. Okay, Bonnie, one sec." To Aly, he said, "He never mentioned us? Boaz and Ruth?"

Aly shook her head.

"Or Moses?"

Aly shook her head again.

"And *Elaine's* working for Darcy. You're not?"

She shook her head a third time. "Neither is Noah."

"That is a lot of information for someone who 'does not know anything'," Tango snarled from his position on the floor. "Imagine if she blabbed like that to one of the factions."

Aly's mouth felt dry. "I wouldn't."

Tango laughed. "Sure."

"If you're his siblings, then you're the only ones who *wouldn't* kill a Faceless on sight," she said. "Please, you need to help—"

"Yeah, yeah," Ross said with a dismissive wave of his hand. "Bonnie will sort him. Still not convinced." He turned away and ran a hand through his hair. "Hard to believe Elijah and Noah aren't working together," he told Bonnie.

Bonnie signed, Ross lifted his hands to sign back and the two of them discussed something. Aly huddled, twisting her wrist as she tried to loosen the bonds.

"When you are done," Tango snarled. "I would appreciate it if someone could get this damn bullet out of my leg."

Bonnie tilted her head at Tango, then gestured at Ross.

"Yeah, I'll do Tango, you do Noah."

Aly closed her eyes and pressed her forehead to the metal beam. Tears leaked out from beneath her closed lashes, sliding down her face to drip from her chin. She didn't know what to do but she knew she needed to be ready for the moment Noah acted. If he woke up.

No. When he woke up. She had to hold onto that

belief. When he woke up.

Ross crouched down by Aly and she peeked at him through her eyelashes. "I still don't know why people want you so much. Three different factions have offered us handsome sums of money for your capture and delivery. You, little lady, have a very, *very* large bounty on your head." Ross smirked. "It's gonna set us up for life."

The man was infuriating. Penelope didn't know what to think anymore. Rex had always been an enigma but something about this whole situation felt *wrong*.

Until the forest, she'd always believed Rex had had Aly's best interests at heart. Then he'd allowed those people to fire upon Aly, locking Penelope in the car so she couldn't get to Aly.

Now, Rex was constantly on the phone. He had numerous cells, with multiple call signs and Penelope wondered how he kept them all straight. When he wasn't on the phone, he was checking some sort of mapping application on a laptop and then making more calls.

And still remaining tight-lipped. He expected her to sit by her cell and wait for Aly to call. He was absolutely fuming about Fletcher-aka-Noah, yet wouldn't explain to her why. Everything was 'shifter' business and therefore not her concern.

Aly seemed so certain it was Fletcher and it made a lot of sense to Penelope. There had been something so familiar about Noah and she desperately wanted to believe Fletcher was still alive and with Aly.

Fletcher was a kid himself. While he might've been living on his own, and obviously survived his own death, he was a teenager. Penelope had so many memories mothering that boy. Helping him learn. Drying his tears and tending skinned knees. Making sure he ate. Fighting with Fletcher's Uncle Lee regarding Lee's willful neglect. Watching Fletcher grow into the kind, sweet, wonderful person he was going to become, alongside her daughter.

Watching him fall in love with Aly and not realize that he was bisexual, not gay. And, if he was Noah and seeing how happy Aly was dancing with him, knowing that he'd figured himself out.

How could Rex possibly say those things about Fletcher? That he was dangerous and manipulating Aly?

Maybe Rex was the manipulative and dangerous one.

Watching Rex spin his webs of deception and with the night growing longer with every passing minute without any news regarding Aly or Fletcher, Penelope lost faith. She wanted her daughter home and safe. Fletcher too. She wanted her family back together.

Rex couldn't be trusted. Not anymore.

Penelope had been approached by many people after Aly had been taken. Shifters, she believed, all trying to glean why Aly was important, dropping hints about what they were and expecting Penelope to bite. Penelope had lied to them all, but one among them had flashed FBI identification and given Penelope her number, saying she was willing to help in any way possible. Tegan had been persuasive and got Penelope in touch with a good psychiatrist to help Aly through her ordeal. Since then, Tegan had called once a week to check on Aly's progress and make sure things were okay. Since Tegan hadn't mentioned shifters at all, Penelope felt the woman genuinely wanted to help Aly.

As Rex lifted yet another cell and relayed *another* call sign, Penelope decided it was time. Lifting her cell, she sent a discreet message to Tegan.

CHAPTER 16

Del woke with a snap as he was dragged from the sofa and dumped on the floor. Lying in a pool of blankets and pillows, he managed a, "Wazzit?"

After glancing at his watch and discovering it was seven in the morning, he squinted at Grace and covered his head with the blankets. "Gracie," he whined. "Too early."

Annoyed that it had taken him this long to become coherent enough to acknowledge her, Grace dropped his ankle and tugged the blankets. "Doesn't matter. You need to get up now."

He wrestled with her in an attempt to keep the blankets and lost. "Don't wanna."

Huffing in exasperation, she made her voice tart, "Your mom called. Plus Dad gets home soon and we need to have breakfast ready for him."

"Five more minutes."

She hoisted his pillow out from under his head and smacked him with it. "You said that thirty minutes ago. Get up."

The pillow had no effect. Del caught it, then plopped it on his face to block out the light. "Comfy."

Grace's patience wore thin. "Dad's been on all night.

After he eats, he's going to bed and you won't get to talk to him."

Del huffed. He grumbled. He whined, "You're relentless."

She rolled her eyes and dug her toes into his ribs. "You're a baby. And you're on toast duty. So get up. Or I'll let Pebbles in."

"Okay, okay!" Del said and flailed. "I'm up! Don't sic your cat on me."

Instead of demanding pats, Pebbles decided she'd rather beg for bacon scraps and remain underfoot as Del and Grace worked in the kitchen. Bacon, eggs, grilled tomatoes and toast, everything her father liked. She made coffee for Del, who gulped it down so fast he almost burned his throat, and left a glass of orange juice on the table for her father.

Jonathan took one look at the spread on the table and turned on his daughter with suspicion. "All right. What are you buttering me up for?"

"Nothing!" Grace insisted, waving her hands at him. "Just want to make sure you get a good feed before bed."

Jonathan fixed a stare on her and removed his jacket and hat, leaving them on the kitchen counter. "Lijuan."

Since he never used her Chinese name unless she was pushing boundaries, Grace sighed and sat on a chair beside Del. "Told you." She waved her hand. "Go ahead."

Del took the lead. "There were some reporters at the lake last night, asking questions about Fletcher's death and we were wondering—"

Jonathan held up a hand to stall Del and looked at Grace, "Honey, you know I don't talk about cases."

"But you can," Grace insisted. "Fletcher's case is closed, right? A matter of public record. You can talk now."

Jonathan sighed and rubbed his face with a hand. He sat at the table and picked up a piece of bacon. "Crispy."

Grace beamed at him and was the picture of a darling

daughter who could do no wrong. "Just the way you like it."

"Bribing an officer is a federal offense," Jonathan joked, then grew serious. "I'm not sure anything I can tell you would benefit either of you. There's a reason I don't talk about my cases. "

Grace and Del exchanged a glance, then Del sat forward and rested his elbows on the table. "The reporter said Fletcher was murdered."

Jonathan looked skeptical. "Did you get this reporter's name?"

"Um… there were two; Elaine and Joseph," Del said, looking at Grace for clarification.

"From the Sacramento Bee," Grace finished. "They didn't give their last names or show id."

"And they implied Fletcher was murdered?"

Grace hesitated as she recognized his 'officer' tone. "They were probably trying to get a rise out of us."

Del, not as versed in Jonathan's various tones, said, "They claimed Noah did it."

Grace frowned. "No, they didn't."

"They implied he knew something," Del argued.

Jonathan focused on Del. "Noah who you invited to the graduation dinner? The one who danced with Aly?"

With a warning glare at Del, Grace said, "Noah wasn't even around then. I mean, the reporters could be trying to stir up something about him, I guess?"

"Did Fletcher speak about anyone called Noah? Had he ever been threatened by anyone with that name?"

Realizing something was going on, Del threw a wide-eyed look at Grace. "Not that I know of."

Graced licked her lips and intervened. "Is there any truth in what they were saying? That he was murdered?"

Jonathan hesitated a moment too long. "No."

"But there *are* things which troubled you?" she asked, honing in on that hesitation.

Jonathan sighed and scrubbed a hand over his face.

Slouching on the chair, he reached for the pepper and dusted his food as he spoke. "Of course I'm troubled. He was your friend and he died in a way that was both tragic and unexpected. The death of a friend was something we hoped you wouldn't have to deal with so young. How you, both of you, and Aly, have reacted to that is troubling." He reached for the salt next. "Aly especially. Losing a lifelong friend and then being kidnapped only to be released without any knowledge of what happened, that's bound to have a deep impact on someone. How's she been?"

"Distracted," Grace admitted. Slouching in her chair, she mirrored her father's position and pulled her hair over her shoulder so she could run her fingers through it. "Quiet. Her drawings are strange and it feels like she's hiding something. But… lately, it felt like she was doing so much better."

"She's gone through a lot," Del said. "But, yeah, she's been smiling like she used to."

The words 'since Noah arrived' hung between them, unsaid.

Grace mentioned, "That woman said Aly was faking but… I mean, she wouldn't have any reason to, would she?"

Scratching his cheek, Jonathan considered, then sighed. "Memories can return. They're tricky and fickle. Perhaps she's getting impressions and doesn't know how to tell you. Or is waiting until they all return."

Del pressed Jonathan, "Don't you think Aly would want to know if someone murdered her best friend? Don't you think it would benefit her? Jog some memories? Maybe, if he was, it was by the same people who took her. What if she's in danger? I mean, the FBI was literally involved in Fletcher's case, maybe there's more to it."

Pursing his lips, Jonathan considered his words carefully. He picked up his knife and cut up an egg, spreading it over his toast. "As far as I'm aware, nothing came from their interest."

"But it's possible that he was—"

Jonathan shook his head. "Del, don't go looking for trouble. There isn't any. It was a tragic accident."

Del wasn't backing down. "If he was murdered—"

"There's nothing to indicate any sort of foul play."

"How about the fact that Fletcher was an incredibly careful driver? He literally wouldn't have had an accident."

"Fletcher was an eighteen-year-old male," Jonathan mentioned. "Being silly on his bike on an open stretch of road when no one is around is plausible."

"It isn't if it's *Fletcher*," Del snapped. "Not when he was on his way to see Aly after she broke her wrist." Riled, Del argued, "Plus—plus—plus, here's the thing. Aly's house is completely in the opposite direction from the pizza place!"

Jonathan nodded in sympathy. "I empathize with what you're going through. Anger and denial are both parts of the grieving process."

"This is not part of the grieving process!"

"Del, chill," Grace interjected. "Don't yell at my dad."

Del, caught in his emotions, protested, "There's something really whacked going on with—"

Footsteps on the stairs stalled Del from continuing as Lan wandered down in a bright pink robe. "Oh, you're home," she said, surprised as she saw them all sitting around the kitchen table. "Lijuan, did you turn off my alarm?"

Grace improvised, knowing her mother wouldn't like her pressing her father for information. "You looked tired. I thought Del and I could make you guys breakfast this morning."

Lan exchanged an amused look with Jonathan. "What'd she ask for?"

Jonathan picked up a piece of toast. "Now, darling, you know Grace doesn't need an excuse to make me breakfast."

Lan laughed. "That doesn't sound like her at all."

Del stared at his food without eating and needed to be

nudged by Grace to get him to eat. He didn't speak again until after breakfast had been cleared away and Jonathan had headed off to bed. "I need to show you something."

With raised eyebrows, Grace followed him to the den. He flopped on the couch where he'd slept and rummaged around in the blankets for his cell.

Perching on the couch beside him, Grace watched him swipe through his cell.

"Couldn't sleep last night," Del muttered. "Feeling... I dunno, but I was looking at pictures and I found something. Just... keep an open mind, okay?"

Uneasy, Grace adjusted her seat. "Okay."

He flipped his battered cell on the side then turned it around to show Grace. "Whose eyes are these?"

Grace looked at the screen. Brown eyes. Slight crinkles at the corners. They took up the entire screen but she couldn't tell at a glance. They were over-enlarged and fuzzy and she didn't know what he was asking. "Ahh... I don't think I can—"

Del pressed, "Noah or Fletcher?"

Grace concentrated. "Fletcher's eyes?"

Without answering, Del turned the screen back toward him, then tapped it a few times, before presenting it to Grace. "Same again, Noah or Fletcher?"

She looked. The image was different, the lighting had changed, but the color of the eyes was the same. Everything seemed the same as the last pair of eyes, including the fuzziness. "They look the same. What's this about?"

Del bounced closer to Grace. "Exactly."

"C'mon, Del, I can't tell who it is."

"No. But watch this." He swiped again to show a hastily cropped picture of both sets of eyes together on the screen.

"Again, they look to be the same eyes, I don't get—"

He patted his hand at her. "I'm getting there. The top one is from the school yearbook photos."

"Okay?"

Del sat forward, intent on her reaction. "The bottom one, you took graduation night. It's Noah."

Grace looked back at the screen and tried to figure out what he wanted her to see. "It's probably a trick of the light or something."

Frustrated with her lack of response, Del blurted, "They're the *same*, Gracie. Same eyes. Same color. Same shape. Same everything."

Pulling a face, she said, "Del. C'mon. This is a stretch. There's a reasonable explanation. They're blurry, over-enlarged photographs on a cell phone. *With* a crack in it. How did you even see this?"

Del shrugged, looking despondent. "Dunno. I was tired and my mind was wandering as I looked through the pictures. My cell glitched mid-swipe and, like, two images meshed."

Looking at Del's shattered screen, Grace said, "You need a new cell. It's probably messing with the picture and making you think you see something that's not there."

"Yeah, yeah." He sighed and covered his face with his hands. "It's stupid. I know. I just…"

She lowered her hands to her lap. "You want to go and see that reporter, don't you?"

His voice was muffled by his hands. "Yup."

She sighed and dropped Del's cell onto his knee. "I'll go get ready."

"I gotta go home first," Del muttered.

"Right."

There were times Grace was grateful Lan had the torment of overbearing parents who wanted her to succeed at all costs, and therefore was more progressive toward Grace's upbringing. Lan and Jonathan wanted her to succeed at her dreams, not theirs. As she watched Cassidy try to reign in her emotions regarding Del being out all night, today was one of those times Grace appreciated her family.

This was precisely the reason Del had asked her to go with him home. Cassidy had pounced the moment Del had opened the front door, scolding him for not calling and staying out all night. Del pushed by her and went straight upstairs, so Cassidy turned her ire to Grace.

"You realize he's grounded," Cassidy said as though it was Grace's fault Del was disobeying her.

Hovering in the front doorway, Grace raised her eyebrows and wished she'd waited in the car. "I'm sorry. He never said."

Cassidy huffed and tossed her twists over her shoulder. "Head in the clouds, just like his father." She gave Grace a searing look. "And I suppose you've been encouraging this 'career' choice of his."

"Absolutely," Grace said, battle stations at the ready. "It's a wonderful medium. Del's put so much work into his channel already, it would be a real shame if he didn't at least try."

"He wants to justify playing games all day."

Grace shook her head. "The sound alone is complicated to balance, let alone timing and editing. Playing games is a small part. There's also lighting and entertainment. Del's a *genius* with sound and effects and he's got a wonderful voice for commentary."

"He should expand his knowledge by going to college and studying like he said he would. If he's that keen, he could be a sound engineer, or whatever you call them."

Correcting Cassidy at this point would be a bad idea, so Grace said, "That would mean he only gets to do one part of the production. If he produces his own content, he gets to be involved in everything. I can't wait to see the stuff he can produce when he doesn't have to worry about homework."

Cassidy's regal face developed a scowl. "He's throwing away everything."

"What's the point of going to school when I could be

doing what makes me happy right now? Life's too short," Del snarled from the top of the stairs.

Exasperated, Cassidy pressed her fingers to her temples. "I don't think Fletcher would've wanted you to throw your life away on—"

"Fletcher wasn't going to college," Del said. "So, I don't think you get to lecture me on what he would or wouldn't have wanted. It's not like I'm doing this on a whim. You saw my projections. I'm already earning just below minimum wage through my videos, and that's just with part-time. I've got partnerships lined up. If I kept up my current growth through college, it could maybe support me through it. If I *fully* commit—"

Cassidy shook her head. "You would fail—"

"I could succeed," Del retorted. "And thanks for the vote of confidence."

"A college degree would—"

"—set me back years when I could be working on my channel. This is what I want to do! YouTube careers are viable; if I wait I'd have so much ground to make up. One year, Mom! That's all I'm asking! Noah is returning to school this year and he had a year off and—"

"I don't believe your new friend is a good role model," Cassidy said. "We know nothing about him, no matter how persuasive he might be—what sort of person who has left school still hangs around with—"

"He's *nineteen*, Mom. That's hardly ancient—"

"It's creepy and manipulative and I don't want to see my precious boy throw his life away by—"

"Oh, for fuck's sake, Mom, you'll use—"

"Language!" Cassidy scolded and raised a finger to Del. "Don't you dare raise your voice to me! I have sacrificed everything to—"

"You never listen! Is that what you're afraid of? That I could do it and ruin all the perfect plans you made for me?"

Grace's eyes felt like they couldn't get any wider as she

listened to Cassidy and Del yell at each other. It didn't feel right that she listen to their secrets like this, but she also didn't want to draw attention to herself.

Del's gaze switched to Grace and he jerked his head to indicate she get out of there. As much as she wanted to support Del, getting in the middle of an argument seemed like a bad idea, so she bolted. Cassidy had been much more reserved at the graduation dinner but now Grace realized Cassidy had bided her time so she didn't make a scene and spoil the banquet.

Feeling like a coward, Grace sat in her car and chewed on her nail while listening to the raised voices inside. Not sure what she could do to help Del, she decided to be practical and picked up her cell to dial Lloyd.

It didn't take long for Lloyd to answer. "Hey-o Grace-e-o, what's shakin'?"

Humored by his greeting, Grace pushed aside her torment to smile. "What have you been watching?"

"Nope. Nah-ah. I plead the fifth."

"I'm telling Tamara."

"*Au contraire, mon ami.* Tammy is here with me."

Grace laughed as she heard Tamara's loud '*hola*' in the background. "Alas, foiled. Listen, you know those reporters from last night?"

Lloyd made a noise of disgust. "Yep. What about them?"

Grace glanced at Del's house. "How long after we left did they stay?"

"Erm… not long."

"They said some things," Grace said and chewed her lip. "And, well… I was wondering—"

"Reporters shit-stir, you know that," Lloyd replied.

"I do. More than anything. But Del's up in arms about it."

A rustling noise, then the background noise vanished as Lloyd paused the television. "What'd they say?"

Grace sighed. "They implied Fletcher might've been

murdered."

"Ahh."

Brow furrowing at the unexpected understanding in his voice, Grace accused, "You know something."

"Nope. Nothing. Nada. Zilch."

Grace shook her head. "You're so transparent. Spill."

Lloyd huffed out a breath. "Okay. Look. You can't tell Aly. I'm not sure she could handle it right now, but"—his voice sounded cringey and rose pitch—"I… kinda, maybe, put in an app for Fletcher's accident report."

Grace nodded to herself. "That's a given." Lloyd was going to college to be a journalist and he wrote stories for the local newspaper on occasion, so often applied for police reports so he could practice.

"Well, I didn't get it," Lloyd continued, his voice normal again. "They cited some nonsense about it being an ongoing investigation."

That confused Grace. "That can't be right. It was closed. Dad said it was."

She could hear the skepticism in Lloyd's voice. "I dunno, but they're not giving out information. Thing is, I overheard someone mention the FBI in the background."

Grace scratched her fingernail against the steering wheel. "Yeah, my dad admitted the FBI had been interested in Fletcher's case and I met the agent who was questioning Aly."

Lloyd made a noise of agreement. "There's no reason for it to be an ongoing case if it was an accident. There are inconsistencies," he said, going into lecture mode and Grace had the sense he'd been sitting on this for a while. "Why was he across that side of town anyway? He picked up pizza and then went over the bridge, in the complete opposite direction of Aly's house. His place isn't that direction either, so he wasn't on the way home. Where was he headed? Also, the speed, there were tire marks on the road which don't match up with the claim of accident. There were burn marks on the railing too hot for a bike and impacts that don't match what they said happened. I got the impression Fletcher was deliberately avoiding something. Or running from something. There's something they're not telling us."

"Del mentioned that too. So many unanswered questions."

"Yeah," Lloyd continued, sounding sheepish again. "We've been talking about it a lot."

That disturbed Grace and she didn't know why. Del hadn't mentioned this to her at all. "So, these reporters might be for real?"

"Might be. Are you going to go talk to them?"

"I think we have to," Grace said. "Del's got it in his head he needs to."

"Do you want backup?"

"Not sure if that's a good idea at this stage," Grace said as she saw Del exit his home, carrying a small satchel. Cassidy came out after him and they continued to argue on the front porch. "But listen, maybe we'll come round after, if that's cool. We could use someone to talk to about this. It depends on what they say."

"More the merrier," Lloyd replied.

"I'll make sure he's dressed," Tamara called in the background.

Watching Del storm toward the car, Grace said, "Okay, thanks, Lloyd."

Del tossed a satchel in the back of Grace's car and flopped into the passenger seat. Eyeing Cassidy and her ball of rage still on the porch, Grace asked, "Del? You okay?"

He grunted at her, turning his face away so she couldn't see how upset he was. "Just go."

Apex Inn was named as such because it sat on a triangular piece of land between two roads. Since it was run by the Owen family, Grace was unsurprised to see Wanita Owen, one of Madison-Lee's friends, manning the front desk for her parents.

Wanita raised her head in surprise as Del held the door open for Grace. "Grace? Del? What…" A sly grin formed on her face. "I never suspected the two of you—"

Del, still angry from the fight with his mother, snapped, "If we were, do you really think we'd be stupid enough to come here?"

The smile melted from Wanita's face. "I—"

Placing her hand on Del's arm to keep him calmer, Grace said, "Those two reporters from last night, they're staying here. They said we should drop in and talk."

Wanita nodded and picked up the phone. "Sure, just lemme tell them you're here." Punching some numbers, she waited, then beamed. "Hello Joseph, this is Wanita from reception. You have some visitors, Grace Locklear and Del Cook, they go to… yes of course." Hanging up the phone, Wanita grabbed up a map of the motel and circled a room before passing the map to Grace. "They've been waiting for you."

"Thanks," Grace said with a smile as Del pushed away from the counter and stalked to the door. Grace hurried after him. "Maybe we shouldn't do this today."

He held the door open for her. "No time like the present."

"Yeah, but I'm concerned about—"

"I'm fine."

She fell into step beside him. "You know I don't believe you for a second. What do you really hope to uncover?"

"The truth. Something. Anything. An answer, a justification. My best friend is *gone* and I—"

Tears pricked at Grace's eyes from the pain in Del's voice. He rarely talked about Fletcher and Grace knew he hurt.

Del threw up his hands. "—I was *replacing* him with someone who could've been involved in his death."

"We don't know that," Grace replied. Placing her hand on his shoulder, she soothed, "It's not a crime to make new friends. Fletcher wouldn't have wanted you to feel that way."

His voice cracked as he spoke, "I want answers. It's wrong. It's all wrong and I need to know why."

She nodded. Anger was a sign of grief and she'd gone through something similar. "So do I, but what if we don't find anything? What if these people are full of shit and preying on us? Noah's nice. I like him. Aly likes him. You like him too."

Nodding grumpily, Del pressed his lips together.

"Why didn't you tell us how you were feeling?" Grace asked, reaching out to catch his arm. "We could've helped."

Del couldn't look her in the eye. "Yeah, yeah."

"Del—"

"Good morning," Joseph called from ahead of them. He leaned his elbows on the balcony railing overlooking the parking lot, slicing at an apple with a sharp pocket knife.

"Hey," Del said, thrusting his hands into his pockets. "We have questions."

Derailed and dismissed, Grace removed her hand from Del's arm.

Joseph straightened and brushed his hand over his pristine white shirt. "Come in," he said and gestured the motel door. "We have motel-grade coffee and chocolate chip cookies."

While Del went straight in, Grace lingered in the doorway.

Working on her laptop, Elaine sat cross-legged in the middle of one of the queen beds in the room. Beside her on the bed rested a tablet, which at present displayed an upside-down photograph of Fletcher. Looking up as they came inside, Elaine smiled and closed the laptop. "Hello. Since you're here, I take it you were unsatisfied with Aly's response."

Del and Grace shared a look. "We haven't spoken to Aly," Grace said.

"We want to know why you think Fletcher was murdered and why you think Noah was involved," Del demanded, his hands clenched into fists and ready to fight.

Elaine sighed. "You know," she said to Joseph. "I still find it odd he went back to that name instead of picking a new one. Didn't he think we'd figure him out?"

"I still say it was a deliberate choice. Bait," Joseph replied. He moved so he leaned against the bench with the television on it.

"He's practically *begging* Darcy to come get him," Elaine said, rolling her eyes.

"Well, he always was a little shit," Joseph said, folding his arms on his chest. "Maybe it's part of the game."

Confused, Grace interrupted their conversation, "What are you talking about?"

Elaine flicked a glance at Grace, then returned her attention to the computer. "We're looking for Aly. We need to talk to her and since she vanished, you're the next best option."

"She hasn't vanished," Del snapped. "She's on holiday with her mom."

"Uh-huh. Right. When was the last time you talked to her? Or to Noah?" Elaine asked.

"I talked to Noah last night," Del snapped and Grace saw Joseph's eyebrows raise at that. A cell beeped a message as Del continued, "I'm asking the questions here. Why do you think Fletcher was murdered?"

As Joseph lifted his cell, Elaine smiled. "Because Fletcher Norman never existed."

CHAPTER 17

Huddled in a ball in the corner of a storage cupboard, Aly rested her head against the wall and stared at the door. Every few minutes her eyes would droop shut before she jerked them open again.

She didn't know what time it was. She didn't know how long she'd been in the cupboard. She didn't know if it was night or morning. She didn't even know if Noah was still alive. She'd felt nothing from him the entire time she'd been locked away and only Ross' promise to kill Noah if she tried anything kept her still.

She knew she slept because the shock of waking up thinking the bang from outside was a gunshot was an experience she didn't want to repeat. Fear kept her motionless, even as she strained her ears for any sounds. Hopelessness and thirst set in as her thoughts tore her up inside. Tears left her feeling numb and broken. Her throat felt scratchy and as she hummed to herself in the darkness, her voice cracked more often than she hit the right notes. Squeezing her eyes shut, she tried to banish the shadows playing tricks along the edges of her vision.

The sound of a motorbike echoed from beyond the door and Aly strained her ears to hear. She'd heard a car engine a little while ago, but because she'd heard movement outside her door, she hadn't thought they'd left.

A voice in the distance called a greeting, then silence grew from beyond the door again.

Stomach grumbling and bladder becoming uncomfortable, Aly curled up tighter.

Footsteps thudded toward the door and a jangle of keys outside.

Aly blinked and shielded her face as the sudden rectangle of light blinded her.

"Bonnie says we need to let you use the bathroom," Ross said. "Behave yourself."

"Can I see Noah?" she asked. As she labored to her feet, her knees creaked in protest from being in the same position for so long.

Ross rolled his eyes. "Do your girl thing, on your best behavior, then we'll see."

The indignation caused a flare of temper. "You're a real insensitive jerk."

He laughed. "Bonnie tells me that too."

Aly tried to memorize everything she could on her way to the bathroom. Entrances, exits, open windows. The place they were in felt like an old manager's office, high above a factory floor, but because of the emptiness and dilapidated appearance of the warehouse, the factory had been closed for a long time. Walls were cracked and the paintwork chipped or covered in graffiti. Windows were cracked or shattered. Newspapers and broken bottles lay discarded on the stained concrete floor. Mold in the corner and other things Aly didn't want to look closely at. A main room, where Tango and his propped up leg lingered, and several offshoots rooms along the hallway beside the cupboard she'd been in.

"Can I have my bag?" she asked, having spotted it beside Tango.

"Why?"

Her eyes skipped over a surveillance camera mounted

in the corner and wondered why the room, which looked so ratty, had surveillance. "I need to clean my teeth and get changed."

Ross smirked. "Sure. If you give us the passwords to your phone and laptop."

That told Aly a few things. They'd already been through the bag and deemed it not dangerous. They'd taken her laptop from her car and couldn't get into it. And they thought she had information on her cell that they needed.

Since she didn't, she bargained, "I'll give you my cell password. Not my laptop one."

Ross raised his eyebrows. "Something to hide?"

"Nope, but it's got all my personal files on that and I don't want you snooping through it without me watching."

"You're not really in a position to bargain."

She stood her ground. "And yet, here I am, doing it anyway."

Ross looked unimpressed. "Tango, bring the bag and her cell."

"You are kidding me, right?" Tango called. "Injured!"

"But not dead."

"I took a bullet to my—"

"I can get it," Aly said. "I'll unlock the cell at the same time."

Ross waved his hand in a vague manner as he stepped to the side to allow Aly by. "Fine. Do it. Cell's on the table."

Picking up her cell, she kept her screen hidden from Tango and Ross to sign in. As discreetly as she could, she disabled her Do Not Disturb function. Maybe if someone called, or even Rex, then she might be able to get some help. Dumping it on the table beside the two laptops, one hers, one Noah's, she said, "There."

Ross scooped it up.

"I don't know what you're trying to accomplish," Aly muttered, picking up Noah's bag. "There's nothing on there."

"You'll be surprised."

Aly nodded. "Yup, I would be. New phone, dumbass. All you're going to see is me complaining to my friends about exams and the fact I like way too many farm games." Noah's number wouldn't be on her recent calls. She made sure to delete their messages and memorized his number. Paranoia meant she kept nothing vital in her cell anymore.

Her laptop was a different story, though, and there was no way she'd give Ross her password for that.

The bathroom had water. Maybe she shouldn't have been surprised at that, or the almost new condition of the toilet, considering the newness of the locks on the doors. She decided this must be a safe house. By all appearances, it was abandoned, until one looked closer. Even though there was no shower, Aly was insanely grateful for the toilet. Ross stood guard outside and could probably hear everything which happened in the room, but Aly didn't care. She washed the dried blood from her hands in the sink, then cleaned the rest of herself as best she could. There was no mirror, so she couldn't check her face from Ross' hit, but splashing cold water on it soothed some of the aches and bruising. Changing her bloody shirt, she repacked everything in the backpack carefully.

A deep breath didn't help settle her nerves, but she knew she couldn't remain inside the bathroom for long, so she gulped and faked bravado.

Bonnie sat at the table beside Tango, with several paper bags ahead of her and four Starbucks coffees, having returned while Aly had been in the bathroom. Spotting Aly, Bonnie lifted a cup and beckoned, then offered the cup to Aly.

Unsure, Aly crept over and accepted the cup from her. Wary, she took the lid off it so she could sniff the contents before taking a tentative sip.

"We didn't poison it," Ross said, his attention fixed on

Aly's phone as he flopped into a chair.

Pressing her lips together, Aly didn't say anything. Gingerly, she sat on one of the chairs and hunched her shoulders. She didn't know what was going on but rather than draw attention, she decided to glean as much information as she could before she was locked up again.

Tango dug through one of the paper bags. "Ooh, yes. Wonderful."

Bonnie's hands fluttered and Tango looked over at Ross.

"Your fave," Ross translated.

Carefully, Tango signed, *'Thank you'*, which made Bonnie beam. She reached over to clasp Tango's shoulder and gave him a friendly shake and Aly saw Tango smile genuinely for the first time.

"Um," Aly said, unsure. "Not to be rude—"

"Bonnie has a form of aphasia," Ross said, his attention still on the phone. He waved a hand at his head. "A bullet damaged her language center." He looked up and smiled fondly at Bonnie. "Took a while for her to relearn how to talk and we still can't manage verbal, but she understands just fine."

"Oh," Aly said, then told Bonnie, "I'm sorry."

Bonnie inclined her head and Ross continued, "Coincidently, same fight which had Noah shot in the heart. I don't suppose you'd know anything about that."

Aly stared at the paper bag and kept as still as she could.

"Yeah, what is the deal with him being bulletproof?" Tango muttered. "I put three into him."

Ross frowned. "We asked you not to shoot him."

"You were the one who said we needed to take her first. Before Noah got to her." Tango shrugged. "He pissed me off. *She* pissed me off by running. She is lucky I was not aiming for her."

If Aly could make herself smaller, she would.

Bonnie lifted her hands, her fingers flying and her face

twisted into a snarl as she glared at Tango.

Ross gasped and pressed a hand to his chest in mock outrage. "Bonnie!" he scolded. "Such language."

The glare swung to Ross and Bonnie's gestures changed into something Aly could clearly identify as rude. She flushed and dragged her eyes away, while Ross laughed at Bonnie and Tango looked amused at the interaction.

Ross said to Tango, "S'all good, bud. Still a lot of instinctual programming you're fighting. Just next time, aim for the legs, please."

Tango sat back and lowered his head. "Yeah. Okay." Looking at Bonnie he said, "I will try. For you."

Satisfied, Bonnie smiled at him and returned to her food.

Concentrating on Aly's cell, Ross said, "You really have nothing on this phone, do you?"

"I told you," she replied with no attempt to hide the sulky tone.

"Since when did a teenage girl have *nothing* on her phone? What has Noah been teaching you?"

Aly shrugged. "Last phone was taken as evidence. Didn't feel like personalizing that one yet."

"Uh-huh."

Lifting her head, Aly kept her voice meek. "May I see Noah?"

Ross looked at her. "Why?" he asked, smirking. "Do you think Noah's going to magically wake and spring to your rescue the moment you step into the room?"

"No," Aly said, even though she suspected he might. "I just need to see him."

"No dice. Eat your breakfast. We have a long way to go today."

"Where are we going?"

Ross grunted. "You know what? Talk again and you'll be going in the trunk."

Shocked, Aly recoiled and pressed her lips together. Tango snickered, while Bonnie seemed to be scolding Ross again. Aly hunched her shoulders and reached mutely for one of the bags on the table.

Unwrapping the paper, Aly picked up a wedge of the bacon and egg toasted sandwich and bit into it without tasting.

Ross pressed Aly's cell to his ear and listened. "Man, your mom is practically begging you to call her."

Aly hunched her shoulders even further.

"Misunderstanding," Ross said. "Things you don't know, blah, blah, you're in danger." He snickered. "Hmm, what does Mommy know that you don't?"

Aly, refusing to say anything, shoved the wedge of sandwich in her mouth and chewed as though her life depended on it.

"Your friend Grace is berating you for not telling her about your vacation," Ross continued. "Now, she's talking about some party. Ugg."

She glared at Ross.

"Boring," he said. "You teenagers and—" He paused and Aly watched as his expression slowly hardened and he sat up straighter. "You said Elijah is going by Elaine."

Mute, Aly nodded.

Ross dropped his hand so he held the cell out ahead of him and thumbed the screen. "Explain this."

"*Hey, so,*" Grace said, "*I really need you to call me as soon as you get this. Del's spouting off conspiracy theories. We had some reporters stirring up trouble at the lake last night and Del's... well, they said Fletcher was murdered and insinuated that Noah was involved. She... I mean, Noah's familiar in a way I can't explain and... Aly, what's his deal? She said... well...*" Grace sighed. "*Del's.... he's... running with this theory that Fletcher was involved in something. This reporter last night fired him up in all the wrong ways and I need you to help calm him down. She said— she said 'Elaine's looking for you'? What does that mean? If Del gets his way, and he probably will, we're gonna go talk to her this morning. Call me.*"

Aly's lungs seized. No matter how she struggled, she

couldn't make them fill. Grace was in danger. So much danger and Aly needed to find a way to warn her.

"Care to lie again about how you're not working for Darcy?" Ross snarled. He jerked out of his seat so hard he knocked his chair over. He pulled a gun out of his holster to wave around to menace her.

Aly's attention honed in on the gun.

"Tell me how—"

Aly flung her coffee at his face. With a pained yelp, Ross reared away from her, trying to sweep the hot liquid out of his eyes. Planting both hands on the table, Aly shoved it as hard as she could at Bonnie and Tango before they could rise, then lunged for Ross' gun.

Grabbing the muzzle, she twisted his wrist back on itself and away from her. She chopped at Ross' wrist with her other hand and kept twisting until the gun was almost pointed at him. He bent, struggling with the gun and she smacked him in the face with the palm of her hand and then kicked him in the shin as hard as she could.

With a wordless cry of pain, Ross' hand went slack. Aly snatched the gun, shoved Ross away and danced clear.

Panting, heart pounding and completely unable to believe she'd managed to pull that move off, she checked the magazine and safety like both Jonathan and Noah had taught her. As Ross swiveled to Aly to confront her, she raised the gun. "Just try it."

Ross scowled at her. "You wouldn't—"

Aly fired at the camera in the corner to show she wasn't messing around. Ross' duck was instinctual, as was the twist to stare at the broken camera in shock. Shifting the muzzle to Bonnie, Aly said, "Gun on the table, right now." She moved to Tango. "You too."

With a cautious glance at Ross, Bonnie obeyed by placing her gun on the table and sliding it away from her. Keeping her gun up, Aly scooted forward and picked up Bonnie's gun. Checking the safety, she tucked it into her belt.

"I am not carrying," Tango muttered.

She didn't believe that for a second. "Hands up," she said, gesturing.

Ross leered, "You won't be able to—"

Relying on bravado and adrenaline, and filled with the certainty the bruise on her face would be the least of her injuries if she failed now, Aly snapped, "You don't know anything about me and what I can do. So you're going to shut up and do what I say."

Ross lazily lifted his hands to show compliance. "Fine. What do you want?"

She had no clue. None at all. She hadn't expected the snatch to work. Adjusting her stance, she fumbled for a plan. Her gaze fell on the room Ross had kept her in. The door had a padlock on it, with the key in the padlock. Taking a step back, she gestured with the gun. "Ross and Tango, in there. Drop the car keys on the table. Bonnie can let you out when I'm gone."

With a sigh, Ross gestured his pocket and said, "Can I?"

Aly nodded, keeping the gun on him. Her heart pounded, her hands felt sweaty and she was hyper-aware of every movement Ross, Tango or Bonnie made. Primed for a retaliation attack, she wasn't going to take any chances.

Reaching into his pocket, Ross pulled out a set of keys and left them on the table ahead of him. "I don't see what this is going to accomplish."

"I will *not* be your hostage." She jerked her gun at Ross and Tango, indicating they should head toward the small room. "Now move. You," she told Bonnie, "stay."

"We're just going to find you again," Ross said as he followed her instructions.

She knew that, but she wasn't going to give him the satisfaction. They probably had a tracker on her, in the backpack or on their cars. She could worry about that later. "Uh-huh."

He sneered at her. "It'll be easy. Next time, we won't be nice about it."

Nervous, she adjusted her grip on the gun. "Shut up."

Certain the exaggerated limping from Tango was a way stall while they figured out a way to unarm her, Aly held her ground a distance from them. She instructed Bonnie to cross the room and padlock the door after Tango and Ross were inside, then forced her to move away while Aly checked the lock.

Satisfied, Aly said to Bonnie, "Of the three of you, you seem to be the only one concerned about the welfare of me and Noah, so thanks for that. But I won't hesitate to shoot you and I don't think you can regenerate like he can."

Bonnie's eyes widened.

Keeping her gun trained on Bonnie and a good distance between them, Aly checked her cell, then open contacts. "Since Noah didn't kill you when he had the chance," Aly said, leaving the cell on the table and backing away, "I assume he's concerned for your welfare too. Put a contact number in there."

Wary, Bonnie stepped forward and picked up the cell. While Bonnie typed, Aly grabbed both laptops and Noah's backpack. "Take me to Noah."

Bonnie regarded Aly, then nodded. Placing the cell on the table, Bonnie walked to one of the other doors and gestured for Aly to follow. Snatching up her cell and the car keys, Aly followed, careful to keep a good distance from Bonnie.

This resistance was a bluff; if Bonnie went after her, Aly knew she was doomed. She was twitching, panic boiling below the surface, threatening to spill from her and into the world. Every sound was Ross trying to escape or a surprise attack from Bonnie. Sweat trickled down her spine and made her grip slippery but somehow she kept her resolve. Aly knew she overcompensated by trying to look everywhere at once, taking note of everything, but she couldn't help it.

Bonnie led Aly down some rickety metal stairs to the bottom floor of the warehouse, to an old shipping container sealed on the outside with a thick chain. Still two cars in the warehouse, as well as Noah's rental bike, and Aly didn't know which car the keys would work on.

Eyeing the container, Aly said, "Yeah, I'm not going inside that."

Bonnie shrugged as she unwound the chain and swung open the doors.

Aly jerked forward a step. Noah sprawled on a dirty mattress beside the wall. Sleeping or unconscious, she couldn't tell. Everything in her wanted to run to his side to check, but she kept herself still and focused on his chest for the rise and fall. She'd seen enough movies to know if she stopped paying attention now, Bonnie would lock her in there too.

She couldn't see his wounds and his shirt was fresh and without blood, with the one he'd been wearing crumpled on the floor beside the mattress.

Pointing her gun at Bonnie, Aly said, "Pull him out."

Lifting an eyebrow at her, Bonnie entered the shipping container and grabbed the mattress, heaving it toward the exit. For a heartbeat, Aly thought the movement would jostle Noah enough that he'd wake, but that hope was dashed as he remained still. She turned and used the car keys to determine which car it unlocked and waited for the beckoning beep. Leaving Bonnie to haul the mattress, Aly hurried to the car which unlocked, the other car than what they'd arrived in last night, and shoved the backpack in the trunk, then opened both the back seat doors.

Bonnie grabbed Noah under the arms and lifted him, dumping him in the back seat, following Aly's request to put a seatbelt on him.

Keeping the gun trained on Bonnie, Aly said, "Open the doors, then I'll give you—" Goose bumps burst onto the skin of Aly's lower back, shuddering up her spine until they reached her shoulders, then traveled down her arms. Not gentle tingles like she felt from Noah, deep shudders which felt like someone walking over her grave.

Shifters. Many of them. There was no mistaking that for idle goose bumps.

At least Noah was in the car and secured. All she had to do was escape.

Frowning, Bonnie tilted her head and signed to her.

What to do? What should she do? If they were friends of Ross and Bonnie, then Aly was doomed. If they *weren't* friends, Aly didn't feel right about leaving several Faceless at the mercy of whatever faction was out there. "Are you expecting anyone?"

Bonnie's frown deepened and she shook her head.

"Then you'd better run," Aly said. She took Bonnie's gun out of her belt, put it on the ground and kicked it away. "There's a bunch of shifters incoming. I can't tell how many, but—" a visible shudder ran through Aly, followed by a stab of pain to her belly. Fire burst against her, the sensation so strong it stole her breath and made her weak-kneed.

Making a concerned noise, Bonnie came toward her. Aly thrust up an arm, displaying the diamond-like goose bumps traveling over her arms. Bonnie's gaze fell on them and her eyes widened exponentially.

"*Lots* of them," Aly gasped and tossed Bonnie the key to Ross and Tango's room. "Within two hundred feet, that way, so you'd better hurry."

Bonnie's hands fluttered as she gestured Aly. Not understanding Aly shook her head and forced her legs to move toward the prickles, toward the chain to open the roller doors. The door rattled upward as fast as Aly could pull it while still holding Bonnie in check. Giving it one last yank, she let it rumble the rest of the way up on its own while she ran for the car.

Clambering into the driver's seat, Aly tossed Ross' gun and her cell onto the passenger seat and locked herself in.

Staring at her, Bonnie's hands dropped down to her sides and moved to the side.

Aly floored it.

From the intensity of the prickles, Aly expected an army to be waiting but the service road was empty. She sped in the direction away from the prickles.

She hadn't been able to get much of a look of the area last night, caught up in concern for Noah's well-being and the lack of light. She was in a warehouse district. Large buildings, some of them splashed with company names. A few trucks parked along the side of the road, ready to pick up their load.

Tense, she followed the signs to leave the area, the prickles chasing her on every turn. They faded in and out so much, she thought that they must be following her. She didn't have a lot of time and if she was going to get caught, she needed to make sure Grace and Del would be safe and not dragged into this too.

Taking a deep breath, she wiped a hand on her jeans and reached for her cell. Spotting an exit sign, she followed it as she thumbed through her contacts to Grace. Putting it on speaker, she settled it on her knee as she continued to drive.

Grace answered, "Aly!"

"Don't talk to Elaine," Aly blurted, taking a corner too fast. The cell slid from her knee and almost onto the floor before she grabbed it. "Frick."

"What?"

Aly puffed out a sigh of relief as she drove out of the warehouse district and spotted a sign for the freeway. The prickles seemed to have disappeared, which was good, but the fear wasn't ebbing. "Don't do it. She's dangerous. I can't explain right now, but you can't go and see Elaine. Don't go near her and—"

"We've already seen her."

Aly's world heaved, making her off-kilter. "And… and you're okay? You're not hurt?"

"Well, we had thought she was full of shit," Grace said, sounding angry. "But now, I'm not so sure. Aly, tell me and don't lie. Are you in Sac?"

Aly's blood ran cold.

CHAPTER 18

Grace spoke fast. "Elaine said Fletcher never existed. She said he was *murdered*. She said Noah was involved and she said you'd know. She said you remembered!"

"I… I can't—"

Grace pressed, a relentless wave of words that forced Aly under. "Aly, do you remember what happened? Do you know?"

"I—I—" Her mouth was dry.

"Joseph got a call and he said they were closing in on you in Sac and they left in such a hurry."

"Ah—"

"So we're following them and—Aly, what's going on? Why are you in Sac?"

Aly's head spun and she couldn't register Grace's questions anymore. She knew her friend spoke, but the words all melded together into a giant entanglement of sound. Without hanging up, she let the cell drop to her lap and stared out at the road ahead. She drove by a large sign giving directions to the freeway and followed it without thinking.

All the adrenaline was leaving her system, leaving her physically and emotionally exhausted. Safety was a luxury she didn't have right now, not with Noah passed out in the back seat. She had to put as much distance between her and Ross as she could.

Her face hurt. Her hands shook and her breathing felt raspy. There was a dull ache in her stomach. "You're okay," she told herself. "You're okay. You're going to get out of this. You're not safe, but you're okay."

"Aly? Aly? What's going on?"

"Did she hang up?" Del's muffled voice asked. "What's happening?"

"I don't know. I think I can hear her but… she sounds weird? Aly, is someone with you?"

Aly checked over her shoulder. "You're okay. You have him and he's… alive. I think. He better be. You're okay. Just drive."

Del suggested, "Hang up and try again."

She needed to calm down or she was going to start shrieking and she didn't think she'd ever stop. Taking a deep breath, she forced herself to exhale slowly and tried to apply some of the self-calming exercises her therapist had taught her.

A glance in the rear-view mirror and then the side ones, before she flicked on her indicator to change lanes. She drove on autopilot, her attention split between controlling her breathing to something which wasn't gasping and the road.

A few moments peace. Nothing but her, the road and a slowing heartbeat.

The world wasn't going to stop but it also wasn't going to end. She could do what needed to be done. To do that, she needed a clear head and air in her lungs. It was so much easier to concentrate on one thing. One thing only. Driving.

It was stupid and some part of her, some distant and far away part, knew that driving given the circumstances was incredibly dangerous. At the same time, she had no real choice. Stopping was just as dangerous.

It was a while before the protective bubble she created around herself decayed enough to let her hear the shrilling of her cell phone. She answered, speaking before Grace had a chance to. "I need you to shut up and listen. Put me on speaker. I don't have a lot of time."

A beep, then Grace asked, "What's going on?"

Panic rose again, bringing with it moments of clarity. "You saw Elaine," Aly said, checking the rear-view mirror for following cars.

"Yes."

"You're following her."

"Yes."

"Stop. Right now. Take the next exit and get away from there."

"Why?" Grace asked, skeptical. "What's going on?"

"Some very... very bad things. Bad people. Bad things. I can't..." Aly laughed mirthlessly. "I don't know how to explain."

Del said, "Aly-cat, what's going on? Does this have something to do with Fletcher?"

An unbidden tear escaped her eye. "Nothing and everything." She hiccupped and wiped her face, then winced in pain from the bruise. "They're dangerous," she continued. "They've killed people and they can be anyone and you'd never even know. You have to stop following them right now. Turn around. Get off the freeway. Take the back roads."

"You're shitting me," Del said.

"You think they'll kill us?" Grace asked, disbelieving. "They're reporters, Aly, they're not going to—"

"They're *not* reporters! There's so much going on I don't have time to explain. Please, trust me."

"Did they kill Fletcher?" Del asked.

"No," Aly said, her eyes darting around to check the car beside her. "Belinda Bell did because she thought he was protecting me."

"You?" Del blurted.

"Belinda Bell? That FBI agent?" Grace asked. "Not Noah?"

Aly laughed. "No way. Noah's… he's…" Aly swallowed. "It's a really, *really* long story and I don't want to do this over the phone. Where are you?"

"On the I-5," Del responded. "About ten minutes out from Red Bluff."

Aly tried to think. "Okay. Okay. Um… We need…"

Silence from the cell, then Grace said, "Aly, you're scaring us."

Scared. They were scared. She couldn't… she couldn't… Realization shuddered through her and she let her mouth wander with her thoughts. "This is… this is the decision he made and now I have to make it too and I can't… I can't involve you… it's dangerous and I'd never forgive myself and… except, he left and they came after me anyway, but that's because of Rex and there's no connection to you and—I need… You need to turn around and go home. You'll be safer at home. Go home, feign ignorance. I'll call you when I'm safe."

"You're not making any sense!"

Her mind went off on a tangent, planning things she needed to do. "I have to burn my cell."

Grace blurted, "We're not going to—"

"And ditch this car. I can't use this. What if they know how to find it?"

"Are you alright?"

She choked on a sob. "Nope. Nope. Not at all. I'm barely holding it together. It happened again and… he got shot and he's not waking up and he's supposed to be able to fix this and he's not and I'm so scared."

"Who got shot?" Del asked.

"Noah." Her hand crept up to clutch at her neck. "God, if I lose him again…" She swallowed the bile rising in her throat. "Please. Go home. I'm sorry. I love you." Fumbling for her cell, she ignored their protests as she hung up on them.

Dialing her mother, she blurted, "I wanted you to know I'm okay and I love you," then hung up on Penelope too. Realizing she couldn't ditch her cell because it had contact details she needed, she switched it off and hoped it couldn't be tracked that way.

Aly drove on a whim, taking roads as she felt like it, weaving on and off the freeway. Leaving Sacramento, she wasn't even sure which direction she headed until she saw a sign to Nevada. Taking the next turn, she headed toward some mountains.

As the gas gauge hit half full, Aly found a secluded place to stop and catch her breath. The scattered tears she'd allowed herself while driving had done little to ease the ache inside her. Even though she knew she shouldn't be breaking down yet, she couldn't help it.

Still wiping tears away, she checked on Noah and was relieved to feel the steady beat of his heart beneath her hand. His wallet still being in the back pocket of his jeans was both a surprise and a moment of sheer hysterical laughter for Aly. Ross and Bonnie hadn't done a good job of divesting them of supplies.

Noah had told her about an application which could create a burner phone on top of her current cell, but she couldn't for the life of her remember how to do that. She found a piece of paper and a pen in the glove compartment of the car and scribbled down Grace's, Penelope's, and Bonnie's cell numbers, then switched her phone completely off again.

Finding Noah's wallet meant she could ditch Ross' car. In the next town she spotted a car rental place and, with a bit of maneuvering, she managed to convince the rental lady she was fine and her 'brother' was suffering car sickness and had been sedated. She didn't think the lady believed her at all, especially with the bruising on her face, but she couldn't worry about it.

Exhaustion settled in sooner than Aly appreciated. Resting her elbow on the door frame and her head in her hand, she picked a road at random. Glancing over her shoulder at Noah, she wondered if perhaps he had been drugged like she'd bluffed at the rental lady and that was why he was still asleep. Thinking that was better than the alternative.

She didn't know what she was doing, but she knew she couldn't keep running waywardly. She needed a long-term plan. She needed a shower and a good cry. She needed food. She needed Noah to open his eyes.

With all her twisting and weaving, she found herself on the outskirts of Lake Tahoe and decided she'd had enough. Picking one of the towns scattered around the edge of the lake at random, she chose a motel off the main road where her rental car could hide in a parking bay out of sight from casual gaze. Paying cash for a room, she bribed the receptionist to help her haul Noah inside.

Once she'd tipped the receptionist heavily, secured their gear in the room, and barred the door as best she could, Aly broke. Large, shoulder-shuddering, chest-heaving sobs wracked her body as she curled up at the foot of Noah's bed.

It was so much, all at once and she knew it wasn't over. Traveling in a strange, detached mode, her entire will focused on keeping them safe and now everything crashed against her.

The tears didn't last long and were more cathartic than anything else. An ultimate release of all the pressure she'd felt in a quick burst. She felt safer than she had all day. In all her rigorous checking and doubling back she'd been unable to spot any cars following her and she hoped with all her unpredictability, they'd lost her.

If they hadn't, she had some time before they caught up. While she had no chance of sensing Ross and Bonnie, if the shifters she'd sensed before had chased her, she'd know. Hoisting herself off the floor, she checked on Noah.

Stroking her fingers across his forehead, she noted the

fine sheen of sweat coating his skin. His health seemed to be progressively worse each time she checked on him. While he seemed to be breathing okay, the blue tinge to his lips concerned her. Any worse and she might have to seek medical attention. She rolled him into a recovery position on his side, so that if he vomited in his sleep, he wouldn't choke.

At a loss for what to do, she double-checked the door, then grabbed a fresh shirt so she could shower, reasoning she should sleep while she had the chance.

As she stood in clean underwear, inspecting the bruising on her face in the steam-fogged mirror, she felt the first tingle trickle along her back. Dropping her hand from her face, she gaped at herself in the mirror. The tingles exploded; they poured over her, cascading and flowing along her skin, stronger and sharper and filling her with such elation.

A thump from outside the bathroom, then a croak, "Aly? Aly!"

She shoved her head into her shirt. "I'm here!"

Another thump and Aly burst from the bathroom, tugging her shirt down. Noah leaned heavily on the bed, his legs struggling to support his weight as he made his way around the bed. He raised his head as she came out of the bathroom. The sheer relief on his face as he lost control over his legs was staggering.

"Fletcher," she cried, darting to him. Ignoring the rivers of bumps on her skin, she looped her arms around his chest and heaved him from the ground so he could sit on the bed. "You're okay!"

His face dotted with sweat as he struggled to move. "Ssssum-ting in… drugged," he rasped, then gasped, his hand rising to hover against the side of her face with the bruise. "Oh!"

"I'm okay," she told him. "I'm more worried about you."

Noah squeezed shut his eyes. "Sssssafe?"

"For the moment."

"'kay. I gotta…" He twitched and rolled his shoulders, flinching his chest upward as he took stock of what had occurred in his body. "Stitches?"

Afraid to touch him, she sat beside him and rested her hands on her lap. "Yeah."

He twitched open his eyes and glanced at her arm. Lifting a shaking hand, he ran his fingers down her skin. "'kay?"

She spluttered out a laugh that turned into a sob. "Not even remotely, but that's not to do with you shifting."

Noah nodded and leaned toward her until their heads rested together.

Aly closed her eyes and concentrated on breathing while Noah's tingles washed over her. Intense and comforting; he was here, he was safe and he was going to be okay. He was fixing the damage done to him, removing whatever was in his system. Choked up and relieved beyond measure, she struggled not to cry.

Noah gagged and covered his mouth with his hand as a wet cough erupted through his chest. Gesturing for her to stay, he rushed for the bathroom.

"Fletcher?"

A gag and the sound of retching, then another liquid cough caused her to follow. She found him spitting blood in the bathroom sink.

"Fletcher!"

Hunched over the sink, he pried one hand away from the counter and waved. "'m fine."

"You're not fine!" she shrilled. Only the fact she still tingled kept her from panicking.

Turning on the tap, he rinsed his mouth out. Staying hunkered over the sink, he said, "I had to shut one lung down. This is old blood. Gotta get it out somehow, I can't absorb it."

She braced one hand on the door frame and pressed the other to her chest. Heaving in a breath, she tried to calm herself. "Shut down one lung, he says, like it's nothing. You scared me half to death!"

Noah rinsed out his mouth again. "I didn't mean to. I had to improvise. I didn't have time."

Turning so her back was on the frame, she slid down to the floor.

Noah winced as he straightened. "Shifting… hurts, Aly. For a complete heal, I need time and… peace. In the middle of a situation like that, I patch enough so that I can escape, but… they surprised me too and I… lost concentration." He glanced at her sheepishly. "I was worried about how so much shifting was affecting you."

"Don't worry about me," she told him.

He narrowed his eyes at her in the mirror. "You were shivering and your skin was—"

"*Your* shifts don't hurt me. Not in any way. Stop thinking they do."

He frowned. "Strange clarification."

"Oh, boy, do I have a story for you," she muttered. "Finish up first."

Peeling off his shirt, he inspected his back, cringing at the three patches. "Wow, he got me good."

"Bonnie fixed you. Did they drug you to keep you under?"

"Yeah." Placing both hands flat on the counter, he sighed and met his gaze in the mirror. "Ruth and Boaz. They're the last people I would've expected."

She felt so mentally exhausted now and it showed in her voice. "They believe you're working with Elaine. They were going to sell me to the highest bidder."

The tingles died as Noah sat down opposite her. Looping an arm around her legs, he hugged them to his chest and put his chin on her knees. "Tell me what happened."

The physical contact grounded her and gave her something to cling to. She told him everything she could, everything she could remember, what they said to her, what they said to each other. Second-hand embarrassment kicked in when she told him about her play for the gun. Cheeks flaming, she muttered, "It was stupid, I know. I could've been killed."

Shaking his head, Noah said, "You are amazing and it *worked*. That's the important bit. You got us both out of a bad situation and you didn't overthink it or doubt yourself. You just acted."

She still doubted. "Maybe I shouldn't have run, though. I mean, they're your siblings, right? Maybe they—"

"Last time I saw them, I'd been sent on a mission to kill them. That was… fifteen years ago. I don't know who they are anymore. They scared you, they taunted you"—he stretched out his hand to touch her face—"they hurt you, so you got us out." The tenderness in his smile did odd things to her stomach. "You're badass, Aly."

Flushing, she basked in his pride. "I don't think they can augment."

"I would be surprised if they could. We learned that after they escaped." Nodding to her, he said, "Keep going."

She told him about the setup of the warehouse and how she trapped Ross and Tango. She mentioned how she sensed the other shifters approaching and how it made her feel, which seemed to concern Noah, even if he didn't have any answers either. She told him of her escape and Grace's call. Grace had been the whole reason for her escape as it was.

Noah nodded thoughtfully. "I was wondering."

"Wondering what?"

He groaned and rubbed his hand over his face. "Del and his theories. It was only a matter of time."

Aly sighed. Leaning her head on the frame, she let her lashes fall closed, completely wrung dry of emotion. "They didn't go home, did they?"

"Probably not."

"I didn't make sense when I was talking to them. I was

babbling and panicked. That would've been…"

"Del would've been all over that." His fingers brushed her cheek. "Go get some sleep. Let me deal with this for a while."

She nodded, exhausted. "Okay."

"Hey," he said, his voice low and husky. "You did good today. You should be proud of yourself."

She tried to smile and caught his hand. Pressing her lips to the back of it, she then rested her forehead on his hand. "Tell me again after I've napped."

Aly's brain refused to stop conjuring up unwinnable scenarios or doubting the decisions she'd made. She lay tucked into bed with her eyes closed while Noah showered, then excused himself from the room to check their location. Even in the dark and quiet, she couldn't sleep.

Eventually, she gave up. Sitting in the middle of the bed, she hugged a pillow to her chest and turned on the television. Within minutes, Noah unlocked the door and slipped inside. "Can't sleep?"

She smiled at him. "'bout time."

Locking the door behind him, he snorted. "Timing me, huh?"

"You stepped into my range for a shift," she said. "I knew you were watching."

He flopped onto the bed beside her. Leaning against the headboard, he stretched out his legs on the bed. "My bad."

"That's okay, I forgive you. What's the plan?"

He shrugged. "I don't have one. Not yet. Couldn't get through to Del or Grace." He patted the air in front of him as he quickly assured her, "Doesn't mean anything. They could be screening calls, or out of range or—"

She didn't know if she had enough strength to panic again. "Del forgot to charge his cell again."

"Yeah. Exactly." He sighed. "I don't know what to do. I left a message. It's a long shot but if they call…"

"Then we deal with it."

"Yeah. I moved the car you hired to a different hotel, then rented a room and rigged up a motion sensor in there. That'll let us know if the room is disturbed. I have another hire car outside in case we need to book it."

He'd done much in so little time. Things she hadn't even thought of doing. "Wow."

"Oh, and I burned your phone for you. New number, but I left your SIM in, so make sure you use the app when you call out. I thought that would be best until we know more. Ross didn't have time to put a tracker on it, and you get to keep your farms."

"Yeah, cause that's important," she said, being sarcastic.

"Yup." He frowned at his shoes.

Sensing her joke fell flat, she cringed. "That's a bad face. Did I do something wrong? I used 'Rose Ward' like you said—"

He jerked his gaze to her. "No," he soothed. "You did everything right. I've been trying to figure something out, that's all. Not much is making sense right now. To clarify, you said Bonnie didn't expect anyone, but you felt a lot of them."

She nodded.

"Okay. So." He rubbed his chin. "Darcy put tracking devices in our bodies that we didn't discover until later, so I have no idea if Bonnie and Ross had them… or if they *still* have them and they're active and she's just… been watching or something."

"Assuming they still work. Wouldn't the batteries have run out?"

"She had the technology to grow people in vats," Noah said, with a shrug. "Maybe it charges off electricity in the body, I have no idea. But I need to see."

"She could've tracked Tango, too," Aly pointed out. "She would've had something in him for sure then."

"Exactly. And, unless Bonnie and Ross have been in

contact with my other siblings, they wouldn't know about the devices."

She ran a hand through her hair as she tried to follow his thoughts. "So you think Darcy's group was outside?"

"That's what's got me confused. Darcy conducts genetic experiments, she doesn't—" he hesitated and amended, "Well, she *didn't* used to have shifters working for her. That may have changed."

"Could it have been Welcher?" Aly asked. All she knew about the Welchers was it was one of the oldest factions, and they believed shifter society should be kept separate and pure. Their faction kept cropping up and that was a worry.

"If it was, how'd they find out?"

Staring at the television without seeing what was on, she worried a thumbnail with her teeth. "Maybe they were buyers? Ross did say there was a bunch of people who were interested in me."

"Maybe."

"What if it was Rex?"

"Maybe. Although I think Rex is trying to keep you a secret even from his people."

She said, "He was in the forest."

"Where his men shot at us," Noah pointed out. "He might've been honest with us when he said they were overzealous. They mightn't have known anything about you."

She puffed out a breath. She didn't like it, but she could accept that. "Good point."

"It's all pretty worrying."

Everything seemed so up in the air. All they had was maybe's. "So, what do we do?"

He was slow to answer. "I don't know."

"I got Bonnie's number. We could call and grill them for information."

Noah countered, "We could call Rex and grill him. He'd probably have more."

Aly pressed her lips into a thin line and stared straight ahead. As much as she was afraid of what Rex would say, Noah was right. He was their best chance of... of what, exactly?

Noah gripped the back of her shirt and tugged to get her attention. "Lovely, you're exhausted. Please, sleep while you can."

Sighing, Aly discarded the pillow she hugged in favor of cuddling him. Tucking herself into his side, she rested her head on his chest and Noah draped his arm down her back.

"What are we watching?"

Aly glanced at the screen. "Spanish sitcom apparently."

"Awesome."

She snuggled closer and closed her eyes. He was right, she was exhausted. It felt thick and heavy against her, and he was warm and safe. Hooking a leg over his, she tucked her toes between his calves then, realizing her shirt had ridden up, tugged it down to cover her. "Sorry."

"Hmm?"

"I'm not very"—she stifled a yawn—"glamorous at the moment. I know it's not something you want to see."

"I don't mind."

Too tired to filter her words, she said, "I could probably walk around naked and you wouldn't notice."

He spluttered and cleared his throat. "I'd definitely notice."

That surprised her. "You would?"

"Sure."

Curiosity piqued and roused her more than she wanted to. "But it wouldn't do anything for you."

"It does stuff for you, though, and I appreciate that. It's not..." he hummed. "Okay, it's not that I can't get aroused. I can. It's... it's a response without a reason. A 'huh, so that happened, it'll go away soon' rather than a 'oh my god, they're so sexy, I *must* have them'."

So warm and comfortable, but she wanted to talk.

"Because you're in control of everything your body does."

"Well… there's that part, but I still get involuntary, um, reactions."

"Oh."

Making a small, contented noise, he rested his hand on the back of her head then ran his fingers through her hair. "It's okay to ask questions. I wouldn't answer anyone else, but you're trying hard to understand. This is stuff we should talk about."

"I don't want to be rude. Or say the wrong thing. Or— or hurt you by asking things that make you uncomfortable."

"I know. And I appreciate that. But you can ask." He bopped her on the nose and she wriggled her nose at him like a rabbit. "After you get some sleep."

A yawn snuck out. "Don't wanna. This is nice."

His soft noise of content warmed her through. Her limbs felt heavy and the warmth of his body seeped into hers. Fingers toying with her hair and a comforting heartbeat lulled her to sleep.

CHAPTER 19

Alyson was more devious than anyone had previously believed. She'd given Belinda and her entire team the slip two months ago. Fooled everyone into thinking she remembered nothing. Escaped the twins. Twisted across California in a route no sane person would've taken.

Belinda wondered what the game was.

The interesting thing was the amount of information on Alyson's location Tegan was able to deliver to Belinda. The twins were quite formidable in tracking. Belinda didn't think she'd have been able to follow Alyson's twisting path. It made her question how they'd done it. Had they managed to get a tracker on her? Or were they following some other form of breadcrumb?

Tegan directed Belinda to an unimpressed Gomez and his mimic detection device, and then on to Lake Tahoe, but couldn't give her any more information than that. Alyson was somewhere in the area, which made Belinda curious because there was still a few hours of daylight left for travel. Who was she meeting?

Tegan said the twins were around, conducting their own investigation, so Belinda needed to be careful. When Tegan suggested that Belinda search the motels around the lake and mentioned that Alyson was also going by the name Rose Ward, Belinda knew.

Rose Ward. Belinda laughed to herself. A pretty clear admission the girl remembered everything. Belinda would've bet her right arm that the person she was meeting up with was a certain Will Ward, the elusive mimic she'd captured protecting Alyson two months ago.

The third hotel Belinda and Gomez visited had a guest called Rose Ward in residence.

Aly woke to a weight beside her, a gentle nudging and the smell of pizza. She groaned and covered her face with her hands.

"C'mon, Als," Noah crooned. "It's got pineapple. Can you smell it? That sweet, tangy goodness mingled with ham and cheese. Your mouth should be watering by now."

"Sweet talker," she mumbled.

With exaggerated chewing sounds, Noah said, "Hmm. *Delicious.*"

A slight heat close to her face and the smell of food increased, but still out of reach. "Meanie."

"I can't waft anymore without leaving this on your face."

Keeping her eyes closed, she opened her mouth expectantly.

"Nope. Sit up. Get it yourself."

Grumbling, she took her time heaving tired muscles and a heavy head upright. "You're not a very good boyfriend."

"Maybe, but I'm an excellent best friend who won't fall for any of your shit."

Giggling, Aly shoved him. "Dork."

He plopped the piece of pizza he'd been wafting in her face in her hands. "Eat up," he said and licked his fingers.

She took a bite of her pizza, smiling as she noticed he'd pulled all the pineapple from his piece and stacked it on hers. "Your pizza habits haven't changed."

"Nasty, filthy stuff," he mocked. Smiling, he sprawled out on the bed beside her, balancing his weight on an elbow. "We haven't done this in ages."

She nodded as she chewed. "Been busy. And trying to hide the fact we know each other."

He nodded. "Hmm. We need to move soon."

Straight to business, which meant he left her sleeping until the last possible moment he could and was now anxious to move. "I figured. How long was I out?"

"About three hours. I wish I could give you longer."

"It's fine. Do we have a plan?"

"Yup. Ross and Bonnie are going to meet us."

Aly paused, her mouth open to take a bite of her pizza. "What?"

"In a crowded place," Noah assured her. "I have a meeting place all mapped out. I need to see if they've got tracking devices so I can warn them."

She lowered the half-eaten slice to her lap. "Oh."

"I owe them that much at least."

"So… you've already talked to them?"

"Short, precise instructions. You don't need to come, Aly," Noah said, reading her mood. "I can—"

"No," she responded with a sharp shake of her head. "I'm not staying behind to worry myself to death. So, we see if they're being tracked, then what?"

"Play the conversation by ear," he said. "See if anyone else shows up following them."

Staring at a spot on the bedspread, she nodded. "Then… call Rex."

His smile dropped. "If you want to."

"I want answers. I want to know why feeling so many shifters at once hurt me like it did. I want… closure."

"Okay." Dusting off his hands, he sat up. "We're not coming back here, so make sure you take all the complementaries."

"Right." She took another bite of the pizza slice and

chewed slowly as she watched him stretch before he stood to check his gun. "I feel guilty about all the money we're wasting."

"Don't," he said with a sharp shake of his head. "Sometimes this is what you have to do to give people the slip. We can make it up when we're safer."

"Is… is this our life now? Running from motel to motel?"

Leaving the gun on the counter, he gave her his full attention. "It's too soon for that, Als. It really is. There's still so much up in the air. So much we don't know. I really think your—Rex will be able to give us a solution. He must've had contingency plans."

"Yeah." Dropping the crust in the box, she headed for her jeans and pulled them on. Doing up her jeans, she said, "Just promise me something."

Noah's eyes were fixed on her, watching her every movement, like he was trying to determine what was going on in her mind. "What?"

Head down, she sat on the corner of the bed and shoved her foot in her shoe. "Don't let yourself be captured to protect me."

Noah looked pained at the suggestion. "Aly—"

"You lost Fletcher because of me. Belinda Bell captured you because of me. Tango shot you because of me. You've lost *everything* because of—"

"I *have* everything because of you." He crossed to her as he spoke, dropping down to kneel in front of her. "Don't do this to yourself. Please. None of this is your fault."

Resting the tips of her fingers on the hollow of his throat, she said, "It feels like it is. I don't want you to get hurt."

"And I don't want *you* to get hurt." Catching her hand, he lifted it to his mouth to kiss the back. "Let's keep each other safe." Swallowing, she nodded and he squeezed her hand. "C'mon, lovely. I promise we'll have that movie night and Snickers galore when this is over."

She smiled, as desperate for normality as he was. "I'm going to hold you to that."

Lake Tahoe was large, with many towns dotted along its edge and a road that threaded along the bank. With Noah driving, Aly could stare out the window and really appreciate how pretty it was. She hadn't been paying attention when she drove in and didn't really know where she was, but Noah drove with purpose, without referencing a map.

"Have you been here before?" she asked as he turned down a road she hadn't seen any signs for.

He flashed her an easy smile. "Yes. Spent about six months here with Rex's group. Really pretty country." With a wink, he said, "I know all the secret haunts."

"Does that mean it's dangerous to be here?"

His smile faded. "No idea. It's been years. We could be shifter central for all I know. Did you feel anything?"

"No."

"Let me know if you do."

"Okay." Glancing out the window of the car, she asked, "We're going down by the water?"

"No. That's too open. There's a park I have in mind. It's usually populated, but it's also secluded and there are several entrances." He grinned at her. "You'll like it. It's very pretty."

Pretty was an understatement. Even in the summer, the park was gorgeous. Tall majestic trees, brilliant green grass for picnics, barbecues and children's play areas, it even boasted a small, ankle deep stream where several young children waded. She wished she had a sketchpad.

With Noah's shifts tingling down Aly's arms, they strolled through the park to a concrete table and chairs surrounded by redwood trees and large shrub-filled garden beds. Secluded and private, hidden away beneath the redwoods, but with a good, angled view out. It wasn't good for Aly to see, but she guessed Noah could.

Adjusting his backpack, Noah said, "Now, we wait."

Aly bounced up on the table to sit and propped her feet up on the seat. "The worst part," she said, then smiled. "For me at least. You can see everything."

He shot her a smile. "I'll warn you when they come." Unhooking the backpack, he placed it beside Aly and gave it a pat. "Our lifeblood. If you get up and move around, take it with you."

She hooked an arm through the strap. "Absolutely. I just got my laptop back. There's no way I'm leaving it behind again."

Noah prowled, constantly shifting as he took in their surroundings. Aly watched him, wishing she could do more than sit and act like bait. Turning her gaze away, she looked through the trees at the other people in the park going about their everyday lives. Parents with their kids. People with their loved ones. Sighing, she cupped her face in a hand and rested her elbow on her knee, watching a couple flirt and laugh and pepper each other's face with kisses as they walked. Tonight, they'd be able to go back to their families, safe in their homes, without caring what else lay out there.

Was she ever going to see her family again? The thought she mightn't pained her.

"What's wrong?" Noah asked.

"Hmm?"

"You made a noise in your throat," he said and tried to follow her gaze to find out what she'd been looking at. "Sounded like a whimper."

"Oh... nothing. I'm okay." He regarded her and Aly dropped her gaze to her shoes. "I'll *be* okay. I was... I was thinking about Tim. I may not get to see him again, and I... I don't want that."

With an expression twisted with pain, Noah made to speak, then jerked his head away. "They're coming."

Tensing, Aly forced herself to stay sitting on the table, rather than finding someplace to hide. It was a tense minute before she spotted Bonnie and Ross walking through the park. "No Tango?" she murmured.

"He's taking up a sniper position," Noah said, indicating the direction with a finger.

Aly swallowed heavily and curled in on herself. "Yeah, this is *so* feeling like a trap."

"I know," he replied, sounding worried. "Do you want to leave?"

More than anything, but she said, "We're here. We need information. Let's see how it plays out."

Nodding, he said, "I want you to get up from where you are and go lean on the trunk of the redwood to my left, back to the creek."

Hoisting Noah's backpack onto her back, she did what he asked. "Okay."

"If he moves from his position, I'll sit on the table and whatever direction I face, move toward that tree. Be discreet."

She swallowed, trying to settle her nerves. "Sneaky. But you'll be exposed."

"I'll be watching him closely," Noah said, still focused on Bonnie and Ross. "There'll be warning. If I suddenly move, cower."

She nodded and wrapped her arms around herself and leaned her shoulder against the bark.

"Hey Als?" Noah asked, waiting until she looked at him before he gave her his lopsided smile. "Love you."

A happy grin burst from her face. "Love you too, bumble-butt."

The sudden proclamation from him soothed her and helped her maintain a calm demeanor as Bonnie and Ross approached. Noah moved so he was standing a little ahead of her, acting like a shield.

"Well," Ross said, stopping ahead of them. "I didn't expect to see you again."

Noah lifted one shoulder in a shrug. "Curiosity got the better of me."

Ross moved his attention to Aly. "And you—you surprised me. I didn't expect that kind of move from—"

"Get your eyes off me," Aly snapped.

Ross laughed softly under his breath. "Such a temperament."

Bonnie gestured Noah, who nodded and lifted his hands to sign in return. Aly recognized a somewhat crude gesture.

Bonnie looked affronted and signed some more, while Ross said, "You know sign language? That wasn't part of our training."

"Maybe not yours," Noah evaded.

Watching them, Aly wished she'd taken the time to learn sign language too.

"I don't care whose idea it was," Noah replied, speaking aloud. "Those drugs could've killed me had I been under any longer." He sighed and ran a hand through his hair. "Let's play a game. You answer one of my questions and I'll answer one of yours. You can go first."

Ross narrowed his eyes and glanced at Bonnie, who shrugged. "Where have you been? Last record of you was over ten years ago."

"California."

Ross frowned. Widening his stance, he crossed his arms over his chest and glowered. "That's real helpful."

Noah shrugged. "Sorry, not giving you specifics."

Brightening, Bonnie clapped her hands and signed something.

Ross started nodding part way through. "That's right. That kid." He pointed at Aly. "That friend of yours. All this started after he died, right? You really weren't lying about knowing him since you were eight?"

Aly snorted. "Nope."

Ross' finger was redirected to Noah. "That was you?"

Noah inclined his head. "Gold star."

"We didn't even *think* to look at him," Ross said to Bonnie. "He was a long-term citizen. Wait. *Wait.* That means…" Ross looked between Noah and Aly with a confused expression.

Noah pursed his lips and answered the question Ross was struggling to ask. "Age shift."

Ross seemed flabbergasted by that. "You can *do* that? *How?*"

Noah said nothing, slipping his hands into his pockets.

Sensing he wasn't going to get an answer, Ross asked, "So… everyone is watching her because of you?"

Noah shrugged and Aly watched him lie with ease. "Seems to be the case. My turn. Who are you working for?"

The glower turned into a scowl and Ross countered, "Who are *you* working for?"

Noah rolled his eyes. "I just told you I spent ten years in Bellhollow."

"Doesn't mean you weren't working for someone."

Noah sighed. "I wasn't working for anyone. I was *living.*"

Ross waved his arms as he spoke. "You really expect me to believe that? We have evidence you were working with Elijah" —he spluttered and corrected—"Elaine. Do you deny that?"

"You have evidence I was *seen* with Elaine," Noah said with a sharp shake of his head. "At the time I accepted her help, I had no idea she was back with Darcy. She led me to believe she was still with Rex."

Ross scoffed. "Yeah, right."

"I didn't have any reason not to trust her," Noah snapped. "I told you to come for a very specific purpose."

Ross frowned. "Oh, and what's that?"

Noah glanced over his shoulder at Aly. "You still have the Institute's tracker chip in your heads. I didn't feel right about vanishing without warning you."

Ross' face pinched. "The Institute had ankle trackers,

not chips."

"The ankle tracker was an explosive designed to kill us if we disobeyed," Noah said. "They also had chips in our head to monitor us." He smirked. "How do you think Elaine and I found you? They knew exactly where to look."

"You're lying."

Noah's eyebrows rose. "What reason would I have to lie?"

Bonnie tilted her head at Noah and signed to him.

Noah raised an eyebrow. "I *don't* trust you. You have yet to give me anything to reassure me. That blind loyalty to my siblings bit me in the ass already. Multiple times. But I can't allow Darcy to get you. I'm here because if I can fuck up any of her plans by removing your chips, then I'm going to do that." He sighed and gestured his face. "It's embedded in your nasal cavity. Easy to miss. We removed ours the night we escaped. If you want proof, I can remove yours now." He scratched his cheek and said, "Although, I suppose that might alert them to its removal, but... well, the batteries should've died a long time ago, but this *is* Darcy."

Ross stared at him. His attention switched to Aly, then to Bonnie, then back on Noah. "You're serious."

"Absolutely."

Bonnie snapped her fingers to gain focus, then signed. Noah pursed his lips and puffed out loudly. "Best guess... either Darcy can use you better if you're free or maybe Rex changed the codes on the night we escaped."

Ross took a step backward. "He did *what*?"

Noah said, "He was at the Institute on the night we escaped. He did a lot of things. I suspect whoever has access to your tracking devices are the ones who followed you to that warehouse. And here."

"He's here?" Ross' voice rose pitch the more he spoke. "Rex is *here*?"

Noah shrugged and Aly wished she knew what he was

thinking, but was more than happy to stand there and watch it unfold rather than participate.

"Chances are high we're being watched." Noah lifted his gaze. "You're not the only one with a tracker. Tango has one too. And since he's *tango*, Darcy definitely knows where you are."

"We need to get out of here," Ross told Bonnie, who shook her head and gestured to Noah.

The longer Bonnie signed, the paler Noah got. "What?" he blurted when Bonnie finished. "Adam's *alive*?" Noah's expression hardened and his hand chopped the air to dismiss the words. "You're lying. Adam would *know* you had trackers."

"He probably does," Ross considered. "We only saw him face-to-face once. After that, it was via webcam or email."

With narrowed eyes, Noah looked between Bonnie and Ross. "You expect me to believe you're working for Adam by infiltrating Welcher's... wait, *fake* Purist front?"

Everything was getting more complicated by the second.

Feeling a faint prick she couldn't place, Aly looked out into the park. She skimmed her eyes over the people in the park, not really seeing any of them until she spotted someone familiar. Aly stifled a gasp, staring at Belinda Bell.

It didn't look like Belinda knew where they were, but she was obviously looking for someone. Belinda turned and waved to someone who was farther away, then gestured to indicate she was going to head a particular direction. Aly looked at the man Belinda waved to. A shifter, but beyond that, she couldn't tell anything about him, he was too far away. Why would Belinda, a Purist, be working with a shifter?

Unless Belinda didn't know. Because Ross spoke the truth.

"Noah." A clear warning tone, even if it was said under Aly's breath.

Noah snapped his head toward Aly. "How did you know where we were?" he asked Ross when he saw where Aly was looking. "How'd you get so close?"

Sounding confused, Ross said, "She left my car outside the place she hired a new one from. We hijacked the rental company's GPS."

Aly closed her eyes, mentally cursing the mistake. She hadn't thought about that at all.

Noah pressed, "Who'd you tell?"

"No one."

Noah pointed toward Belinda Bell. "Then there's your proof you're being tracked."

"How do we know *you're* not being tracked?" With a wary glance at Noah, Ross moved to a position where he could see who Noah pointed to. Blood drained from Ross' face as he saw Belinda. "Oh. Shit."

"Well, he knows who that is," Aly muttered.

Noah continued, "It's possible she followed us from the hotel, but there's no way she would've known we were in this town without following you. If she's working for your fake Purist front, and I'm pretty sure *she* believes it's real, then *Welcher* is the one who has your location."

Ross regarded Bonnie, who seemed at a loss. Aly shuffled, then changed her grip on Noah's backpack.

"I can get the implants out," Noah said, backing away from Ross and Bonnie and toward Aly. "But that might kill your infiltration. I am *not* allowing Belinda to get us, not even so you can keep your cover. I don't trust you that much." His tingles changed from gentle blows to shudder across her skin as he augmented a lot at once.

He held out his hand for the backpack and Aly gave it to him. He heaved it onto his back then reached for Aly's clammy hand. "Choice is yours, Ross, but I'd hurry. We're leaving." He lowered his voice to talk only to Aly. "Walk. Don't run. Keep your head down. Stay on my left."

Aly nodded and squeezed his hand.

"This was a bad idea," Noah muttered and shot Aly an

apologetic look. "We shouldn't have come."

"Too late now," Aly said, then swallowed heavily and tried to be brave. "Let's just get out of here."

Bonnie's hands flew. Noah watched her sign, then he nodded. "Fine." With a squeeze, Noah released Aly's hand and approached Bonnie. Lifting his hand, he spread his fingers. "Hold still," he told her in a tender, yet demanding tone. "I'll be quick." Wrapping his arms around Bonnie, they hugged. It was an awkward hug, especially since Bonnie was taller than Noah and Noah's hand was on Bonnie's face.

Aly turned away, not wanting to see, not wanting to hear Bonnie's strangled noise. Aly fixed her eyes on Belinda and watched as the woman walked in the opposite direction of where they were. They had some time, but not long. Even though she knew Noah was probably watching, she said, "She's moving away."

"Good." Removal of the implant didn't take long. Noah released Bonnie and stepped away, offering her something on the palm of his hand. "It's different than what I had. I suspect it's been replaced. Any missing chunks of time?" he asked, his tone mild.

Shaking her head, Bonnie plucked the tracker up, dropped it to the ground and stomped on it.

"How are you able to do that?" Ross asked.

"It's called augmentation," Noah muttered, wiping his hand on his shirt. "Same way I can heal. It's something Adam knows. So ask him."

"What do we do about Tango's?" Ross asked, stepping toward Noah.

"Whatever you like, but we're leaving," Noah said, embracing Ross and lifting his hand to Ross' face.

Prickles and spikes jittered their way down Aly's spine, completely overwhelming Noah's tingle. Not harsh and painful like the other shifters had been but different. Unexpected. With a yelp, she danced away from the tree she was leaning on and looked in the direction the sense came from. The prickle she recognized as Elaine's but the spikes were new. "Two," she blurted. "One is Elaine." She thrust her hand in the direction she felt, at an angle to the tree she'd been hiding behind. The tree she was no longer using as cover.

Panic brimmed.

A splattering of gunfire, loud, echoing, unmistakable. Bullets pelleted the ground, casting up clouds of dirt. Screaming; high pitched and panicked. People rushing to get their kids. Teenagers hunkering. People running. Complete terror and chaos.

Aly shoved herself up behind the tree.

"Tango! Stand down!" Ross yelled.

Noah grabbed Ross, forcing him toward a tree for cover. "It's not him!"

The rational side of Aly's brain vanished. She felt disconnected. Like she was on hold. She couldn't think. Couldn't feel. Everything felt slow and sluggish. She couldn't move. Why couldn't she move?

Blood. There was blood on her shirt. On her jeans.

Some subconscious thought made her press her hands to the bottom of her ribs. She slumped to the base of the trunk, tucking into a ball to keep herself small.

"Aly?"

She rolled her eyes to her left. Noah and Ross hunkered behind a tree a short distance away. Bonnie cowered behind a stone trash can, gun in hand. Both Bonnie and Ross were trying to see where the shots originated, quick snatching looks before they re-hid, but Noah looked at Aly.

She didn't want to move her hands. Couldn't move her hands. Warmth welled between her palms and she had to keep it inside her. She lost eye contact with Noah to stare at her knees. Pain set upon her like a ravenous beast. It ripped apart her insides and shredded her skin. It clamped its icy hand over her mouth, making it difficult to breathe. Prickles and tingles and spikes battled for patches of her skin until she couldn't tell who augmented.

More gunfire, Noah exchanging shots. More screaming from people in the park. "Goddamn it, Elaine, what are you playing at?!" Thudding footsteps and then Noah slid into cover beside her. "We need to—" the words died in his throat, choked off in horror. "Oh no." Both hands buried in his hair, pulling at his scalp.

One hand fluttered, lifting away from her stomach to catch the sleeve of his flannel shirt. "Fletcher?"

Fumbling for the backpack, he dumped it beside her, then reached for the buckle of his belt. "Oh, God. This is my fault. I was so stupid—just breathe, it'll be okay—"

The world spun. "I don't wanna die."

Noah's expression was fierce. "I'm not going to let you." He pried her leg away from her chest, pulling her out of the ball and set her leg flat on the ground, then slipped his belt beneath. She'd barely registered the pain in her leg but as he pulled the belt tight, she cried out. In a sweeping motion, he tore the sleeve off his shirt and then ripped a hole in her jeans where the bullet went in. Stuffing the sleeve into the hole he created, he applied pressure to her leg.

Ross returned fire, the crack of his gun overpowering the screaming people. "We need to move!" he yelled as Bonnie darted across to take refuge behind a tree.

"No," Noah called back. His eyes darted around, taking in everything. "Just cover!"

"If Elaine's the one shooting, then that's *Darcy* out there. We *can't* stay!"

"We can't move Aly! It's in her liver. She'll bleed out."

Oh God.

Tears pricked as a weight set upon her. She was going to die. Here, in this place, so far from home. Alone, because her last moments on this world were going to be spent ensuring he wouldn't return to the nightmare he was born into. "You gotta go."

Noah ignored her. Another sweeping look before his

gaze fell on Aly's hands. "You need to move your hands."

Battering at him weakly, she tried to shove him away. "Please, you gotta—"

With an exasperated look, he touched her wrist to coax, "Let me look."

A burning sensation overwhelmed her skin. Her shifter sense. Many of them who were not Noah. Or Elaine. Or the third spike. Many of them who would do bad things if they found him. Aly closed her eyes and refused to move her hand. "I'll be okay. You need to—"

"Don't be a martyr."

It hurt to breathe, hurt to talk, but she needed him to understand. "They want you—"

"They want Rex. You're bait. She wants me out of the fight and it's working."

His words made little sense but she had to make him leave. She struggled to speak, gasping between each word. "I don't want to be the reason she gets you." She gripped his shirt. "Shifters coming."

"I know." Swiveling his head, he called, "Ross, you need to leave! A large group of shifters coming in!"

Startled, Ross shrilled, "What?"

Noah yelled, "Get out of here!"

"What about you?"

Turning back to Aly, Noah said, "I'm right where I need to be."

Aly protested, shaking her head, "I don't want—"

"I'm not leaving you."

Aly whined, "I can't—"

He cupped her neck and smiled gently. "I know, lovely, I know."

She had no energy left to protest when he pulled her hands away and hiked up her shirt so he could see. It took effort to form words which were coherent enough not to be mistaken for a groan of pain. "What—?"

"I'm going to lend you my regeneration," he said as he rested his hand on her wound and hunkered over her until he could place an arm across her collarbone, pinning her to the tree. "It'll hurt. I need you to be as still as you can."

Aly swallowed.

Noah cast another look around and flinched from what he saw. "I love you. Ready?"

She shook her head but it didn't matter. Shoulders hunched, he curled until his forehead rested on hers. His eyes went glassy. Tingles intensified, eclipsing all other sensations until there was nothing but fire blazing inside her. Crying out in pain, the muscles of her back spasmed and she arched. The pressure of Noah's arm across her collar increased. She grabbed his arm, trying to pull it to escape. Her legs thrashed and he sat on them to hold her still.

"Please."

She didn't know who said it, her or him. Squeezing shut her eyes and clenching her teeth, Aly gripped his arm and forced her body still. Pain kept her stiff but it also kept her awake. Sweat dotted her forehead and made her clammy as she endured.

Time lost its meaning. It narrowed to heartbeats, snatches of breath and his soothing voice in her ear as he tried to keep her calm. It didn't matter what he said, what mattered was tone.

Aly threw her head back and dug in her heels as she felt a strange pressure within her. Lifting and tugging, tearing at her as it rose.

"Easy. Stay with me."

She couldn't tell where the pain was coming from. Was it from the hole in her? Was it from her leg? Or was it from the shifters circling around?

The pressure seemed to pop. Blood ran free. She couldn't stop the strangled cry.

Hair tickled her face and she struggled to open her eyes. Noah's head was down, his shoulders slumped, and his breath coming in ragged gasps. It occurred to her, among the great rolling waves of agony, that whatever he was doing caused him great pain as well. Words echoed in her head. *Too fast or do it wrong and there's no coming back. Shifting hurts.*

He said he was lending her his regeneration, rebuilding her insides using parts of him. He was hurting himself for her.

Prying open her hand to release his arm, she touched his neck. He raised his head to meet her gaze. His smile was full of echoed pain but also full of love. Tears pricked at her eyes and her lips quivered, trying to form his name. Holding her gaze, he continued to help her.

A shout, too close for comfort and the sound of fighting. Feet thudding on the ground, scuffles and yelling. Noah turned his head, then huffed a laugh. "Outta time."

A deep voice she didn't know yelled, "There!"

Noah's head dipped until it rested against hers again. "Hold on."

Aly whimpered and her eyelashes fluttered as she wrestled with consciousness. Head lolling, her eyes skipped across the surroundings. Shadows filled the sky. People in dark clothing forced anyone who was still in the park to the ground. Ross, face-first in the dirt not far, staring at them. Bonnie, beside the concrete table, a foot pinning her and a gun at her head. Hapless bystanders received the same treatment, all cowering against a small army of shifters.

Aly didn't want to leave Noah alone, resisting the pain as it tugged at her to succumb. If she slept now, she might never wake. Blood soaked the ground. Burning, writhing, twisting, pain seared diamond scales into her skin.

"Don't shoot!" Noah bellowed. "*Please!*"

Men with rifles gathered, guns pointed directly at Noah. "Step away from her. Get on the ground."

"I can't," Noah hastened. His weight lifted from Aly's legs as he moved aside, but his hands stayed where it was. "We're attached right now. She's been shot. Please, you need to let me finish!"

"You're what?" Murmurings of disbelief and guns dipped with indecision then someone blurted, "Holy fucking shit, look at his hand!"

The man's astonishment compelled Aly to look down. Noah's index finger was missing; instead, it was comprised of writhing tubes and blood vessels which disappeared into her body. Aly's stomach rolled. She groaned and her head flopped.

"My name is Noah and I am willing to come quietly if you allow me to finish healing her. We are both worth more alive and—"

"My God," one of them said. "He's one of those immortal Faceless! He's gotta be!"

"I thought they were a myth!"

Shoulders slumping, Noah closed his eyes. "Great."

A commanding voice cut over the mumbles. "Take the weapon and step back. Guns trained, if he moves wrong, shoot him."

"Which faction?" Noah asked.

Someone brought out a phone and it pinged as it began to record. "Boss'll want proof."

Distraught, Aly turned her face away from them and stifled a wretched sob. The pain morphed into cold. The chill swept over her, her fingers trembling and her teeth chattering. Eyes slipped closed and no amount of effort allowed her to open them.

"Which faction?" Noah repeated. When no reply came, he asked, "Can I fix her leg?"

"No," the commanding voice said. "We'll patch it. When we get to the boss, then you can do whatever it is you're doing. Show him."

Sapped of strength, Aly concentrated on her breathing. Deep breaths in, slow ones out.

So many voices, swirling and murmuring. She could hear so much and yet it felt like nothing but noise. "Anyone else feeling sick watching this?" "Yeah. I feel weird." "Secure the traitorous twins."

Noah brushed the fingers of his free hand along her abdomen, then took her hand. "Aly," he coaxed, squeezing her hand.

Her eyes fluttered open in response to his voice.

"I'll see you soon," he promised, smiling at her.

Despair settled into her chest. He was going to give up. He was going to submit. She mouthed 'no', shaking her head.

"It'll be okay." Bracing, he extracted both his hands and raised them in submission.

Men fell upon Noah, brutal as they forced him face-first to the ground. The sound of his head colliding with the dirt echoed in Aly's ears. His arms were twisted behind his back and he grimaced in pain. Someone grabbed her wrist, dragging her across the ground away from him.

Aly squawked in both pain and surprise. She didn't want them close. She didn't want them touching her. Touching him. Extending her arm toward Noah, she reached and tried to crawl. His eyes were fixed on her as the men manhandled him and he wasn't protesting his rough treatment.

"There's not even a scar." A hand slid over her bare abdomen, too close for comfort.

Violated, her hands battered at theirs. Her shifter sense went haywire. They were everywhere, all around her, touching her. Rolling barbs across her skin the longer their hands were in contact and she went into convulsions. Froth formed in her mouth while her arms and legs thrashed.

"Sir!"

The more they held her down, the harder she seized. Blood pounded in her ears. Strong waves of intensified dread, unease and fear swept through her, crashed against her, destroyed her. Voiceless yells and calls filled her ears as her vision spun out of control.

She could feel each and every one of them, see them in her mind. Pillars of flame, standing tall in the dark. The flame marked them.

Something in her broke free. Went out instead of in.

Snuffed out the flames.

The man with his hand on her abdomen crumpled. Glassy eyes stared at nothing as his mouth hung open and his flesh rippled. Another man who held her collapsed with the same ripple overcoming his features. Then a woman farther away hit the ground. All around the park, shifters dropped. With each one that fell, their flames were extinguished, the convulsions dimmed.

Then it was only Noah, Ross, Bonnie and any non-shifter bystanders who remained. Noah's familiar and comforting tingle engulfed her as she stared at a blade of grass. Exhaustion made her limbs heavy. Her tongue felt thick against the roof of her mouth. She existed in a void, safe and free.

Sneakers and jeans filled her vision. Warm fingers on her icy face tilted her head. Noah's expression was close to panic while he checked her pulse and then the inside of her mouth. Tender as he brushed the hair from her face, he looked stricken. She was so lost she couldn't claw her way back to reassure him. Sliding his hands beneath her body, he hoisted her up and cradled her to his chest. The small movement was enough that she lost her tenuous grip on consciousness.

She faded.

CHAPTER 20

Frantically trying to navigate through a swathe of injured and terrified people escaping from the park, Belinda searched the crowd for Alyson Gale and Will Ward. While whatever guise Will held would keep him hidden unless Gomez found him first, Alyson was not a shifter. Belinda was certain once she spotted Alyson, Will wouldn't be too far away.

While the gunfire had resounded, Belinda had been forced to cower behind the closest concrete trash can. Not sure what was occurring, but certain Alyson was somehow involved, Belinda had tried to get her bearings. Men and women in combat gear had appeared with the gunfire, moving among the terrified masses with weapons brandished and calling for everyone to get down. Not knowing if they were friend or foe, Belinda had stayed quiet, watching and waiting, ready to act.

No one had been prepared for every single one of the combat gear clad people to collapse without warning.

Now that the gunfire had stopped, people were edging out from their hiding places and taking stock of the situation. People told each other different stories as they ran, yelling details which may or may not have held a grain of truth; a man in a hoodie, a bomb, armed gunmen, a swat team, people were injured, people were dead.

People were on their cells. People huddled in groups. Belinda could hear sirens in the distance.

Some were bleeding but no one was screaming out that they'd been shot. The injuries seemed minor, occurring when they'd tried to flee. Others helped carry injured, elderly, or children toward the parking lot. Some screamed hysterically, frozen in place, while others checked those unmoving.

So far, the only unmoving people Belinda could see were those in combat gear.

And Gomez.

Concerned, Belinda hurried to his side. Had he been shot in the crossfire? The other downed people Belinda ran by seemed to be convulsing, their limbs shuddering. As she reached Gomez, she found he was suffering a strange rippling across his face. Dropping to her knees, she reached for him, then snatched her hands back. "Gomez?"

He couldn't hear her. He couldn't see her. A strange film had come down over his eyes as he convulsed. His skin seemed to be almost liquid as it rippled over his face.

Frowning at him, she considered, then sat back to look around at the others and found herself staring straight into the steady gaze of Will Ward, who stood a few paces away from her.

At least, she thought it was Will. The only clue she had was that he held Alyson, and the way he held her suggested he cared about her. Carefully carried, she was limp in his arms, pale and sweating and soaked in blood. It was obvious she'd been shot. Beside Will stood two other people, both of them staring at her and she recognized the pair known as 'the twins'. The way they flanked Will suggested that they were protecting him.

Which meant...

Belinda's mind reeled.

Will spoke and his voice sounded like death, "Your

organization is corrupt. If you want to hunt shifters, I suggest you start looking at them instead." Before Belinda could question further, Will spun on his heels and stalked away, carrying Alyson with him.

The male twin smirked at her and mocked a salute. "Try looking into the name 'Welcher'. Start with Tegan. Might help," he said as he fell in behind Will, while the female twin simply shook her head and turned away.

Belinda looked at Gomez and saw a different face flaccid on his features. Rocking away in horror, she exclaimed, "Mimic detection device my ass!"

More pain riddled through Tango Eight's body than he had ever experienced. Even with Smith's impossible shift experiments, Tango Eight had never felt so much at once. He was burning, fire beneath his skin which seared him away from the inside out. There was no end. He couldn't move, could barely breathe, couldn't call for help.

He was dying. He was dying and he'd only just gotten a taste of freedom.

Why did it have to hurt so much?

What had happened? He wasn't sure.

He'd taken up a sniper position at Ross' request. He'd waited. He'd watched. He'd held his ground like he'd been asked. Asked. Not told. His opinion was valued and considered, a luxury which had never been offered before.

When the gunfire started, he'd searched for the instigator to no avail. Ross and Bonnie had been captured and Tango Eight knew if he revealed himself he'd be dead before he could save them.

He *would* save them. They'd been kind to him. Firm, but kind, showing him what family really was. Offering freedom and a place of his own. Teaching him about how the world really worked, instead of the lies Smith had taught them. Smith had instilled loyalty in them, Tango Eight had chosen to be loyal to Ross and Bonnie.

As Tango Eight contemplated his next move, everything had gone to hell.

The sky was so blue. He could see it through the leaves of the towering tree above him. Blue and bright and endless. Rocks against his back, arms splayed and lifeless, the fire consumed him, but the sky... the sky gave him peace.

He wanted to see more of it. He wanted to be filled with the blue. He wanted to be smothered by it.

A shadow loomed above him, interrupting his view. "What happened to you?"

Tango Eight gasped, his world an ocean of agony he couldn't break free from. "Please."

"I'm sorry. There's nothing I can do. Your body's breaking down."

With effort, Tango Eight lifted his arm and splayed his fingers in front of his face. "The sky."

The shadow above him lifted their head and looked upward. "Ahh. Yes. Of course."

Strong arms slipped under his body, lifted him up and moved him from beneath the shade of the tree into an open space, before gently laying him down again.

Tango Eight sprawled out in a patch of sunlight and gazed upward. Blue. So very blue.

Echo One hunkered down to sit beside him and clasped his hand. "I'll sit with you," Echo One said, his voice soft. "Look to the sky and embrace freedom."

CHAPTER 21

Sweltering and stifled, Aly kicked off the blankets and rolled over. Lifting her head up, she dragged out the bottom pillow and hugged it to her chest. It was a struggle to get comfortable and while her body craved sleep, a nagging feeling crept up on her that she should be awake.

Huffing in a sigh and wondering why the room had a strong scent of mothballs, she swung her feet over the side of the bed and hoisted into a seated position. There, she froze as she realized she had no idea where she was.

The room was small. Dark log walls. Floral bed sheets. Queen bed with an empty wooden bedside table. Polished wood floors with a dark square rug by the door. Peering down at herself, she found her clothes had been changed; Jeans and tee swapped for a button-up flannel shirt she recognized as Noah's. While her hands were clean, the edges of her fingernails were rimmed with dried blood.

Gasping, she grabbed her leg and found nothing wrong with it beyond a dark bruise and an ache she felt all the way through. She ran her fingers across her ribs. Except for another large and painful bruise, there was no evidence a bullet had ever struck her. No scars. No wound. Nothing.

She looked around, wondering what she should do. Where was Noah? Had they been captured? She struggled to remember. An agonizing release, then nothing.

It was so silent. No voices. An odd bird chirp every now and then, but no other noises. Where was Noah? Would he hear her? Or would her calling for him distract him? His shirt was a comfort, but it was the only familiar thing in the room. Casting aside the blanket, she eased her legs out of bed. Perhaps if she was quiet, she could find out what was going on and not cause a disaster.

Her leg didn't want to hold her. Pain shot up her thigh and her knee buckled. With a small cry of protest, she grabbed the bed for support.

Alerted by her noise, a chair scraped across the floor and then footsteps approached. Aly bit her lip, working hard to keep her feet supporting her. Staggering to the closest wall, she braced and lifted her fists ready to defend herself.

"Aly?"

Fletcher's voice. *Fletcher's.*

The door open and his beloved face poked through. Dark mop of hair. Chocolate eyes. Lopsided smile as he spotted her.

Heart feeling like it was going to burst, Aly's legs crumpled. Fletcher rushed to catch her before she hit the floor. Arms around her, Fletcher crushed her to his chest. "I got you."

Unprepared, Aly burst into tears. She clutched his shirt and buried her face against his neck, hugging him as tight as she could. They slid to the floor together, wrapped up in each other's arms. Large, ugly sobs, tears dripping onto his shirt and embarrassing herself by whimpering wasn't enough to stem the flow of tears, but she wasn't the only one. Fletcher's shoulders shook; tiny movements which could easily be mistaken for something else, but Aly knew.

He was here. He was here and he was safe and *they* were safe and she didn't care about anything else right now except him.

He was faster to compose himself than she was. The desperate clutch gradually turned into soothing strokes. "I thought I was going to lose you," he mumbled, his voice cracking.

Not knowing what to say, she hummed. Pulling back, she flopped the cuff of the flannel shirt over her hand and wiped her face on the wrist in an effort to compose herself. "I'm sorry. Not very elegant of me."

"I really don't care. Are you okay?" He cupped her face as he stared intently at her. "How do you feel?"

"I feel... tired. Confused. Very sore."

Releasing her face, his fingers brushed over her leg. "I did what I could but there's still a bit you need to heal on your own. We have painkillers."

Wincing at the thought of how loopy she tended to get when taking painkillers, she said, "Yeah, cause we really need me talking about unicorns in potato sacks right now."

"It's an option. If you need it."

Snuggling against him, she rested her forehead on his neck. "I didn't know you could do that."

"I wasn't going to let you die," he said with absolute certainty. "Not when I could help."

"Thank you."

He cuddled her. "It's... it's very hard because I can't... I can't see what I'm doing. I have to attach all these nerves so I know and... well, you don't need to know."

She wanted to, though, so she stored the conversation for later. "Are we safe?"

"Yes."

She was so relieved to hear that, she couldn't stop the heartfelt sigh. "Good. Then I'm not moving for about a year."

His cheek pressed against the top of her head. "There are decisions to be made and things... things I need—we need to talk about."

She huffed out a breath. Sliding her hands from around

his neck so that her palms pressed flat on his chest instead, she made to rise. "Okay," she pouted. "Alright. Fine. Buzzkill."

Fletcher didn't let her pull away, and tugged her back. "It can wait five minutes."

Smiling to herself, she tucked into him. "Good, cause I was gonna whine." She stroked her finger along the hollow of his throat. "You're okay? You're not hurt?"

"I'm fine. A hundred percent A-Okay."

She rolled her head back on his shoulder so she could peer at him. "You sure?"

He smiled contently. "Yup. Tired and confused too, but much better now you're awake."

Feeling sentimental and running on an emotional high she couldn't explain, she nosed the rough stubble of his cheek. "I missed your face." She touched a lock of hair by his ear. "And the hair."

Fletcher chuckled. "Me too, although—" Aly ran her fingers along his jaw until she reached his chin, then coaxed his head to turn toward hers. His voice died as he met her gaze and her eyes were drawn to his throat as he swallowed. "Um…"

Stroking her thumb from his bottom lip, down to the point of his chin, she whispered, "So, so much."

"I…" he swallowed again, his eyes roaming around her face. "I… ahh… thought you might need a familiar face."

She cooed, "I *like* that face."

"Are these the so-called doe eyes you accuse me of?"

"Yup." She wet her lips. "I'd like to kiss you, if that's okay?"

"Oh. Okay." With a soft, delighted sigh, he met her halfway.

Gentle and sweet, his lips felt warm and soft against hers. As natural as breathing, a pleasant and simple progression of their relationship. No demands, no urgency. Only a wish to be with one another and rearrange their boundaries to something they always wanted to be.

Pulling back, she kept her face close as she checked, "Is this…?" She couldn't finish, not because she was afraid of an answer, but because kissing him made her breathless.

"More than," he whispered and closed the distance again.

Delicious butterflies churned in her belly and her heart caroled with joy. If she'd had doubts before about how she felt about him, the kiss swept everything away. This was about sharing. Joining. Her other first kisses had been more of a surprise, a spur of the moment thing and while she enjoyed them, Fletcher's kiss made her feel special.

Loved.

It wasn't long. Long enough to make her heart thud and butterflies in her belly sing. Long enough to make her want to bury her fingers in his hair and open her mouth to taste him, but she was keenly aware that while this was the first kiss among many, they needed to take things slow. She needed to let him lead the way and reshuffle his limits at a pace he could handle. Sighing, she rested her face against his to bask in the afterglow and he snuck in another kiss.

Although she wanted nothing more than to remain curled up on the floor with him for the remainder of the day, common sense won the struggle. Fighting a flush, she asked, "Where are we?"

"Safehouse. We're in Nevada, in the mountains on the other side of Tahoe. I didn't want to go far." He cleared his throat and said cautiously, "Bonnie and Ross are here."

She didn't know how she felt about that. "Oh."

Fixing his gaze on her, he said, "I know… I know they hurt you, Aly, but I needed to find out—"

She nodded to show she understood. "There are things we need to know. And they stood with us when it mattered."

"Yeah. I've spent most of the time talking to them trying to figure out what was going on. Plus…" he coughed, cleared his throat. "Um. This is one of Rex's safe houses. He's, er, waiting for the go-ahead to come."

She stared at him. The implications of Fletcher reaching out to Rex for assistance was staggering, but she couldn't fault him. He must've been panicked.

"We needed answers," he continued. "That was just… um… do… do you remember what happened?"

Curling in on herself, she didn't want to think about what happened, but she knew she needed to. "Yeah… I had some sort of… reaction to the shifters. Had a fit or something? It was… pretty awful."

He swore vehemently. "Has that… has it ever happened before?"

Cuddling into him for comfort, she said, "No."

"I… don't even want to begin to…" he cleared his throat, struggling with the words. "Rex has answers and… well, he gets bonus points for staying away until you woke up. If you don't want to talk to him, I'm going to go down and see him. Ross and Bonnie can stay here to act as protection—"

She gripped his shirt. "You're not going anywhere without me. We stay together. I'll talk to him, I have questions of my own."

"You probably want to clean up," Fletcher said, studying her hair. "I did my best, but you've got dried blood in places."

Wrinkling her nose, she said, "Eww. Gross."

Tapping her on the small of her back, he said, "C'mon. I'll show you where the bathroom is. I've even chased away all the spiders."

"Awesome."

The house seemed like a hunting cabin. The water had a slightly brown tinge when she started running it, which gradually became cleaner. A bath/shower in a tiny bathroom and a separate toilet. Two bedrooms, a kitchenette in the living room and a wooden porch. All the furniture was outdated and there were several white sheets bundled up in the corner. Outside she thought she could hear a generator running.

Studying her reflection in the mirror, Aly grimaced. Dark circles under her eyes, a bruise on her cheek. Lifting up Fletcher's shirt, she studied the dark purple mark on her belly. Tender and painful, it pulled at her with every movement, as did the one on her leg. She wasn't going to be running anywhere for a while.

Regretting not taking the offer of painkillers, Aly mumbled, "Hey, Fletch, do we have ice?" A double tap tingle indicated that they did, so that cheered her up a little. "Thanks. Now, turn the ears off."

A tickle which felt akin to a burst of laughter followed Aly as she limped into the shower.

When she limped out of the bathroom, she found Bonnie, Ross, and Fletcher sitting around the small wooden dining table, their hands flying as they talked to each other. The three of them stopped the moment she entered, looking at her in greeting.

"Hey," Fletcher said, smiling. He stood from his chair to move to her side to offer assistance.

Aly put the repacked backpack on the floor by the wall. "Hey," she said, taking his elbow so he could help her to an armchair.

"We were making contingency plans," he told her.

"I still think it's a bad idea to talk to Rex," Ross said.

"Objection noted," Fletcher chirped, settling Aly in the chair. "Still going to do it. I'll get ice."

"Fine," Ross said, planting both hands on the table as he stood. "But leave us out of the conversation. Less he knows about us, the better."

"The conversation wasn't going to be about you," Fletcher assured him as he headed for the small bar fridge.

Smiling at Aly, Bonnie signed.

"She wants to know how you're feeling," Fletcher called, rummaging in the freezer.

Aly returned Bonnie's smile. "Tired but alive."

Bonnie signed and Fletcher answered her, "Yeah, we're

completely confused about that too. Which is why we need to talk to Rex." He wandered back to Aly carrying two small bags. "He, apparently, has answers."

"Is that, whatever that was, why they're all after her?" Ross asked.

Since she wasn't sure what Fletcher had told them or was willing to share, Aly shrugged as she accepted the bags from Fletcher.

"We'll let you know," Fletcher said. To Aly, he said, "It's all we have."

Planting one of the bags on the bruise on her leg, she tucked the other one under her shirt. "It's fine, thank you."

Ross didn't look like he believed Fletcher. "I've never seen *anything* like that. Bonnie said you knew about the shifters before they came to the warehouse. How?"

"I really don't know," Aly mumbled.

"She's a sensor," Fletcher said. At Ross' questioning look, he elaborated, "Like how we can tell each other no matter what form we take. Aly can feel them, even if she's not looking at them."

Ross and Bonnie exchanged a look. "That's handy. Didn't know they existed."

Fletcher nodded. "It has its adverse effects as we've found out."

Aly made a noise of agreement and refused to say anything else.

Ross breathed out a hard sigh. "Right. C'mon, Bonnie, time to make ourselves scarce."

Adjusting the ice pack, Aly nodded and Fletcher reached down to rest his hand on her shoulder.

"Call when you're done," Ross said, holding the door open for Bonnie and the two of them ducked outside into the evening light.

As the door closed behind them, Aly asked, "Do they even know what Rex is to me?"

"That's not for me to tell." He sighed. "Ross thinks our best course of action is to find Adam."

"And you don't?"

One hand on his hip, he clutched the back of his neck and looked up at the ceiling. "I'm not even sure if it *is* Adam. Elaine said he was dead."

"Elaine hasn't exactly been a fountain of truth."

Fletcher sighed and scrubbed his face. "I know. Ross said Adam never allows face-to-face visits, it's hard to know if it's really him and not someone masquerading. I need to see him in person, but I doubt it's going to be easy to do that."

"Ahh."

"With their chips out, we have a better chance. It could be he never let them close because of the chips. I don't know."

"Where's Tango?" Aly asked and adjusted the ice pack on her leg.

"Vanished during the fight," Fletcher said, with a shrug. "It's why we didn't go too far. He might be hiding, so we're going to hang around a bit to see if he contacts us. I may be able to remove his chip." Sighing, he stroked his hand down Aly's arm. "I have to change back."

She gave him a puppy dog expression and whined, "Why?"

Laughing, he poked her nose. "Stop it."

"But why?" she asked, dragging out the 'why' as long as she could.

"Because Fletcher's form is just for you. I'm not going to share it with Rex."

That thought made her warm inside, but she still pouted, wanting to keep him around for longer. "Aww."

"I'll keep the floppy hair, though," Fletcher said, lifting up a handful at the front to check the color. "Don't feel like re-growing it again today."

Aly cocked her head. "Is that how you did it?"

He nodded. "Hair is dead cells," he said. "I had to regrow it to change the color. Hence the shaggy look."

"I love it."

He snorted and wandered away from her so he could shift. "I know."

Night fell and Aly remained curled up in the armchair icing her bruises until her shifter sense flared a warning. Heart hammering, she lifted from her chair and limped to the window to watch headlights flicker up the path. The car halted a small distance away from the cabin and Rex climbed out, illuminated by the porch light and wearing the same form she'd seen outside her house. Aly watched him circle the car to fetch a plastic bag from the front seat. As he approached the door, she retreated across the room.

"You okay?" Noah asked and Aly squeaked at him in reply. When Rex knocked, Noah asked, "Can I let him in?"

Twisting her fingers together, Aly squared her shoulders and nodded.

Noah opened the door and blocked it with his body and Aly felt his tingle flit across her skin.

Rex gave Noah the once over. "Noah. Do I pass inspection?"

Without answering, Noah stepped away from the door and allowed Rex access into the cabin.

Standing in the doorway, Rex's sternness vanished as he smiled at Aly. "Hello, Alyson." Lifting up the plastic bags, he said, "I bought take-out. I wasn't sure what you liked, so there's a range."

Aly alternated between looking at Rex and Noah. Adjusting her stance, she took her weight on her good leg. "Umm… thanks."

Rex's smile was full of the fatherly pride Aly preferred to see on Roger's face. "It's good to see you."

Uncertain, she raised a finger, then dropped her hand. "This isn't your natural form."

"Hard to be near me?" Rex asked, then inclined his head. "I hoped you'd outgrow that."

"Well, I didn't."

"Unfortunately, I'm not returning to my natural form. Not with him here." Rex threw a scowl at Noah. "For security reasons."

Noah snorted as he secured the door and Aly felt a tingle from him as he checked the windows. "I've already seen it. Aly's a brilliant artist."

Unperturbed, Rex said, "I'm aware of how good she is. I have commissioned several pieces in the past."

Nothing would surprise Aly anymore and if Rex wanted the gratification of her being shocked at something he'd done, he'd have to earn it.

Lifting the bags, Rex moved around the room toward the table, taking care to remain at distance from Aly. "My separation from you was not by choice. I had to make the hard decision to leave you with Penelope."

"With..." Aly glanced at the door and felt a surge of disappointment. "Mom's not here?"

Placing the bags on the table, Rex started unpacking cardboard pails full of food. "She's getting the rest of your family out of Bellhollow for a time as a safety precaution."

From the smell of the food, Aly guessed Thai. "Oh."

"She doesn't know you're here," he continued. "There were factors I needed to take into consideration."

"Factors?" Noah asked and thrust his hands into the pockets of his jeans. "That doesn't sound good."

"In her ignorance, she's the one who called in Welcher's men."

Aly bristled and had to bite back a retort.

Noah made a disgruntled noise. "Welcher. How'd he get to Penelope?"

"By accident. When you were taken, it drew attention from everyone. Tegan—she's Welcher's head of communications—can be very persuasive and Poppy fell for it. She nearly got you killed." Rex glanced at Noah. "Thank you for saving her."

Noah narrowed his eyes. "I didn't do it for you."

"Regardless, thank you." Rex sat at the table and opened the paper to get the wooden chopsticks. "Please, join me."

Unnerved, Aly held her ground. She didn't like this. She didn't like Rex's casual dismissal of Penelope or his glaring hatred of Noah. Her mom always did the best she could and there wasn't any way for her to know who could be trusted and who couldn't.

"It's better she's not here for this," Rex continued after a moment's study. "Poppy can be rather emotional and we need an open conversation."

"And there are things she's safer not knowing," Noah noted.

Rex nodded. "She made a poor decision to trust Welcher."

"Which you kept her in the dark about, anyway, so don't try and blame any of this on Penelope. She's always done what she thought was best and, obviously, she thought that wasn't you." Noah's stance was casual but for Aly, it seemed Noah shared her anger concerning Rex's dismissal of Penelope.

"I have always had Alyson's best interests at heart."

"Uh-huh," Noah scoffed and changed the subject. "I heard Welcher was assassinated."

Rex regarded Noah. "He was. Assassinated and replaced. They like to keep it in the family." Rex clicked his chopsticks together and reached for a box. "Sit. Eat."

Hugging her arms to her chest, Aly muttered, "Fine where I am, thanks."

Noah crossed the room from the door and inspected the boxes. Choosing one, he delivered it to Aly. "You might only manage one or two bites," he mumbled, helping her limp to the armchair. "But try. Let me know if it doesn't want to stay down."

"Do I have to?" she muttered as she took the box and tucked her feet up beneath her.

"Yes. For me. Don't worry," he said, with mock-joviality. "It's not poisoned. I checked."

Aly snorted.

Grinning, Noah returned to the table and picked up a

chair. Swinging it so it was backward to the table, he straddled it and took a box for himself. "There's only one reason I called you," he said to Rex. "So start talking."

Leaning back and arms extended to rest on the table in what Aly recognized as an attempt at dominance, Rex considered Noah. "A question first."

Stirring his noodles with his chopsticks and completely uncaring of Rex's display, Noah nodded. "I may or may not answer."

Rex sat forward, intent on Noah's reaction. "How does Alyson feel to you? Does she make you uncomfortable to be around? Does being in her presence make it difficult to shift?"

Noah stuffed noodles in his mouth, chewing while he stared at Rex. Taking longer than was necessary to swallow, Noah's tone was tart when he finally spoke, "Do you really think I'd tell you if she did?"

Rex's lips thinned as he pressed them together. "I can assume that's a 'no'. You wouldn't have been around her for as long as you were if she did."

"You're free to assume what you like," Noah said and readied another chopstick full of food. "Just as I can assume she makes you just as uncomfortable as you're making her."

Aly sat up straighter. "Really?"

Rex grimaced. "I forgot how many tricks you had at your disposal to read a person."

Noah chewed, indicating Rex with his chopsticks. "How close do you need to be before she starts affecting you?"

"I felt her as I walked in the door."

"Nothing before that?"

"No."

Noah took another bite. "Huh."

Rex's gaze swung to Aly. "And how about you, Alyson? How does he feel to you?"

She decided to be as standoffish as Noah was. "That's

none of your business."

Rex was insistent. "But you can feel him?"

"Only when I shift," Noah conceded, which was more than Aly would've given him.

"Interesting." Rex scratched his neck as he considered. "Must've been difficult for you. Ten years not being able to shift whenever you wanted to."

Noah shrugged. "Not really. My augments are much cleaner and quicker now."

"It's hard to believe you lasted so long in one place. I should've kept a better eye on—"

"You can't sense me and I'm fairly certain, knowing Penelope, she would've sent you pictures of me and Aly, and no one can tell from pictures. Ultimately, if I'd ever seen you, this whole thing would've been bust."

Rex nodded, looking disgruntled. "True."

"Although… you did get me with this not being your natural form," Noah admitted.

"Poppy told me a lot about you. Or at least the person you're pretending to be. It was a surprise to hear that you were gay, I thought all of you to be sexless."

Noah's eyes snapped from the food to Rex's and he rocked back. "Oh, for fuck's sake… *really*? You want to discuss *that*?"

"You don't get to do that," Aly announced. "You don't get to be part of the"—she lowered her voice to a tenor "— 'What are your intentions for my daughter?' deal. That's my *dad's* job."

Rex sighed and pinched the bridge of his nose. "Alyson, I know how upsetting this must be for—"

"You *don't* know," she snapped, indignant at being treated like a child. "So let's not pretend to sit here and be civil."

"I don't know if I can trust him with—"

"It's not about you trusting him," Aly grated out. "Right now, it's about *me* trusting *you*."

"I don't know who he's working for," Rex continued,

undaunted. "I don't know who he'll report this conversation to."

"Right," Aly said and made to stand. "C'mon, Fletch, we should—"

Rex raised his hands, suddenly frantic. "Alyson, please."

Noah lifted his noodles with his chopsticks. "You're supposed to be talking. Not fishing for details." Glancing at Aly, he nodded in the direction of her food.

Rex sighed and placed his food on the table. "It's a long story."

Aly scoffed as she folded back into the armchair and opened the box. "It's always a long story."

"Please try to keep an open mind," Rex said, addressing Aly. "This will probably be hard to hear. I assume you know where he came from?"

Aly nodded, dread sinking into the pit of her stomach. She took a bite to calm her nerves as she settled in to listen.

Rex threaded his fingers together and looked at Noah. "Have you ever noticed there's no Alpha group?"

Noah frowned. "I assumed they failed."

"Darcy's techniques were not as… refined. She had no way to accelerate growth, the first of the Faceless were born to surrogates. Raised as normal children." He sighed. "Died as normal children. The Bravo group had their share of genetic mutations and none of them lived beyond a year. Two members of Charlie and all of Delta survived to escape their torment and… well, you killed all of them, didn't you? Part of your 'training'."

Noah didn't say anything. Aly took her cue from him and stared blandly at Rex.

Seeing no reaction, Rex continued, "Then we have Echo group. The success. Shifters without equal, training second to none. No other group has surpassed your standard."

"Because any group following were already dying," Aly

said. "You changed the formula."

Rex hunched his shoulders. "He told you."

Aly nodded.

"I had to," Rex implored. "There were mitigating—"

Noah interrupted, "How are you coping with them still coming out, only to die because of something you did?"

Rex shook his head. "There's been no sign since Lima. Darcy moved on from that experiment."

Noah frowned and exchanged a glance with Aly. Aly was as confused as he was, considering they'd both seen Tango. Elaine said they'd been coming out every year, so someone was lying. Or didn't know. Not knowing what else to do, Aly held her tongue.

"What does this have to do with Aly?"

With regret, Rex spoke, "There were ten doors. Alyson is not a natural sensor."

CHAPTER 22

Dumping his food on the table, Noah pushed away from the chair. It slammed into the table and the whole thing shuddered from the force. "That's complete bullshit," Noah thundered. "Aly is *not* Faceless."

Eyes wide, heart pounding and noodles part way to her mouth, Aly sat frozen to her chair.

Undeterred, Rex said, "Experiment Ten was designed to be a virus to infect natural shifters. All failed. Darcy tried to create Ten as a shifter *and* a toxin. She burned herself out each time. All of them, except Echo's."

Noah shook his head. "Echo Ten burned too. I heard them talking."

"There were two Echo Tens."

"That's *impossible*."

Rex scratched his fingers through his beard as he chose his next words. "Among the genetic team working on the creation of Charlie through to Foxtrot was a brilliant geneticist. Ahead of her time."

Aly slowly lowered her chopsticks of noodles back into the box. She could see what was coming. She could see what Rex was going to say and there was nothing she could do to stop it. "My mother worked for Darcy."

Inclining his head, Rex said, "I met Maddie at a genetics conference a few years before you were born. She made quite a splash, astounded a few genetic scholars with her theories and discoveries, left with a job offer which would change her life."

"I'm not sure I want to hear this," Aly said as she put her food aside and tucked up into a ball.

Rex looked sympathetic. "You need to hear it to understand."

"Do I really?" Aly shook her head. "This is like straight out of a movie. You meet. You fall in love. It's romantic and passionate, but wait, you're from two separate worlds, you can't possibly be together. Only, she's a genetic scientist, she can create a child who can remove the separation between the worlds." She waved her hands dramatically. "Problem solved."

Rex shook his head and drummed his fingers against the table. "Life is not like a movie. I respected Maddie, I enjoyed her company, but I didn't love her. Maddie was brilliant but she had very little empathy. She looked at what she created and she didn't see people, she saw projects." He nodded at Noah. "Weapons. She was *exactly* what Darcy wanted and when she started working on the Faceless, things began to come together. We needed Intel into Darcy's operations and Maddie was an opportunity."

"She was your mission," Noah said in a bland tone.

Rex admitted to that with an incline of his head and Aly felt appalled. "Maddie had a lot of flaws. One of which was she brought her work home with her and forgot to secure it. That's how I gained access to the project. How we learned what they were doing." He sighed. "I wasn't always a leader. That came out of necessity."

Noah glanced over at Aly, then returned his attention to Rex. "You used her."

Rex met Noah's unforgiving gaze. "Maddie returned the favor. She knew why Ten failed. She theorized Ten poisoned herself but Darcy was so set on Ten being able to do both, be a shifter and a toxin, that she wouldn't listen. So, when Echo was being concocted and grown, Maddie took matters into her own hands. She took my…" Rex looked awkward for the first time. "We were in a relationship and Maddie assumed. She created one Ten in a lab as per Darcy's instructions and the other…"

Horrified, Aly covered her mouth with her hand. "She created me."

Looking sympathetic, Rex took a deep breath. "While she had the tools to… engineer you, she didn't have the tools to grow a human, and Darcy would have discovered and terminated if she used the Institute's. So Maddie used the next best thing, the natural way. Her intent was to show Darcy how Ten was meant to be. Present you when you were born."

Noah said, "And you found out."

Rex nodded and continued, "She… was excited about it. She didn't see what she was doing was wrong or unethical. It didn't matter to her that I was a shifter; she even had the gall to say that's why it worked. I managed to convince her to elope. Big romantic gesture since I was going to be a father. She agreed and I…" He hunched his shoulders. "I am not proud of what I did to ensure you would not be given to the Institute, Alyson."

Dread filled Aly. "You kidnapped her."

"She was free to go after you were born. But I couldn't allow…"

Aly shook her head and closed her eyes so she didn't have to look at him.

A scrape of a chair made her open them again. Rex crossed the room to stare out the window. "When you were born, I—I don't have other children, Alyson. I never wanted them but you were so perfect and you were *mine*. I would've given up everything to protect you and… I didn't expect that." He sighed. "I would've been able to deal had it just been me but watching you tremble every time I held you was heartbreaking. Maddie had made you toxic, but there was a high price for you. I… Maddie was… confused. She'd expected you to take my ability away and you didn't."

At Rex's pause, Noah asked, "If you knew she was trying to take shifter abilities away, why did you stay?"

Rex lifted the curtain away from the window to peek out. "Maddie said 'enhance', I stupidly believed her. I didn't realize I was going to be her first test subject."

Noah pointed out, "That doesn't explain what happened before."

Rex dropped the curtain and turned toward them. "Exponential reaction. One shifter is in no danger of losing their abilities to Alyson. It causes discomfort to both parties, but it doesn't seem to endanger either. Two has a larger reaction, but there's no danger. Any more than three in close quarters…"

Noah nodded. "Increases the rate of reaction, speeding up the toxicity process." He flicked his gaze to Aly and his expression was unreadable. "She's a ticking time bomb for natural shifters."

Aly's throat closed up in horror. Swallowing hard, she managed to blurt, "All those shifters before, they're no longer shifters?"

Rex inclined his head. "You struck a massive blow to Welcher. My people are moving to capitalize, but it does mean they're aware of you. The next attack will be more precise."

Her stomach bubbled, threatening to rebel. She covered her mouth with her hands to help keep her meal down.

Noah focused on Aly's reaction rather than Rex's prediction. "You didn't know, Als."

Fighting tears, Aly wanted to believe him. "Doesn't make it right."

"Even if you did know," Rex included. "There wouldn't have been a lot you could've done to warn them. There would've been one incident before they took you seriously."

She didn't want Rex's pity. "Why would Darcy want to remove shifter abilities?" she asked Noah. "You said she was more focused on shifters being the next step in evolution."

"She's unlocking shifter genetic code," Rex said. "Imagine if you controlled who could be a shifter and who couldn't."

Deep in thought, Noah nodded. "Equalize the playing field."

"Or destroy it completely."

"So… I'm basically allergic to shifters," Aly muttered, trying to get her head around what she'd been told. "And make them allergic to themselves?" Looking to Noah she asked, "How would that even work? Is it in my blood?"

"No," Noah said and waved his hand. "Well, I mean it could be, but I copied your blood so I could give you some and it didn't feel unusual. It's probably a combination of things."

"If you copied me completely, could you be toxic?"

A muscle in Noah's cheek twitched. "Probably not a good idea. Ten died. That'd probably happen to me, too."

Aly's stomach lurched and she had to fight against throwing up. "Oh. But you duplicated—you could—"

"Don't panic," Noah soothed with a smile and a wave of his hand. "I feel fine."

Rex made a soft noise of consideration as he watched the pair so Aly turned her attention back to him. "What happened to Maddie?"

He dropped his gaze and scratched at the collar of his polo shirt. "Alyson… maybe it would be better—"

It wasn't up to him to protect her, so she demanded, "Tell me."

Rex sighed. "Regardless of what she deemed as a failure, she still wanted to present you to Darcy. She thought since there was evidence *something* was going on, if she had the tools to refine it or study you, she could… I wasn't about to let that happen. I had to protect you."

Aly's eyes widened. "You... you said she was dead. Did you...?"

"Alyson..." Rex began, then stopped, an admittance in itself.

Her insides twisted and the world spun. In response, Noah came and sat on the arm of the chair. Clutching at herself, Aly curled against his side and let him rub small circles on her back to offer comfort. He didn't say anything and she appreciated that.

After a time, and many glances backward, Rex returned to the table. "It was difficult to locate Poppy. She and Maddie were estranged and Poppy was so much younger. Maddie mentioned her only once in passing, so I knew Darcy wouldn't know. It was selfish, I guess, but I wanted you with family. I wanted you loved. I wanted you to have a chance for a normal life. The minute Poppy saw you, her face lit up and I knew I'd made the right decision."

Aly accepted a tissue from Noah and wiped her face.

"Poppy knew from the beginning why I couldn't be around. I left her everything she needed. She was only twenty-one and I knew what I asked was a hard burden on anyone. I bought your house. Paid her college fees and set up a fund for you. She always made sure to keep me updated on you, letters, pictures, and videos. She didn't have to but she did. I visited when you were younger and watched from a distance. Every year, when you went to the cemetery in Sacto, I was nearby." His laugh was brief. "When she married, she sought permission for Roger to adopt you. I met him, under the guise of being a distant cousin of Poppy's in town for one night. He is a good man. I couldn't ask for anyone better to raise my daughter."

Unable to bring herself to speak, Aly nodded.

"I wanted to be part of your life, Alyson, but I couldn't."

Seeing Aly wasn't able to deal, Noah filled the silence,

"You had your natural form."

With a shake of his head, Rex said, "My natural form would have caused even more problems."

"And why is that?"

Rex switched his gaze from Aly to Noah. "For the answer to that, I need you to answer a few of mine."

"Of course you do," Noah muttered. "Go ahead."

"You've been in Bellhollow for the last ten years?"

Not caring if Rex saw, Aly snuggled closer to Noah, who answered with a, "Yup."

"And in all that time, you've never left?"

Noah laughed. "'Course I did," he said, nudging Aly to include her in the joke. "We've traveled all over. Redding, Sac, summer camp at Lake—"

"Never left as anyone other than… well, this isn't Fletcher's form, but you know what I mean."

Noah's humor died. "No."

"Something to hide?" Rex pressed, his tone shy of accusatory.

"Absolutely. You're trying to finger me for something and I won't play. You're just going to have to believe I haven't been part of your war since I left your group."

Rex stroked his beard, his expression guarded. "You really haven't been involved in any shifter politics?"

"No," Noah said with a shrug. "It's not my fight. I had nothing to protect, no stake in who won. All the sides would prefer if me and my kind up and died. Why would I involve myself?"

"And now?"

Noah adjusted his seat on the arm of Aly's chair. "Now, everything's a mess. Everyone's after Aly because of you. I still couldn't give two shits about the politics or your super-secret war. I just want my family safe." Noah's hand clenched on his knee. "I have no love for you, Rex. As far as I'm concerned, this whole war is inane. I want no part in it. Will take no part in it beyond keeping Aly out of it. Given her reaction, I'm pretty sure she doesn't want to be around shifters ever again."

Aly nodded.

Rex didn't look convinced. "Why did you choose Bellhollow?"

Noah said nothing, staring at Rex with an even expression, but his hand on Aly's back clenched.

Rex narrowed his eyes. "Here's where I have a hard time trusting you. You walked away and yet *somehow* ended up with my daughter. That's no coincidence."

"I had no insider knowledge," Noah said. "No ulterior motive for becoming friends with Aly, if that's what you're asking."

"I heard a lot about you from Poppy. How much your friendship mattered to Alyson. How you made her a better person." Rex shook his head sharply. "You were grooming her."

"For what purpose?" Noah countered. "What would that gain? I want *nothing* to do with you."

"Look at how she clings to you," Rex snapped.

Rousing in reaction to the rising tension in Noah, Aly bristled.

Outraged, Noah spat, "Because *you* tore away what remained of her world. All I did was live my life and share it with her. You're a fucking hypocrite, Rex. Making Maddie out to be the villain. She saw weapons, which is exactly what *you* see when you look at us. All that garbage about Faceless not intermingling and whatever crap you're spewing now—"

Responding with his own anger, Rex yelled, "Do you know what we're up against? Have you *seen* the new abominations Darcy's been pumping out?"

Noah shrugged, nonchalant. "Seen, fought one. No big."

Rex's jaw dropped. "You *fought* one?"

"You gave us crap for years and now you claim your own daughter is—"

Aly pinched the sleeve of Noah's shirt and tugged to

restrain his words. He was speaking out of anger and fear and she didn't want him saying anything he'd regret. Startled, Noah's gaze swung to her, then his teeth clicked as he shut his mouth.

"You're a murderer," Rex snarled.

Noah shot back, "So are you!"

"An assassin; that's what the Faceless were created for—"

Aly was done. Done with the yelling and the lies and the twisted half-truths. "The same Faceless which you insinuated I was a part of." Turning her head, she frowned at Rex. "You called him an abomination. Is that what you think of me, too?"

Rex flinched at her accusation and was quick to attempt to pacify her. "No. Of course not. I saw you born; he was grown—"

Aly cut him off with a wave of her hand. "I already said you weren't allowed to do the whole overprotective parental thing. I've known Fletcher for ten years. That much shared history would make it pretty hard to fake a personality. I had boyfriends who cracked in less than a month and showed their true colors. So don't you *dare* sit there and say he groomed me for anything when you're manipulating both of us. So many people seem to be lying to us, why should I believe anything you say?"

Rex shook his head. "You're telling me you see no change in his personality? None at all?"

She wasn't going to allow Rex to influence her. "People change in stressful circumstances. I've changed, I can't be stupid enough to think he wouldn't change. Fletcher is an adorable dork, who can have his stern and trying moments and isn't afraid to yell at me when I'm dumb."

Noah gave Aly a lopsided smile. "Thanks, I think."

Rex said, "And it hasn't occurred to either of you that maybe he doesn't remember who he's working for."

Noah's head snapped to Rex. "What do you mean by that?"

"Brain shift. You could've implanted compulsions, then removed your own memories. You could be working for anyone."

Noah was as solid as a rock beneath Aly's hand. "I can't shift my brain."

"How would you know?" Rex replied, looking entirely too smug. "If you removed the knowledge along with the shift?"

"If I was going to do something stupid and shift my brain, I'd want to make damn sure I had a way to restore those memories. Something—" Noah paused, then his eyes widened in horror and he lifted his hands to dig them into his skull. Pushing away from the armchair, he paced across the room still clutching his head. "No. No. That can't be right."

Aly's heart sank like a stone into the pit of her stomach.

Rex lit up in triumph. "See? I *knew* you were—"

"Shut up," Noah snarled. "Just shut up! You don't know anything!"

"You think he brainwashed himself into being my friend?" Aly asked, incredulous.

Rex shook his head. "No one knows what kind of programming Darcy embedded in them."

"Programming?" Aly asked.

Stalking in tight circles, Noah snapped at Rex. "Elijah went back voluntarily, didn't she? She wasn't ordered. She left on her own."

Rex inclined his head. "Elijah was with me for years, then Jonah comes back, male and wanting to be called Joseph and suddenly Elijah calls herself Elaine and leaves. Months later, I find she's working for Darcy. What am I supposed to think?"

Shoulders slumped in defeat, Noah swore viciously.

Rex said, "Now do you see why I don't trust you?"

"What sort of programming?" Aly asked.

With a glare at Rex, Noah was vitriolic. "We all were programmed. Lessons were a reminder of something we already knew. Being taught to read, to talk, it was all... fast-tracked somehow. They fed us some bullshit story about how we chose what happened to us, how we volunteered to fight. Real dystopian type shit so I already know it's within the scope of Darcy. If she could implant those memories, then—if there was somehow a compulsion to return if we ever escaped—" Noah flinched. Clutching at his head, he grabbed two fistfuls of hair and tugged.

He looked so distraught, she wanted to hug him but doubted he'd accept it. "Fletcher—"

"It's okay," Rex said to Aly and his voice turned soothing and understanding. "You are young. Impressionable. He's trained in the art of manipulation."

Aly frowned, affronted. "What are you—"

Noah swung his attention to Aly to plead, "I swear, I never—"

Rex continued in the same infuriating understanding tone. "It's not your fault you fell under his sway—"

"You make it sound like I didn't have a choice," Aly snapped. "I did. I *do*." She pushed out of her seat and limped toward Noah. "It's okay, we can—"

"No," Noah snapped, holding up his hand to keep her away. "No, it's not okay. This all makes sense now and I wish to fuck it didn't." Noah backed away and his retreat hurt. "I told you I felt drawn to you. What kind of person feels drawn to an eight-year-old?" His face twisted in disgust. "What if—what if I *made* it so that—"

"You see what he is," Rex pressed, and she knew he tried to make her doubt. "Alyson, I know I haven't been the best father but—"

"Don't imply what I think you're implying," Aly snapped and turned her back on Rex. Limping toward Noah, Aly lowered her voice. "You are not going to tell me ten years of friendship is null because of something he says, are you? Don't tell me ten years means *nothing*."

"Alyson, we don't have time for his theatrics—"

Noah looked devastated but let Aly approach him. "Maybe you should go with him."

She knew why he said it. She also knew it was never going to happen. "Don't you *dare*," she snarled. "Why do you always assume the worst?"

"Because it always is," Noah retorted. "Anything good in my life has always been taken away."

"There are people after you," Rex continued, vying for attention. "I can—"

Ignoring Rex, Aly snapped at Noah, "I'll try not to be offended." She balanced on one leg, tilting dangerously and Noah's grab to steady her was done without thought.

"You don't understand—" Noah began.

Rex made a frustrated noise and demanded, "Alyson—"

Aly thrust a hand to Rex, palm facing him. "Give me a minute!" Taking Noah's arm in her other hand, she spoke to him in hushed tones. "Let's think about this logically for a sec. If you shifted your brain, who's to say you didn't take *out* the programming?"

Noah closed his mouth and blinked rapidly.

"Because that would be, like, the number one thing, wouldn't it? Mess with Darcy, remove your programming." She frowned, mulling things over. "But your siblings— family is important to you. So, *so* important. You couldn't leave them in the lurch, right? It's the same reason you couldn't leave me and you couldn't leave..." Aware Rex was listening, she wasn't about to mention Ross and Bonnie now.

Mute, he nodded.

"So, hypothetically, you'd find a way to tell Elaine, because of your siblings, she's the one more likely to be able to do it too. And yet, she's gone back to Darcy. What's that tell you?"

Noah frowned. "Umm... I don't..."

"Either a brain shift *can't* be done—"

Noah's shoulders slumped in defeat. "Or there's still

programming in place."

Aly waggled her finger at him. "*Or* we've walked into something big and are making a mess of some long-term planning." She limped a step closer and put her hand on his chest. "Because I bet, if you knew you could shift your brain and escape whatever programming Darcy'd put in you, if there's any at all, you'd be all up on her thing, mucking up every single plan she made on the sly. Right?"

Noah snorted and relaxed a little.

"And Elaine would be right there with you, wouldn't she? So… what if *Elaine* figured out she could shift her brain?" Aly asked, casting a glance at Rex, who looked back anxiously, and lowered her voice even further. "Those photos, that's what you were thinking. A trail, right?"

Noah's eyes widened. "Yes. Exactly."

"And you don't have any sort of trail like that, do you?"

"I… maybe I didn't leave one?"

"C'mon. That's a stretch. Even for you."

Noah scowled at the ground. "*Elaine* shot you. That wasn't an accident. She deliberately—"

Aly's head jerked back and her fingers on Noah's shirt loosened. "She did?"

"Yes. So don't try to justify it, there's no logical—"

It threw her thought processes into a tailspin as she tried to figure out how that could fit in. "Elaine knew you could heal me, though, right? I assume she's seen you do that before?"

He breathed out through his teeth in an attempt to settle himself. "She also knew I'd be at Welcher's mercy if I did."

"Maybe that was her plan. We just don't know. There's not enough information and—and!" Her voice rose as something occurred to her and she tugged on his shirt to illustrate her excitement. "Here's another thought! What if you feeling drawn to me was *Maddie's* fault?" Ignoring the sudden confusion on his face, Aly pressed on. "I'm supposed to be a weapon, right? Well, a weapon needs guards."

Noah's jaw dropped and he gaped at her.

She gestured the two of them. "If he's to be believed, we're of the same… well—batch. You said you always know your siblings, no matter what."

"But that…" he swallowed. "That would mean we could be—"

"Is Elaine genetically related to you?"

He shook his head, still looking lost and withdrawn.

"C'mon, bumble-butt. Brain cells. Use them." She pulled a face at him, then studied his expression.

A myriad of emotions flittered across his face, as wave after wave of thoughts washed over him. When he finally met her eyes, when all the pieces of her logic had fallen into place, his expression was clear.

Aly murmured, "Have I thrown enough spanners in the works? There's still so much we don't know and we can't believe everything, because—to be honest, I can't tell who is lying, can you?"

He shook his head.

Fingers splayed over his heart, she patted his chest. "You and me, Fletch, we have to trust in *us*."

With a tender smile, he lifted a hand to curl it over hers. "What would I do without you?"

"Let's not find out." She waved her free hand at Rex and raised her voice. "Fuck that noise."

Swearing produced the desired effect in Noah as his lips quirked up into a smirk.

"Alyson!" Rex scolded, looking flabbergasted.

Keeping her hand on Noah's chest, she turned on Rex. "It doesn't matter to me if Noah works for someone else. You can't erase years of friendship."

"That's the point," Rex told her. "He *could*."

"But would he?" Aly snapped. "Memories are important. Why would he remove some?"

Rex didn't believe her. "What if—"

304

Aly clenched her free hand into a fist. "If that's why he came to Bellhollow in the first place, then that's the reason. What happened afterward, *we* did that. Our choices. Our life. Our friendship." Aly took a step back until she stood beside Noah. Determined to show a united front, she pulled their joined hands from his chest and left them entangled by their sides. "He could've left at any time and he didn't."

"Because—"

Aly wasn't going to let him speak or try to sway her mind. Forging on, she spoke over Rex. "There's so little I trust right now. People telling me different things, words are twisted into knots but there's one thing I've *always* held on to. No matter what, I'd never give up Fletcher's friendship for anyone."

"Except he's *not* Fletcher," Rex snarled, gesturing Noah with large, cutting motions. "He's a Faceless!"

"According to you, so am I!" Aly responded.

"I think it's time for us to leave," Noah said in a tone devoid of emotion.

Rex dropped his hands, stunned. "What?"

Noah continued in the same even tone, "Aly and I have things to discuss regarding what we've learned today and what we're going to do next. I'm not comfortable spending any longer in this cabin than I need to. We'll be in touch."

Lurching a step forward, Rex blurted, "You can't be serious. You're in danger!"

Aly was determined to remain strong. "That's a given. But we'll be okay."

"I won't allow you to—"

Gritting her teeth, Aly asked, "Are you going to lock me up like you did my mother? Is that your plan? Smuggle me away somewhere and expect me to stay?"

"She would've had you dissected or raised you like they were. I didn't want that for you! I wanted you to have a normal life—I didn't miss eighteen years of your life keeping you safe to have it all thrown away now!" Shaking his head, Rex cleared his throat and blustered, "There's more you need to know."

Noah laughed under his breath. "Of course there is."

Rex seemed desperate to stop them as he moved to stand between them and the door. "Where are you going to go? What are you going to do?"

"We'll figure things out." Noah was tense even if his words were blasé. Aly didn't need to wonder if he'd go through Rex if he had to. He would. She knew.

"That's no life!" Rex scolded, waving his arms around to emphasize his words. "Always on the run. Alyson deserves better than that."

Noah gave Rex a deadpan look. "Really? And you think you can offer her more? *Everyone's* after you, what sort of life would that be? I lived for ten years without detection. And now I know it's not just me they're after, I can do that again. At least she'll have a chance."

Aly frowned, not looking at either of them now. "I don't need to be looked after. It's my choice."

Rex ignored her protest. "Everyone knows she exists!"

Noah stepped toward Rex and Aly went with him. "So make her die! Claim whatever happened killed her. Blame it on Welcher. Blame it on Faceless. *Lie*, you're good at that."

"That'll never work!"

"You've been after something to ignite this war for ages. What better way than an innocent caught in the middle?"

The veins on Rex's neck bulged. "How dare you insinuate I would—"

"You're just bent I said it out loud," Noah scoffed.

Rex thrust a finger at Noah, "Don't you be cocky with me, boy! You have no idea what you're dealing with!"

Watching a grown man have something akin to a temper tantrum, Aly said, "It really frustrates you when you don't get your way, doesn't it?"

Noah squeezed her hand. "Sad, isn't it?"

Visibly trying to control himself, Rex spoke to Aly. "You were shot under his watch! He's a danger to you."

Aly bristled. "You can't blame him for that!"

"I can and I do! They'll *never* give up."

Noah shook his head. "Do you really think we don't know that?"

"I have a compound!" Rex snarled. "Up in the forests of Washington. Near the border. She'll be safe there for however long she remains and no one knows about it—"

"So, your solution is for her to *hide*?"

"For *both* of you to hide!" Rex snapped. "You can stay out of this war. You can protect her if that's what you want!"

A snarl tore out of Noah's throat before his voice rose. "Right, so you can have your toxin and her bodyguard Faceless tucked away—"

Limping between the yelling men, Aly put her hand on Noah's chest. "Stop it."

Hands clenched into fists, Rex stepped forward. "How dare you!"

Aly thrust her hand at Rex, palm flat toward him. "*Stop it*." She widened her stance, intending to be a barrier between the two of them, only to have her leg fail her. Staggering, she felt Noah grab her to keep her steady.

Contrite, Noah's voice was husky, "Easy, lovely."

Quick to add his voice, Rex blurted, "Alyson, you shouldn't—"

Making a stern face, she jabbed her palm at Rex again. "Stop." Dropping her hand down, she covered Noah's hand on her hip and glared at Rex. "Here's what's going to happen. You're going to give us a contact number and the address of this compound, then we're going to leave." Keeping Noah's hand, she turned from side on to face Rex. "You've given us a lot of information and I know we're having knee-jerk reactions to it. But seriously, you need to give us time to process this."

"We don't have time!" Rex said. "They know about

you. They'll be moving to take you down."

"I am not going to make a rash decision right now," Aly snapped.

"This *is* a rash—"

Aly had had enough. She was hurt, sore, exhausted and emotionally compromised in more ways than one. She needed time to think, to feel, to talk to Noah. To be hugged. "You're going to let us do this our way if you *ever* want to see me again."

Rex paled and took a step back. His eyes darted between Aly and Noah as though he was trying to determine if she was serious. Breathing out through his nose, he muttered, "Fine." Reaching for his pocket, he pulled out his wallet. Extracting several cards, he left them on the table with a thick wad of cash.

With a shake of her head, Aly protested, "We don't need—"

Rex grunted, "I don't expect you have many supplies right now. You'll need clothes. Food. Money for transport. Rainy day funds. It goes quickly. There are several fresh credit cards, you just need to activate them. I'll ensure they're paid off." He glanced at Noah. "Untraceable."

Noah laughed. "Yeah, don't believe you." Giving Aly a squeeze, he released her so he could fetch their bag.

Defeated, Rex's arms dangled by his sides. "You can't pick your old life up, Alyson," he said. "You can't go to college. You can't work in the animation industry. You need to fly under the radar and you need money to do that. If you come with me, there's a chance—"

"Don't," Noah snarled, shouldering the backpack as he glared at Rex. "That's not fair."

Rex's words brought with them a stabbing pain in Aly's chest. Her entire life slipped through her fingers and she fumbled. "I… I can still do commissions."

"You can't talk to any of your friends again. I'll…" Rex ran a hand over his head. "I'll make you die, but if you talk to anyone from Bellhollow, the ruse won't work."

The gravity of the situation finally dawned on her. She was leaving everyone behind. Everything she ever knew. All of it. There was no other choice. "Even Mom?" she asked, her voice wavering.

Rex was sympathetic, yet firm. "Even Mom. If you contact anyone from your old life, there's a chance you'll get them killed. This is the consequence you have to deal with if you go with him."

Her heart broke at the finality of it all. It all felt so real. She wrapped her arms around herself and hunched her shoulders. Her mother, Roger, her baby brother Tim, Del, and Grace, they'd lost Fletcher and now they'd lost her too.

"If I can't find you, they can't find you." Rex shifted his gaze to address Noah. "I couldn't find you for ten years and you were right under my nose. You can do that again?"

Noah nodded. "Absolutely."

Rex swallowed and flopped into a chair at the table. He rested a business card on top of the cash. "You can contact me at this number. If you call, just say… you've got a delivery of poppies, and… if it's safe to talk and it's me, I'll say 'oh, good, they're for the back garden'. If I say front, then it's me, but it's not safe to talk. Got it?"

"Yes."

"If you really want to stay away from this war, make sure you stay hidden. I can give you twenty-four hours head start."

Noah strode forward to collect what Rex left on the table, shoving it into his bag. Coming back to Aly's side, he slung an arm around her waist. "Time to go."

Nodding, she looped her arm around him so she could use him as a crutch. "Okay." Limping toward the door, Aly waited until she was level with Rex before Penelope's ingrained politeness forced her to say, "Thank you." It felt inadequate but she didn't know what else to say.

Staring at the table of discarded food, Rex looked like a

broken man. "If you are ever captured, don't use my name. It won't protect you. You're better off if they believe we have no connection." He lifted his head and met her gaze. "I can't help you if you choose to go with him, Alyson."

Freezing in place, Aly felt lost. Her world tumbled down around her and there wasn't anything she could do anymore. The events of the last two days were fast catching up with her. She couldn't think. Didn't want to think. Just wanted everything to stop.

She turned away from Rex, meeting Noah's gaze. His face was an impassive mask, but his eyes were awash with emotion. "It's your choice, Als."

She could choose to go with Rex. To hide away and be a kept daughter. To force Noah into another kind of servitude because she knew he wouldn't let her go alone. They'd be stuck wherever Rex put them, dependent on him for everything.

She could choose to go with Noah. To be scared and run. To live and experience. To make decisions and stand by them. For them to choose how to live their lives. It would be hard, she had no illusions about that, but it would be their lives.

So really. No choice at all.

Since *Noah* was her choice, and would always be her choice, she stepped through the door.

Noah helped her into the passenger side of the car. "I didn't want this."

Aly nodded, staring at the dashboard. Her choice, but that didn't mean she couldn't grieve for those she was leaving behind. "I told them I'd call." She lifted her feet onto the seat and buried her face in her knees. "They're going to believe I'm dead. They're all going to think... I'll never see them again. Oh, Tim... this is... I can't..."

He squeezed her shoulder. "I know. Aly... I..."

She waited, desperately hoping he had something to make all this better but he seemed at a loss for words. With a sigh, Noah closed the passenger door. She felt the trunk thump as he put his bag away, then he slid into the car. "Aly?"

"Just go," she mumbled.

"I just—we should—I mean, I really think—"

"I don't want to talk." Keeping her face buried, she stretched out her hand and groped for his, giving it a squeeze before she retreated into a ball.

Silence, then a meek, "Okay," as he started the car. A beep as he unlocked his cell and placed it on his lap before starting down the dirt trail which led from the cabin.

"Secret rendezvous done?" Ross asked, answering the call.

"Yeah," Noah mumbled. "We have twenty-four hours head start. Then all hell breaks loose."

Ross let out a long whistle. "Well. *Shite*."

"Any word on Tango?"

"Not a peep. So, what's your plan?"

Noah let out a long breath. "We need to find Adam."

CHAPTER 23

"All of them?"

Tegan checked her nails and readjusted her cell against her ear. "Yes. The entire squad."

On the other end of the call, Alistair Welcher sounded astonished, a rare emotion from the man. "How many dead?"

"Ten, sir. All those within a thirty-foot radius. The ones holding her went first. Those who survived report they were forced into their natural forms and are now experiencing overwhelming pain, headaches, and a lack of connection to their abilities. We're trying to determine if this is a permanent loss of—"

"All of them?" he repeated, seeking clarification.

"Yes, sir."

There was no mistaking the anger now. "You've lost an entire team of shifters because you sent them all in at once. I gave strict orders for all groups to stay clear—"

Tegan raised an eyebrow. Clearly, Alistair hadn't spoken to his brother. "Nicholas ordered us in. We didn't know this was possible."

An exasperated noise. "Nicholas."

"There's more, sir. Initial reports say a Faceless was

involved. Apparently, the girl was shot and one of the others overheard the deceased say the Faceless was healing her. There's evidence of the twins involvement but we're unable to confirm. One of the men who survived said there was a recording of the incident which we're searching for now."

"Send me a copy," Alistair said. "Any sign of the instigator?"

"None."

"I want this girl captured. Unharmed."

Tegan hesitated at the unusual order. "Sir?"

"She's worth more to our cause alive."

"Not if we can't go near her."

"I'll have the video analyzed. Current instructions for your team are: find the girl. Watch her and do not approach. When the time comes, we'll tell you how she can be captured."

Tegan pressed her lips into a thin line. "Yes, sir. One last thing. Belinda Bell was also in the vicinity when the event occurred and I'm now having trouble locating her—"

"She's a liability. Cut her loose."

The line went dead.

Sighing, Tegan stopped leaning against the railing outside her motel and headed back into her room.

A news report played on the television. "*A lone gunman tore through a park at Lake Tahoe late today, ending the lives of at least eleven people and leaving many more injured before the gunman turned his gun on himself—*"

Joseph muted the television and threw the controller on the bed and looked over at Tegan expectantly. "Well?"

With a loud sigh, she scooped some of her long black hair over her shoulder and ran her fingers through it. "Belinda was cut loose. Welcher wants Aly alive. Gomez is missing and I suspect that's Belinda's doing."

Joseph cringed. "You shouldn't have assigned him. You shouldn't have assigned *her*."

Tegan tossed her cell on the bed and shook herself, allowing her body to return to its preferred form with ease. Sighing, Elaine said, "There wasn't much choice. She was necessary in case we weren't there in time. We were stuck, and I needed loyal eyes." Nodding to the television she said, "Think she'll be declared among the dead?"

"Yup."

"Rex worked fast."

Joseph nodded. "He's still trying to play all sides. We expected he would."

Elaine stretched tired arms over her head. "That was the *only* thing we anticipated. Her range is incredible as was the speed of her toxicity. We projected slow infection, not… not *that*."

Joseph stared at a spot on the comforter, his face devoid of expression. "She works on Faceless. Tango was too close when she went critical."

Aware of the emotions surging through Joseph right now, Elaine kept her voice soft, "We always knew the later ones were doomed. That's not our fault."

Joseph nodded. "It's not a good way to die."

Sympathetic, Elaine turned her attention to the muted television. "Think Darcy will buy she's dead?"

Putting his arms behind his head, Joseph flopped on the bed to stare at the roof. "Doubt it."

Sighing, Elaine scrubbed her face with her hands.

"And I suspect Noah's going to shoot first, ask questions later."

With a nod, Elaine glanced over at Del and Grace huddled in the corner, who watched with wide, fearful eyes. "We'd better move fast. There are things to be done."

TWIST

ABOUT THE AUTHOR

Rikkaine Thompson lives in the Northern Territory of Australia with her wonderful husband, three boisterous children and a dog.

Twist is her second novel. She is currently working on the third instalment, *Tangle*.

CONNECT WITH RIKKAINE

I really appreciate you reading my book. Here are some social media site you can find me at:

Follow me on Facebook
   https://www.facebook.com/rikkainethompson/
Follow my blog
   http://rikkaine.tumblr.com/
Follow me on twitter
   https://twitter.com/rikkaine